John R. Russell

Recollections and Suggestions, 1813-1873

John R. Russell

Recollections and Suggestions, 1813-1873

ISBN/EAN: 9783337218003

Printed in Europe, USA, Canada, Australia, Japan

Cover: Foto ©Andreas Hilbeck / pixelio.de

More available books at **www.hansebooks.com**

PREFACE.

———◇———

SOME persons who may cast their eyes upon this book, with the hope of finding that the whole work is new, may be disappointed, and even consider themselves deceived, by discovering that they have at second-hand what they have already read in the introduction to my report of my ' Speeches and Despatches.' But I hope my explanation will satisfy them that I have acted for the reader's benefit in thus repeating what has been already read, instead of furnishing him with an article entirely original.

The fact is, that after I had proceeded some way in my task I found that my memory of past transactions was not, after the lapse of some years, so lively as it had been when I wrote the original introduction. I have, therefore, satisfied myself with copying in the first pages the work which I had already published.

It may interest some persons to learn what education I had received before I entered Parliament. That education was in part broken and disturbed. After being at a private school at Sunbury, I went to Westminster, but was so ill there that, by the care and affection of my step-mother, the Duchess of Bedford, my father was persuaded to remove me, and I was sent with several young men of riper age to receive private tuition from the Rev. Mr. Smith, of Woodnesbury, in Kent. There I formed relations of friendship with the Earl of Clare, the late Duke of Leinster, his brother, Lord William Fitzgerald, and others. But I had not remained there long, when Lord and Lady Holland proposed that I should accompany them on a journey to Spain in the troubled year 18??. When I returned from Spain, in 1810, I asked my father to allow me to go to the University of Cambridge. But he told me that in his opinion there was nothing to be learnt at English Universities, and procured for me admission to the house of Professor Playfair, at Edinburgh.

There I had my studies directed and my character developed by one of the best and the noblest, the most upright, the most benevolent, and the most liberal of all philosophers.

Some years afterwards I travelled again in Spain with my cousin, the late Earl of Bradford, and Robert Clive, the son of Lord Powis. In the course of these travels I became acquainted with the Duke of Wellington, and had occasion to admire the calmness, the directness, and the patriotism which distinguished his character.

But I need not follow this narrative any further. I was about to accompany my companions to Constantinople, and return home by way of Moscow and St. Petersburgh, when I was informed by a letter from my father that his old friend, the acute and witty Fitzpatrick, was dead, and that he intended to propose me as candidate for Tavistock. Thus I became a member of Parliament before I was of age, and from that time my political life begins.

Before I conclude this Preface, I may mention that at Edinburgh a public dinner was sometimes held to commemorate the birthday of Mr. Fox. At one of these dinners, presided over by Lord Kinnaird, the following toast was given : —

' The Houses of Russell and Cavendish. May they ever be united in the cause of freedom ! '

I was called upon by the chairman to acknowledge the toast. I then said : —

' It gives me great pleasure to acknowledge the

toast which has just been announced by the chairman. It is a satisfaction to me to reflect that
your favor is obtained, not by the accidental qualities of talents and power, but by a steady adherence to those principles which animated Mr. Fox
through life, and, holding it by that tenure, I trust
that it will never be forfeited.'

RUSSELL.

ALDWORTH, *October* 30, 1874.

CONTENTS.

CHAPTER I.

I WAS elected a Member of Parliament for the borough of Tavistock in July, 1813, just a month before I became of age.

The state of public affairs at that moment was one, if not of anxiety, yet of the highest interest. The great Revolutionary War, which had continued with intervals from the invasion of France by the Duke of Brunswick in 1792, was evidently drawing to a close. That war may properly be divided into two very distinct periods. First, the vain, weak, and ineffectual struggle of the Powers of Europe against the insane strength of the French Revolution, terminated by the Treaty of Campo Formio, and the Treaty of Ratisbon, on the Continent of Europe, and by the Peace, or more properly, the Truce of Amiens, between England and France. Secondly, the struggle maintained on the one side by Napoleon Bonaparte with infinite ability, infinite ambition, and an entire disregard of moral or religious scruples, with a view to make himself despotic master of every country in Europe; on the other side, by the resisting power of England, and by the spirit of national independence, first roused on the Continent in the breasts of the Spanish people, and extending from them, as

1

opportunity arose, to the people of Russia, of Germany, of Holland, and of Northern Italy.

For some years the conduct of the war on the part of the Allies, forms a strange contrast to the skill with which William III., Marlborough, and Prince Eugene had conducted the Grand Alliance against France, and to the spirit and military talent which Frederick the Great and Lord Chatham had displayed in the Seven Years' War against the forces of France, Austria, and Russia. In 1792, the Duke of Brunswick, in contradiction to his own views and opinions, had issued a proclamation inspired by the French Royalist emigration, threatening with condign punishment the National Assembly of France, and all who held political, municipal, or other offices under the French Republic. This atrocious attempt to deprive France of the rights of an independent nation was soon defeated in the field, and, by the just resentment which it provoked, was the main cause of the repeated and splendid triumphs of the French Republic. The beginning of the war was a trial of energy between the combatants, and in point of energy, as Mr. Burke has confessed, the French far excelled their opponents. In fact, the Allies were not only without energy, but without any motives by which enthusiasm could be excited. Each great Power had its own separate object. Austria wished to increase her territory, either by annexing Bavaria, or by conquering part of the French territory, as far as the banks of the Somme. Prussia wished only to enlarge her share of the partition of Poland, and employed the subsidies of England in conveying her army to fight the Poles, and acquire new provinces. Russia was intent solely upon the conquest of Poland, and her crafty Empress expressed in many pious phrases and moral maxims the utmost horror and detestation of the Jacobin Convention of Paris, while her real object was to inflame the English and the Germans against France. In the mean time, her political intrigues and overwhelming legions secured and consolidated her Polish conquests. While she betrayed every Polish party, and crushed those to whom she had promised protection, she indulged in unbounded licentiousness at St. Petersburg, and laughed at the pious zeal excited by the atheism of France.

The course of England, though more honest than that of the Continental Powers, was less definite, and less likely to obtain success. The restoration of the Bourbons was the wish, but not the object of the English Government.[1] The maintenance of the Austrian province of the Netherlands was the immediate object of Mr. Pitt, but it was pursued with little vigor by means of subsidies inconsiderately thrown away, of negotiations defeated by the insincerity of Prussia, and of military operations conducted by an English general, totally ignorant of the art of war, in co-operation with treacherous allies.

It was no wonder that hostilities thus conducted, failed of success. Nor when the energy of the Jacobin democracy abated, was the contest of military skill which followed more auspicious to the Allies.

---

[1] This wish was openly avowed by Mr. Pitt, in the debate on the Peace of Amiens : —

> Me si fata meis paterentur ducere vitam
> Auspiciis, et sponte meâ componere curas,
> Urbem Trojanam primum, dulcesque meorum
> Reliquias colerem, Priami tecta alta manerent,
> Et recidiva manu posuissem Pergama victis.

A natural wish in the breast of Æneas; a very strange one in the mouth of Mr. Pitt.

The military men who arose in France, Pichegru, Moreau, Hoche, Massena, and lastly Napoleon Bonaparte, defeated and dispersed the Allies and compelled them to agree to ignominious terms of peace. The allied armies were usually commanded by men of little reputation at the time, and of complete obscurity in the present age. The military knowledge of the Archduke Charles, and the barbarous ferocity of Suwarrow, shine out alone amidst the dearth of talent and of skill.

The second act of the great tournament of Europe was of a very different description. Napoleon, flushed with success, pretended that peace never could be made between France and the ancient monarchies, and considered his own supremacy over all the states and nations of Europe as the only security for what he and others called the principles of 1789.

This pretension alienated those in England and on the Continent who had been quite willing to see France constitute herself as she pleased, and even enlarge her boundaries to a considerable extent. In 1805, Mr. Fox, in opposition, wrote to his nephew, Lord Holland, that it was no time to talk of peace. In 1806, Mr. Fox, in office, conducted the negotiation which broke off not merely, as he told his nephew, on the point actually in dispute, but on account of the evident insincerity of the French Government. After this there remained nothing for those who were not disposed to allow England to be absorbed in the French Empire but to resist and to persevere.

The task seemed not only a difficult, but almost a hopeless one; no amount of subsidy, no coalition of Powers, seemed likely to end otherwise than in such defeats as Austerlitz, Jena, and Friedland.

Happily, from an unexpected quarter appeared the

dawn of better times. Napoleon invited the King of Spain and his heir apparent to Bayonne with the view of betraying and dethroning them. Many Spanish grandees bowed their necks beneath the yoke, but every Spanish peasant felt his own honor assailed in the persons of his unworthy, contemptible, but still national Sovereigns.

The signal fire was lighted on every hill, the flame of independence blazed up in every bosom.

Here was indeed a crisis in the affairs of Europe. The cause of national independence, which in the first portion of the war was defended by France, was now about to be upheld by the other nations of Europe. No matter how ignorant, how ill-armed, how ill-led the Spanish people might be, here was a nation animated by a real enthusiasm; ready to fight in the field of battle, in the town, in the village, in the farm-yard and in the peasant's cottage for the sacred cause of national independence.

It behooved England, therefore, to welcome this reviving spirit, to expend her growing treasures, to employ her extensive credit, to dispatch her most skilful officers, to marshal her bravest troops in defence of this sacred cause. England might be exhausted in the struggle, but by lifting up her heart to meet the mighty danger, and by an attempt to free herself and other nations from intolerable slavery, she could never be disgraced.

Unhappily Lord Grenville (who became head of the Ministry in 1806), and the leaders of the Whigs, did not perceive the nature of the change that had taken place.

Lord Grenville in the former war had directed Lord Malmesbury to insist upon retaining the Netherland provinces for Austria, when the attempt was hopeless. Indeed Austria herself, when beaten in Italy, was willing to yield those provinces to France. Again, when Napoleon, as first Consul, had invited England to make peace, Lord Grenville had informed him that the best way of giving peace to Europe was to replace the Bourbons on the throne of France.

With all the integrity, and with more than the abilities of the first George Grenville, he exactly answered the description which Burke has drawn of that statesman. When the waters were out, Lord Grenville, like his father, was unable to discern the means of safety. Now the waters were out. Lord Grenville and the Whig party dwelt on precedents of former wars; on the inability of Sir Arthur Wellesley to maintain himself in Portugal, and on the exhaustion of the finances which a war in Spain would entail, but they thought too little of the grandeur of the struggle, and the obvious certainty that England or Napoleon must fall to rise no more. Towards the end of the year 1813, when Lord Grenville had begun to see more clearly the new aspect of affairs, Mr. Horner wrote to Mr. Allen, at Holland House, in the following terms : —

'Your account of the view which Lord Grenville is expected to take of Continental affairs, in a speech upon the first day of the session, has relieved me from an anxiety which I felt on that subject; for I have had fears that we were to make the same false step respecting this German war that has been so fatal to the party, and deservedly so, with respect to the Spanish cause. That the financial difficulties of the country will be increased by our embarking so deeply with the Allies, as I think we ought to do, is true and ought not to be disguised; that the sanguine expectations, professed by the friends of Government, of a speedy settlement of the affairs of Europe have apparently no just foundation in the present aspect of them, ought likewise, in my opinion, to be stated; but I cannot hesitate now in believing that the determination of the French military force, and the insurrection of national spirit in the north of Germany, form a new conjunction in which the Whigs ought to adopt the war system, upon the very same principle which prompted them to stigmatize it as unjust in 1793, and as premature in 1803. The crisis of Spanish politics in May, 1808, seemed to me the first turn of things in a contrary direction, and I have never ceased to lament that our party took a course so inconsistent with the true Whig principles of Continental policy, so revolting to the popular feelings of the country, and to every true feeling for the liberties and independence of mankind. To own that error now is a greater effort of magnanimity than can be asked for; but the practical effects of it will gradually be repaired, if a right line of conduct is taken with respect to German affairs.' [1]

Such were the opinions of Francis Horner, a man thoroughly imbued with Whig principles, who had mastered in early youth the soundest doctrines of political economy, who spoke in Parliament in a clear and manly style of eloquence, who acted on every occasion of his short public life in the highest spirit of honor, and whose premature death caused deep and lasting affliction to all who knew him and to all who valued liberty.

But it is time to explain how it was that I embraced with warmth the opinions of Lord Holland and Mr. Horner in reference to Spain, rather than those of Lord Grenville and Lord Grey.

In the autumn of 1808, when only sixteen years of

---

[1] Life of Francis Horner.

age, I accompanied Lord and Lady Holland to Corunna, and afterwards to Lisbon, Seville, and Cadiz, returning by Lisbon to England in the summer of 1809. They were eager for the success of the Spanish cause, and I joined to sympathy for Spain a boyish hatred of Napoleon, who had treacherously obtained possession of an independent country by force and fraud — force of immense armies — fraud of the lowest kind.

In 1810, I went on a visit to my brother, Lord William Russell, at the Isla de Leon. He then served on the staff of Sir Thomas Graham, who was gallantly defending Cadiz against two French divisions.

When my visit was over, Colonel James Stanhope, who likewise was on the staff of Sir Thomas Graham, proposed to me to go with him and Colonel Walpole to the head-quarters of Lord Wellington, who had just occupied with his army the lines of Torres Vedras.

This offer I joyfully accepted, and, after a voyage to Faro, and a pleasant journey by Almodovar, we arrived at the quarters of General Hill.

The next morning we rode with General Hill through the small town of Alhandra, beyond which *abattis* were placed to stop the French cavalry, as this was the farthest English post. Indeed, it had been intended to leave Alhandra to the French; and I remember that Lord Grey, whom I met at dinner at Holland House on my return to England, was much surprised when I told him that I had ridden through the place within a fortnight.

My friends and I proceeded next day to Pero Nero, where we were most kindly received by Lord Wellington. We were furnished with bedsteads though not with beds, and the next morning before daylight we accompanied our general to the fort of Sobral.

Never was I more struck than with the physical, military, and political spectacle which lay before me. Standing on the highest point, and looking around him on every side, was the English General, his eyes bright and searching as those of an eagle, his countenance full of hope, beaming with intelligence, as he marked with quick perception every movement of troops and every change of circumstance within the sweep of the horizon. On each side of the fort of Sobral rose the entrenchments of the Allies, bristling with guns and alive with the troops who formed the garrison of this fortified position. Far off, on the left, the cliffs rose to a moderate elevation, and the line of Torres Vedras was prominent in the distance.

Below us, over a large extent of hill and valley, plain and eminence, was the position of the French army. The villages were full of their soldiers; the white sails of the Portuguese windmills were actively in motion for the supply of flour to the invading army. There stood the advanced guard of the conquering legions of France; here was the living barrier of England, Spain, and Portugal prepared to stay the destructive flood, and to preserve from the deluge the liberty and independence of three armed nations. The sight filled me with admiration, with confidence, and with hope.

Impressed with these sentiments I returned to England. Being some time in the succeeding autumn at Lord Grey's at Howick, I betted a guinea with his brother-in-law, Lord Ponsonby, that at that time next year Lord Wellington would still hold the lines of Torres Vedras. Lord Grey thought that I had made a foolish bet, and referred to the lines of Marshal Villars, called the *ne plus ultra* of Marlborough, and which

Marlborough successfully penetrated, as a proof that the lines could not be held. At the end of a year Lord Ponsonby paid me my bet.

I remember that in the year 1812, being at dinner at Lord Wellington's head-quarters, he called to Lord March (afterwards Duke of Richmond), ' What are you talking of at that end of the table?' Lord March: ' We are discussing, sir, the question whether if we went back to the lines at Torres Vedras, we should again be able to hold them.' Lord Wellington said: ' That may be a political question, but as a military question, I would go back twenty times to the lines, and be confident of holding them.' I saw Lord Wellington on three other occasions during the Peninsular War.

The second was, when in company with my cousin George Bridgeman, and my friend Robert Clive, I entered Spain from Oporto. We joined the army at the time when Lord Wellington, after the victory of Salamanca and the capture of Madrid, had failed in his siege of the castle of Burgos. I sat next to him at dinner in the evening when he had made up his mind to retire, and to withdraw his army both from the siege of Burgos and the occupation of Madrid. I knew nothing of this important and mortifying decision, nor could any thing less prepare me for it than the conversation of the great commander. He said he was sorry he could not show me the castle ; talked of the advance of the French army, of which I had been a witness, as a *forte reconnaissance*, and laughed at the luxury of a Highland soldier, who had piled up a whole tree and set it in a blaze, in order to make himself a comfortable fire-side. The rest of his conversation was taken up by comic descriptions of the defects of his three iron guns — Thunder, Lightning, and Nelson — of which one had a severe wound in the mouth, and another had lost its trunnions by the fire of the enemy. After dinner, my companions and I were informed by Colonel Ponsonby that a retreat was resolved upon for that night, and we were advised to pack ourselves off as quickly as we could. We lost no time in following that advice, and, for my part, I found a very comfortable bed on a heap of chopped straw some leagues from Burgos. We tried to reach Madrid by San Ildefonso, but were again driven back by the French advance, and forced to proceed by Salamanca and the Sierra de Gata to Badajoz, Seville, and Cadiz.

.At Cadiz, during the winter, I met Lord Wellington when he paid a visit to that town, to concert with the Government and the Cortes as to future measures. Lord Wellesley had been urging in Parliament the expediency of sending large reinforcements to the British Army in the Peninsula, but Lord Wellington did not share in this opinion. He related at some length the difficulties encountered in transporting two regiments from Lisbon to the army on the frontier of Portugal, and observed how little statesmen at home knew of these difficulties, in the emphatic words, 'My Lord Wellesley does not know all this.' Lord Wellington was no less solicitous about the arrangements to be made for transporting and provisioning the army, than about the military operations themselves. Mr. Bissett, who acted as Chief Commissary during the absence of Mr. Kennedy, told me that on the day of the battle of Salamanca, Lord Wellington sent for him. He found the General lying on his camp-bed, having devoted an hour or two to repose, while a division which he had sent for, to take part in the battle, was coming up from a distance. Mr. Bissett told me that Lord Wellington entered with the greatest detail into the arrangements to be made for the transport and supply of the army with provisions. Thus, on the eve of a great battle, Lord Wellington could refresh his bodily energies by a short repose, and dictate the complicated arrangements necessary for an army whose means of transport and whose food were paid for and not extorted by force. While he did so, his mind was undisturbed by the immediate prospect of an impending battle, in which his fame and his life were to be exposed to a hazard which might have appalled men of the greatest courage.

In the autumn of 1813, I again saw Lord Wellington at his head-quarters in the Pyrenees. It was either at Lesaca or at Vera that I was for a day at the British head-quarters. I could not but feel admiration and joy at beholding the General whom I had visited in a critical position, defending with difficulty the capital of Portugal, now advancing in command of an admirable army to the invasion of France. The same coolness, the same imperturbable judgment in the midst of danger, distinguished him in the advance as had marked his prudent defence of the lines of Torres Vedras. My brother, Lord William Russell, who was on his staff, told me that on one occasion a single division of the army having crossed a river, Lord Wellington with a few officers of his staff likewise crossed with a view to observe the enemy. In the evening the river was flooded, and it swelled with such rapidity that it was impossible to pass from one bank to the other. The officers of the staff showed much anxiety lest the French should take advantage of the dangerous position of a single division of the army and overwhelm General and troops with their superior forces. Lord Wellington,

alone, remained perfectly calm, and never betrayed the
slightest symptom of uneasiness or anxiety. Such was,
in fact, the strength of mind upon which the whole
British Army relied, stronger than the arms they bore,
unconquerable as the discipline by which they were
united and controlled. Thus Ovid, in describing Cad-
mus when about to encounter the Python, says, —

> telum splendenti lancea ferro,
> Et jaculum ; *teloque animus præstantior ullo.*

Such was the spirit by which, at the end of this great
contest, the constancy, courage, and perseverance of the
British people, animating the prostrate nations of the
Continent, at length achieved a triumph over the most
formidable combination of military genius, warlike population, conquering armies, and political talent, which
ever threatened the independence of our country.

In 1814, happening to be with my father at Florence,
I found there was an opportunity of going to Elba in
a brig of war, and I eagerly availed myself of the
occasion to have an interview with the late master
of Europe. To Lord Ebrington (afterwards Lord
Fortescue) he had spoken fully of his past life, and the
accusations which history might bring against him, but
when I saw him he was in evident anxiety respecting
the state of France, and his chances of again seizing
the crown which he had worn for ten years. I was so
struck with his restless inquiry, that I expressed in a
letter to my brother in England my conviction that he
would make some fresh attempt to disturb France and
govern Europe.

In speaking of the Duke of Wellington, Napoleon
said it was a mistake to send him as Ambassador to
Paris : — 'On n'aime pas un homme par qui on a été
battu.'

The coalition of 1815 and the Battle of Waterloo put an end to Napoleon's enterprise, and restored peace to Europe.

I have pointed out what I conceive to have been the error of policy of the Whig party, when they failed to see that the war of 1808 was a war in a great popular struggle, linked closely with the cause of the independence of Europe. After the peace of 1815 the Tory party committed an error as great, and still more irretrievable.

During the continuance of the war, men readily listened to the saying of Windham, that it is dangerous to repair our house in the hurricane season, and thus Lord Eldon, Lord Sidmouth, and other bigoted Tories were permitted to leave 'windows which shut out the light, and passages that led to nothing,' in the Palace and the Parliament. But when the storm was over, men would naturally survey the building, repair the crumbling walls, and admit the excluded rays of the sun. A wise Ministry would have studied Mr. Pitt's policy from 1784 to 1792, and would have found how little ground there was for considering him as an enemy to extended commerce and religious freedom.

As, however, the majority of the ministers preserved in 1816 the attitude their great leader had taken in 1793, it behooved the Whigs, who had toasted in the worst of times 'The cause of civil and religious liberty all over the world,' to come forward and under happier auspices to propose the reform of our foreign policy, our financial system, our commercial exclusions, our intolerant laws, and lastly of our Parliamentry representation.

The foreign policy of our Government was at this time a timid repudiation of all those doctrines of national liberty and independence which had been inscribed on our flag at the end of the war, and which had led Madame de Staël to declare that the Tories of England were the Whigs of Europe.

Our financial system was based on the necessity of keeping up a Navy and Army suited to our high position, and of paying the interest of a debt which, having amounted to one hundred and thirty millions before the American War, had risen to eight hundred and thirty-six millions at the death of George III. In order to defray these expenses, the taxation of the country had penetrated to every corner and cranny of an Englishman's life, in the manner described with so much humor, and no less truth, by Sydney Smith.

With the same object of collecting a large revenue, and also of promoting native industry, prohibition and protection pervaded our commercial code.

No Roman Catholic could hold high civil office, or be admitted to a seat in Parliament. No Protestant dissenter could hold any official position without nominally, at least, submitting to what, in his eyes, were degradation and profanation.

Last of all, our Parliamentary representation was a mockery and a scandal.

But I must explain these various matters of grievance somewhat further. The Treaty of Paris had replaced the elder Bourbons on the throne of France, and the Congress of Vienna had divided the territories of Europe among the Sovereigns whose arms had defeated Napoleon. It was to be desired at that time that the wishes of the people of Europe should be consulted both in the choice of the Sovereign whom they were in future to obey, and the form of the institutions by which they were thenceforth to be ruled. Both these conditions were set at nought by the armed monarchs at Vienna. The Belgians wished to be Belgian ; they were made Dutch. The Lombards wished to be Italian ; they were made Germans. The old Republics of Holland, Genoa, and Venice were not restored ; the Prussians, who had indulged the hope of having a Constitution granted to them, were not gratified ; the charter granted to the French people by Louis XVIII. contained ambiguous phrases by which Charles X. was enabled, fifteen years afterwards, to assume the power of dispensing with its most important provisions.

Lord Castlereagh was not to blame for the violation of the solemn promises which the military rulers of Europe had made to the people of Europe, with a view of obtaining their aid against Napoleon. At Chatillon Lord Castlereagh had been powerful ; he held the key of the strong-box of England, and could dispense at pleasure million after million of treasure to the coalesced Sovereigns. Again, in 1815, ten millions of pounds sterling had been granted in subsidies to the German Princes, and Great Britain spent about a hundred and forty millions in that war of a hundred days. But, after Waterloo, the work was done, and the statesman who had been all-powerful at Chatillon was powerless at Vienna. He tried to save Poland from the arms of Russia, and he assisted Talleyrand in defending Saxony against the ambition of Prussia. But neither Russia nor Prussia required any more subsidies; immense armies were employed to watch any symptoms of resistance, and

> Ease will recant
> Vows made in pain as violent and void.

Mr. Canning, as Foreign Secretary, might have done better, but he had unhappily excluded himself from that office, and was content with a useless embassy at the Court of Lisbon.

Thus it happened, that after the gigantic efforts made by Spain, by Russia, and by Germany, the Continent lay almost as much enslaved by its old, and for the most part dull Sovereigns, as it had been since the beginning of the century by the marvellous genius of Napoleon and his victorious legions; only, instead of the improvements and material benefits gained by the efforts of the French National Assembly of 1789, the Continent of Europe returned to the old feudal laws and corrupt administration of the despotic monarchies of Europe.

Thus, the English Government, in conquering Napoleon, and quenching the flame of Jacobin revolution, did not succeed in establishing a satisfactory or permanent settlement. Pitt, in 1805, had drawn out a sketch of a restored Europe, such as he wished it to be, should fortune crown the arms of the Powers then at war with France. In this sketch Belgium was given to Prussia. A military Power of that magnitude might have had a chance of suppressing a Belgian insurrection; but the supremacy of Holland was sure to tempt a foreign people to resistance, and to provoke a combat in which the Belgians might meet the Dutch on equal terms, and thus bring on European intervention. In 1830, such an insurrection took place, and nothing but the temperate wisdom of the then ruler of France, and the judicious firmness of Lord Grey and Lord Palmerston, prevented a European war.

Italy could only be coerced, not governed, by Austrian archdukes and Austrian armies.

The treaty by which France was given over to the Bourbons, and liberty kept in check by the passive submission of the French, was attacked by Mr. Horner in a most able argumentative speech. The cause of the ancient republic of Genoa, and of the old public law of Europe, was pleaded with great weight of reason and authority by Sir James Mackintosh.

But a question touching England more nearly than the state of the Continent was now to be submitted to her Government, her Parliament, and her people. What was to be thenceforward her home policy? Before the great convulsions of France, in 1785, Mr. Pitt had proposed parliamentary reform, not indeed as Minister, but with all the weight of his personal talents. In 1786, in concluding a commercial treaty with France, he had founded his measure on the principles of free trade, temperately and gradually introduced. In 1792, Pitt and Fox had lauded, as the source of all our prosperity and all our greatness, the principles of the British Constitution. In 1801, in framing the measure for a legislative Union with Ireland, Pitt had proclaimed as its basis, that England, Scotland, and Ireland were to be placed on a footing of equality. He contemplated the admission of Roman Catholics to seats in Parliament, and, with few exceptions, to all civil and military employments. He projected a permanent grant to the Roman Catholic clergy, which would have placed them on a footing of virtual equality with the clergy of the Established Church.

In 1806, the Duke of Bedford, then Lord Lieutenant, directed Mr. Ponsonby, the Chancellor, Mr. William Elliot, the Chief Secretary, and Mr. Grattan, to prepare a measure for the commutation of tithes. They proposed to give the Church a compensation for the tithe of agistment, which had been abolished, without any regard to justice, by the Irish Parliament. The plan was transmitted to England, but the Ministry soon after resigned, and the Government which succeeded them was not prepared to do justice, either to the people as against the Church, or to the Church as against the landlords. Ireland was again given up to that monopolizing minority, who, by intolerance, corruption, and oppression kept her in a miserable subjection.

Any one who will read the descriptions given of Ireland by Burke, by Bishop Doyle, by Grattan, by Ponsonby, and by Plunket, before the Union, will find in them a picture of 'a country ill-governed, and a government ill-obeyed.'[1] The system of intolerance and corruption there described prevailed from the period of the Union till 1806, and from 1807 till 1830. Lord Grey then undertook the double task of putting down sedition and inaugurating justice.

Questions of this importance, which occupied Pitt's mind before and during the war, were thrust aside by the imminent perils of the war itself, and by the necessity of combining the elements of a majority who might agree upon the policy of continuing the war, although they might differ upon all other questions.

Thus Pitt renounced his views on reform of Parliament in gratitude to the supporters who had opposed what he called the Jacobin party; he put free trade in abeyance in order to raise the supplies for the year; and, after a temporary retirement from office, he consented to suspend the pacification of Ireland in deference to the King's scruples and the strong religious prejudice which disturbed his mind.

But now, with the war concluded, a very large debt contracted, trade embarrassed, and manufactures de-

---

[1] Grattan.

pressed, these questions were sure to arise. Free trade, parliamentary reform, pacification of Ireland, might each be expected to excite popular discussion and parliamentary movement.

Had Pitt lived till 1815, he might have recurred to his study of Adam Smith, and promoted freedom of trade with foreign countries; he might have introduced a temperate reform of the representation; he might have pacified Ireland without waiting for the threat of civil war, or fearing the conscientious scruples of the Prince Regent. For the Prince Regent, in 1812, had empowered Lord Wellesley to form a Ministry on the basis of granting what was called ' Catholic Emancipation.'

But these are questions belonging to the hypothesis of what might have been; my task is to record what was the policy of the Ministry of Lord Liverpool.

Lord Liverpool, of whom Lord Melbourne said after his resignation, 'that he had been clear in his great office,' had the merits of unblemished character, of great fairness in debate, and of avoiding extremes in policy. He was a man of very moderate understanding, not averse to some relaxations in matters of trade, but utterly averse to parliamentary reform, and too much imbued with the prejudices of the Tory party to admit the claims of Roman Catholics to seats in Parliament or political office. He had been the butt of Canning at Oxford; he was his master in Downing Street. Lord Castlereagh, who was leader of the Government in the House of Commons, had in fact the superior power in domestic as well as in foreign affairs.

Lord Castlereagh had entered the Irish House of Commons early in life. He had professed opinions favorable to parliamentary reform. But having re-

ceived from the Irish Government the offer of the high
and responsible office of Chief Secretary, with the
lead of the Irish House of Commons, he accepted it,
and became the exponent of the policy of the Government on the critical questions of the Rebellion and the
Union. There can be no doubt that the insurrection
was suppressed with little regard to humanity, and that
the Union was carried by means of political corruption.
But Lord Castlereagh, while he obtained the praise of
Lord Cornwallis for his ability, judgment, and habits of
business, did not incur any peculiar reproach for want
of feeling or want of integrity. After the Union it
was proposed to him to lead the Irish supporters of
Government in the House of Commons. But he declined this separate position, and chose rather to be
merged in the general body of the ministerial party
than to be the leader of the Irish members. He did
not resign with Pitt; on the contrary, he held an important office in the Addington administration. Yet he
was favorable to the claims of the Roman Catholics,
and gave them his support as soon as George III.
ceased to have personal control over public measures.
It is said that many years afterwards, when Grattan's
friends were assembled round his sick-bed, the dying
patriot said to them, ' Don't be hard upon Castlereagh
— he loves our country.' It is added that when Lord
Castlereagh heard of these words of his great opponent,
he burst into tears. I cannot vouch for the truth of
this anecdote, but I think it probably authentic.

Lord Castlereagh, who had been often pointed out
as the successor of Pitt, wanted the large views of that
great man. Still more obviously did he fail in emulat-
ing the magnificent march of Pitt's eloquence. Lord
Castlereagh was an obscure orator, garnishing his
speeches with confused metaphors. He took three-

quarters of an hour in telling the House of Commons that he did not mean to make any motion on the Treaties of Vienna, but that any private member was at liberty to do so. On another occasion, he had gone on for an hour speaking upon what subject no one could guess, when of a sudden he exclaimed, 'So much, Mr. Speaker, for the law of nations.' On another occasion, when he had spoken for an hour tediously and confusedly, he declared, 'I have now proved that the Tower of London is a common-law principle.' Of Spain he declared, that 'the pendulum had swung so far on the side of Jacobinism, that it afterwards swung quite as far on the side of anti-Jacobinism, which had prevented its settling in a middle point.' Every one has heard of his exhortation to the country gentlemen not to turn their backs upon themselves. He is said to have ended one of his long orations with the little word 'its.' He had no classical quotation, no happy illustration, no historical examples with which to adorn argument and enforce conviction. Yet his influence with his party was very great, and he was, till near the close of his life, a successful leader of the House of Commons.

For this end he possessed, besides the halo of glory encircling his brow as the Minister who had successfully concluded an arduous war, very considerable advantages. He was, as a man of business, clear, diligent, and decided. His temper was admirable — bold and calm, good-humored and dispassionate. He was a thorough gentleman; courteous, jealous of his own honor, but full of regard for the feelings of others. No one doubted his personal integrity, however much they might dislike his policy. That policy was detestable. None of the great subjects which had been in abeyance during the war — free trade, parliamentary reform, the grievances of Ireland — were made the basis of ministerial measures. The Tory party dreaded free trade doctrines, as likely to lead to the subversion of the corn-laws. Mr. Canning, who had again become one of the Ministry, was a vehement opponent of parliamentary reform. On a motion of mine to disfranchise Grampound, he said to his constituents at Liverpool, ' In disfranchising Grampound, if that is to be so, I mean to preserve Old Sarum.' With respect to the Catholic question, brought forward in 1816 by Mr. Grattan, Mr. Peel, then Chief Secretary of the Lord Lieutenant, made a powerful speech on the argument, that if the higher Catholics were admitted to Parliament, the great mass of the people would make a demand — an irresistible demand — for the abolition of the Protestant Church. Lord Castlereagh and Mr. Canning were permitted to vote for the motion, but Lord Liverpool maintained that his Ministry must continue divided upon a question vital to the empire; and for fourteen years after the peace this perilous and discreditable see-saw continued.

Even upon questions of social progress remote from party politics, Lord Castlereagh resisted innovation. Sir Samuel Romilly, a man of austere virtue and the most enlightened humanity, tried to amend our criminal law; Lord Castlereagh obstructed, and successfully obstructed, his progress. The same great and liberal man proposed to make freehold property subject to the payment of simple contract debts; the law-officers of the Crown would not hear of so dangerous an innovation.[1] So with regard to the Slave Trade and slavery;

---

[1] One of the Crown lawyers said that it was a mistake to say the law dated from the reign of Henry VIII.; that its origin was as far back as the time of Edward I. 'What care I,' retorted Romilly, 'whether this law was made by one set of barbarians or another?'

in speaking of the omission of Lord Castlereagh to insist on the condition that France should not revive the Slave Trade, and of our own acquisition of new colonies, Sir Samuel exclaimed, ' These colonies have been bought with the blood of Africa ! '

His look of stern indignation added to the effect of these words. Never was purer integrity, more enlightened philosophy, or a more profound love of mankind shown in the application of political science to practical legislation.

The conduct of the Government in refusing all measures of improvement or relief amid the distress which soon after the peace befell both the manufacturing and the agricultural classes, produced its natural effects — anger, discontent, disaffection, and secret conspiracies. Lord Sidmouth had recourse to the usual weapon of arbitrary government ; he employed spies to discover the plans of the conspirators, and the spy, as usual, fomented the disaffection which he was sent to investigate. A knot of disaffected persons in Derbyshire were told by the spy that 70,000 men in the neighborhood of Manchester were ready to rise in insurrection, and some of these unhappy dupes having appeared in arms to support their allies, were, on the evidence of the Crown, condemned and executed.

In 1817 the Habeas Corpus Act was suspended in England ; in 1819 six bills for the suppression of disturbance and for the repression of discussion at public meetings were introduced and passed. Lord Castlereagh, with his usual boldness, in bringing forward his portion of the bills, said, — ' I rise for the purpose of proposing to the House measures of severe coercion.'

It was evident that, if such was to be the peace policy of the Government, it behooved the Opposition to declare their own policy, and take issue on their proposals, as contrasted with those of the Government.

The Opposition of that day was neither a strong nor a compact body. Except Lord Grey, who had, much to his annoyance, been transferred from the House of Commons to the House of Lords, and who was not at this time very active in political life, the Opposition had no leader fit to inaugurate a policy or to lead a party. I remember being summoned to a meeting of the members of the party, both in Lords and Commons, at Burlington House, early in the year 1817. Lord Grey, in a few clear, bold, and dignified sentences, sketched the policy expected from the Ministry, and his own determination to oppose to the uttermost such of those measures as should be brought forward in the House of Lords. He ended by saying, 'Mr. Ponsonby will explain to you what is expected on the part of the Government in the House of Commons.' Mr. Ponsonby then addressed the meeting, and declared that he knew nothing of the proposals to be made by the Government in the House of Commons, or of the course that it was fit to pursue.

While such was the inability of the leader who had been set over us, there was little concord as to the measures to be resisted, or the motions to be brought forward by members of the Opposition. On foreign policy, little was to be done at this time. On the question of retrenchment, I moved in 1816, by the advice of Mr. Tierney, that the estimates should be returned to the Government with a prayer for their reduction. This motion failing, the question was taken up by Mr. Joseph Hume, who had great knowledge of details, unblemished honesty, and dogged perseverance.

With regard to parliamentary reform, as I took the lead upon that question from the end of 1819, it may be as well to explain the notions prevailing in the party. The abuses which had existed in the representation, and which had gone on increasing ever since the Revolution, had from time to time excited violent bursts of indignation, but the flame of reform, after blazing fiercely for a while, flickered and sank, and like a fire of straw had burnt itself away.

Impracticable theories or weak palliatives had been suggested instead of a wholesome remedy. The Duke of Richmond and Major Cartwright were in 1780 the advocates of personal suffrage. Pitt and Fox had both professed themselves favorable to a temperate reform. But the majority of Pitt's adherents did not follow him upon this subject, and on the Whig side while Fox, Sheridan, and Grey were favorable to parliamentary reform, Lord Rockingham and Burke were opposed to it. With these traditions, the Whigs of 1819 were much divided in opinion, many dreading, with the old Whigs and the Grenvilles, the agitation of so serious a subject, and others, left to their own inspirations, promoting impracticable schemes. Lord Milton opposed reform. Lord Althorp and Mr. Brougham supported it.

It seemed to me that this question was the test by which the popular principles of the Whigs, and of the Liberal party in general, were to be tried. As a question of men, I could not understand how any Ministry could be formed with a fair prospect of stability while a phalanx of members for close boroughs could be marshalled at any time, and drive Liberal statesmen from office, to expiate by a penance of ten or twenty years the crime of having brought forward measures favorable to religious liberty, or hostile to corrupt expendi-

ture. As to measures, similar reasoning might be
applied so long as a selfish cabal could feel certain of
defeating any plan of reform injurious to their personal
interests. There was no hope, therefore, unless parliamentary reform were seriously taken up and resolutely
pursued, of arresting the course of political repression,
religious intolerance, and wasteful expenditure, which
was upheld by all the strength of a great party, victorious in foreign war, fortified by the possession of boroughs which gave a majority in the House of Commons,
and apparently invincible from long possession of Government patronage, spreading over the Church, the
law, the army, the navy, and the colonies.

In assailing such a power, it behooved the Opposition
to be very cautious ; indeed, I had, like many others,
somewhat of a superstitious reverence for a system
which seemed entwined with our liberties, and almost
linked with the succession to the Crown. There was
besides the danger of touching public credit, which
was rightly compared by Lord Chatham to the sensitive
plant, shrinking from the slightest contact with a rude
hand. It was necessary to exorcise what Mr. Bentham
called the ‘hobgoblin argument,’ and this could not be
done by bell and candle, but must be met by clear argument, and dispelled by the light of day.

Such, then, was the problem which in 1819 I had to
examine and consider.

On the question of financial economy, I am convinced that when the sums proposed in the yearly
estimates are excessive, and show profusion or carelessness, the motion suggested by Mr. Tierney in 1816
is the proper course for the House of Commons to
adopt. Mr. Hume, however, with indefatigable industry and perseverance, in 1822, and following years,

attacked the various items of expense, and succeeded in persuading the country that the general character of the Government was not marked by economy.

The motion which I made in 1816 produced able speeches in debate, but no adequate result on the division.

In fact, the men of property, who had the representation in their hands, still feared a fresh explosion of the . French Revolution, and were disposed to trust blindly to those who had ended the war with glory, and replaced the Bourbons on the throne of France.

I have said that in 1817 the Habeas Corpus Act was suspended. At this time I had felt attendance in the House of Commons to be too fatiguing for my health, and I resolved to give up my seat in Parliament — at least for a year. Before doing so, I opposed the Suspension Bill in the speech contained in the volume of my speeches.

I was returned to Parliament in 1818 for the borough of Tavistock, and in 1819 I spoke on parliamentary reform.

The state of the representation of the people in the House of Commons, which in 1780 had excited so much popular discontent, had in the course of a long lapse of time become more and more unsatisfactory. Successive Sovereigns had granted the right, or imposed the burden, of returning members to Parliament on the corporations, freeholders, or burgage-tenants of numerous small towns. Powerful peers and wealthy commoners had bought property in these small boroughs with a view to increase their political influence. One noble lord used to go out hunting followed by a tail of six or seven members of Parliament of his own making. Another, being asked who should be returned for one of his boroughs, named a waiter at White's Club; but as he did not know the man's Christian name, the election was declared void, and a fresh election was held, when, the name having been ascertained, the waiter was duly elected. The object of the boroughmongers, as they were called, was generally to buy up the freeholds or burgage tenures in a small borough, in order to reduce the number of electors to a manageable number. If a freeholder or burgage-tenant refused to sell, it was not a very uncommon practice to blow up his house with gunpowder, and thus disfranchise a political opponent.

In this manner a number of boroughs, called nomination boroughs, were created, and became valuable property. A seat for the whole duration of a Parliament was sold for 5,000*l.* But as Parliaments were subject to sudden death, prudent men made a bargain to pay 1,000*l.* a year so long as they sat in the House of Commons. Mr. Ricardo, and many others, were members of the House of Commons in virtue of such payment. Sir Francis Burdett entered Parliament by purchase of a seat from the trustees of the Duke of Newcastle — a minor. Other proprietors of boroughs sold their seats to the Treasury for rank, office, or patronage. A friend of mine was concerned for a friend of his in a transaction of this kind. A valuable sinecure was part of the assets to be allotted to the seller of a portion of the representation of the people — I think not less than four seats. The partial remedies applied from time to time by Parliament did little to cure a wide-spread and notorious evil. Shoreham, where rich nabobs from India were all-powerful, and where a club, called the Christian Club, sold the borough and divided the profits, was thrown into the Rape of Bramber. Lord Chatham expressed his satisfaction that Shoreham

was taken away from Bengal and restored to the county
of Sussex. Similar treatment was applied to Aylesbury.

But these rare punishments were ineffective while
the general system was so corrupt.

The prevailing notion in 1780 was to diminish the
representation of the boroughs and increase that of the
counties; or, at all events, to add one hundred to the
representation of the counties, by way, as it were, of
diluting the noxious ingredients. Lord Chatham highly
approved of this remedy; but Lord North, with char-
acteristic humor, said — 'Some ask, with Lear, for a
hundred knights; and some, with Goneril, for fifty; but
I say, with Regan, what need of one?'

It was clear that no efficient remedy could be applied
unless by means of a strong party organization, or a
strong public opinion; and both were then wanting.

In 1801, Pitt, in his speech on the Union, declared
not only that he would not propose reform while the
war required the undivided energies of the nation, but
that the resistance to Jacobinism displayed by the House
of Commons during the French War persuaded him that
no reform of Parliament was necessary.

Fox, on his side, induced Grey to bring forward
reform in 1797, not with a hope of carrying any measure,
but as a protest against the whole foreign and domestic
policy of the Government. Thus reform became in men's
minds closely connected with revolutionary change.

Sir Francis Burdett, in later years, proposed reform
in the spirit of Bolingbroke and the Tory party of the
reign of Queen Anne. The Tory theory of that time
was, that the House of Commons ought to be a check
upon the Crown, but that no Minister ought to sit in
the House of Commons. The Whig theory, which was
adopted by a compromise called 'West's Expedient,'

from the name of its proposer, admitted Ministers into the House of Commons, if duly elected after the acceptance of office, and instead of leaving to the Sovereign the free choice of his political servants, insisted that the Ministry, as a united and responsible body, should possess the confidence of the House of Commons. Sir Francis Burdett, reverting to the notion that the prerogative of the Crown, in choosing its servants, ought to be unfettered and uncontrolled, said, in bringing forward a motion for reform of Parliament, 'If a country gentleman were to offer to a servant out of place to make him his butler, and the man were to answer, " I will not be your butler unless you will take Harry for your coachman, and Thomas for your groom, and Dick for your footman," the gentleman would be greatly astonished.' This remark proves that Sir Francis Burdett was, as he sometimes avowed himself to be, a high prerogative Tory of the days of Queen Anne. Indeed, this mode of arguing the question of reform was an arraignment of the whole course of constitutional government, as it had existed from the accession of the House of Hanover, and tended to no practical result.

Yet the case against the House of Commons, as an imperfect and distorted image of the people, was stronger than ever. On the one side, the strength of the nomination system was such, that even Mr. Canning felt the weight of the chain he was unable to burst. When he was going to India, Mr. George Vernon Harcourt, meeting him in a passage of the Opera House, said to him, ' I cannot but lament your going to India ; I was in hopes that one day you would have been leader of the House of Commons.' Mr. Canning answered that at one time he had entertained a similar hope, but that when he saw that the Ministry were obliged to yield to the dictation of the Duke of —— and the Duke of ——, he no longer had a wish to be leader.

On the other hand, while a few men governed the Government, large commercial and manufacturing cities had grown up which had no representatives in Parliament. Mr. Stuart Wortley conducted all the local business of Yorkshire — of Leeds, Halifax, Bradford, and Sheffield; Lord Stanley that of Lancashire — that is, of Manchester, Oldham, and other populous towns. On public affairs these great centres of industry, skill, intelligence, and wealth had no representative voice whatever.

With a view to work my way to a change, not by eloquence — for I had none — but by patient toil, and a plain statement of facts, I brought before the House of Commons the case of Grampound. I obtained an inquiry; and with the assistance of Mr. Charles Wynn I forced the solicitors employed in bribery to reveal the secrets of their employers: the case was clear; the borough was convicted.

At this time Lord Castlereagh, who had always been personally very kind to me, invited me to speak to him on one of the benches behind the Treasury Bench. He told me that the Government would cordially support me, if I would content myself with extending the right of voting for Grampound to the neighboring hundreds. I answered him that I could not agree to that proposal, and that I must persist in proposing that the franchises of Grampound should be transferred to the town of Leeds. This was, in fact, the whole principle at issue between the Government and the reformers. The hundreds of Cornwall represented the stationary policy of the Ministry; Leeds, the new population which I sought to admit, and with them, the principle of reform. When, twelve years afterwards, I proposed a bill of reform, on behalf of Lord Grey and his colleagues, Mr. Alexander Baring said, ' The plan takes away representation from the barley-field and gives it to the coal-field.' This was the truth in 1819, as in 1832. My proposal took away representation from the dead bones of a former state of England, and gave it to the living energy and industry of the England of the nineteenth century, with its steam-engines and its factories; its cotton and woollen cloths; its cutlery and its coal-mines; its wealth and its intelligence. The present vindicated its rights; the past lost its privilege.

But to return.

After a long conversation, Lord Castlereagh persisted in his view and I in mine. I carried my bill in the House of Commons; but when it went to the House of Lords, the town of Leeds was expunged, and the two disposable seats were given to the county of York. Thus the introduction of new representation was avoided. It is singular, however, that the Government of 1820 should have thought that by excluding Leeds, Manchester, and Birmingham from representation, they were consulting the Conservative interests of the Constitution! Such, however, was the spirit of the Government of Liverpool and Castlereagh.

After the disfranchisement of Grampound, I revolved in my mind a plan for the reform of the whole state of the representation.

In meditating upon this subject, I had to survey not only the danger of shaking an edifice which resembled rather a strong fortress than an ordinary dwelling-house, but also party objections which would be brought against me.

Mr. Tierney told me that the notes to members

usually sent out when a party motion was in contemplation, could not be allowed to me on the question of reform. An old and powerful Whig member of Parliament told me that he never knew the question of parliamentary reform brought forward without doing harm to the party.[1]

Thus discountenanced by my betters and my elders, I had to consider the position, the character, and the principles of the Whig party.

It seemed to me then, as it does now, that the Whig party had from the Revolution of 1688 endeavored to accommodate itself to the wants of the time, without binding itself slavishly to precisely the same course.

In the reigns of William III. and Queen Anne, the party had devoted its energies to wars against the ambition of Louis XIV. That contest rendered necessary the exclusion of Roman Catholics from all those vantage points of power of which James II. had availed himself, to subvert the liberties of Englishmen.

During the reigns of George I. and George II., Walpole had confined his home policy to the single point of maintaining the House of Hanover on the throne. When asked by a leading dissenter to support the repeal of the Corporation and Test Acts, he urged that the time was inopportune. The dissenter, ill-satisfied, wished him to be so good as to point out when he would support such a measure. The Minister said he would answer in one word, ' Never.' [2] Walpole was probably as little inclined as any man to favor the exclusion of Protestant dissenters, or the enactment of harsh penal laws against Roman Catholics. But he knew that if

---

[1] Lord George Cavendish.
[2] See Coxe's ' Life of Sir R. Walpole.'

he favored religious liberty, the Church would rise
against him, and would probably overthrow the Protestant succession. His maxim was, therefore, *Quieta
non movere.* Lord Chatham, who was intrusted with
the lead of the House of Commons when the country
had drifted into war, carried on that war so gloriously,
that the peace of 1763 marked the ascendancy of England both in the East and in the West. After this time
the Whig party fell into a state of decline, and for
several years there was scarcely a perceptible difference
between Whigs and Tories.

The American War and the debating powers of Mr.
Fox led to a revival of party distinctions, and the
new Whigs engaged in the pursuit of objects which
the old Whigs had not dreamt of. These objects may
be shortly defined.

1. Not to interfere in the internal government of
other countries.

2. To make peace with our American colonies by
acknowledging their independence, and to satisfy the
people of Ireland by conceding their demand of political
equality.

3. To promote religious liberty, and to remove the
political disabilities affecting Protestant dissenters and
Roman Catholics.

4. To favor parliamentary reform and liberty of the
press.

Had these principles prevailed from 1770 to 1820,
the country would have avoided the American War
and the first French Revolutionary War, the rebellion
in Ireland in 1798, and the creation of three or four
hundred millions of National Debt.

Such were the principles which Fox and those
whom Burke afterwards called the 'New Whigs'

professed. They had been powerful in argument, but weak in numbers. Both the American and the French wars had the support of the great majority of the country. Sir George Savile and Sir Gilbert Elliot are witnesses to this preponderance of warlike opinion during the American War; Mr. Fox himself and his few adherents testify to the warlike temper of the majority during the French War.

Among these adherents were my uncle, Francis, Duke of Bedford, and my father, who succeeded him.

On a visit which I paid to Sir James Mackintosh, at his country house, he said to me, with some significance,

> Ecquid in antiquam virtutem, animosque viriles, /
> Et pater Æneas et avunculus excitat Hector?

He urged me especially to undertake the question of reform of Parliament.

Thus animated, I brought forward the whole question in 1822.

My friend Mr. Lambton had a little while before made a motion in favor of reform. But his plan of electoral districts was not generally approved, and a premature division put an early stop to the debate.

That carelessness and forgetfulness which are so common about events a little preceding our own time, are well illustrated by a passage in the 'Quarterly Review' of January, 1869, which I proceed to copy : — 'Any thing on the scale of Mr. Pitt's Reform Bill of '86, or Mr. Grey's of '95, never entered into the heads of statesmen as a practical object to be attained from the beginning of the nineteenth century to the death of Canning. The extreme Radical party, led by Sir Francis Burdett, did, in 1819, move for something of the sort: but Lord John Russell opposed it as revolutionary, and substituted for it his own little pop-gun against Grampound. From that time to 1826 the Whigs never stirred in the matter.' The inaccuracy of this statement in a publication which professes to be the organ of the great Tory party is something marvellous. In the first place, Mr. Grey's Reform Bill was brought forward, not in '95, but in '93 and '97. Admitting this to be a slip of the pen, or an error of the press, the assertion with regard to my exertions in the cause of reform is directly opposed to the fact.

In 1822, in a speech of three hours on the subject of reform, I suggested that one hundred members should be added to the House of Commons, and that they should be chosen by the larger counties and the great commercial and manufacturing communities of the kingdom. So little did Mr. Canning consider my motion as a mere pop-gun, at which no one could be alarmed, that he gave me a solemn warning, in words which, thus challenged by the Quarterly Reviewer, I will not refrain from copying : — ' Our lot is happily cast in the temperate zone of freedom, the clime best suited to the development of the moral qualities of the human race, to the cultivation of their faculties, and to the security as well as the improvement of their virtues; a clime not exempt indeed from variations of the elements, but variations which purify while they agitate the atmosphere that we breathe. Let us be sensible of the advantages which it is our happiness to enjoy. Let us guard with pious gratitude the flame of genuine liberty, that fire from heaven of which our Constitution is the holy repository; and let us not, for the chance of rendering it more intense and more radiant, impair its purity or hazard its extinction ! The noble lord is entitled to the acknowledgments of the House, for the

candid, able, and ingenuous manner in which he has
brought forward his motion. If, in the remarks which
I have made upon it, there has been any thing which
has borne the appearance of disrespect to him, I hope
he will acquit me of having so intended it. That the
noble lord will carry his motion this evening, I have no
fear ; but with the talents which he has shown himself
to possess, and with (I sincerely hope) a long and brilliant career of parliamentary distinction before him, he
will, no doubt, renew his efforts hereafter. Although
I presume not to give any weight to observations or
warnings of mine, yet on this, probably the last opportunity I shall have of raising my voice on the question of parliamentary reform, while I conjure the House
to pause before it consents to adopt the proposition of
the noble lord, I cannot help conjuring the noble lord
himself to pause before he again presses it upon the
country. If, however, he shall persevere — and if his
perseverance shall be successful — and if the result of
that success shall be such as I cannot help apprehend-
ing — his be the triumph to have precipitated those
results — be mine the consolation that to the utmost,
and the latest of my power, I have opposed them.
(Loud cheers.)' [1]

Mr. Canning's speech was eloquent and successful.
But his peroration showed that he did not expect that
the representation, as then existing, would very long
endure. And my friends were encouraged not only by
the large number who supported me, but by remarking
that among those who appeared in the division, and
who had never voted for reform before, were three
members, each said to be worth a million. In the

---

[1] Canning's Speeches.

days when it was said that reform threatened property, such substantial support was worth a great deal.

The melancholy death of Lord Londonderry (Lord Castlereagh) produced a change, at first gradual, but afterwards abrupt, in the state of public affairs. Lord Liverpool considered Mr. Canning as the only fit successor, and being supported by the Duke of Wellington, did not fail to obtain the reluctant consent of the King. The transfer of power from a man of business, endowed with common sense and discretion, but bound by traditional Toryism, to a man of genius, a brilliant orator, and a no less shining wit, was in itself a novelty. But the change was far greater from one who professed adherence to principles of non-intervention with the supremacy of the Holy Alliance, and who spoke coldly in favor of Catholic relief, to one whose impulses were strongly in favor of freedom abroad, and religious liberty at home. The expedition to Portugal, and the speeches which heralded its departure from our shores, gave assurance to the Continent that the arm of England was yet powerful. The eloquent speeches of Canning in favor of granting the petitions of the Roman Catholics, and the speeches of Huskisson and Canning in favor of free trade, created a new feeling in the country. Neither the expedition to Portugal nor the measures of Mr. Huskisson with regard to free trade were of themselves very important. But every Liberal felt that

> Night's candles are burnt out, and jocund Day
> Stands tiptoe on the misty mountain tops.

Lord Holland, observing the cooling zeal of the Tory party on behalf of the Government, said that their feeling was like that of Nisus: —

> Absistamus, ait, nam lux inimica propinquat.

The first step of Canning in regard to the French invasion of Spain was not, and could not be, successful, but, in my opinion, was not open to censure. I could not, therefore, concur in the motion made against it, and I absented myself from the House of Commons on that occasion. .

The substitution of Mr. Peel for Lord Sidmouth gave the country a criminal law reformer and a friend of free trade, in place of a Minister who was the incarnation of prejudice and intolerance. Upon one great subject, however, no advance was made. In 1825, a last attempt was made in Parliament to settle the Roman Catholic question on the basis originally laid down by Pitt. In 1805, on a motion made by Fox, Pitt said: — 'My idea was not to apply tests to the religious tenets of the Catholics, but tests applicable to what was the source and foundation of the evil; to render the priests, instead of making them the instruments of poisoning the minds of the people, dependent in some sort upon the Government, and thus links, as it were, between the Government and the people.'[1]

In 1825, it was proposed by Lord Francis Egerton, 'That it is expedient that a provision should be made by law towards the maintenance of the secular Roman Catholic clergy, exercising religious functions in Ireland.'[2] The motion was carried by 205 to 162. It was proposed at the same time that the 40s. freeholders should be disfranchised. These two measures were called the wings. They would have settled the Catholic question without the evil and the reproach of yielding to intimidation; without uprooting the Protestant

---

[1] Pitt's 'Speeches,' vol. iii. p. 424.
[2] Hansard, vol. xiii. new series, p. 318.

Church Establishment ; civil, political, and ecclesiastical equality would have been attained ; peace with Ireland would have been permanently concluded. The Roman Catholic clergy, who would have rejected a pecuniary provision taken alone, would hardly have refused it as part of a settlement by which the Roman Catholic laity would have been admitted to Parliament and political office.

Lord Liverpool, a man of honest but narrow views, would not allow this civil crown to be placed on his brow. He told Lord Harrowby that he would not agree to the words ' by law ' in the resolution respecting the provision to be made for the Roman Catholic clergy. He said to Mr. Arbuthnot, ' Even if I were to give way, Peel would not.'

Thus, from weakness, from the want of a directing mind in the Ministry, from the jealousy of Canning entertained by the Tories, and from some personal feelings on the part both of Government and Opposition, this promising scheme fell through ; a great man was wanting in the Cabinet, and a great opportunity was neglected by Parliament.

In 1827, Lord Liverpool was disabled by a fit, which removed him from office, and which was soon followed by death. Thus ended a Ministry of fifteen years, marked by great events, but not by the predominance of any great statesman.

But Lord Liverpool's disappearance from the political scene gave rise to a great *débacle*. The fragments of the old system rushed against each other, and for a time all was confusion.

The question who was to succeed Lord Liverpool in the King's Council gave rise to much conversation in ministerial circles, and to some, if not much, intrigue in the cottage where George IV. resided during the rebuilding of Windsor Castle. What passed in Parliament, and among the members of the Liberal party in Parliament, was sufficiently interesting and exciting.

Canning was pointed out to be First Minister by the usual order of succession; by thirty years' experience of political life, begun under the immediate guidance of Pitt; by his eloquence and his genius; by his Liberal sympathies, and his Conservative tendencies; by his position as the official representative of the Government in the House of Commons.

Objections both political and personal were raised against his appointment. The intolerant party, who had enjoyed the greater share of patronage, and especially of ecclesiastical patronage, under Lord Liverpool, would not consent to the transfer of bishoprics and deaneries to men who might be favorable to the grant of equal rights and privileges to Roman Catholics. This change was especially distasteful to Mr. Peel, the Home Secretary.

But there were likewise objections of a personal nature. The quarrel with Lord Castlereagh had left disagreeable impressions. The frankness with which Canning had urged the reasons for free trade, and had told men who objected to improvement, because it was innovation, that if they persisted they might have to submit to innovations which were no improvement, had offended and alarmed the real Tories, as much as it had attracted and conciliated the real Whigs.

The apparent objections to Canning were of little weight. If the Roman Catholic question was to be treated as an open question in the Cabinet, it was obviously unfair to deny to a pro-Catholic leader that supremacy which had been long and quietly yielded to an anti-Catholic Prime Minister. The quarrel with

Lord Castlereagh was owing rather to the weakness of
the Duke of Portland and Lord Camden than to any
fault of Canning. It was no wonder, therefore, that
Canning felt deeply the wound inflicted upon him,
when (upon his selection for the post of Prime Minister) six of his colleagues sent in their resignations. In
a debate upon this subject, in the House of Commons,
he said : ' My position is not that of gratified ambition.'
But he went on to say that he could not be a consenting party to his ' helotism.' This was, in fact, the
question to be decided. Canning, with all his powers
of debate, his experience in public affairs, his conduct
of foreign affairs, which had raised England in the
scale of nations, was to be reduced to execute the
orders of some man evidently his inferior !

He justly resented these resignations as a proof of
want of confidence on the part of his Tory colleagues,
but he also, from his excitable nature, felt them as
personal attacks : and when, like Burke, he saw Blanche,
Tray, and Sweetheart all barking at him ; the clerks and
underlings of Lord Liverpool's Ministry assailing him
from every quarter, his spirit rose to meet the open
attack, but his heart sank under the secret hostility by
which it was prompted.

With the alteration of one word, I may apply to him
Dryden's lines on Shaftesbury —

> A fiery soul, which, working out its way,
> Fretted the fragile body to decay,
> And o'er informed the tenement of clay.

In the conduct of affairs he had not preserved
the calm and cold demeanor of Castlereagh. When
Brougham attacked him for his tergiversation, he rose
with passion to repel the imputation. When an anony-

mous pamphleteer threatened him with death,[1] he was so imprudent as to send a personal challenge to the antagonist whose mask was worn for the very purpose of evading responsibility.   Thus easily exasperated, thwarted in his foreign policy by the King and half his colleagues, holding a position on the Catholic question which kept Ireland in perpetual ferment, distrusted by many of his party, and prevented by his opinions on reform from cordially uniting with the Whigs, it is no wonder that his temper and health gave way.   I remember the impression made upon me painfully by a single word, uttered by him in answer to a question evidently intended to vex and embarrass him.   The resignation of all the anti-Catholic members of the Government placed at Mr. Canning's disposal the office of Judge-Advocate.   There was some delay in naming a successor.   The question was asked whether the office had been filled up.   The answer was the monosyllable 'Yes,' but pronounced in such a tone of mingled scorn, anger, and grief, that it seemed as if the heart of him who uttered it were breaking with vexation and disappointment.   I remember nothing like it but Kean's answer to Iago, 'You are moved,' when he replied, 'Not a jot,' in a voice of the deepest anxiety and emotion.

Lord Lansdowne and Mr. Tierney joined the Cabinet of Mr. Canning.   Mr. Tierney stipulated that he should be free to vote in favor of parliamentary reform.   Mr. Abercromby, Mr. Stanley (the late Lord Derby), and Mr. Macdonald accepted office.

The new pieces were not very well dovetailed into

---

[1] Trecenti conjuravimus principes juventutis Romanæ, ut te in hac viâ grassaremur. — Livii Hist., ii. 12.

the remains of the Tory Ministry, but the importance of the change thus indicated was enormous. The Tory party, which had survived the disasters and the follies of the American War, which had borne the defeats and achieved the final glories of the French War, was broken by its separation from Mr. Canning into fragments, which could not easily be reunited.

It is singular to observe how this well-disciplined Tory party was ready to break forth into mutiny when any one of its favorite errors or rooted prejudices was abandoned. Neither the eloquence, nor the financial talents, nor the experience of Pitt, prevented his being left with only fifty followers, when the King refused to conciliate Ireland, and to repair injustice. Neither the brilliant genius nor thirty years of experience saved Canning from desertion, obloquy, and hatred. The great services and patriotic disinterestedness of the Duke of Wellington availed him little when he preferred the pacification of Ireland to civil war. The eminent qualities of Peel did not protect him from invective and vituperation on the part of his followers, when he proposed to free from taxation the daily food of the laborer.

The period from 1820 to 1827 was the most brilliant period for oratory in the House of Commons within my recollection. The graceful, finished, well-prepared speeches of Canning, sparkling with classical quotation, happy illustration, and refined wit, were delightful to all who heard him. Sometimes, indeed, the *purpurei panni* did not well combine with the plain broadcloth of a business argument, but, on the whole, the effect was entrancing and attractive to all the young members, who cared rather to support a cause well defended than to examine the solidity of the defences themselves.

Mr. Ward, himself an orator of no mean rank, said once. to me, ' I like what is polished and perfect — I admire Virgil, Racine, and Pitt.' To such men the eloquence of Canning was irresistible. Those who above all admired what was sublime, though not fault-less, and who preferred to finished poetry and elaborate oratory Homer, Dante, Shakespeare, and Fox were, however, not ready to yield altogether to the seduction of a statesman who, while he fought for Roman Catholic relief and the reduction of protective duties, contended for restrictions on political freedom, and utterly opposed parliamentary reform.

On one occasion, when Canning was concluding a speech in favor of coercion he deprecated the forth-coming reply of Brougham by the quotation —

> Stetimus tela aspera contra,
> Contulimusque manus; experto credite, quantus
> In clypeum assurgat, quo turbine torqueat hastam.

Brougham well earned a great reputation. With pro-digious force of argument he struck down any common adversary, pouring fiery sarcasm, and unsparing, over-whelming refutation upon his head, and leaving him an object of ridicule or of pity, crushed beneath the weight of accumulated epithets and a burning mass of invec-tive.

The third whom I have to mention, Plunket, was, in the opinion of the best judges, the most perfect orator of that time. Plunket so restrained his brilliant fancy, that it was ever ready to help, to adorn, to illustrate, while it was never used to eclipse or encumber his argu-ment. He usually confined his speeches to the subject of Roman Catholic disabilities, but his defence of his own conduct, in answer to Mr. Brownlow, was a great

triumph of oratorical art; and his answer to Brougham
on the proposal to make a provision for the Roman
Catholic clergy, was a memorable display of wit and
wisdom.

On the Catholic question, while Copley and Peel
made the most of a bad cause, the union of Plunket,
Brougham, and Canning, in defence of justice to Ireland, produced three speeches in different styles, unequalled in power to convince, combining the eloquence
of great orators with the counsels of wise statesmen.

This brilliant period was about to terminate. Canning died in 1827 at Chiswick, where Fox had died in
1806. Plunket accepted a seat in the House of Lords;
Brougham remained only three years longer in the
House of Commons. But the fire which these three
men had kindled blazed on for many years after their
disappearance. After a short period of official rule,
Lord Goderich, First Lord of the Treasury, who had
taken no means to strengthen his Government, resigned,
and the King sent for the Duke of Wellington, who
retained the Canning portion of the Cabinet, and got
rid of the Whig members of the Ministry. Mr. Tierney said he had been killed in a chance-medley.

Mr. Peel was the new leader of the House of Commons.

In 1828, at the request of a body of Protestant dissenters, I brought forward a motion for the repeal of
the Corporation and Test Acts, and to my great surprise
carried it by a majority of forty.

Peel, finding himself defeated, after a vain attempt
to avoid a total repeal, proposed a useless and feeble
declaration, which the Bishops accepted in the House
of Lords, after adding a mischievous barrier against the
admission of the Jews, in the words ' on the true faith

of a Christian.' The whole of this declaration was repealed in 1868; it had kept out nobody, and its removal will admit nobody.

Huskisson and the friends of Canning voted against the repeal of the Corporation and Test Acts.

The successive steps which brought on the Roman Catholic Relief Bill are to be found in Sir Robert Peel's Memorandum upon this subject. It has always seemed to me, that, however pure his motives, and however clear his integrity, he would have done better, both for himself and his country, if he had resigned office, and given his support, either to the Duke of Wellington with another leader in the Commons, or to Lord Grey and the Whig party, in the settlement of a question which, since the peace, had been the apparent cause of their proscription.

The only reason alleged in the Memorandum alluded to, is the King's personal dislike of Lord Grey. But this dislike was not so strong as that which his father entertained to Mr. Fox. Fox had, notwithstanding this dislike, when an emergency arose, been admitted to the councils of the King, and when he died, George III. said to his daughter, the Duchess of Gloucester, who told it to me, 'I did not think I should ever have regretted the death of Mr. Fox, as I find I do.' But George III.'s religious scruples, and even his personal prejudices, were respected by the nation, and formed real barriers so long as he did not himself waive them; the religious scruples of George IV. did not meet with ready belief, nor did his personal dislikes inspire national respect or obtain national acquiescence.

However, as Mr. Peel had thought it his duty to remain in office, the Whig party determined to give him a cordial support. I was present at a small meeting of the leaders of the party, at Sir Francis Burdett's, when Lord Althorp was authorized to communicate to Peel our objections to part of the ministerial measures. But when Lord Althorp reported to us the answer of Peel, that the Ministers could not go further than they had done, we all acquiesced, and waived every objection, in order to give a thorough support to the Government which had undertaken this mighty task.

One of the shrewdest of the Tory party, who afterwards held a Cabinet office, is reported to have observed that he should not have felt so much objection to Catholic emancipation, had he not felt sure that it would be followed by reform of Parliament.

He was not mistaken. The Catholic question having been moved out of the way, attention was more eagerly directed to the faults of the existing state of the representation of the people.

Standing one day at the bar of the House of Commons, in the year 1830, I showed Mr. Huskisson some resolutions on parliamentary reform which I intended to move. Huskisson said: 'I cannot vote for these resolutions, but something to this effect will be carried before long.'

The events which immediately preceded the General Election of 1830 had prepared the way for the fall of that Tory supremacy which had for sixty years, with little interruption, ruled England; had carried on the American War and the French Revolutionary War, and had placed the country in a position of immense power, enormous debt, and great internal difficulty.

The sudden change of the Duke of Wellington and Sir Robert Peel on the policy to be pursued towards Ireland, had struck men with astonishment and inspired them with distrust. That the same man who in 1827

4

had declared, with six of his colleagues, that not only could he not consent to admit the Catholics to Parliament and to high office, but that he could not even submit to serve as Secretary of State under a Prime Minister who was favorable to their claims, should, two years afterwards, have come forward, and, in a speech of great length and ability, have recommended concession on all those points, without conditions and without security, produced a very natural and very general distrust. 'If,' they said, 'Peel, while he was opposing Canning in 1827, knew that concession must be the end of his policy, what becomes of his honesty? If such was to be the inevitable termination, why should he not rather, even out of office, have assisted Canning, who, by his genius, by his eloquence, and by his great reputation, was entitled to that assistance, rather than have proclaimed a continued and determined resistance to claims which he then declared to be inconsistent with our political Constitution and our religious Establishment? But if, in 1827, Peel hoped to resist successfully all further concessions to Roman Catholics, and in 1829 perceived that it required only a continuance of the balanced state of the House of Commons, and the agitation of a skilful demagogue in Ireland, to make the defence of all those buttresses which he had so long and so pertinaciously defended, hopeless, where was his wisdom?' In fact, the whole framework of our representation, the whole machinery of government by which Lord North, Mr. Pitt, and Lord Liverpool had ruled, seemed to be tumbling into ruins after this great political earthquake.

Few men saw justly and clearly the consequences at home of the course pursued by the Duke of Wellington abroad. The Revolution in France, overthrowing Legitimacy, and crowning a monarchy founded upon popular resistance; the excitement of a General Election, and the accession of a new Sovereign; the internal state of the country, resulting from long mismanagement; all contributed to bring about, on the one side a desire of change, and on the other discouragement and despondency.

When, therefore, at the meeting of Parliament, November the 3d, the Duke of Wellington declared that the constitution of the House of Commons was perfect, and that the wit of man could not *à priori* have devised any thing so good, the general feeling was one of dismay. The House of Lords, usually so calm, showed signs of amazement and perturbation. The Duke whispered to one of his colleagues, 'What can I have said which seems to make so great a disturbance?' 'You have announced the fall of your Government, that is all,' replied his more clear-sighted colleague.

Accordingly, when Sir Henry Parnell, in the House of Commons, moved an amendment respecting the appointment of a Committee on the Civil List, which Mr. Tierney had frequently brought forward unsuccessfully, it was carried by a majority of upwards of thirty. Although, in ordinary times, this victory of the Opposition would have been of little consequence, it was now thought so serious, that Mr. Peel went at once to the Duke of Wellington, at Apsley House, to declare he could no longer remain in office; the following day the whole Ministry resigned. Lord Grey was sent for by the King, and desired by his Majesty to form an administration.

At this period the situation of affairs at home was very critical. The fifteen years which had elapsed since the peace had not been employed to good pur-

pose; the currency, indeed, had been restored to its
old value, and the guinea no longer represented more
than the twenty-one shillings which it professed to be
worth; but, generally speaking, old abuses which had
been left uncorrected during the pressure of war had
been still uncorrected during the leisure of peace, and
the new abuses which had arisen in times of scarcity,
and at periods of emergency, had been allowed to grow
up in rank luxuriance, till they overspread the land.
Among these abuses, there was none more contrary to
sound principle, none more destructive to the peace and
prosperity of the country, than the perversion of the
Poor-law of Elizabeth. During the years of scarcity
which had afflicted the country at the end of the last
and the beginning of the present century, the poor had
suffered grievously from the great rise in the price of
provisions, unaccompanied by a similar rise in the rate
of wages. It occurred to some not very wise country
gentlemen, that the laborers might be enabled to maintain themselves and their families, without putting their
employers to the expense which a general rise in the
rate of wages would involve. They accordingly framed
a scale: so much to an unmarried laborer; so much to
a married laborer with one child; so much to a married
laborer with two children; and so on, till the allowance
given to a laborer with ten or twelve children was
equivalent to a very high rate of wages. In the course
of years, this foolish scheme produced the evils that
might have been expected. The individual laborer was
no longer paid according to the value of his strength
and skill as a laborer, but according to the number of
his family, without reference to the work he might perform. The population of a parish increased, not in
proportion to the demand for labor, but in proportion to

the readiness of farm laborers to take advantage of the
perverted law to marry, and live on the public as parish
pensioners. The mischiefs produced by this system in
the agricultural counties were extensive and appalling.
In Buckinghamshire whole parishes were pauperized,
and farmers abandoned tillage rather than attempt to
pay a rate of nineteen or twenty shillings in the pound.
A farmer in Huntingdonshire, giving evidence before a
Committee of the House of Commons, over which I
presided, stated that the young laborers said to the
members of the vestry, ' We will marry, and you must
maintain us.' In Bedfordshire, a state of society existed, which is portrayed with much fidelity in a petition
presented to the House of Commons in 1830. In the
agricultural parishes, gangs of forty or fifty laborers out
of employment were sent nominally to repair the roads,
but in fact loitered all day by the side of their wheel-
barrows, and passed the night in poaching, and spend-
ing the fruits of their plunder in the public-houses. In
the parish of Woburn, where there were forty of these
able-bodied laborers unemployed, I asked a farmer why
he did not give wages to two or three of them in return
for work upon his farm. He answered, ' They would
do me no good ; they would be more likely to steal what
I have than to do any work on the farm.' In the western counties, large bodies of these idle young men went
about destroying thrashing-machines, and setting fire to
ricks of hay and stacks of corn. At night, the whole
atmosphere was lighted up by fires, the work of lawless
depredators. The yeomanry were called out and captured many offenders, but still the evil went on. Farmers were alarmed for their property, members of parish
vestries were afraid to refuse the demands of sturdy

beggars, and the whole framework of society seemed about to yield to force and anarchy. Sir Robert Peel, the Home Secretary, confessed that he had no remedy to propose for this diseased condition.

The state of the metropolis was not better than that of the rural districts. The King was advised not to pay that visit to the city which is customary upon the accession of a Sovereign, lest his presence should excite tumult and disorder. A tradesman in Westminster, being asked why he had provided himself with a musket, answered, ' In the first place to get reform of Parliament, and in the next place to defend my house against a mob.' A certain vague desire, and a fear equally undefined, seemed to possess all classes of men. The events of the three glorious days of Paris had filled the mind of England with a notion that the public good was to be sought by revolution, by barricades in the streets, and by force employed to obtain popular measures. But of what nature, to what extent to be carried, or what were the precise benefits to be attained by these measures, no one well knew. It was therefore the task of the new Government to frame measures large enough to satisfy expectation, and at the same time to maintain the dignity of the monarchy and the authority of Parliament.

The aspect of affairs abroad was at the same time disquieting. The weak and unnatural connection which the treaties of 1815 had formed between Holland and Belgium had, after many years of jealousy and discontent, ended in a general insurrection of the Belgium people. A proclamation beginning ' To arms! to arms!' had been signed by men of the first rank and ability as leaders of the insurgent party. It was to be feared

that the French appetite for annexation, which had
been indulged by the Jacobin Republic of 1792, might
revive under the excitement of a recent revolution, and
the sympathies of the popular party. The great Powers
had already communicated to each other their anxieties
upon this subject, and a conference under the auspices
of Lord Aberdeen had been assembled in London.

It was in this state of affairs that Lord Grey was
called to the councils of his Sovereign, and, happily,
his abilities and his experience were found equal to the
emergency.

Lord Grey determined to construct his administration upon a broad and comprehensive basis. He invited Lord Goderich, Lord Palmerston, and Mr. Charles
Grant, who had been members of Mr. Canning's Ministry, to accept offices in the Cabinet. He placed Lord
Palmerston at the head of the Foreign Department,
and confided the Home Office to Lord Melbourne, who,
having belonged from his early youth to the Whig
party, had accepted the office of Chief Secretary in
Ireland when Mr. Canning was Prime Minister. It is
even supposed that Lord Grey would have consented
to leave the Great Seal in the hands of Lord Lyndhurst. The chiefs of the Whig party, however, were
not willing to see this high office in the hands of any
other person than Mr. Brougham, whose splendid eloquence and extraordinary talents had won for him the
applause of the country and the admiration of his party.
Lord Althorp, therefore, on the part of Lord Grey,
offered him the Great Seal, and, after a long discussion,
succeeded in persuading Brougham that he might render greater services to his country and to his party by
accepting this very eminent post than by remaining in

an independent position in the House of Commons.[1]
Lord Althorp himself accepted the post of Chancellor
of the Exchequer, with the lead of the House of Commons.   He was very unwilling to take office, but Lord
Grey assured him that he could not make his Ministry
without him, and it was some consolation to him to
reflect, in accepting the office of Chancellor of the
Exchequer, that he could only hold it as a member of
the House of Commons.   Mr. Stanley was made Chief
Secretary to the Lord Lieutenant of Ireland, an office
for which he was qualified by his great abilities and
his unequalled powers of debate; but his declarations
in favor of the Established Church of Ireland, and his
temper, little tolerant of opposition, gave warning of
storms.

The Ministry being thus constituted, the first and
most important object to which their attention was
turned was the great question of parliamentary reform.
Lord Durham, by Lord Grey's desire, invited me to
consult with him on the formation of a committee for
the purpose of framing a plan; Lord Durham proposed
that the Duke of Richmond should be a member of
the committee, but, as the Duke had never been a
reformer, I objected to this proposal, and we agreed
to invite Sir James Graham and Lord Duncannon to
form with us a committee for the proposed purpose.
Lord Durham and Sir James Graham were in the
Cabinet; Lord Duncannon and I were not.   Lord
Althorp was not a member of the committee.   An

---

[1] Brougham had at this time made up his mind that no office but that
of Lord Chancellor could properly be offered to him, but he did not till
the last moment make up his mind to leave the House of Commons, and
give up his seat for Yorkshire. His mother, who had much sense and
much talent, always regretted his decision.

outline of a plan of reform, to which I have elsewhere referred, was laid by me before that committee, and, with some alterations, adopted by them. On the proposition of Lord Durham, vote by ballot was added to the outline, and the whole scheme was submitted to Lord Grey.

The Cabinet of Lord Grey contained very few members who had supported proposals for reform of Parliament. Lord Grey himself, and Lord Durham, had brought forward motions on the subject. Lord Brougham and Lord Althorp had warmly supported the principle of reform, without favoring any particular plan. Lord Durham had proposed to introduce a bill dividing the country into equal electoral districts; and Lord Brougham had, if I recollect aright, opened to a meeting of members of the House of Commons, in Lord Althorp's room at the 'Albany,' a scheme for taking away one member from a certain number of the smaller boroughs.[1] Lord Palmerston and Mr. Grant had, with Lord Melbourne, followed Mr. Canning in his opposition to parliamentary reform. Lord Lansdowne and Lord Holland had never been very eager on the subject; but the circumstances of the country required decisive measures, and Lord Grey was persuaded that nothing but a large reform of Parliament would ward off revolution. In this opinion the Cabinet participated, and adopted our plan, but without the ballot.

I was so fully persuaded that the country would respond with enthusiasm and ready assent to a large proposal of reform, that I entreated Lord Grey to im-

---

[1] I see, on referring to Lord Brougham's 'Speeches,' vol. iv., that he says he was in favor of the disfranchisement of some boroughs, though not to the extent proposed in the bill of 1831.

press upon his colleagues the necessity of secrecy, in order that the plan might come with all the freshness of novelty upon the public ear, and deprive our opponents of the advantage of making adequate preparations to resist the first assault upon the well-fortified entrenchments of the enemy. So little were the opposite party prepared for the bill, that a few days before the first of March, Sir Robert Peel, in a careful speech, derided what had been done on the subjects of peace and retrenchment, and predicted that when the plan of reform should be developéd, it would occasion disappointment by the meagreness of its proportions, and the trifling nature of the changes recommended.

The effect, therefore, of the revelations of the first of March was astounding. I had purposely omitted, or passed slightly over, those arguments in favor of reform, which in 1822 I had developed at length. Sir Robert Peel observed sarcastically that I had said that many ingenious arguments were urged in favor of the ballot, but that I had not stated any ingenious arguments in favor of my proposition of that night. This was substantially true. It seemed to me that the arguments in favor of reform had made their impression — a very deep impression — upon the country; but that those arguments had become trite and familiar, and that the great novelty of my speech must consist in a clear and intelligible statement of the nature of the proposition I had to make. The extinction of one hundred and fifty seats in the House of Commons, all taken from the class of boroughs which were either dependent or venal, would amount, if carried, to a revolution.

It was no wonder, therefore, that this proposition, when placed boldly and baldly before the House of

Commons, created feelings of astonishment, mingled with joy or with consternation, according to the temper of the hearers. Mr. John Smith, himself a member for a nomination borough, said the proposal took away his breath. Some, perhaps many, thought that the measure was a prelude to civil war, which, in point of fact, it averted. But incredulity was the prevailing feeling, both among the moderate Whigs and the great mass of the Tories. Sir Henry Hardinge told Sir James Graham that he supposed we should all go out the next morning. Many of the Whigs thought it impossible the Government could succeed, either in the existing House of Commons or by an appeal to the people.

The Radicals alone were delighted and triumphant. Joseph Hume, when I met him in the streets a day or two afterwards, assured me of his hearty support of the Government. He said (on another subject, in a public speech) that he was ready to vote black white in order to carry the measure of reform. Lord Durham, who was sitting under the gallery on the first of March, told me he was inclined to doubt the reality of what was passing before his eyes. A noble lord who sat opposite to me, and who has long ago succeeded to a seat in the House of Lords, cheered me so vociferously that I was myself inclined to doubt his meaning. I found afterwards that his cheers were meant derisively, to show his thorough conviction of the absurdity and impracticability of my proposals.[1]

For my own part, my impression had always been that if the Reform Bill of Lord Grey could go down to

---

[1] I had thought it due to the Cabinet to conceal in my speech the part which I had taken in preparing the measure. In this concealment I was not justified; I ought to have told the whole truth.

the country, it would receive such an amount of support as would ensure its ultimate, if not its immediate, success. I was, therefore, much pleased when I found that the leaders of the Opposition did not intend to dispute the introduction of the bill, and still more satisfied when, by nine nights of debate, time was given to the country to hold public meetings, and to communicate to their members the popular, and, what turned out to be the almost universal, opinion in favor of the proposed measure.

The second reading was fixed for an early day, and both parties prepared anxiously for the coming conflict.

Before the day arrived, many members who had never voted for reform on previous occasions, and who were really hostile to any change in the representation, received such accounts of the ferment existing in the country, that they made up their minds to vote in favor of the second reading. Among these may be reckoned Sir Thomas Acland and Mr. Wilson Patten, the one member for Devonshire, and the other for Lancashire, both excellent country gentlemen. The second reading was carried, after a long debate, by a majority of one. I never saw so much exultation expressed in the House of Commons as upon that occasion. One member threw his hat up in the air, and the vociferous cheering was prolonged for some minutes.

Yet this majority, trifling as it was, was far from expressing the intention of those who composed it to give a cordial and thorough support to the bill in the shape in which it was introduced. Many amendments, destructive of its chief provisions, would have been introduced and carried, had the bill been proceeded with in that House of Commons.

The cry, which owed its origin to Lord Brougham, of

'The Bill, the whole Bill, and nothing but the Bill,' was intended to meet this disposition, and gave the Government a very powerful lever in raising the country to the height of their lofty proposals, while it did not prevent them from modifying some clauses which were ill-considered or unpopular.

The indisposition of the House was soon manifested. Upon a resolution moved by General Gascoigne, that the number of members for England and Wales should not be diminished, this latent hostility burst out. Mr. William Holmes, in the course of the debate, said privately to a friend of the Government, 'For good or for ill, there is a majority of eight in the House in favor of this motion.' So it appeared on the division, a majority of eight voting in favor of General Gascoigne's motion.

Upon this event, it became the duty of Lord Grey and his colleagues to consider seriously their position. They had brought forward a great measure affecting the constitution of the country and the course of legislation for generations to come. They could neither tamely abandon their situation, nor allow their measure to be frittered away, and rest contented with the fragment of a plan, the whole of which had been enthusiastically accepted by the country. It was manifest that the existing House of Commons would endeavor to destroy in detail that which they had sanctioned in the bulk. It was evident that the country was ready to follow Lord Grey, and to adopt his measure as a satisfactory settlement of a question which, since 1780, had always been in the minds of Liberal politicians, and which was now rooted in the heart of the people.

Lord Grey, therefore, prepared the King for the decision to which the Cabinet arrived, to advise his Majesty to have recourse to an immediate dissolution of Parliament. The King, though averse to the adoption of such a proceeding, little more than six months after the general election, was disposed, at this time, to trust implicitly to Lord Grey, and I am inclined to believe the popular story, that when it suddenly appeared necessary, in order to prevent remonstrance from the House of Lords, that the King should appear in person to dissolve Parliament, and some trifling difficulty of plaiting the horses' manes in time was interposed as an objection, the King said at once, ' Then I'll go down to Parliament in a hackney-coach.' Had such been the spirit of Louis XVI. he might have been the leader instead of the victim of the French Revolution.

The scenes which occurred in the two Houses of Parliament, so far as I was a witness of them, were singular and unprecedented. Before the King arrived, the House of Commons was assembled, and Sir Robert Peel and Sir Francis Burdett rose at the same time to address the House. Lord Althorp, amid the confusion and clamor of contending parties, following the precedent of Mr. Fox, moved that Sir Francis Burdett be now heard. Sir Robert Peel, on the other hand, imitating a precedent of Lord North, said, ' and I rise to speak to that motion.' But instead of saying a few words, as Lord North had done, to put an end to all further debate, Sir Robert Peel quite lost his temper, and in tones of the most violent indignation attacked the impending dissolution. As he went on, the Tower guns began to fire, to announce the King's arrival, and as each discharge was heard, a loud cheer from the Government side interrupted Sir Robert Peel's declamation. Sir Henry Hardinge was heard to exclaim, ' The next time those guns are fired they will be shotted ! ' Presently we were all summoned to the House of Lords, where

the King's presence had put a stop to a violent and unseemly discussion.   The King in his speech announced
the dissolution and retired to unrobe.   The scene that
followed was one of great excitement and confusion.
As I was standing at the bar, Lord Lyndhurst came up
to me and said, ' Have you considered the state of Ireland ? do not you expect an insurrection ? ' or words to
that effect.   It so happened that in going into the House
of Commons, I had met O'Connell in the lobby.   I asked
him, ' Will Ireland be quiet during the general election ? '
and he answered me, ' Perfectly quiet.'   He did not
answer for more than he was able to perform.   But of
course I said nothing of this to Lord Lyndhurst, and
left him to indulge his anger and his gloomy foreboding.

Many good Liberals were in great despondency about
the election, and fancied, as they well might, that an
appeal to the condemned boroughs to sanction their own
extinction, would meet with a very unfavorable reception, while, on the other hand, Manchester, Birmingham,
Leeds, and Sheffield, and the principal manufacturing
towns of Lancashire and Yorkshire, would be unable to
take part in the election.

But the forty-shilling freeholders, both in those towns
and in the rural counties, made themselves heard in
favor of reform.   Middlesex, Yorkshire, Lancashire,
Devonshire, were unanimous in their choice of reform
candidates.

The members for the English counties, with the addition of two members for Yorkshire in place of Grampound, were altogether 82; of these upwards of 70, I
think 76, pledged themselves to support Lord Grey and
the Reform Bill.   The proportion of the two parties
appeared on the second reading, when there divided in
favor of the bill 367, making, with 9 pairs and 2 tellers,
378; against it 231, with the same addition of pairs and

tellers, 242, giving a majority of 136 for the Government
and the Reform Bill. This was a majority which no
skilful manœuvres, nor even the authority of the time-
honored House of Lords, although led by such men as
the Duke of Wellington and Lord Lyndhurst, were
likely to counteract or overbear.

The Parliament met on June 14, and after the election
of a Speaker, and a debate on the address, the new
Reform Bill was immediately introduced. The second
reading, as I have said, was carried by a large majority,
and the opponents of the bill, no way dismayed, reserved
their opposition for committee. For forty nights the
subject was discussed, in its principles as well as in its
details. Sir Robert Peel, besides objecting to the large
amount of disfranchisement and to the ten-pound franchise, took special exception to the partial disfranchisement in Schedule B, and, after a very neat and
well-arranged speech of Mr. Praed, Sir Robert argued,
with his usual force and ability, that more room should
be left for the entrance into Parliament of men of retired
and studious habits. Subsequent legislation seems to
indicate that, according to public opinion, too many
seats, rather than too few, were left to men of retired
and studious habits. But, besides these fair and plaus-
ible objections to the extent and democratic tendency
of the bill, skilful lawyers like Sir Edward Sugden and
Sir Charles Wetherell, tried to unpick it thread by
thread, leaving no remnant of the original texture.
That which Penelope did to keep off her suitors, they
attempted to do to keep off reform. But, at the end of
forty nights, on the seventh of September, the debate
was closed, and after much labor, and considerable sacrifice of health, I was able, on that night, to propose,
amid much cheering, that the bill should be reported to
the House.

The bill was then carried to the House of Lords, and on October 2, the second reading was proposed by Lord Grey. There never was a debate of greater importance, or one marked by more ability. Lord Grey's opening speech recording that, in 1786, he had voted with Mr. Pitt in favor of reform of Parliament; his clear and able statement of the reasons which seemed to him to require that the bill should be adopted by Parliament, and that in order to be safe and enduring, it should be large and commensurate with the evil to be abated, was powerful and convincing.

One of the greatest speeches ever delivered in the House of Lords was spoken on this occasion by Lord Brougham; and among the most striking parts of that speech, was the reference to the events in Ireland which preceded the grant of Catholic emancipation. I copy this remarkable passage : — 'Those portentous appearances, the growth of later times, those figures that stalk abroad, of unknown stature and strange form — unions, and leagues, and musterings of men in myriads, and conspiracies against the Exchequer — whence do they spring, and how come they to haunt our shores? What power engendered those uncouth shapes — what multiplied the monstrous births, till they people the land? Trust me, the same power which called into frightful existence, and armed with resistless force the Irish volunteers of 1782 — the same power which rent in twain your empire, and conjured up thirteen republics — the same power which created the Catholic Association, and gave it Ireland for a portion. What power is that? Justice denied — rights withheld — wrongs perpetrated — the force which common injuries lend to millions — the wickedness of using the sacred trust of government as a means of indulging private caprice — the idiocy of treating Englishmen like the children of the South Sea Islands — the frenzy of believing, or making believe, that the adults of the nineteenth century can be led like children or driven like barbarians. This it is that has conjured up the strange sights at which we now stand aghast. And shall we persist in the fatal error of combating the giant progeny, instead of extirpating the execrable parent? Good God! Will men never learn wisdom, even from their own experience? Will they never believe, till it be too late, that the surest way to prevent immoderate desires being formed, ay, and unjust demands enforced, is to grant, in due season, the moderate requests of justice? You stand, my Lords, on the brink of a great event — you are in the crisis of a whole nation's hopes and fears. An awful importance hangs over your decision. Pause, ere you plunge! There may not be any retreat. It behooves you to shape your conduct by the mighty occasion. They tell you not to be afraid of personal consequences in discharging your duty. I, too, would ask you to banish all fears; but, above all, that most mischievous, most despicable fear, — the fear of being thought afraid. If you won't take counsel from me, take example from the statesmanlike conduct of the noble Duke (Wellington), while you also look back, as you may with satisfaction, upon your own. He was told, and you were told, that the impatience of Ireland for equality of civil rights was partial, the clamor transient, likely to pass away with its temporary occasion, and that yielding to it would be conceding to intimidation. I recollect hearing this topic urged within this House, in July, 1829; less regularly I heard it than I have now done, for I belonged not to your number — but I heard it urged in the self-same terms. The burthen of the cry was—"It is no time for concession: the people are turbulent and the Association dangerous." That summer passed, and the ferment subsided not. Autumn came, but brought not the precious fruit of peace—on the contrary, all Ireland was convulsed with the unprecedented conflict which returned the great chief of the Catholics to sit in a Protestant Parliament. Winter bound the earth in chains; but it controlled not the popular fury, whose surges, more deafening than the tempests, lashed the frail bulwarks of law, founded upon injustice. Spring came, but no ethereal mildness was its harbinger, or followed in its train—the Catholics became stronger by every month's delay, displayed a deadlier resolution, and proclaimed their wrongs in a tone of louder defiance than before. And what course did you, at this moment of greatest excitement and peril and menace, deem it most fitting to pursue? Eight months before, you had been told how unworthy it would be to yield when men clamored and threatened. No change had happened in the interval, save that the clamors were become far more deafening, and the threats beyond comparison more overbearing. What, nevertheless, did your Lordships do? Your duty—for you despised the cuckoo-note of the season, "Be not intimidated." You granted all that the Irish demanded, and you saved your country. Was there in April a single argument advanced that had not held good in July? None, absolutely none, except the new height to which the dangers of longer delay had risen, and the increased vehemence with which justice was demanded—and yet the appeal to your pride which had prevailed in July was in vain made in April, and you wisely and patriotically granted what was asked, and ran the risk of being supposed to yield through fear. But the history of the Catholic claims conveys another important lesson. Though, in right and policy and justice, the measure of relief could not be too ample, half as much as was received with little gratitude, when so lately wrung from you, would have been hailed twenty years before with delight; and even the July preceding, the measure would have been received as a boon, freely given, which, I fear, was taken but with sullen satisfaction in April, as a right long withheld. Yet, blessed be God, the debt of justice, though tardily, was at length paid, and the noble Duke won by it civic honors, which rival his warlike achievements in lasting brightness — than which there can be no higher praise. What if he had still listened to the topics of intimidation and inconsistency which had scared his predecessors? He might have proved his obstinacy, and Ireland would have been the sacrifice.'

Lord Grey concluded the debate, and closed his speech in the following remarkable manner: —

'The noble and learned lord has said, that if I were to resign office, it would be a culpable abandonment of the King. It is my duty to consider what course I shall follow under the circumstances in which I may be placed. I certainly will not abandon the King as long as I can be of use to him. I am bound to the King by obligations of gratitude, greater, perhaps, than subject ever owed to a sovereign, for the kind manner in which he has extended to me his confidence and support, and for the indulgence with which he has accepted my humble but zealous exertions in his service. Therefore, so long as I can be a useful servant to him, I trust that it never will be a reproach to me that I abandoned so gracious a master. But I can only serve him usefully by maintaining the character which belongs to a consistent, conscientious, and disinterested course of public conduct; this character I should deservedly forfeit, if, by any consideration, I should desert principles which I believe to be just, or give up, for any consideration whatever, measures which I believe to be essential to the security, happiness, and honor of my Sovereign and of my country. If I could fall into such disgrace, I should be at once disqualified from rendering to his Majesty any useful service. As to abilities, I am too sensible of my own deficiency, which is not less in those other qualifications which long habits of office give. All that I can pretend to is an honest zeal, an anxious desire to do my duty in the best way I can; as long as he is content to accept my services on those terms, no personal sacrifice shall stand in the way of my performing the duty which I owe to a Sovereign whose claims upon my gratitude and devotion can never be obliterated from my heart, whatever may happen, to the last moment of my existence. I had no desire for place, and it was not sought after by me; it was offered to me under such circumstances that nothing but a sense of duty could have induced me to accept it. To such as have observed my public conduct, I think I need make no such professions, for I can appeal to the history of my whole life to prove that I have not been actuated by an unworthy desire for office. But I found myself placed in a situation in which, to shrink from the task imposed upon me by the too partial opinion of a benevolent master, would have been the dereliction of a great public duty. I have lived a long life of seclusion from office —I had no official habits—I possessed not the advantages which those official habits confer. I am fond of retirement and domestic life, and I lived happy and contented in the bosom of my family. I was surrounded by those to whom I am attached by the warmest ties of affection. What, then, but a sense of duty could have induced me to plunge into all the difficulties, not unforeseen, of my present situation? What else, in my declining age,

> What else could tempt me on those stormy seas,
> Bankrupt of life, yet prodigal of ease ?[1]

I defy my worst enemy, if he has the most moderate share of candor, to find ground for charging me with any other motive. I have performed my duty as well as I am able. I shall still continue to do so, as long as I can hope to succeed in the accomplishment of an object which I believe to be safe, necessary, and indispensable ; but should this hope fail me, and should the Parliament and the public withdraw the confidence with which I have been hitherto supported, as, in that case, I could no longer prove a useful servant to my King or to my country, I would instantly withdraw from office into the retirement of private life, with the consoling reflection that, whatever my other defects may be, I had not been wanting, according to the best of my ability and judgment, in a faithful, conscientious, and zealous discharge of what I felt to be my duty.'

The House divided about six o'clock in the morning, at the end of five days and nights of debate. The 'not contents,' including proxies, were 199, the 'contents'

---

[1] Dryden's lines are —

> Punish a body which he could not please,
> Bankrupt of life, yet prodigal of ease.

Either Lord Grey altered the lines, or quoted only the last line, and the reporter supplied the first.

158, giving a majority against the second reading of 41.
It became now a very serious question with Lord Grey,
whether he should remain in office, or whether he should
throw upon his opponents the entire responsibility of
carrying on the Government in the midst of an excitement of a very dangerous character. Lord Grey decided,
rightly, as I think, that he would not desert his Sovereign nor abandon his high post, while he had any hopes
of being able to carry a great measure of reform. On
the seventeenth of the same month (October), in ex-
plaining what he was alleged to have said to a deputa-
tion, he gave the following account of his position : —
' He did state that some alterations in the late bill would
be necessary before it was re-introduced, and that it
would be for his Majesty's Ministers, during the recess,
carefully to consider what those alterations should be ;
but he distinctly added that he would never be a party
to, or recommend any measure of reform which was not
founded on any similar principles, and as effective, as
regarded its declared object, as that which was lately
before Parliament. This was the whole of what passed
between him and the delegates from the parishes, except
that when they represented to him that if satisfaction
was not given to the public, as to the length of time on
which Parliament was to be prorogued, it would tend to
increase the agitation and excitement which prevailed ;
he felt himself called upon to inform those who communicated with him, that it was their duty to use all the
means in their power to repress agitation and excitement, and to keep the people in obedience to the laws
of the country, that the Ministers might not be placed
in the painful situation of being compelled to use those
powers which, as a Government, it was their duty to
use, for the preservation of the public peace. With

respect to the prorogation, he would only say, that whatever might be the length of the period to which his Majesty's Ministers thought it their duty to recommend his Majesty to prorogue Parliament, it would be regulated by a sincere desire to do that which they considered most conducive to the advancement of the great measure of parliamentary reform.'

The rejection of the bill in the House of Lords made it necessary to review some of the most important provisions of the original bill, so as to preserve its principles and maintain its efficiency, correcting at the same time some of the details which, from the ignorance and inexperience of its authors in matters of government and legislation, had proved to be defective. The first list of boroughs to be entirely or partially disfranchised had been made out by consulting the tables of population for 1821. These tables contained the population of parishes, not of boroughs or towns ; and the boundaries of parishes were sometimes widely different, either in excess or deficiency, from those of the boroughs which were to be the objects of penal extinction. Commissioners were appointed by the Secretary of State for the Home Department to rectify these details, and they were instructed to ascertain the boundaries of the boroughs to which the right of sending members to Parliament had been granted. Further than this, a new test of importance was taken, borrowed very much from the tests of defranchisement applied in the Act of Union with Ireland, and announced by Pitt at the time. We took, therefore, the number of houses as a test of the existing population, and the amount of assessed taxes paid as the test of property in boroughs.

From these two elements combined, a list of the boroughs was formed, with a view to their relative importance. The compound ratio was calculated by Mr. Drummond, on a scientific principle. This was approved by Mr. Davies Gilbert, a mathematician of eminence, who was at one time President of the Royal Society. Mr. Croker, who seemed to be ignorant of, all mathematical science, alone doubted the accuracy of the rule adopted.

With regard to the boundaries of boroughs, of towns newly enfranchised, and of counties to be divided, the reports of commissioners were sent up to London, and were referred to Mr. Littleton, afterwards Lord Hatherton, a liberal but moderate politician, and to Admiral Beaufort, whose views were purely scientific. I sometimes assisted at their deliberations, especially when there was any discrepancy in the opinions of the different commissioners. But the whole process, whether of singling out small boroughs, and placing them in the list for disfranchisement, or of enlarging the boundaries of old boroughs, or of marking the limits of new boroughs and divisions of counties, was performed, so far as I am aware, with an entire absence of party bias.

Of course, the addition or subtraction of particular districts had an effect favorable to one party or the other; thus the Liberal party at Stamford, who had succeeded in returning Mr. Tennyson D'Eyncourt, in opposition to the influence of the Marquis of Exeter, lost all chance of opposing that influence with success when a suburb was added, which properly formed a part of the town of Stamford, but which was chiefly inhabited by the tenants of Lord Exeter. Thus, in an opposite political direction, the influence of the Duke of Somerset at Totnes was increased, by adding to the borough a part of the town which lay on the opposite side of the river Dart. Thus, in particular counties,

Whig or Tory proprietors derived some advantage from
the particular line of boundary adopted, but without
any intention on the part of the Government to secure
any advantage to themselves. In fact, the Boundary
Bill, framed upon these reports, was adopted with very
little discussion, and, except with regard to the borough
of Arundel, now disfranchised, with no important alteration.

The number of boroughs to be wholly or partially
disfranchised had been, in my original sketch, arbitrarily
fixed. Lord Durham had suggested that the penalty
of total disfranchisement should be confined to towns,
or rather villages, of less than two thousand inhabitants,
and that none under four thousand should return more
than one member. But the arbitrary line was now
again resorted to ; the number of boroughs to be wholly
or partially disfranchised was copied from the bill rejected by the House of Lords, and the test I have mentioned was applied to that number, so that fifty-six
boroughs, returning one hundred and eleven members,
were placed in Schedule A for total extinction, and
thirty boroughs, returning sixty members, were condemned to lose half their representatives. In this manner, one hundred and forty-one seats belonging to
boroughs which, since the days of Charles I., had regularly sent members to Parliament, were cut off on account
of their dependence or their insignificance. By my
original sketch, one hundred and forty-nine seats would
have been disfranchised.

This was the most popular part of the Reform Bill.
The country argued that from these boroughs, in
scarcely any of which the element of popular representation existed, had arisen all obstructions to the reforms
and retrenchments which the people so evidently de-

sired. As this was the strong and popular position of the Government, it would evidently be a great mistake, on the part of our opponents, to direct their attack against it; yet, as we shall presently see, this was the part of our lines singled out for attack in the House of Lords.

The obstruction and delay from which the former bill had suffered in its passage through the House of Commons were only partially renewed. On March 9, the bill was in committee for the twenty-first day, and on the next day, March 10, the report was received. On March 22, the bill was read a third time, after a division, in which the ayes were 355, and the noes 239; majority, 116.

Throughout the debates which took place upon the Reform Bill, while Lord Althorp and I had the greater portion of the labor, and a still larger portion of the responsibility, the palm of eloquence in debate belonged undoubtedly to Lord Stanley. Conscious of my own deficiencies, I had, on the first introduction of the Reform Bill, stipulated with Lord Althorp that Mr. Grant, and not I, should undertake the task, the weightiest that belongs to a leader, of reply at the end of the debate. But Mr. Grant contented himself with general adherence to the principles of the bill, while Lord Stanley, by his animated appeals to the Liberal majority, by his readiness in answering the sophisms of his opponents, by the precision and boldness of his language, by his display of all the great qualities of a parliamentary orator and an able statesman, successfully vindicated the authority of the Government, and satisfied their supporters in the House of Commons.

While Sir Robert Peel was the most eminent, both in weight of argument and in oratorical ability, of the opponents of the bill, Mr. Croker, by his profusion of words, by his warmth of declamation, and by his elaborate working out of details, was perhaps a still more formidable adversary. He told Lord Althorp, in private, that when he discovered the error we had made of confounding the limits of parishes with those of Parliamentary boroughs, he thought himself sure of defeating the bill. But his own statements of details were singularly inaccurate; and even where the particular point upon which he insisted was not mistaken, his exaggerations of its importance were repulsive to the House of Commons. Above all, the tide of opinion flowed so rapidly, that all obstacles were swept away, like Canute's chair, by the advancing waves. Thus the bill which had been introduced to the notice of the House of Commons on March 1, 1831, was finally passed on March 22, 1832, but little impaired in efficiency. It overthrew a system which had been left untouched at the Revolution, — a period when the wisest patriots, forced by necessity to transfer the Crown to a foreign prince, had been careful rather to maintain the ancient privileges of the Constitution than to disturb other parts of the existing edifice. The same system had enabled Sir Robert Walpole to consolidate the throne of the House of Hanover, amidst internal and external dangers. But the same system enabled Lord North to maintain his power against the fair demands and justifiable insurrection of the North American Colonies, even after the people had become tired of the contest against our fellow-subjects in America. The same system enabled Mr. Pitt and his successors to increase the public debt from about two hundred and thirty millions to eight hundred millions, and to restrict, by the most severe laws, the right of public meeting, and the liberty of the press. The fidelity with which the majority of the House of Commons had supported the French War, and its costly armaments, led Pitt to renounce all his early theories upon reform, and induced him to rely on the construction of that House as a firm barrier against democratic, or, as it was then called, Jacobin revolution. But the same willingness to sanction expense on the part of the Government, and to punish excesses on the part of the people, which had conciliated the opinion of Pitt, had estranged the public mind. Government, by nomination-boroughs, had become odious to the community at large; and the House of Commons, which voted by a majority of more than a hundred its own extinction, did but sanction the judicial sentence of the country.

New perils, however, awaited the measure in the House of Lords. In view of the large majority which had rejected the bill in October, Lord Grey had thought it right to consider what should be done if the same obstacles should recur. He and his colleagues could perceive no other resource than that of advising the King to create a large number of peers.

From 1784 to 1830, the prerogative of the Crown to create peers had been exercised almost entirely by the chiefs of the Tory party. The addition of about eighty or one hundred peers, solely from one party, had entirely overthrown the old balance of parties in the House of Lords. Besides the new creations, many peers who attached themselves to the Minister of the day had received higher titles as the reward of their political attachment. Earls had been made Marquises; Viscounts and Barons had been made Earls. The old and venerable titles which they had received from their ancestors were exchanged for coronets of a more ex-

alted degree, significant of their adhesion to Tory policy
and Tory Ministers. They could not be expected to
forget these recent favors, or the hands by which they
had been conferred. At the same time, the creation
of sixty or seventy peers for a particular purpose,
though undoubtedly within the prerogative of the
Crown, and not more than an adequate exercise of the
power which had secured a majority to the Tory Ministers of Queen Anne, was felt to be a measure likely
to shake the confidence of the country in the stability
of our ancient institutions. Admitting that the prerogative of creating peers had been abused by Pitt,
and still more by Lord Liverpool, Lord Grey, as a follower of Fox, was sure to be averse to any steps which
might seem inconsistent with unbounded reverence for
the Constitution of these realms. It was thought, therefore, by the Ministry and their supporters, that every
effort ought to be made to secure a majority by con-
ciliating the opponents of the bill. Lords Harrowby
and Wharncliffe, who were in that day called the
waverers, met Lord Grey and Lord Palmerston, in
order to suggest alterations which might conciliate some
who were not hostile in principle to reform, but who
considered the bill of 1831 as dangerous and revolutionary. It was found, however, that the alterations
proposed would seriously impair the efficiency of the
bill. Lord Harrowby and Lord Wharncliffe, therefore,
while they agreed to support the second reading, were
left at liberty to propose their own amendments in
committee, without the promise of any concession on
the part of Lord Grey. Various members of the Ministry wrote to their friends in the House of Lords,
pointing out to them the danger of a large creation of
peers, and exhorting them to ward off that danger by

supporting the Reform Bill. Of three peers to whom
I wrote with this object, one supported the second
reading, one abstained from voting, and the third repeated his vote against the bill.

It was considered by the Cabinet that these endeavors to procure a majority were not of themselves sufficient, and that the King should be asked to consent to
a creation of peers as guarded and limited as possible,
in case of the rejection of the bill on the second reading.
This proposal, although very unpalatable to the King,
received his Majesty's sanction. Whether the leaders
of the Tory party had any inkling of what had passed
I cannot tell, but they seemed to have framed their plan
of campaign on the supposition that the second reading
would be carried by the Government. On April 13,
the House divided: contents, 184; non-contents, 175;
majority, 9. The bill was read a second time, and ordered to be committed on the first day after the recess.
The House adjourned at a quarter past seven o'clock in
the morning. On April 17, the House adjourned for
the Easter recess, and on May 7, when the House met
again, the bill was considered in committee. It was
understood that Lord Lyndhurst meant to move the
postponement of the disfranchising clauses of the bill.
On that day I met Lord Grey riding in the Park, and
rode with him to the Park door of his official house in
Downing Street. I was anxious to ascertain what language he intended to hold, and was gratified to find that
he considered Lord Lyndhurst's proposal one of vital
importance, and that he meant to hold firm language in
the debate. With this assurance from Lord Grey, I felt
quite certain of a speedy and triumphant issue of the
contest. The debate was anxious and interesting, but
was not protracted. The Tory peers who had supported

the second reading of the bill, with an unconquerable aversion to its principles and its objects, now went over in a body to the Opposition. Some of the more prudent of the Tories were alarmed at the near prospect of their temporary triumph.

The Earl of Harewood, who had had much experience in the House of Commons, said: 'He wished to exonerate himself from being a party to any project or indirect contrivance to defeat the bill. If the proposition (the amendment) contained in it any thing which he did not understand, or any thing sinister, he would not support it. He wished that more time were allowed to promulgate what was meant to be proposed, if the proposition were successful; and if that were the case, he was sure all feelings of acrimony on the other (the Ministerial) side would be done away. He thought, if the amendments to be proposed were seen and known, they would remove all the objections which the noble Lords opposite might have to the amendment. He had no idea that the object was to get rid of Schedule A; and if it were, he certainly would not join in any such object. He believed that the plan of enfranchisement to be proposed would include all Schedule A, and perhaps more, and he had no predisposition to defeat that schedule. There might be some variations, perhaps, in the places to be disfranchised, but he believed if the enfranchisement were first agreed to, the places to be disfranchised would be identical with those places in Schedule A. There were difficulties about the question which the plan proposed by the noble and learned Lord might get rid of. If the noble Earl (Grey) did not look on the proposition in a hostile light, much might be done to bring about a satisfactory settlement of the whole question.'

Lord Wharncliffe, who spoke before Lord Harewood, said he could assure the noble Lords opposite that there was no disposition on the Opposition side of the House to be niggardly as to the amount of disfranchisement. The Duke of Newcastle, he remarked, had said that he would give his support to the amendment, in order that the bill might not pass; but that was not his view. After what had passed, he could not do any thing to violate the pledge he had given; and he was prepared to go the whole length of Schedule A. If the amendment succeeded, he should vote, he believed, for the whole of Schedule A, and would not give his consent to any amendment which would reduce the amount of disfranchisement.

Earl Grey was not, however, to be intimidated or cajoled. 'He hoped,' he said, 'the noble Lords present would not deceive themselves; but he must say that if the motion was successful, it would be fatal to the whole bill. Should the amendment be carried, it will be necessary for me to consider what course I shall take. More I will not say than what, on a former occasion, was stated by the noble Earl on the other side, — and it was not denied by any other person, — that this bill had found support in public opinion. Noble Lords deceive themselves if they suppose that opinion in favor of this bill is relaxed; and certainly I dread the effect of the House of Lords opposing itself as an insurmountable barrier to what the people think necessary for the good government of the country, and a sufficient representation.' 'More he would not say, than that to the motion of the noble and learned Lord he meant to give his most determined opposition.'

The committee divided on the amendment: con-

6

tents, 151; non-contents, 116; majority in favor of the amendment, 35.

On the motion that the next clause be postponed, to which Lord Grey did not object, Lord Ellenborough took the opportunity, ill-timed as it appeared to be, to propose a scheme of his own. He said he should not object to the disfranchisement to the full extent of Schedule A, making, with the members for the borough of Weymouth, one hundred and thirteen seats to be placed at the disposal of Parliament. Neither did he object to the ten-pound qualification, provided it were better defined.

The immediate consequence of the vote on Lord Lyndhurst's amendment was a meeting of the Cabinet to consider their new position. It was evident that the House of Lords had determined, by a large majority, to defeat the bill, which had the enthusiastic support of the House of Commons. With the exception of the Duke of Richmond, the Cabinet were unanimous in thinking that no course was left to them but that of proposing to the King to sanction a creation of peers sufficiently numerous to overbear the opposition of the Lords. Lord Grey as Prime Minister, and Lord Brougham as Lord Chancellor, carried this advice to Windsor. The King, anxious as he was to see a Reform Bill carried, and even willing to go to a considerable extent in favor of Lord Grey's bill, shrank from the alternative now proposed to him. It seemed to him, that to overbear the majority of the House of Lords was to destroy the independence of that body. He therefore at once rejected the advice of his Ministers. Lord Grey and Lord Brougham returned to London to report this decision to their colleagues.

The next day Lord Lyndhurst was sent for, and

informed that the King had accepted the resignation of
his Ministers, and was determined, if possible, to form
a Government on the principle of carrying an extensive
reform in the representation of the people.　The Duke
of Wellington, impelled by that honorable feeling of
loyalty to the Crown which induced him to incur any
risk, and almost to surrender any opinion, rather than
show himself wanting in zeal for his Sovereign, informed
Lord Lyndhurst that he would endeavor to form a
Government in compliance with the King's wishes.
From Sir Robert Peel Lord Lyndhurst received a very
different answer. , He declined to make himself responsible for a bill which, in his opinion, as he had often and
publicly declared, would entail great calamities on the
country.　He therefore refused to accept office, while
he professed his readiness to give such support to the
efforts of the Duke of Wellington as his opinions would
permit him to afford.

There was something remarkable in the contrast
between the conduct of the Duke of Wellington and
that of Sir Robert Peel at this crisis.　They were both
men of high character, both anxious for the honor of
their Sovereign and the welfare of their country.　Their
position appeared similar, if not identical.　Yet the
Duke of Wellington declared that if he had refused
to assist in the formation of a Government he should
have been ashamed to show his face in the streets;
while Sir Robert Peel declared in the House of Commons
that if he had accepted the task proposed to him he
could not have walked upright into that House.　The
Duke of Wellington's feeling was one of excessive loyalty as a subject, Sir Robert Peel's that of dignity and
consistency as a statesman.　We have no right to withhold our meed of respect from either of them.

It has been commonly supposed that, after the refusal of Sir Robert Peel, the Duke of Wellington had recourse to Mr. Alexander Baring, a man of great experience, of great ability, and intimately acquainted with the means by which the credit of the country was upheld. But while these negotiations were pending, and while Mr. Baring, whose mind was irresolute, doubted as to the course he should pursue, events rushed rapidly on, and turned his hesitation into despair.

London and the country were not only awake, but highly excited at the crisis before them. Men who would have accepted with satisfaction the disfranchisement of ten small boroughs, and the enfranchisement of ten large manufacturing towns three years before, were now not in the least appeased by Lord Ellenborough's offer to sacrifice one hundred and thirteen seats, and to fill them up from unrepresented places. Nine years previously I had said that if reform were not allowed to follow its course with the majesty of a river, it would rush on with the madness of a torrent. I had been laughed at by one of my Tory friends for this phrase, but he and others were now carried away by that torrent, the approach of which they had so little foreseen. This was indeed a moment of peril. It was the only time during my political life in which I have felt uneasy as to the result. Fortunately, in this as in other cases, the House of Commons proved the safety-valve of society.

On the very day, May 9, when Lord Althorp announced the fact of the resignation of Ministers, Lord Ebrington gave notice of a motion, for the next day, for an address to the Crown, to implore his Majesty to call to his councils such persons only as will carry into effect, unimpaired in all its essential provisions, that bill

for reforming the representation of the people, which
has recently passed this House. Notice was also given
of a motion for a call of the House. On the next day,
accordingly, Lord Ebrington made his motion, and was
opposed by Mr. Baring, who said that if the opposition
had been imputed to personal motives, he would only
ask those who made such an imputation to look to the
fact that almost all the members of the Government
opposite had been opposed to reform, except the noble
Lord (Lord John Russell), and there was hardly a
public man in the country, and more particularly in the
King's councils, who had not, at one time or another,
been opposed to such a sweeping measure of reform as
that introduced by his Majesty's Government. Mr.
Baring pretended to be ignorant of the causes of the
resignation of the Ministers. In answer to this assertion, Lord Althorp gave a clear and manly statement
of the causes which had induced the Ministers to resign.
'I stated last night,' he said, 'that the advice which we
gave was occasioned by our finding that it was impossible to carry the Reform Bill. We, therefore, Sir, asked
his Majesty to enable us to take such steps as were necessary to carry the bill; and to carry it where, Sir?
Why, in the House of Lords. That was the statement
which I made last night. But as my hon. friend does
not think that was enough, I have no objection to state,
for his better satisfaction, that the advice which we
thought it our duty to offer to his Majesty was, that he
should create a number of peers sufficient to carry the
Reform Bill through the other House of Parliament in
an efficient form.' A division took place the same night,
when there appeared for the motion, 288; noes, 208;
majority, 80. Before the debate began, the Sheriff and
Remembrancer of the city of London had presented a

petition from the city, praying the House to stop the supplies till the Reform Bill was passed. On the next day, May 11, Mr. John Wood presented a petition from Manchester, which, he said, was signed in the space of three hours ·by 25,000 persons, and which, he believed, would be followed by thousands of other petitions, praying the House not to vote any supplies until a measure essential to the happiness of the people and the safety of the throne shall be carried into a law.

The excitement continued to increase. At a meeting at Brooks's Club, Mr. Stanley made a most violent speech against the formation of a Ministry which was not prepared to carry the Reform Bill in its integrity.

This occurrence is said to have taken place on Saturday, the 12th. I was not present at the meeting. On Monday, the 14th, the Ministry of the Duke of Wellington was nipped in the bud in the House of Commons. After a debate upon a petition which had been passed at a meeting of the livery of the city of London, in the Common Hall assembled, in which debate Mr. Baring, Lord Althorp, Sir Henry Hardinge, Lord Palmerston, and the Attorney-General spoke, Sir Robert Inglis rose. He said, ' that while he held, as an old Tory, that the King had the same right to give his decision on any measure which might pass the two Houses, he could not forget also this other great constitutional truth, that the opinions and wishes of the King were known to the House in no other way than by his public acts, for which his known confidential advisers were responsible. He was told that the new Government was actually to take charge, had, indeed, already taken ·charge, of the Reform Bill.·

' He was willing to make the greatest allowance for changes of opinion in young men ; but, when he was told of men of mature age — statesmen who all their lives had been opposed to a particular measure, who had in April protested against it as revolutionary, adopting it and making it their own measure in May, he must own that he could imagine no consideration which could justify such a change of conduct. He did not accuse any one of love of pelf, or even of power; he did not say that ambition, that last infirmity of noble minds, had misled any one : but the conduct itself, from whatever motive, he must deprecate as fatal to that singleness and consistency of public character which, as he had already stated, he considered to be the best property of public men, and, in them, of their country.' Sir Robert Inglis's character, universally respected, added great weight to these words, and, when it became quite clear that the new Government would neither be joined by Sir Robert Peel nor supported by Sir Robert Inglis, Mr. Baring saw that his task was hopeless. Accordingly, before the end of the night, he intimated clearly that the attempt would not be proceeded with, and that he wished to see the former Ministers resume their offices. In reviewing these events, it is impossible to refuse to the Duke of Wellington the tribute at all times due to · him of having acted from conscientious motives and a high sense of honor. But while the Duke of Wellington was actuated only by undeviating loyalty to his Sovereign — and it is not surprising that this feeling should take deep root in the mind of a military man used to obedience as a soldier, and attached to the throne — it was indeed strange that Mr. Baring and others should have supposed that to such a principle could be sacrificed the character of a public man, and the Constitution of these realms. I had stated in the debate of the 12th that if a Cabinet was formed it would be a Cabinet into which honor could not enter. I ought to have excepted the Duke of Wellington. The failure of this attempt to set aside the very basis of the Constitution was a happy event, on which the House of Commons might justly pride itself.

As soon as the Duke of Wellington perceived, from the discussions in the House of Commons, that it was impossible to form a Government which would obtain the confidence of the country, he felt it his duty to report that he could not fulfil the commission with which his Majesty had been pleased to honor him. The King thereupon resolved to renew his communications with his former Ministry.

When Lord Grey received this communication, he merely informed the King that he was aware that the Duke of Wellington had failed in forming a Ministry, and that he would consult his former colleagues on the state of affairs.

When the Cabinet assembled, very serious discussions took place. It was unanimously resolved that the bill must be carried in its integrity, and the question was, how this object was to be effected. It was understood that Sir Herbert Taylor, on the part of the King, would use the royal influence, and that the Duke of Wellington, on his part, would do all in his power to induce the peers to abstain from further opposition to the bill. Sir Herbert Taylor was very active in concert with others in reconciling the King to a course which, although it did not directly overpower the House of Lords by a large creation of peers, yet, upon this occasion, and on a question of the gravest importance, absolutely destroyed their privileges as a House of Parliament, and reduced them to a cipher in the working of the Constitution.

But the Cabinet was not satisfied with the probable effect of the influences thus brought to bear upon the peers ; they thought it necessary that Lord Grey should be armed with the power' to create peers in a number sufficient to carry the bill, should any of its essential provisions be interfered with in its further progress through the House of Lords. It was not until the King had given to Lord Grey his solemn promise that, if called upon, he would create peers in a sufficient number for this purpose, that the Ministers consented to resume their offices.[1]

Lord Althorp, in announcing the restoration of the Ministry, said he could not reveal the nature of the securities for carrying the bill which Lord Grey and his colleagues had obtained, but that he trusted the House had sufficient confidence in him to be satisfied with his assurance that they had that security.

After this the bill passed triumphantly through committee without much debate, and with no important alteration. It was read a third time by a majority of eighty. The Reform Bill received the royal assent on June 7, 1832. A Boundary Bill, complicated in its details, was successfully carried through both Houses. The Reform Bills for Scotland and Ireland were likewise carried, and on August 16 Parliament was prorogued.

A session more successful for the Ministry could not well have been. The manly and straightforward conduct of Lord Grey, and the enthusiastic support he received from the people, overcame all opposition.

It may be a question, however, whether the manner

---

[1] See 'Correspondence of King William IV. and Earl Grey,' vol. ii. p. 464.

in which the vote of the House of Lords was nullified by the compulsory absence of a great many of the majority, was not more perilous for their authority than the creation of peers which the Cabinet of Lord Grey proposed. In the reign of Queen Anne there had been a decided majority in the House of Lords which had interfered so far with the royal prerogative as to address the Queen not to consent to any peace which should leave the Crown of Spain in the possession of any branch of the House of Bourbon. This was a most unconstitutional interference with the prerogative of the Crown, and the discretion of its advisers, who could not fail to be influenced by the events of the war. The Tory Minister of that day, strong in the confidence of the Queen and of the country, obtained from the Crown the creation of a sufficient number of peers to overbear the majority, and secure the harmonious working of the Constitution. In those days, when the House of Peers was not crowded by the host of partisans who were added to it by Mr. Pitt and his successors, the creation of twelve peers was sufficient for the purpose of Harley and St. John; but whether twelve or one hundred be the number requisite to enable the peers to give their votes in conformity with public opinion, it seems to me that a House of Lords sympathizing with the people at large, and acting in concurrence with the enlightened state of the prevailing wish, represents far better the dignity of the House, and its share in legislation, than a majority got together by the long supremacy of one party in the State, eager to show its ill-will by rejecting bills of small importance, but afraid · to appear, and skulking in clubs and country houses, in face of a measure which has attracted the ardent sympathy of public opinion.

Yet such was the state in which the House of Lords was left by the forbearance and regard for royal scruples of Lord Grey and his colleagues. Mr. Pitt, in a few years, had advised the creation of one hundred peers. Lord Liverpool had sanctioned the creation of fifteen in a single day. Lord Grey, on succeeding to power in 1830, found in the House of Peers a majority of at least eighty party adherents arrayed against him. After the Reform Bill had been carried, this majority was held back with scrupulous care by the Duke of Wellington, but it was unscrupulously employed by Lord Lyndhurst to stop the course of wholesome legislation, and to nip in the bud measures which, while they were useful, were at the same time unpretending, and were not likely to rouse popular enthusiasm, or to justify in the eyes of the country a large addition to the House of Lords.

After the passing of the Reform Act, a duty of the highest importance, of the gravest responsibility, but at the same time of the clearest necessity, devolved upon the Government.

The long war in which England had been engaged had brought with it immense burdens, an enormous debt, an inconvertible currency, an entire derangement of the relations between capital and labor, and an abuse of the poor-laws which had placed the rural population in a state of idleness and discontent, and threatened to absorb all the funds of the land-owners and farmers. To these permanent disorders was to be added a condition of Ireland destructive of life and property, which urgently required immediate remedies.

Of these evils, the last, as being the most urgent, required the earliest attention. A measure of coercion containing very strong provisions was sent over by the

Government of Ireland. Lord Grey accepted it, because, in his opinion, the protection of life and property was a duty incumbent upon every Government. Lord Althorp accepted it also, because, in his opinion, the stronger the measure the more likely was it to be temporary, and to give way after a short time to the restoration of the ordinary law. But while Lord Althorp was as fully persuaded as any member of the Cabinet of the necessity for this bill, he was little fitted to persuade a Liberal House of Commons to acquiesce in a proposal repugnant to their dispositions, and at variance with their settled opinions. It was thought right, however, that he, as the leader of the Government in the House of Commons, should introduce the Coercion Bill. He did so in a manner tame and ineffective. His detail of the outrages committed in Ireland was like reading a few of the blackest pages of the 'Newgate Calendar.' The Liberal majority were disappointed, sullen, and ready to break out into mutiny against their chief. Mr. Stanley, who was sitting next to me, greatly annoyed at the aspect of the House, said to me, 'I meant not to have spoken till to-morrow night, but I find I must speak to-night.' He took Lord Althorp's box of official papers, and went upstairs to a room where he could look over them quietly. After the debate had proceeded for two or three hours longer, with no change of temper in the House, Stanley rose. He explained with admirable clearness the insecure and alarming state of Ireland. He then went over, case by case, the more dreadful of the outrages which had been committed. He detailed, with striking effect, the circumstances attending the murder of a clergyman, and the agony of his widow, who, after seeing her husband murdered, had to bear the terror of running knocks at the door, kept on all night by the miscreants who had committed the crime. The House became appalled and agitated at the dreadful picture which he placed before their eyes; they felt for the sorrows of the innocent; they were shocked at the dominion of assassins and robbers. When he had produced a thrilling effect by these descriptions, he turned upon O'Connell, who led the opposition to the measure, and who seemed a short time before about to achieve a triumph in favor of sedition and anarchy. He recalled to the recollection of the House of Commons, that at a recent public meeting, O'Connell had spoken of the House of Commons as six hundred and fifty-eight scoundrels. In a tempest of scorn and indignation, he excited the anger of the men thus designated against the author of the calumny. The House, which two hours before seemed about to yield to the great agitator, was now almost ready to tear him to pieces. In the midst of the storm which his eloquence had raised, Stanley sat down, having achieved one of the greatest triumphs ever won in a popular assembly by the powers of oratory.

On February 12, a bill was brought into the House of Commons by Lord Althorp, for the reform of the Church of Ireland. Ten bishoprics were to be suppressed, the Church-rates entirely abolished, and arrangements made for the transfer to other districts of the income of benefices where divine service had not been performed for three years. Three members of the Cabinet, Lord Althorp, Lord Durham, and I, had wished to transfer some of the revenues of the Established Church to general purposes of education; but Lord Grey having declared himself strongly against any such provision in the bill, Lord Althorp gave way, and Lord Durham and I followed his example. But the difference of opinion which was at this time stifled broke out with irresistible force in the following year.

The year 1833 was, in my opinion, the most distinguished and the most memorable of Lord Derby's political career. In the course of the discussions which arose upon the subject of slavery in the West Indies, Lord Grey had thought it desirable that Mr. Stanley should be transferred from his post in Ireland to the office of Secretary of State for the Colonies, and the measure for the abolition of slavery fell, consequently, into his hands. But he was not thereby freed from the responsibility of mastering and defending the details of the Irish Church Temporalities Bill; and, therefore, besides the Irish Coercion Bill, which he had carried by the force of his eloquence, he had to conduct through Parliament and defend, clause by clause, the Irish Church Temporalities Bill and the Colonial Slavery Abolition Bill, two of the largest and most important measures that were ever proposed for the consideration of Parliament. He performed these tasks with infinite skill, readiness, and ability; and, for my part, I felt and expressed to my friend the Duke of Richmond the opinion which I firmly entertained, that whenever Lord Althorp should retire, or, by his father's death, be removed to the House of Lords, Mr. Stanley would be fully qualified to assume his place as leader of the Liberal party in the House of Commons. It will be seen how subsequent events destroyed this prospect, and produced a disastrous rupture in the Ministry.

In the year 1834, Parliament met early in February. The King remarked in his speech, that during the last session more numerous and more important questions were brought under the consideration of Parliament than during any former period of similar duration. In fact, the embarrassment of the Government and of Parliament arose rather from the abundance of subjects and the difficulty of considering them in due order, than from any want of diligence either on the part of the Ministry or of the House of Commons. In the royal speech, attention was called to the state of the municipal corporations, to the administration and effect of the poor-laws, and to ecclesiastical revenues and patronage in England and in Wales. With respect to Ireland, the King recommended the early consideration of such a final adjustment of the tithes in that part of the United Kingdom as might extinguish all just causes of complaint without injury to the rights and property of any class of subjects, or to any institution in Church or State. These subjects occupied four or five years, and their consideration was constantly interrupted by topics of immediate interest, by events connected with foreign policy, and by the impatience of the more eager reformers to introduce into debate proposals of change which would have required fifteen or twenty sessions to deal with. Besides these topics, there were other proposals, compliance with which would either have been inconsistent with the due faith to be observed to the Crown, or injurious to the interests of the country.

Among the subjects recommended to consideration in the King's speech, there was none more urgent or more important than the reform of the Poor-laws. A commission had been appointed upon this subject, and their labors had for result a valuable report, which formed matter for anxious deliberation in a committee of the Cabinet of which Lord Althorp was the principal member. Lord Brougham did not attend the committee, but took much interest in the subject. The report of the Commissioners of Enquiry was presented to the

Government in February, 1834, and on April 17 of that year Lord Althorp introduced a bill into the House of Commons. This bill underwent much discussion, and had to encounter a violent, though by no means a party, opposition in the House of Commons. But the patience, the good sense, the practical experience, the unremitting labor, and the just influence of Lord Althorp overcame the obstacles which ignorance, prejudice, and the violent opposition of a person of much influence in the press, interposed against this great measure. The bill was sent to the House of Lords July 1, and received the royal assent August 14 of this year.

Increase of the amount raised for poor-rates had been enormous in three-quarters of a century. In 1748, '49, '50, the average amount raised within the year for poor-rates and county rates was 730,000*l*. In 1775, it was 1,720,000*l*. In 1801, the sums expended for the relief of the poor exceeded 4,000,000*l*. In 1811, these sums exceeded 6,600,000*l*. In 1821, they amounted to 6,959,-000*l*.; in 1831, to 6,798,000*l*; and in 1832, to upwards of 7,000,000*l*.

But within three years after the passing of the new law the decrease was equally remarkable. In 1837, poor-rates amounted only to 4,000,000*l*., and in the years 1838 and 1839, they did not reach 4,500,000*l*. It cannot be denied, however, that the sound principles inculcated by the commissioners of 1834 have been relaxed in practice by the ignorance, the carelessness, or the fear of unpopularity, which have checked the due administration of the law. With respect to other subjects, but little progress was made; and dissensions in the Ministry produced a fatal effect on the union of the Cabinet. I have already stated that, on the subject of

the Irish Church, I had the misfortune to differ from
Mr. Stanley, and on May 6, after Stanley had spoken,
and had declared that he adhered to his former opinions,
I made the following statement: ' With respect to the
proposition of the hon. and learned member, that one-
fifth of the composition should be paid out of the public revenue, he was quite certain that this contribution
of the nation would be entirely thrown away, unless
some new principle were established by Parliament with
regard to appropriation. Upon the subject of appropriation, the hon. and learned member for Tipperary
alluded, the other night, to an opinion which he (Lord
John Russell) gave, when out of office, which the hon.
and learned member said was contrary to the opinion
he had since given when in office. But the only opinion
he had ever given on this subject, when out of office,
was by giving a silent vote in favor of a motion made
by the hon. member for Middlesex. He did not understand that this bill contained any proposition on that
subject. As he understood it, the object of this bill
was to ascertain and secure the amount of the tithe.
The question of appropriation was to be kept entirely
distinct. If the object of the bill were to grant a certain sum to the Established Church of Ireland, and the
question were to end there, his opinion of it might be
very different. But he understood it to be a bill to
secure a certain amount of property and revenue destined by the State to religious and charitable purposes ;
and if the State should find that it was not appropriated
justly to the purposes of religious and moral instruction,
for which such revenues were intended, when given to
any Church Establishment, it would then be the duty
of Parliament to consider of a different appropriation.
His opinion upon that subject was declared — not when

7

out of office, but when in office — and that opinion was, that the revenues of the Church of Ireland were larger than necessary for the religious and moral instruction of the persons belonging to that Church, and for the stability of. the Church itself. The more he had seen and reflected since, the more had that opinion been confirmed. He did not think it would be advisable or wise to mix the question of appropriation with the question of amount of the revenues; but when Parliament had vindicated the property in tithes, he should then be prepared to assert his opinion with regard to their appropriation; and if, when the revenue was once secured, the assertion of that opinion should lead him to differ and separate from those with whom he was united by political connection, and for whom he entertained the deepest private affection, he should feel much regret; yet, considering himself pledged, not only by his general duty as a member of that House, but by the resolution which had been passed the other day, to attend to the just complaints of the people of Ireland, and considering that if there ever were a just ground of complaint on the part of any people against any grievance, it was the complaint of the people of Ireland against the present appropriation of tithes — he should then, deeply lamenting the decision he should feel himself. bound to come to, but at the same time reflecting that he had to the utmost of his power resisted all projects for the repeal of the Union, and that he had, by the support he gave to this and former bills for the maintenance of tithes, vindicated the right of property against those who wrongfully withheld them, he should, at whatever cost and sacrifice, do what he should consider his bounden duty; namely, do justice to Ireland.'

This speech was prompted by what I understood to

be a declaration of Mr. Stanley, that he meant to persevere in the opinions he had given respecting the permanence of the Church of Ireland, and I thought that
if that declaration were received in silence by his colleagues, the whole Government would be considered
pledged to the maintenance of the revenues of the
Church of Ireland, undiminished. I do not find in
Hansard any such declaration; but it was strongly fixed
in my mind at the time, and is so fixed in my memory
at present. Perhaps Stanley's words were not so peremptory as I supposed; perhaps the words he uttered
have been omitted in the reports. Be that as it may,
my speech made a great impression, the cheering was
loud and general, and Stanley pronounced his sense of
it in a well-known note to Sir James Graham: 'Johnny
has upset the coach.' When the Cabinet next met,
much dissatisfaction was expressed; some wished me to
retract what I had said, but that I positively refused to
do. Lord Althorp testified to the hearty cheering from
all sides of the House of the Liberal party. The question
of the Irish Church was evidently advancing to a crisis.
Redress was not immediately granted; justice was not
done then; but a commencement had been made, and
that which was not performed at the Union by Pitt, and
which the Duke of Wellington and Sir Robert Peel left
undone in 1829, was yet to be accomplished. Mr. Ward
did not fail to bring forward a motion upon the Irish
Church. He quoted the opinions of Lord Brougham,
and those which Lord Althorp had stated in 1824. He
ended with the following motion: 'That the Protestant
Episcopal Establishment in Ireland exceeds the spiritual
wants of the Protestant population: and that, it being
the right of the State to regulate the distribution of
Church property in such manner as Parliament may

determine, it is the opinion of this House that the temporal possessions of the Church of Ireland, as now established by law, ought to be reduced.' The debate was interrupted after the motion had been seconded by Mr. Grote, who said that when the advocates for the repeal of the Union put forward the evils arising from the Irish Church Establishment, no man replied to them. He continued: ' When the magnanimity of England in her conduct to Scotland, as compared with her conduct to Ireland, with regard to their respective Churches, was urged, no man replied to them; and why? Because no reasonable answer could be given to such objections. The first step towards the reform of an abuse was to lay down a good principle; such a principle was laid down in this motion, and, as a first step, he earnestly hoped that the House would concur in it.' After this speech, Lord Althorp rose and spoke to the following effect: ' Since my hon. friend who rose to support this motion commenced his address, circumstances have come to my knowledge which induce me to move that the further debate upon this subject be adjourned to Monday next. I cannot now state what those circumstances are, but I hope the House has sufficient confidence in me (the noble Lord was interrupted by loud and long-continued cheering from all parts of the House) — I hope, I repeat, that the House will have sufficient confidence in me to believe that I would not make such a proposition unless I were convinced of its propriety. I now move that the further debate on this motion be adjourned to Monday next.'

On the Monday following, it was well known that four members of the Cabinet, and those among the most important, had resigned. The Cabinet, previously to their taking this step, had resolved on advising the

Crown to appoint a commission to inquire into the revenues of the Church of Ireland, and the number of members belonging to that Church, compared with the whole population of Ireland. The consequence was, the resignation of the Earl of Ripon, Lord Privy Seal, Mr. Stanley, Secretary of State for the Colonies, Sir James Graham, First Lord of the Admiralty, and the Duke of Richmond, Postmaster-General. The issuing of this commission was considered by these four members of the Cabinet as a preliminary step towards the partial disendowment of the Established Church of Ireland. The motives of the seceders were thus explained by the Earl of Ripon, on June 6, in the House of Lords, in answer to a speech of Lord Grey: 'As his noble friend (Lord Grey) had correctly stated, the proposition to appoint a commission arose out of peculiar circumstances, and was not taken up suddenly. The question was deeply considered, and certainly great objections were felt by himself, as well as by his colleagues, to the adoption of that measure. He had no particular desire to avail himself of the compliment that had been paid to himself and his colleagues, in adverting to their having been described as the " drags " of the Government of which they were members; but he might remark that possibly they had been useful "drags." At all events, he certainly did feel, with regard to the commission, that if he assented to it, the question as to the appropriation of the revenues of the Church to secular purposes was settled; and when he asked himself if he could assent to such a proposition, his answer was, no. He thought that the principle of inquiry into the state of the population of parishes, to ascertain the number of resident Protestants therein, as compared with the number of Catholics, if it meant any thing, must mean something that had a direct tendency to effect an alteration of the principles on which the Church Establishment was based. His noble friend stated that he did not contemplate the possibility of any great change as the result of appointing the commission; but it was because he (the Earl of Ripon) believed that the effect of the commission must be to alter the footing on which the Established Church stood, that he could not concur in that preliminary step.' Lord Ripon went on to argue, that if the revenue of the Church in a particular parish was to be regulated by the number of the Protestant population in that parish, then they destroyed the principle on which alone the Established Church existed.

Such was the commencement of the contest on the subject of the Established Church of Ireland. Had it been continued in every session, from 1834 to the present time, a period of thirty-five (now forty) years, it is probable that little progress would have been made; parties would have been marshalled against each other every year, and popular interest on the subject would have languished, and perhaps have perished. During the truce of this long period, discussion has taken place, information has been given, floods of light have been poured upon the subject; Parliament has divided and disestablished the Protestant Church; and public opinion has perceived the absurdity, the injustice, and the insult of a monopoly kept up for the benefit of one-eighth of the population of Ireland, and repugnant to the sentiments of at least three-fourths of the people.

An event of far greater importance than the secession of four members of the Cabinet, important as that was, occurred in the same session. The head of the Cabinet himself retired from office, and thenceforth took little part in public life, leaving, however, a brilliant example of unstained honor, of consistent public principle, and of success in legislation achieved in strict conformity with the principles which, in conjunction with his great leader, Mr. Fox, he had always strenuously maintained. It is well that those who embrace politics as the occupation of their lives should have before them the example of two such men as Fox and Grey, who having early in life distinguished themselves by their attachment to the cause of civil and religious liberty, of peace abroad and of reform at home, should have persevered in those sentiments in spite of the proscription of a court, and the mistaken passions of a people — should have vindicated in Parliament the suppression of the Slave Trade, the abolition of slavery in our Colonies, and the cause of justice in Ireland, together with all those measures which flow from the adoption of sound principles, maintained, during many years of political contention, and cherished to their last breath with unswerving rectitude. If the seventeenth century saw, in Sunderland and Shaftesbury, examples of selfishness and faction, the names of Fox and Grey should ever be used to incite men who enter public life to keep their honor unstained, and to look to the welfare of their country as the object of all their exertions.

The immediate occasion of Lord Grey's retirement was in itself not very creditable to those by whom it was caused. Lord Wellesley, the Lord Lieutenant of Ireland, was led by private correspondence to suppose that he should facilitate the course of the Government on the Irish Coercion Bill by departing partially from the sentiment he had expressed in a public dispatch — that political agitation and rural outrage were joined together, ' by one unbroken chain of indissoluble connection.'

Lord Althorp, in a manner quite inconsistent with his
usual guarded conduct, allowed Mr. Littleton, Chief
Secretary of Ireland, to inform O'Connell that in all
probability the Cabinet would not renew the Coercion
Act in its full rigor.   When, therefore, Lord Grey proposed to his Cabinet the renewal of the Coercion Act
without alteration, although he carried with him a
majority of his colleagues, he was strongly opposed by
Lord Althorp, who was followed by Mr. Grant, Mr.
Spring Rice, and Mr. Abercromby. Upon the proposal
being made in the House of Commons, in conformity
with the opinion of the majority, O'Connell referred, in
a way that Lord Althorp could not misunderstand, to
the assurances he had received, and protested with his
usual power and eloquence against the Government proposal.   Lord Althorp that same night called together
those who had agreed with him in the Cabinet, and with
their concurrence sent his resignation to Lord Grey.
Lord Grey, in laying this letter before the King, accompanied it with his own resignation.[1]

A Cabinet was summoned for the following evening ;
meeting Lord Melbourne in the Park he said, ' I believe
we are summoned to-night to consider a decision already
made.' . At the meeting of the Cabinet in the evening,
Lord Grey placed before us the letters containing his

---

[1] I was sitting by Lord Althorp when he announced, after O'Connell's
speech, in his own homely way, his resolution to resign. ' The pig's
killed,' he said.   A porcine illustration was not new in our history.
When Henry VIII. was considering of the best means of procuring his
divorce from Catherine of Aragon, he gave his decision in favor of Cranmer's opinion by saying, ' Cranmer has got the right sow by the ear.'
When Sir Robert Walpole was asked how he had overcome Sir Spencer
Compton, to whom the King was partial, he replied, ' He got the wrong
sow by the ear, and I the right.' So vulgar and idiomatic are the phrases
of English monarchs and ministers.

own resignation, and that of Lord Althorp, which he had sent early in the morning to the King. He likewise laid before us the King's gracious acceptance of his resignation, and he gave to Lord Melbourne a sealed letter from his Majesty. Lord Melbourne, upon opening this letter, found in it an invitation to him to undertake the formation of a Government. Seeing that nothing was to be done that night, I left the Cabinet and went to the Opera.

The acceptance of Lord Grey's resignation by the King was somewhat hurried; there was no reason why, upon friendly discussion between Lord Grey and Lord Althorp, the difference with respect to the clauses in the Coercion Bill, objected to by Lord Althorp, should not have been arranged. The whole measure was at that time one rather of precaution than of urgency; and had the dangers of the former year again arisen, Parliament might have been called upon to supply the want of authority.

But the King's purpose in this hasty acceptance soon became apparent. His Majesty desired Lord Melbourne to consider whether the Duke of Wellington and Sir Robert Peel might not be invited to join the Administration. Lord Melbourne, who was very averse to coalitions, declined in positive, though very courteous, terms, to undertake any such task. He had in view the maintenance of the Administration, taking himself the place of Lord Grey, and giving Lord Duncannon the Home Department. Lord Grey asked me, at the levee, whether I had any objection to continue in office under Lord Melbourne? I told him I had not.

But the great difficulty which every one felt, was how to secure the continuance of Lord Althorp in his post as leader of the House of Commons. It was obvious that he would not consent to the renewal of the Coercion Act, unless those clauses to which he had objected were omitted. But there was a still greater difficulty ; it might seem that Lord Grey's resignation was forced upon him by Lord Althorp, and that Lord Althorp's object had been to remain in office himself without Lord Grey. This supposition was totally inconsistent with the known inclinations and wishes of Lord Althorp. One of the ministers who had seceded on the question of the Irish Church, said to me that if he had been told that Lord Althorp had engaged in an intrigue to get out of office he might have believed it, but an assertion that Lord Althorp had intrigued in order to remain in office was utterly incredible. In fact, Lord Althorp detested office, and it was only at the earnest solicitation of his friends, the leaders of the Liberal party in the House of Commons, that he very reluctantly consented to retain his official position under Lord Melbourne. He told me that every morning when he woke, while he was in office, he wished himself dead. His acquiescence thus cost him a painful effort, and he no doubt determined at this time that if any event should set him free, he would never again take office upon any terms.

The death of Lord Spencer put this resolution to the test. Lord Althorp ceased to be the leader of the House of Commons, and no entreaties could induce him to accept, as a peer, the post of Secretary of State for the Colonies. Mr. Spring Rice becoming Chancellor of the Exchequer in his place, he retired for ever from public life.

There had been an impression in the Liberal party, that no one but Lord Althorp could lead the party in the House of Commons, and the difficulty was very great. Lord Melbourne informed me that he had consulted all his colleagues, and that each had said, with more or less warmth of expression, that I was the person to whom that position should be offered. Thus invited, I considered it my duty to accept the task, though I told Lord Melbourne that I could not expect to have the same influence with the House of Commons which Lord Althorp had possessed. In conversation with Mr. Abercromby I said, more in joke than in earnest, that if I were offered the command of the Channel fleet, and thought it my duty to accept, I should not refuse it. On this private and casual remark, Sydney Smith afterwards constructed an elaborate charge; and as I had consented, in the ecclesiastical commission, to a proposal that the patronage of the deans and chapters should be transferred to the bishops, he was so angry as to impute to me a want of feeling with which I trust I am not justly chargeable.

Lord Melbourne went to Brighton, and proposed to the King that I should succeed Lord Althorp as leader in the House of Commons. The King objected. Lord Melbourne then proposed successively the names of Mr. Spring Rice and Mr. Abercromby. But the King objected to both; and the next morning gave Lord Melbourne a written paper, saying that he had no further occasion for his services, or those of his colleagues. Lord Melbourne returned to London that day, bringing with him a letter for the Duke of Wellington. He saw no one that evening but Lord Brougham and Lord Duncannon, and he earnestly impressed upon them the importance of keeping the whole matter secret till after the meeting of the Cabinet, which was fixed for twelve o'clock on the following day. Before that time arrived, however, two of the morning newspapers, the

'Times' and the 'Morning Chronicle,' had announced the dismissal of the Ministry, and the 'Morning Chronicle' added to the announcement the words, 'the Queen has done it all.' This comment gave just offence to the King. He required the Duke of Wellington to deprive the Ministers at once of their offices. Lord Duncannon was interrupted at church, during the time of divine service, by a messenger commanding the instant delivery of the Seals of the Home Department. The Duke of Wellington recommended that a messenger should be sent for Sir Robert Peel, who was at Rome, and that to him should be entrusted the formation of a new Administration.

This whole proceeding was a very ill-judged step on the part of the King. Whatever might ultimately be the views of Lord Melbourne's Ministry on the Irish Church, no measure upon that subject had hitherto been matter of agreement, or even of deliberation in the Cabinet. Lord Melbourne and his colleagues possessed the confidence of a great majority of the House of Commons. If no one of the Ministry should be found to inherit the confidence so freely accorded to Lord Althorp, that fact would be tested by debate and division in the House of Commons itself. If the measure which the Ministry should introduce on the Irish Church should prove in the opinion of the House of Commons dangerous or impracticable, the vote upon that subject would involve their fall. Thus the King would have been relieved from responsibility; but by taking upon himself the initiative, he naturally offended the whole body of the people, who considered the exercise of the royal prerogative an act of caprice rather than of reasonable judgment. Sir Robert Peel was placed in a most unfavorable position; and he aggravated his own disadvantages by advising an immediate dissolution. Had he boldly met Parliament, and been thwarted in his attempt to govern, he might fairly have appealed to the country, and would probably have had a majority in his favor.

As it was, the very large majority which had followed the dissolution of 1832 was very sensibly diminished, but not entirely destroyed. The confidence placed in Sir Robert Peel, and the fear of any interference with the Irish Church, were the chief reasons of the diminished number of the Whig members. Still the Liberal party had a clear majority on the elections, but that majority consisted of every shade, from the most moderate of the Whigs to the most resolute of the Radicals. It seemed to me, as commander-in-chief of an army so variously composed, that they could not be too soon brought into action, and that motions ought to be framed in which the whole party could agree. With this view, Mr. Abercromby was proposed as Speaker, in the place of Mr. Manners Sutton, and was elected. An amendment was proposed to the address, advising a popular reform of corporations, and censuring the dissolution, the only act of importance for which the Ministers of the Crown were actually as well as virtually responsible. This amendment was carried. A motion for constituting an unsectarian University of London was carried by a majority of eighty. It was made evident that Sir Robert Peel had not the confidence of the House of Commons. His position, therefore, was not consistent with the principles of the Constitution. But he determined to remain as Minister till that want of confidence was shown by some overt act, and the difficulty was to frame a resolution by which a proof should be given that the Minister was not supported by the House of Commons. A notion prevailed, even among Liberals, that Sir Robert Peel should have a fair trial, — an advantage which had been denied to Lord Melbourne. It seemed to me that this fair trial would be given, and the House of Commons would still have in its hands the power of the purse — the citadel of its strength, if the supplies were only voted for three months. But when the party was consulted upon this suggestion, it was found that there were several who feared that any limitation of the ordinary vote in supply would affect public credit and alarm the country. I therefore reluctantly renounced this intention.

As leader of the Liberal party in the House of Commons, I had no smooth path before me. To turn the majority into a minority by a direct vote of want of confidence would have been easy. But my object was to keep the majority together; and in the whole twenty years during which I led the Liberal party in the House of Commons, I never had so difficult a task. The plain and obvious plan of voting the supplies for three months being given up, the question naturally occurred, in what manner could Sir Robert Peel obtain that fair trial which his own partisans and many independent Whigs called for on his behalf? There appeared no question so well fitted for an *experimentum crucis* as the question of the Irish Church. The proposal for a commission, made by Lord Grey's Government, had been considered by four of the leading members of the Cabinet as a test of principle; and the Liberal members of the first reformed House of Commons had accepted the question of the integrity and perpetual endowment of the Irish Church, as marking the frontier line between Liberal and Tory principles. I therefore proposed to bring forward a resolution, which, on the one hand, would be supported by Lord Howick, and was, on the other, the basis of an alliance with O'Connell and the Irish members. Compact there was none; but an alliance on honorable terms of mutual co-operation undoubtedly existed. The Whigs remained as before, the firm defenders of the Union; O'Connell remained as before, the ardent advocate of repeal; but upon intermediate measures, on which the two parties could agree consistently with their principles, there was no want of cordiality. Nor did I ever see cause to complain of O'Connell's conduct. He confined his opposition fairly to Irish measures. He never countenanced the Canadian Catholics in their disaffection, nor promoted a recurrence to physical force, nor used trades-unions as a means of discord and separation among classes.

I may pass over the interval between the first proposal of interference with the revenues of the Irish Church and Sir Robert Peel's surrender of power. Those proceedings are amply detailed in the 'Parliamentary Debates.'

On Lord Melbourne's return to power, a question of great interest arose. He had determined, some months before the dissolution of Sir Robert Peel's Ministry, that he would not again sit in the same Cabinet with Lord Brougham. What were the reasons for this determination? In order to form even a conjecture, it is necessary to give a sketch, however slight, of the character of Lord Brougham.

Lord Brougham was a man of extraordinary powers of mind. It must be said also that, with many aberrations, those powers of mind were generally directed to great and worthy objects, — to the abolition of the

Slave Trade and of slavery, to the improvement of law, to the promotion of education, to the furtherance of civil and religious liberty. His speech on the trial and condemnation of missionary Smith combined the closest and most pressing logic with the most eloquent denunciations of oppression and the most powerful appeal to justice. It contributed, no doubt, in a very marked degree, to the extinction of slavery throughout the dominions of the Crown of England. His speech of six hours on the amendment of the law was large and comprehensive in its general view, searching and elaborate in its details. The institution of the Judicial Committee of Privy Council was a most valuable result of his exertions as a law reformer. His labors regarding the endowed schools and misapplied charities of England destroyed many flagrant abuses, detected the perversion of a large amount of charitable funds, and led the way to those further inquiries, and those remedial measures, of which we have seen the commencement and progress, but of which the consummation is yet to come. It would be taking a narrow view to complain that large sums have been spent upon inquiries, and we have not as yet had an adequate return. Lord Brougham's speeches at the bar of the House of Lords, on the Bill of Pains and Penalties against Queen Caroline, were striking specimens of a powerful understanding; and his great speech in opening the defence was the most wonderful effort of oratory I ever heard. Nor can any one who heard him remember with any other feelings than those of the highest admiration his speech on the second reading of the Reform Bill in the House of Lords. The speech which he made at the assizes, in defence of Ambrose Williams, in 1821, carries satire and sarcasm to a height

that may be called sublime. But his speech on the
conduct of the continental powers of Europe towards
Spain — a country which had been guilty of the offence
of endeavoring to dispose of its own destiny, and to
establish a free government — was certainly one of his
brightest flights. His allusion to the protest of the
Russian Minister at Madrid, who had declared, with
horror, that blood had been shed in the Royal Palace,
was at once a withering invective and a just condemnation of despotism. 'If I had been one of the counsel-
lors of the Emperor of Russia,' he said, 'the last
subject I would have advised my master to touch upon
would have been that of " bloodshed in the Royal
Palace." ' The reigning Emperor of Russia was Alexander I. At the epoch of his coronation, a lady, writing from St. Petersburg, had described the ceremony in
these terms: 'The Emperor entered the church preceded by the assassins of his grandfather, surrounded
by the assassins of his father, and followed by his own.'

The question recurs, if such were the qualities and
such the achievements of Lord Brougham, why was
the Great Seal not restored to him? After one of his
most striking speeches against Lord Melbourne, Lord
Melbourne replied in these terms: 'My Lords, you have
heard the eloquent speech of the noble and learned
Lord — one of the most eloquent he ever delivered in
this House — and I leave your Lordships to consider
what *must be* the nature and strength of the objections
which prevent any Government from availing themselves of the services of such a man.'

What, then, was the nature of the objections which
prevented Lord Melbourne from offering to return the
Great Seal into the hands of Lord Brougham when he
himself resumed office? These objections came first

from Lord Melbourne, and were frankly communicated
by him to Lord Brougham, before he finally decided to
form an Administration. In the next place, these objections could not fairly be said to imply any charge of
treachery· towards his chief, or his colleagues, during
the former Administration. He had not written to
Lord Wellesley with a· purpose to undermine Lord
Grey; he had willingly assented to the selection of
Lord Melbourne as Prime Minister. He had not
attempted to carry measures to which the Prime Minister was opposed, nor, like Lord Thurlow and Lord
Loughborough, to thwart measures which the Prime
Minister had approved. His faults were, a recklessness
of judgment, which hurried him beyond all the bounds
of prudence, an omnivorous appetite for praise, a perpetual interference in matters with which he had no
direct concern, and, above all, a disregard of truth.
This spirit of interference led him to promise his support to Mr. Canning, without any communication with
Lord Althorp, and with great indiscretion to influence
Lord Wellesley on the renewal of the Coercion Act
without any communication with Lord Grey. I remember Lord Dudley saying to me, many years before this
time, ' What a character Brougham would have been
for the pen of Lord Clarendon! " Lord Appleby (supposing he had got his peerage) was a man who, if the
solidity of his judgment had been equal to the preg-
nancy of his wit, would not have been surpassed in
this or any other time." ' This was the truth. Lord
Brougham's vast powers of mind were neutralized by a
want of judgment, which prevented any party from
placing entire confidence in him, and by a frequent
forgetfulness of what he himself had done or said but a
short time before.

Lord Melbourne was a man of a very different character. His ease of manner and apparent indifference tended to conceal the excellence of his understanding and the warmth of his feelings. He would have been ready, perhaps too ready, from the easiness of his temper, to yield to the incessant urgency of Brougham's interference. But his understanding would have condemned the concessions he made, and his feelings of pride and shame would have made him deeply sensible to the reproach that, while nominally Prime Minister, he was adopting decisions which he could not approve, and was degraded by the very elevation upon which he apparently stood. It was for these reasons, I conceive, that, many weeks before the change of Government, he resolved not to offer the Great Seal to Lord Brougham. He told me of his fixed resolution on this head many weeks before the dissolution of Sir Robert Peel's Ministry. When his resolution became known, Lord Melbourne exposed himself and his party to the charge of ingratitude to a man whose vast powers and splendid services made him an object of general admiration. Observing as I did the characters of the two men, I thought Lord Melbourne justified in his decision, and I willingly stood by him in his difficulties. Nor did Lord Brougham ever act towards me with less cordiality on account of the part I took. Indeed, I should have been glad to see Brougham in the Cabinet, and it could not be denied that a Liberal Ministry, deprived of the assistance of Lord Grey, Lord Althorp, and Lord Brougham, opposed by the Duke of Wellington, Lord Lyndhurst, Lord Aberdeen, Sir Robert Peel, Lord Stanley, and Sir James Graham, and resting its claims to support on the justice of its Irish policy, of which the merits were little understood, stood daily in great risk of overthrow. Yet, from April, 1835, to August, 1841, the Ministry stood its ground, and was able to pass measures of great importance to the public welfare. But these measures encountered much opposition, and the task was one of constant labor and anxiety. To add to the public discontent and impatience, Lord Lyndhurst contrived to induce the peers to throw out measures which were of undoubted public utility, but had no strong breeze of popular approbation in their favor. Among the measures which owed their success to the restoration of a Liberal Administration, I may mention three.

First, the commutation of tithes. The unsettled state of this question was deeply injurious to the interests of agriculture, and to those of the Church. In many instances, where waste lands might have been brought into cultivation, or the produce of cultivated lands and the supply of food to the people largely augmented, the right of the Church to appropriate a tenth of the produce, without regard to the expense of the improvement, was a positive bar to cultivation. In many other instances, the attempts of the farmer to abate the rights of the Church, and to force the clergyman to be content with a twentieth part of the produce, or even less, instead of his legal tenth, had been the source of wrangling and ill-will between the farmers and the clergymen, to the destruction of Christian charity, and of the harmony that ought to prevail between the pastor and his flock. Pitt had attempted in vain to frame a complete measure on this subject. Peel had endeavored to remedy the notorious evils by a voluntary commutation; but a commutation short of compulsory would have left many of the worst cases untouched — cases in which the Church had insisted un-

wisely upon its full rights, or a combination of farmers
had determined to vex and worry a clergyman of easy
disposition, till they reduced him to penury by their
obstinacy and injustice.   All the evils of the tithe system were the subject of fair compromise and permanent
settlement by the Act of 1836.   Three commissioners,
two of whom were appointed by the Crown and one by
the Archbishop of Canterbury, were empowered, after
examination, to proceed by certain fixed rules to a final
adjudication.   In about seven years this process was
completed, and a work from which Pitt had shrunk was
accomplished.   The progress of agriculture was freed
from vexatious impediments, and the clergy were spared
the unseemly contentions which had fostered ill-will
and disturbed social relations.

Other questions affected religious liberty.   The Church
had taken possession of the registers of baptism, by
which alone the number of births was ascertained.
Marriage was legally a religious ceremony, and although
by the ancient laws it was a civil contract, those who
did not belong to the Church could neither be married
in their own places of worship, nor in any building of
a civil character, nor by any other form than that of
the Establishment.   So, likewise, the performance of the
Burial Service was confined to those who had been
baptized according to the Anglican rite, and there existed no civil registration of deaths.   These matters
were made the subject of legislation.   An Act was
introduced providing for the marriage of Protestant
Dissenters, Roman Catholics, and Jews, according to
their own rites, and enacting a civil marriage in the
office of a registrar for those who were contented with
a civil contract only.

The question of civil marriages raised much objection, on the part of Sir Robert Inglis in the House of Commons, and of the Bishop of Exeter in the House of Lords; and although the Tory party did not generally join in the opposition, the principle is so important that I may be excused for dilating upon it.

Generally speaking, Scripture is unfairly or unwisely quoted in political controversy; but there are some words of Christ's uttered on a memorable occasion, which it is impossible for politicians to keep out of view, in the course of discussions on government and legislation. Those words are, ' Render unto Cæsar the things which are Cæsar's, and unto God the things that are God's.' [1] The immediate question was the payment of tribute: but the precept is general, and statesmen must ask themselves what things are Cæsar's and what things are God's, or, in other words, what are the limits of the temporal and spiritual power.

The spirit of priestcraft, or, as the present age, fond of long words, calls it, the spirit of sacerdotalism, has been continually engaged in extending the spiritual, and restricting the temporal, power. Time was when in England a priest who had committed murder was withheld from the civil, and claimed by a spiritual tribunal. In the same spirit, the birth of a child was not acknowledged or recorded by the State until it had undergone the rite of baptism as ordained by one sect of Christianity.

Other distinctions have been made, and other usurpations attempted. Some of these have been repelled, others quietly withdrawn. But there are two points upon which disputes still exist, and with regard to

---

[1] St. Matthew, xxii. 15.

which what is called by diplomatists a rectification of frontiers, appears to be urgently required.

One is marriage, the other education.

The question of marriage is one that obviously concerns civil interests of the highest importance. The succession to property, to political rights of subjects and citizens, nay, the very succession to the throne, is decided, if we attend to the priesthood, according to the law of marriage which prevails in the Church. If we listen to some of the highest Roman Catholic authorities, the divorce of Napoleon I. was null and void, and the prince whom the French call Napoleon II. must have been an illegitimate son.[1] According to the same, or still higher Roman Catholic authorities, the marriage of George, Prince of Wales, to Mrs. Fitzherbert was valid, and if that lady had had a son, he must have been considered by Roman Catholics as the true heir of the Crown of England.[2]

Thus far and thus high reaches the question whether the State or the Church is supreme in regard to the validity of marriage. Property in all its forms, legitimacy of birth in every class of society, depends on the decision.

The Marriage Bill of 1836, in contradiction to these sacerdotal authorities, considered marriage as a matter within the competence of the State, and not as part of the jurisdiction of the Church.

Sir Robert Inglis, a firm supporter of Church pretensions, said in the committee on the bill, ' With the single exception of the time of the Great Rebellion,

---

[1] See ' Memoirs of Cardinal Gonsalvi.'

[2] See the statements of Mr. Langdale in ' Memoirs of Mrs. Fitzherbert.' 8vo. 1856.

there was no one instance in the history of the country of marriage having been considered otherwise than as a religious ceremony. This was a solitary attempt to give a civil character to a religious contract.'

In reply to this speech, I said, ' That the great object of the bill was to allow every person to be married according to whatever form his conscience dictated. Here were, first, members of the Church of England, next the Dissenters, who considered marriage a religious ceremony, and preferred being married in their own chapels; the first were left in their present situation, the second were permitted to carry their wishes into effect. There were other classes of Dissenters who considered marriage not a religious but a civil ceremony. Taking the broad principle of religious liberty, I felt that we were bound to provide for all these classes; I did not think that the House had a right to tell one class of men that their scruples were just and reasonable, and to reject all regard for those of others. If the bill were carried with that clause, I entertained no doubt but that ninety-nine marriages out of one hundred would still be considered as religious ceremonies. Although the number of marriages celebrated upon any other principle might be few, the principle was a great one, and we were bound to maintain it.'

In the House of Lords, the Bishop of Exeter spoke on behalf of the Church, and thus shortly summed up his objections: 'This bill, in his opinion, went the length of inviting the members of the Church of England to contract marriage without any religious ceremony, and that was a principle he hoped the legislature never would adopt. By this bill parties would be able to contract marriage without uttering a syllable as to the nature of the contract, beyond that they desired to live together as man and wife. They would not even be obliged to say that it was a contract for life, notwithstanding it was a contract of the most solemn and binding description. The only period in the history of this country at which a similar attempt was made was during the time of the usurpation ; but, although marriage might *then* be contracted before a magistrate, a strictly solemn and religious *formula* was enjoined. Here, however, the contract was to be purely civil, and attended with no greater solemnities than would be required for a contract entered into between parties for mere service. He must insist that a contract so sacred and indissoluble should be accompanied with suitable solemnities, and, unless this were done, no earthly inducement could prevail with him to allow the measure to progress another stage without opposing it.'

Although much was done by the Act of 1836, I stated, when the bill was returned to the Commons, that I accepted the amendments of the Lords, on account of the great principle they admitted, but not as a final settlement of the question.[1] 'In France and Italy, by the prevailing laws of these countries, the civil marriage is alone recognized, and alone gives the right of succession. In the United Kingdom various laws prevail. The pretensions of the clergy were got rid of by the Act of 1836, so far as England is concerned. But in Scotland and Ireland the law is still very uncertain, and Sir Roundell Palmer has wisely proposed, in a very clear and able speech, that there shall be one uniform law for the United Kingdom. It will be matter for consideration whether the future law, instead of recog-

---

[1] Hansard's 'Debates,' vol. xxxv. p. 1805.

nizing the marriage registers of every Christian communion, and every Jewish synagogue, should not be
founded on the same principle as the law of France and
Italy, constituting civil marriage the only bond recognized by the State, and leaving to the parties concerned
to add any religious ceremony or ceremonies they may
think proper.

Upon this subject I should have liked to listen to the
opinions of the Lord Chancellor of Ireland, and the Lord
Justice-General of Scotland; but as Lord Malmesbury
will not admit life peers into the House of Lords, I
fear we have no chance of hearing the voices of those
eminent and learned persons in that assembly.

Still I hope, although we have no promise from the
Government to that effect, that a bill on marriage will
be introduced by them during the next session. I trust,
above all, that Sir Roundell Palmer will not lose sight of
this great matter, so worthy of his large capacity and
undoubted zeal for the public welfare.

On the subject of Education, the Church of England
has not been slow to follow the traces of the Church of
Rome by an attempt to monopolize the question.

In 1807, the British and Foreign School Society commenced its work, with the flag of 'Schools for all!'
The Established Church pronounced at first the opinion
that the children of the poor should not go to school at
all; but, finding that George III. had expressed a wish
that every child in his dominions should be able to read
the Bible; that the Duke of Kent, the Duke of Bedford, and others were promoters of the British schools,
and that national opinion was favorable to education,
changed its ground, and in 1809 set up the so-called
National Society on a narrow and exclusive principle.

In 1832, Lord Brougham induced the Government to

propose a vote of 10,000*l.* each to the National and British and Foreign School Societies.

In 1839, with her Majesty's sanction, I wrote a letter to Lord Lansdowne, President of the Council, proposing a scheme of National Education. The principles I laid down were, that ' the youth of the kingdom should be religiously brought up,' and that ' the rights of conscience should be respected.'

These last words raised a storm. Mr. Stanley quoted, in a great speech, a *dictum* of Henry IV., only four centuries old, assuming for the Church the monopoly of education. The Archbishop of Canterbury carried, in the House of Lords, an address adverse to our unhallowed scheme. The grant proposed was only carried in the House of Commons by a majority of two.

In these circumstances, Lord Lansdowne and I met the Archbishop of Canterbury (Dr. Howley), the Bishop of London (Dr. Blomfield), and the Bishop of Salisbury (Dr. Denison), and agreed to a compromise.

Inspection, which Lord Lansdowne especially insisted upon, was to be conducted in the schools of the National Society by inspectors, in the appointment of whom the bishops were to concur, and whose reports, comprising religious as well as secular instruction, were to be communicated to the bishop of the diocese, as well as to the Committee of the Privy Council. Tuition in British schools, and in Protestant Dissenting and Roman Catholic schools, was likewise to be subjected to inspection, but only so far as regarded secular teaching.

This arrangement, in which, with Lord Lansdowne, I was glad to concur, has no doubt done much to promote education, and to dispel the darkness of ignorance; but, as a plan of National Education, it left much to be desired.

In the first place, it was evident that where education was most wanted, least would be given. Where the land-owners were rich and public-spirited, where the clergy were zealous, and the farmers generous, schools would flourish. But where land-owners and farmers would give no encouragement, schools would be altogether wanting, or miserably conducted.

Then, again, where Dissenters existed, but were not numerous enough to keep a school of their own, the clergy would exclude the Baptist, the Independent, and the Unitarian. The British schools, where Christianity is taught pure and simple, are sure to be distasteful to the Church of England, to the Church of Rome, and to sectarian zealots of all denominations.

It was not easy to supply these deficiencies; and indeed I never considered the plan otherwise than as a step in the education of the people, till the tide of public opinion should set more strongly in favor of National Education.

The Duke of Newcastle's commission has done much to open the way to a National plan. Their scheme, if adopted on the basis that every county should be divided into separate districts, that every district should be bound to furnish an adequate number of schools, on a scale to be fixed by Parliament; that if supported by rates, the ratepayers should decide on the religious instruction to be given, or, if they preferred it, give a secular character to the school; and, lastly, that when any religious instruction is given, it should be either in the first or the last hour of school attendance, and that during the hour of religious instruction every parent should be at liberty to withdraw his children, by a strictly defined conscience clause, — might form the outline of a plan of National Education.

With a compulsory provision for the building of schools, I should not be disposed to insist on the compulsory attendance of children. It will probably be expedient to impose a fine upon employers who have in their service boys or girls between twelve and eighteen years of age, who cannot read and write; but this power must be used with great moderation. English farmers are gradually becoming enlightened, but have still a long way to go before they are on a level with the farmers of Scotland, or the artisans of our great towns.

It is, in fact, from the great towns that light must proceed. From them was spread the knowledge of Christianity, from them proceeded the revival of letters, from them have come reform of Parliament and free trade.

I have elsewhere given the reasons which induced the Government to abandon, in 1838, what was called the appropriation clause. The public mind of Ireland, guided by O'Connell, wished to go much farther; the public mind of England and Scotland, having neither knowledge of Ireland nor sympathy with its inhabitants, was not prepared to go so far. But, in giving up the appropriation clause, the Government not only maintained a just administration in Ireland, for which Burke had written in vain, but had passed through Parliament a settlement of the Irish tithes, for which Grattan had so long and so fruitlessly labored.

I may take this opportunity of considering the state in which Ireland was left by the Government, when the appropriation clause was abandoned. I need say nothing here of the administration; that subject is treated in the speech of 1839, when I proposed a vote of confidence in the Administration, so far as Ireland was concerned.

The law abolishing tithes and substituting a rent-charge met with so general a concurrence from all parties in Parliament, that, as usually happens in such cases, its importance was very much overlooked. It is extraordinary that Mr. Bright, who has spoken with so much force and eloquence on the Irish Church, and who has devoted so much study to Irish affairs, has not even enumerated, among the measures of importance to the welfare of Ireland, which have been passed during the last fifty years, the Act of 1838. Yet if he will look to Grattan's speeches made before the Union, and to the speeches made in 1832–33, on the subject of tithes, he will see how deeply the people of Ireland were tormented, and the whole course of peaceable government disturbed, by the collection of tithe in kind.[1] Any one who will read this part of the history of Ireland will see that a measure which changed the collection of tithes from a question between tithe-proctor and peasant, into a question between landlord and tenant, with a percentage of twenty-five per cent to the landlord for the cost and trouble of collection, and thereby put an end to all the oppression, all the ill-will, and all the bloodshed of former contests, was one of immense value to the whole body of small occupiers in Ireland. No measure has tended more to the peaceful progress of Ireland than the Tithe Act of 1838.

The legislation of that year, taken together with the Catholic Relief Act of 1829, the abolition of the Church cess by the Church Temporalities Act, and the Poor-

---

[1] See especially Mr. Grattan's 'Speeches,' vol. ii. March 13, 1787; February 14, 1788; April 14, 1788; May 8, 1789. See also the debates on the outrages that took place, and on the blood that was shed in Ireland on the subject of tithes from 1832 to 1835.

law of 1838, left, however, three subjects of immense importance for future consideration.

The first of these was the Established Church of Ireland. Every author who has written on the subject of Church Establishments has taken for granted that where a Church has to be established by the State, it should be the Church of the people, and the Irish Established Church never was, never had been, and never could be, the Church of the people.

It has been said, blinking the question in dispute, that the clergy of the Established Church of Ireland taught religious truth, that they were a respectable body of men, that they were well educated, and that they were kind and charitable to their neighbors, whether Catholic or Protestant.

These arguments put me in mind of a story told at some length, in verse, by Dr. Herbert, afterwards Dean of Manchester. He relates how a traveller, hospitably received by a friend, in course of conversation, lays down as an incontrovertible maxim that that which is excellent *per se* can never be misplaced. His host does not dispute the maxim, but at supper places upon the table a plate of salted cherries. When his friend makes a wry face at the nauseous mixture, the host tells him that his maxim is thus refuted.

So it was with the Established Church in Ireland. The English fruit was wholesome, the Irish salt was pungent, but the fruit and the salt together make a most unpalatable dessert.

Happily this whole mischief has been abated by the Act of 1869. Although many supplementary provisions may be required, the main principle of that Act will remain a permanent benefit to the people of Ireland.

The Minister who brought forward and carried a

bill to disestablish and disendow the Protestant Church of Ireland had to put forth all his strength in bearing so heavy a weight upon his shoulders. He had to unite in one phalanx the old Liberal party, who wished to maintain the Church of England ; the Voluntaries, who wished to abolish all Church Establishments ; the nominees of the Irish priests, who wished to compensate the Church of Rome in Ireland for what she has lost in Italy and in Spain ; and the representatives of the stern Presbyterians of Scotland, who, in the words of an anonymous letter which I received from Glasgow, thought that the Church of Scotland was God's truth, and the Church of Rome was the devil's lie.

To combine these parties, so as to gain and to keep a majority of one hundred and twenty-six in favor of the measure, and at the same time not to depart from justice, was a task of unparalleled difficulty ; those who have long been convinced of the iniquity of maintaining a Church Establishment for a minority must be grateful to the able Minister who achieved a success so speedy and so complete.

But we must not be surprised if the wants of Ireland have been in a great degree overlooked ; if the hatred entertained by a large proportion of the Low Church, of the Protestant Dissenters of England, and of the Presbyterians of Scotland, whether endowed or seceding, against the Pope and the Church of Rome, should have been allowed to prevail over policy, rather than incur any risk of seeing the majority divided and disbanded.

Moderate men ought to rejoice that the words of the preamble, upon which the Liberation Society appeared at one time disposed to insist, have been expunged at the desire of a majority of seventy-eight in the House of Lords, and that the disposition of the surplus in all future times, instead of being employed in the degradation of the Irish people, has been reserved at the suggestion of Lord Cairns. It is a valuable treasure rescued from the wreck. It is said by desponding Protestants that the free Protestant Church of Ireland cannot flourish; that the Roman Catholic priest has in his armory weapons more potent than any which his Protestant adversary can wield; that by absolution he can relieve from thousands of years of flames and torture those among the departed whom his penitent most loved in life, whom he fondly cherishes beyond the tomb.

But this is entirely to mistake the strength, and forego the true arms, of Protestantism.

If, indeed, the Protestant clergy rely on a faint copy of the doctrine of the Roman Catholic real presence, — if they rely on candles and incense, fine music and gaudy vestments, then, indeed, their Protestantism is, what Mr. Sheil called it, Popery with a bar sinister. Such an imitation can never compete successfully with the legitimate Roman Church. The Queen of England might as well order her army to fight the Chinese with gingals and tomtoms, or President Grant send his troops against the Indians armed with bows and arrows.

The strength of the Reformation lies in a totally different direction. Shakespeare has pointed out the true source of Protestant power: —

> Sure he that made us of such large discourse,
> Looking before and after, gave us not
> Such capability and god-like reason
> To fust in us unused.

It is because men feel that their 'capability and god-like reason' is not given to fust in them 'unused,' that they endeavor to find out what they ought to think and

to believe on the most deeply interesting of all subjects.
Hence the right of private judgment, hence the Bible
of Wicliffe, and the Bible of Luther, and the Bible of
Great Britain.   Hence, men throw aside the pseudo-
popery of. Oxford, with the time-hallowed popery of
Rome ; hence they reject the allurements of splendid
churches, gilded vestments, soft music, and all that can
entrance the senses ; hence they seek, in the words of
Christ, of St. Peter, and St. Paul, and St. John, the true
spiritual food for their souls, and leave below them the
mists of theology and the stars of earthly splendor.

It is in such a spirit that the Protestant Church of
Ireland must act ; it is with such weapons that she will
prevail.

Archbishop Murray said, ' Let the children of Ireland read the Bible, and then I am sure they will be
Catholics.'   Archbishop Whately said, ' Let the children of Ireland read the Bible, and then I am sure they
will be Protestants.'   I admire the bold and confident
spirit in which these two prelates proved the sincerity
of their faith.

The Roman Catholic Church of Ireland has unfortunately sadly fallen off from the confidence of Archbishop Murray.   It is now considered dangerous that a
Roman Catholic child should be made aware that there
are Protestant children in the land, that he should play
with them, talk with them, learn arithmetic with them,
be on friendly terms with them, or consider them otherwise than as outcasts from heaven.

A better prescription for sowing hatred and ill-will
between Catholics and Protestants in Ireland cannot
well be imagined.   Let us reflect a moment.

Before the Church of Ireland was disestablished, it
was usual, natural, and even right, for Liberals to look

upon the claims of Roman Catholics with some degree of partiality, and to make concessions, both as to men and measures, with a view to redress the balance which Protestant ascendency so greatly disturbed.

But Liberal Protestants have now a right to be strictly just, and to grant to the Roman Church no more than that Church can fairly claim.

The two principal questions which remain for consideration are, that of National Education and that of Land.

In considering Irish education, a very large question arises, which must not be permitted to slip through Parliament without being handled, weighed, and examined.

For two centuries after the death of Julius Cæsar, writers of great ability and eloquence endeavored to teach morality to the senate and people of Rome. The old gods, who had never, either by precept or example, encouraged a strict observance of morals, had lost their authority. The god of Epicurus was

> A jolly god, who left mankind alone;
> Who unconcerned could at rebellion sit,
> And wink at crimes he did himself commit.

In place of divine rulers, Cicero, Seneca, and Marcus Aurelius endeavored, by elegant exhortations and pungent sentences, to inculcate morality. Their influence in reforming morals was scarcely perceptible.[1] A more dissolute society than that of Rome could not well be. The philosophers had entirely failed to improve the morals of the Roman Empire.

After the death of Jesus Christ upon the cross, a new society arose.

---

[1] See Lecky's admirable 'History of European Morals,' from Augustus to Charlemagne, vol. i.

Pliny, the Proconsul of Trajan in Bithynia, informs the Emperor of the existence of a sect called Christians, and asks for his instructions. He states that this sect having been denounced to him, he had taken pains to ascertain their doctrines and their conduct. They admitted that they sung early in the morning a hymn to Christ as to God, but they affirmed that their teaching was innocent and irreproachable. They taught the members of their society to refrain from theft, from robbery, and from adultery; to act with punctual good faith to their neighbors, and to restore scrupulously to its owner any property confided to their care.

Two maid-servants who belonged to the society, and who, like Rhoda in the Acts of the Apostles, waited upon them, were put to the torture by Pliny, but nothing further was extracted from these noble-hearted damsels. Pliny thereupon desired the Christian culprits to worship the Emperor and to curse Christ. Those who did so were dismissed; those who refused he ordered to be led to execution.

The Emperor Trajan approved of what had been done, but desired that no search for Christians should be made, and that they should only be punished when duly convicted of worshipping Christ, and of refusing to adore the divinity of the Emperor.

Since the time that Christ began to teach, morality has been connected with religion. Christianity has been persecuted, and persecutor; has been perverted and corrupted. Alva put to death his thousands; Cranmer consigned to the flames a maiden guilty of some error in theology; Calvin burnt Servetus, and defended the thesis that errors in belief ought to be punished by the civil magistrate; Presbyterians have been oppressed in the Old World, and have been oppressors in the New;

but in spite of all alterations of fortune, in spite of wickedness in high places, amid the affliction of the good and the triumph of the bad, the divorce of religion and morality has never taken place.

In Ireland, religious teaching cannot be given by a Protestant Established Church. The church of a minority cannot teach the mass of the people. Mr. Grattan said, 'I love the Protestants; I love the Catholics; I love the Presbyterians: and my affection only abates when the members of those communions hate each other.' Mr. Grattan might have added, with St. Paul, 'and I will very gladly spend and be spent for you; though the more abundantly I love you the less I be loved.'[1]

Grattan also said, more than seventy years ago, that as the Roman Catholic priests must be the teachers of the people, he wished them to be well-informed; and, as the classes from which the priesthood were drawn were not usually able to afford a good education for their sons, he thought it would be wise to found a college for their instruction. Hence the College of Maynooth.

Some men think we have grown wiser since those dark ages — of Grattan and of Burke, of Fox and Pitt.

Yet I confess I still cling to their notions, and those of their predecessors. I cannot admit that in a country where, in the case of a murder, the sympathy of the people is with the murderer, and not with the sorrowing family and friends of the murdered man, there is no need that the State should assist and promote the 'teaching of religion.'

Yielding, however, to the sense of Parliament, that

---

[1] 1 Corinthians, ch. xii.

there can be no endowment of the Roman Catholic Church, and that even concurrent endowment is hopeless and impracticable, it may be permitted me to inquire whether the doctrines of Christianity cannot be imparted to the young by a school establishment, founded on the system at present in force.

The object and fundamental principle of the system of National Education in Ireland is thus officially stated : —

1. The object of the system of National Education is to afford *combined* literary and moral, and *separate* religious instruction, to children of all persuasions, as far as possible, in the same school, upon the fundamental principle, that no attempt shall be made to interfere with the peculiar religious tenets of any description of Christian pupils.

Next, as to the description of schools.

2. The schools to which the Commissioners grant aid are divided into two classes, viz. : — 1st, Vested Schools, of which there are two sorts; namely, those vested in the Commissioners, and those vested in trustees, for the purpose of being maintained as National Schools. 2d, Non-vested Schools, the property of private individuals. Both these classes of schools are under the control of local patrons or managers.

The rules for religious and secular instruction are thus stated : —

1. Opportunities are to be afforded (as hereinafter provided for) to the children of all National Schools for receiving such religious instruction as their parents or guardians approve.

2. Religious instruction must be so arranged, that each school shall be open to children of all communions; that due regard be had to parental right and

authority; that, accordingly, no child be *compelled* to receive, or to be present at any religious instruction, of which his parents or guardians disapprove; and that the time for giving it be so fixed, that no child shall be thereby, in effect, excluded, directly or indirectly, from the other advantages which the school affords.

3. A public notification of the times for religious instruction must be inserted in large letters in the ' Time Table ' supplied by the Commissioners, who recommend that, as far as may be practicable, the general nature of such religious instruction be also stated therein.

*   *   *   *   *   *

The reading of the Scriptures, either in the Protestant Authorized, or Douay Version — the teaching of catechisms, — public prayer, — and all other religious exercises, come within the rules as to religious instruction.

Religious instruction, prayer, and all other religious exercises, may take place at any time, before and after the ordinary school business (during which all children, of whatever denomination they may be, are required to attend), but must not take place *at more than one intermediate* time, between the commencement and the close of the ordinary school business. The Commissioners, however, will not sanction any arrangement for religious instruction, prayer, or other religious exercises *at an intermediate time*, in cases where it shall appear to them that such arrangement will interfere with the usefulness of the school, by preventing children of any religious denomination from availing themselves of its advantages, or by subjecting those in attendance to any practical inconvenience.

The following note to the 13th rule is of great importance : —

Note. — The Commissioners earnestly recommend that religious instruction shall take place either immediately before the commencement, or immediately after the close, of the ordinary school business ; and they further recommend that, whenever the patron or manager thinks fit to have religious instruction at an intermediate time, a separate apartment shall (when practicable) be provided for the reception of those children whose parents or guardians may disapprove of their being present thereat.

It may be here observed that these rules are far more full and more complete than the Conscience Clause of the Committee of Privy Council in England.

The managers or teachers of a National School in England might so arrange and intermingle the secular and religious instruction as to give the parents no choice but either to leave their children in school during the hours of religious instruction, or to lose their lessons of secular instruction. This, it will be said, is not a probable occurrence ; but, as such cases do happen, it is well to guard against it.

With regard to management, the rules of the Irish National Board direct that —

1. The local government of the National Schools is vested in the local patrons thereof.

The rules go on to declare that the person who first applies to place the school in connection with the Board becomes, unless otherwise specified in the application, the local patron ; that the patron has the right to nominate any fit person to act in his place as the ' local manager ; ' that when a school is vested in trustees, they have the right to nominate the local manager.

The 12th clause, in regard to management, is of great importance. It provides as follows : —

'The local patrons (or managers) of schools have the right of appointing the teachers, subject to the approval of the Board as to character and general qualifications; the local patron (or managers) have also the power of removing the teachers of their own authority.'

This rule gives a vast power to the local patrons or managers — the landlord or clergyman of the Episcopal Church, the Presbyterian minister, or, more frequently, the parish priest.

Observe, that the salaries of the teachers of the ordinary National Schools are miserably small. In 1865, the principal teachers of the 2d division of the 3d class received, men, 18*l.*; women, 16*l.*; or, in other words, the men little more than seven, and the women little over six, shillings a week. Men and women thus rewarded for the devotion of their whole time to teaching are, of course, entirely dependent on the local manager, who can dismiss them at pleasure. If the parish priest happen to be that local manager, and, if he find the teacher deviating into broad Christian principle or rising to the higher regions of science, he may dismiss the teacher or school-mistress at once to poverty and destitution.

But Cardinal Cullen and his colleagues are not satisfied with this degree of denominational exclusiveness.

There are mixed schools, which are attended by 24,000 Protestant children in various proportions; in some ten, in some five, in some one or two.

In many of these schools, images of the Virgin Mary and of saints are enclosed in cases, or closets, and only exhibited at the hours of religious instruction. The Roman Catholic bishops require that these images should be exhibited at all hours, with a view, no doubt, to induce the Protestant children to pay their reverence and devotion to Roman Catholic saints. They require, also, that Protestant teachers should not be permitted to teach reading and writing, arithmetic and geography, in schools where the pupils are altogether or mainly Roman Catholic. And this in schools where, according to the report of 1865, of 303,723*l*. 11*s*. 9*d*., received by the teaching staff of the schools, only 16·95 per cent was locally provided, while 83·05 per cent was provided by the State. Is not this too much for the priesthood to ask?

Parliament may consistently give large sums for National Schools in England, where a religion defined by the Church in Convocation, adopted by the State, and confined within bounds, approved by Parliament, and interpreted by judges named by the Crown, is taught at the expense, partly of the State, and partly of local subscribers. But the Roman Catholic prelates require that the State should furnish eighty three per cent of the salaries of teachers, the majority of whom will be constrained by the priests to stigmatize Protestants as rebels to Divine authority and objects of Divine wrath; perhaps to teach that William III. had no right to the throne, and that his successor is a usurper. Surely the House of Commons of the United Kingdom can never sanction such a scheme!

The system of National Education in Ireland, introduced by the Government in 1831, under the sanction of Lord Grey, by the instrumentality of Mr. Stanley, and with the co-operation of Archbishop Whately, was no branch of the poisonous tree of Protestant ascendency. Its object and intention was to unite the Protestant Episcopalian, the Roman Catholic, and the Presbyterian in one scheme of secular and religious instruction; to leave religious teaching free; to respect the rights of conscience, and to persuade all communions to live in harmony and peace.

The principle of the National School system of Ireland is, we may conclude, one befitting the State, which is bound to provide instruction, not for the children of one church, or one sect only, but for all. But it is open to the following objections: —

1. In the non-vested schools, the Roman Catholic parish priest is frequently the patron, and holds the school-master in very servile subjection. A very efficient school-master, popular with the scholars, may be dismissed at will, if he does not follow the directions of the priest.

2. The school-masters and school-mistresses are divided into three classes.

The payment of the third class, as already stated, is very inadequate.

Having no dwelling-house, and often a very wretched school-house, their teaching is much disturbed and restrained by physical discomfort and inadequate means.

The remedies for these deficiencies are not far to seek.

The school-masters and school-mistresses should be more liberally paid. They should have comfortable dwelling-houses, and adequate school-houses, built and repaired by the Board. They should be independent of the caprice of the patron, and not liable to be removed without the consent of the Board.

With these changes, and 400,000*l.* provided by Parliament, for twenty years to come, a well-educated generation would form the majority of the Irish people.

I am almost afraid to avow that I prefer the simple words of Christ to any dogmatic interpretation of them, whether taught by the Pope, by Luther, or by Calvin. If I am in error in this respect, I am in error with Dr. Arnold, with Dean Milman, and with still higher authorities.

The Pope, who was called upon to judge between Fénelon and Bossuet, said, Fénelon has erred by having too much of the love of God; Bossuet, by having too little of the love of his neighbor. I prefer the error of Fénelon to that of Bossuet. Nay, more, I think that the spirit of the Christian religion is to be found, not in dogma, but in reverence to God, and love of our neighbor. In my opinion, Fénelon and Tillotson were better Christians than Bossuet and Laud. Men have endeavored to ascertain, by metaphysical research, whether the Son is of the same substance as the Father, whether the Holy Ghost proceeds from the Father only, or from the Father and the Son. These are subjects upon which men may differ, and yet respect one another.

But there are matters of infinite importance, upon which the words of Christ are plain to all understandings.

He taught his disciples to love one another. He taught them to pray to God to forgive us our trespasses, as we forgive them that trespass against us.[1] He taught that when the traveller was robbed and wounded, it was not the priest, nor the Levite, but the heterodox Samaritan who relieved him. He pointed out that the Samaritan was the neighbor of the wounded man. He said, ' Let those who love me obey my commandments.'

Those commandments were not dogmatical definitions

---

[1] Singularly enough, our Church Catechism, in its paraphrase of the Lord's Prayer, omits this great lesson, and inserts a passage which has no counterpart in that divine prayer.

of the nature of God, but practical and clear expositions of great truths.

Let us teach these great truths to the people of Ireland, and we may hope that they will cease to applaud murder.

In wishing to see Christianity thus taught, whether by Protestant or Roman Catholic teachers, I may be accused of wishing to promote 'indiscriminate endowment.'

Be it so ; I know that tares must be mingled with the wheat, and I am willing, like our Great Master, to see them both grow together till the harvest. God, who has neither our imperfect vision, nor our limited charity, will punish the obstinate reprobate and forgive the repentant sinner. ⋅

Let us now take stock, and compute what means will remain to Parliament, if they should hereafter determine to consider, in an impartial spirit, the welfare of Ireland as part of the United Kingdom.

1. A surplus which we may fairly take at six millions, remaining from church property, after discharging all the life-interests and commutations charged upon it by the Act of 1869.

2. A yearly grant, which has of late amounted to from 300,000*l.* to 360,000*l.* on an average, voted by Parliament for National Education in Ireland.

The surplus of the late Established Church has been increased, we are told on authority, by a sum of 4,000,000*l.*, derived from the credit of the Exchequer. This sum is, according to the Irish Church Act, to be applied 'mainly' to the relief of 'unavoidable calamity.'[1]

---

[1] Act of Parliament, 1869.

Never were 4,000,000*l*. so recklessly thrown away.

The application of public or local taxes to the relief of absolute destitution, whether of the old and infirm, the sick or the lame, the blind or the insane, may well be defended against Dr. Chalmers and other writers of great authority.

But when the State gives relief for physical or mental disease to those who are able to pay for their medical care, or who have relations and friends of sufficient means to help them, the State does a great mischief. Imposture is promoted to a large extent; the charitable zeal of relations and neighbors is dried up; a great rush is made on the public funds, and the overwhelmed tax-payer, scarcely able to meet the demands of the collector by unremitting industry, sinks under the weight of the fraudulent mendicant and insane drunkard.

Yet such is the character of many of those objects of charity who are sufferers from what is called in the late Act of Parliament ' unavoidable calamity.'

Let us, at all events, take care to substitute the term ' partly ' for the term ' mainly.' Otherwise Roman Catholic charities will absorb and misapply the whole of the funds which the wisdom of Lord Cairns has saved from dilapidation.

In the ' Report of the Commissioners of National Education in Ireland for 1865,' called the Thirty-second Report, we have an account of the number of children on the rolls for the year ending December 31, 1865. They amounted to 922,084. The total number of schools in operation was 6,372. 'The calculation made by estimate of the number of children of various denominations for the entire year, gives the following results : —

Established Church	. . . .	61,492
Roman Catholics	. . . . .	752,328
Presbyterians	. . . . . .	101,616
Other Persuasions	. . . . .	6,648

Total, 922,084.

The following list contains the names of the Commissioners of National Education in Ireland : —

Rt. Hon. Lord Bellew.

Rev. Dr. Henry, President, Queen's College, Belfast.

Rt. Hon. Alexander Macdonnell.

The Lord Bishop of Derry and Raphoe.

Hon. Judge Longfield.

Rt. Hon. Mr. Justice O'Hagan.

Rt. Hon. the Earl of Dunraven.

Rt. Hon. Lord Chief Justice Common Pleas (Monahan).

Rt. Hon. Lord Chief Baron (Pigot).

The Marquess of Kildare.

Rt. Hon. the Lord Chancellor (Brady).

James Gibson, Esq.

Rt. Hon. the Attorney-General (Lawson).

Rev. John Hall, D.D.

Laurence Waldron, Esq.

John Lentaigne, Esq.

John O'Hagan, Esq., Q.C.

Hon. Thomas Preston, D.L.

Rt. Hon. Mr. Justice Fitzgerald.

James William Murland, Esq.

The then Lord Chancellor (Brady) has since that time ceased to be so; and that office is now held by Mr. Justice O'Hagan. But both these learned persons remain Commissioners of National Education. It is said that the Board have relied on returns often inaccurate. But these errors will not affect the general result.

The funds for education are so fairly applied in Ulster, that the proportion of Roman Catholics to Protestants in the population returns, and the proportion of Roman Catholics to Protestants in the National Schools, are nearly identical.

Let us, then, supply the want of a National Church Establishment by a more complete National School Establishment, of the benefits of which all communions, Protestant and Catholic, may partake.

The 360,000l. of tithe rent-charge, instead of being given up to the landlords, after fifty-two years, might well be maintained as a provision for National Education. Thus a great question will be solved, and a large sum appropriated for Irish purposes.

I now approach the important and critical question of the Land Tenure of Ireland. The evils of the present law of landlord and tenant are much complained of, and great oppression is in some cases exercised. Two kinds of remedies have been proposed. The first kind consists of proposals to abolish practical abuses, to favor tenures of thirty-one years, to oblige the landlord to compensate the tenant for all the practical improvements he has made, and to pay for the value of the house he has erected. The other is far different; it takes for granted that all which has been done for the last seven hundred years is usurpation and tyranny; that, consequently, the Acts of Elizabeth, of James I., of Charles II., and of George I. are null and void, and it would therefore give the land to the occupier, and restore that state of possession by the strongest which prevailed before the Norman Conquest. The object, however disguised, is, in fact, to drive out all Protestant owners, and to put an end to British rule in Ireland. I need not say that, in my opinion, the first class of remedies, when properly defined and justly applied, ought to be cordially adopted, and the latter class peremptorily rejected. Every indication favors the conclusion that Government will act with temper and wisdom.

Lord Hartington says: —

'It is not only the property of Irish landlords which is at stake, it is not only the property of English landlords, but it is property of all kinds which will be at stake.' Lord Clarendon has spoken firmly and judiciously, both as to the wrongs of the tenants and the rights of the landlords. In fine, unless the Government and the House of Commons should adopt some of the revolutionary plans of the Irish newspapers, property of all kinds will not be at stake. I quite admit that if Irish landlords are robbed of their property, no other kind of property will be safe ; but no man of sense imagines that the Government will be wild enough to propose such a robbery, or the House of Commons unprincipled enough to sanction it.

Supposing, however, the Government to confine itself, as Lord Spencer intimated, to what is practicable, the task is still difficult, though far from impossible.

Guicciardini, an experienced politician and an accurate historian, says that statesmen commit no greater mistakes than when they apply a successful precedent to circumstances of a different nature.

There is much danger of such a mistake in Ireland. In the north of Ireland, tenant-right is the established custom. Lord Granard and others say, ' Let us transfer the custom of the north to the south of Ireland. It is successful in the north, therefore it will be successful in the south.'

But stop a moment. Ulster was colonized by the Scotch. We are told, on good authority, that the Irish were not sufficiently industrious, and the English not sufficiently used to hard fare and poor dwellings to make good colonists. The Scotch were accustomed to work hard and to fare hard ; they improved the soil, they built fit dwellings ; one Scotch tenant succeeding another, came into the occupation of land well cultivated, and farm-buildings stored with corn and implements. He could, therefore, afford to pay the outgoing tenant for the good-will as well as a shopkeeper coming to succeed a successful tradesman in Bond Street or in Regent Street.

But shall we transfer this custom of Ulster to Munster and Connaught? In the first place, although it may be equitable to sanction by law a custom established for generations, it is by no means equitable to introduce compulsory copyhold where tenancy from year to year has been the general custom.

In the next place, tenant-right may be practically a custom quite unfitted for Kerry or Cork. A tenant may have left his marshy land undrained; his fences full of gaps, by which his cattle, tired of the sour grass of the meadow, may break into the field of oats; his farm-buildings may be ruinous; his implements broken and antiquated. Still a farmer, eager to hold land, may pay a few pounds for the occupation, and he may go on, leaving the marshes undrained, the ploughs broken, the fences full of gaps. Is the landlord to be bound to respect the tenant-right of the thriftless, lazy occupier? Is such a man to be compared to the active, industrious tenant of Ulster? Because a custom succeeds with the landlords and tenants in Ulster, is it to be made compulsory in Cork and Kerry? This were to adopt the practice of workmen upon strike, when they insist that the man whose labor is worth to the master 9s. a week, should have the same wages as a man whose work is worth 30s. a week. Yet such is, if I understand it, the principle adopted by Mr. Butt as the flag of a great national movement.

An illustration occurs to me. Some persons wonder how it is that since the Italians have obtained independence and freedom, the crime of assassination is still so common.

The answer is, that habits and usages transmitted from father to son are not changed by the best written constitution. Lord Holland, when he was asked by

Murat, then King of Naples, to furnish him with a constitution, replied in effect, ' You might as well ask me to build a tree.'

It is well known that the Papal government punished severely men who ate a chicken on a Friday, but were very lenient to robbers, brigands, and assassins. A gentleman who acted as Procurator-General at Rome when the First Napoleon assumed the government, informed me that in one year there were reported to him two thousand cases of assassination! that term comprehending, in Italian phrase, cases of killing, maiming, cutting, and wounding with intent, &c.

Does any one expect such habits to be changed in a year, or in twenty years? The saying that ' Rome was not built in a day ' and other similar proverbs show that the popular mind is not so unreasonable as political speculation.

Another illustration occurs. In the sixteenth century, the Spaniards brought from Peru heaps of gold and silver. Spain declined. Men of grave authority said ' See how the importation of gold and silver ruins a country.' In the nineteenth century, the United States discovered in California, and Great Britain in Australia, immense quantities of gold. The United States flourished, Great Britain flourished; California and Australia rose to unheard-of prosperity. How could this be? Historians had forgotten to mention that Spain imported in the sixteenth century not only gold and silver, but political and religious despotism. Spaniards, no longer free, became, as Homer says, only half men. Thus it appears, as our grandsires tell us, that ' one man's meat is another man's poison.' Thus it may happen that what makes Ulster rich may make Munster poorer than before.

The difference in the price of land in the county of Down, where it fetches thirty years' purchase, and in the county of Kerry, where it scarcely reaches twenty-five, shows the effect, not of tenant-right, but of habits of order and industry on the one side, laziness and improvidence on the other.

The 'Times' newspaper has a very intelligent correspondent in Ireland, who is charged especially to report on the land question. His letters remind me of the saying of a witty diplomatist who, in the last century, returned from time to time to England, his native country.

'When I arrive in England,' he said, 'if I open my eyes and shut my ears, I think the country very flourishing. But if I shut my eyes and open my ears, I find that England is the most wretched country on the face of the earth.'

The 'Times' correspondent very properly opens his eyes. He sees much improvement — farmers selling their cattle and their crops to great advantage, laborers well clothed, earning 8s. or 9s. a week where their fathers earned with difficulty 5s.

He then opens his ears, and forthwith imbibes a storm of complaints. 'Our landlord is very kind, and never raises his rents. But what if he should suddenly turn tyrant? and what if, when we ask for a lease, he should choose to have the land valued, and demand a higher rent than we now pay?' Then, as to the laborers, 'they are tolerably well off, much better housed, and much better clothed than they used to be; but they think that eight centuries ago their ancestors possessed the land, and that, as they are the people of Ireland, they ought to possess it now.'

To grumble is the prescriptive right of Englishmen,

and on principles of equality, cannot be refused to Irishmen. But to legislate on such vague notions would be most unsafe.

Lord Portsmouth says, with just pride and satisfaction, 'Since 1822, the experiment of thirty-one years' leases, with free liberty to sell them, and practically vesting all buildings in the tenant, has been tried on my estates in the county of Wexford, with the following results:—Badly cultivated patches of land, with wretched hovels on them, have been changed into well-cultivated farms, with first-rate homesteads. The rental has more than doubled, is punctually paid, instead of irregularly paid. Discontent and misery existed in 1822: prosperity and contentment exist in 1869. Vinegar Hill was the head-quarters of the Rebellion in 1798; now no more loyal and contented population exists than that which surrounds it.'[1]

This, however, is not 'fixity of tenure.' In fact, 'fixity of tenure' is but another term for property in land, which the agitators propose to take from the owner and give to the occupier.

A writer in the 'Daily News' very sensibly remarks, that fixity of tenure would 'diminish progress,' and 'stereotype desolation.' 'The Spectator' seems to have no objection to 'desolation,' and says that 'the more wealth Ireland has accumulated, the more loudly and bitterly she has protested against our rule.' But surely it is not the business of Parliament to 'stereotype desolation,' to stop the 'accumulation of wealth,' and to foster the agrarian murders which, instead of being stopped, would be promoted by such legislation.

In the midst of the conflicting evidence of his eyes,

---

[1] Letter to the 'Times,' September 11, 1869.

and of his ears, the 'Times' commissioner arrives at a very rational conclusion. After stating the case of Mr. Pollok, who, as a landlord, has greatly improved his land at his own expense, the commissioner continues thus: — ' Yet, on the other hand, in the case of these village communities, how idle it is to say, that it is consonant to justice to abandon them to the rules of the common law, to ignore the existence of the property they have created, to subject them to eviction without full compensation, or without an equivalent prolongation of tenure. He evidently will be the true statesman, and will be entitled to claim the merit of solving this complicated problem justly, who, recognizing the coexistence of these modes of tenure, and the variety and conflicts of rights under them, shall devise a law that shall be applicable to each, and, as far as human legislation can go, shall protect the interests arising under both, and shall then give them complete freedom. Without venturing to dogmatize, I am, not without hope that a reform of this kind is quite feasible, without endangering, in any rational sense, the rights of property.'

This is the result arrived at by an intelligent observer acted upon by all he sees, and all he hears, but reserving his powers of reasoning and sense of justice.

To sum up shortly the whole matter, we may say, ' Property has its duties as well as its rights ; ' let those duties be enforced by law.

But ' Property has its rights as well as its duties;' let those rights be preserved by law.

In point of fact, the attempts made to overthrow the barriers of law and prescription, by pure reasoning, are flimsy and shallow enough. First, it is said that great oppression is exercised by the landlords. But as every impartial inquirer finds that this charge of oppression, true and revolting as it is, does not practically apply to more than one in fifty of the landlords, it is absurd to say that fifty shall be deprived of their property because one of them has been guilty of oppression. Then it is said that the proprietors are Protestants, while the majority of the occupiers and laborers are Roman Catholics. This is in effect to propose a new religious disability; to make an odious inquisition into religious faith; to introduce a new element of discord into Ireland, when, for forty years, harmony, good-will, and religious equality have been the objects of all wise statesmen. Nor could the rule be restricted in operation. For, if the Duke of Devonshire and the Duke of Leinster are not to hold property in Ireland, because they profess a faith differing from that of the majority, how can the Duke of Norfolk and Lord Arundel be permitted to own land in England?

It is not even pretended that Protestant land-owners in Ireland are worse landlords than Roman Catholics.

But lastly, it is urged, that the titles of the Irish land-owners are derived from the confiscation of property held by ancient Irish chiefs, and forfeited by rebellion.

No one, however, who has the slightest regard for the peace of the country, will go back seven centuries, to inquire what lands were declared forfeit by Henry II., by Henry VIII., by Elizabeth, by James I., by Charles II., and by William III. Still less will any one pretend to point out the heirs of the expelled rebels.

Upon this question there can be no compromise. Either British rule in Ireland must be renounced, and all that has been done to improve and civilize, for the last forty years, must be exchanged for anarchy, bloodshed, and desolation, or the law must be quietly amended, and steadily maintained under the authority of the Queen.

Ireland must be governed by the British Parliament, which cannot abdicate its supremacy; which must protect life and property; must reject frantic theories and treasonable projects; must punish the wrong-doer, and throw its shield over the peaceable subject.

Yet, rejecting all these theories as impracticable, infinite care must be taken to protect the real rights of the Irish tenant.

Upon this difficult land question, I suggested, in my third letter to Mr. Chichester Fortescue, that every tenancy less than a yearly tenancy should hereafter be by law a yearly tenancy.

That any contract between landlord and tenant, by which the tenant agrees to give up his holding on any other terms than those in force in the case of a lease, or of a yearly tenancy, shall be utterly illegal, and *ipso facto* void.

That upon a notice to quit, the case of the tenant shall be heard, as usual, and that he shall be empowered to bring forward evidence to show the improvements he had made on his farm, and the buildings which he had erected at his own expense.

That the chairman of quarter sessions should be authorized by law to accompany his decree by an award compelling the payment of compensation for the value of the improvements made, and the buildings erected, or granting the tenant power, equivalent to what is called tenant-right, of selling the good-will of his farm to any other person.

I added — 'The chairman might also, I think, be empowered to quash the ejectment, and to direct the grant of a lease of twenty-one years by the landlord, in terms to be settled by the judge.'

I have only to add to these suggestions, that I think a special court should be created at Dublin, similar to the court erected by the Encumbered Estates Act, and that erected by the Irish Church Act.

This letter was published early in 1869. Later in the year, a pamphlet has appeared, written by Mr. Gerald Fitzgibbon, a Master in Chancery, a man of great ability, well acquainted with the law, and sincerely desirous to find a solution which may prove beneficial as well to landlord as to tenant, and be productive of peace to Ireland.

His suggestions are very remarkable; his experience and his suggestions may be summed up as follows : —

He states that the Court of Chancery often takes into its charge an estate in land. He has himself had to deal with about four hundred estates, occupied by nearly twenty thousand tenants. When one of these tenants applies to the Court of Chancery to allow the receiver to supply slates and timber for roofing a farm-house or a cow-house, upon an undertaking to build the walls and complete the structure at the tenant's own expense, Mr. Fitzgibbon, as representing the Court of Chancery, uniformly complies with it. I may remark that I believe every just and liberal landlord does the same. Mr. Fitzgibbon likewise complies with applications from the tenant for assistance to drain or otherwise improve the farm.

I believe that most landlords would comply with similar applications.

But as the distrust of the tenants is so wide-spread as to be almost universal, Mr. Fitzgibbon would enforce the duties of landlords in the following manner : —

Pass an Act by which every tenant in the country, great and small, having a term of less than seven years in his land, shall be entitled to transmit to some public functionary a written notice that he desires to improve his farm, and undertakes, within three years, to add some substantial and specific amount to the present yearly value. If his proposal is approved, and he fulfils what he has undertaken, let him have a grant at the old rent, in proportion to the addition he has made to the permanent value of his farm. 'Let an addition of twenty-five per cent entitle him to thirty years. Give him sixty years if he adds fifty per cent, ninety years if he adds seventy-five per cent, and so on.'

Mr. Fitzgibbon deserves great credit for this proposal, intended to reconcile equity with popular demands, and encourage industry by conferring property upon honest exertion. Yet I cannot but think there is some danger in the process by which the tenant is to be enabled to oust the proprietor, and become the owner of the fee. Lord Portsmouth speaks of his grants of leases for thirty-one years, but not at the same rent as the leases of his progenitors. Neither would it be easy to prove the exact twenty-five or fifty per cent which, with lawyer-like precision, Mr. Fitzgibbon requires as a pre-existent condition. It seems to me, therefore, that if my scheme is somewhat too vague and too rough, Mr. Fitzgibbon's plan is too positive and too minutely guarded; that it holds out hopes which would not be realized, and would hardly stand the test which he himself proposes of being fit for adoption in England and in Scotland.

Still I cannot doubt that in this direction lies the solution of the land difficulty of Ireland, and that we want only the combination of a great lawyer with a great statesman to arrive at a peaceable and happy termination of this perilous and impassioned controversy.

To sum up this question of Irish grievances, let us reflect that, in 1829, the Roman Catholics of Ireland, as of England, were made competent to hold offices in the political government of the country and in courts of law, excepting only the offices of Lord Lieutenant and Lord Chancellor of Ireland. This last exception has since been repealed.

That, in 1833, the Church of Ireland was freed from many abuses, and that church cess (the church-rate of England) was totally abolished.

That about the same time 'Schools for all' were established by Lord Derby, then Mr. Stanley, for the purpose of improving and extending National Education.

That, in 1869, the Protestant Church of Ireland was disestablished and disendowed.

That, by Acts passed in 1839 and subsequent years, the paupers of Ireland obtained relief, furnished from rates.

That, by Acts relating to the Poor-law of England, a short industrial residence in England enables an Irish workman to obtain all the advantages in the labor market of English manufacturing towns which an English workman enjoys.

That, in 1838, the chief evil of the tithe system was remedied by converting tithe into rent-charge, payable by the landlord.

The consequences of these and various other Acts have been —

That there is now complete civil, political, and religious equality in Ireland between Protestants and Catholics.

That the rent of the landlord, the capital of the farmer, and the wages of the agricultural laborer, have all, since 1829, greatly increased.

That the commerce of Ireland and the revenue from the custom-house have been considerably augmented.

That, between 1832 and 1868, agrarian crimes were much diminished.

That the disorders which prevailed from 1792 to 1838, arising from the collection of tithe, have totally ceased.

That the evils arising from the deeply mortgaged condition of many landed estates have been, by the operation of the Encumbered Estates Act, greatly diminished, and landed property to the amount of thirty millions has been sold to solvent purchasers.

That the appointment of judges without reference to religious creed, and the selection of juries fairly chosen from Protestant and Roman Catholic qualified persons, has removed all just cause of complaint against the administration of justice.

Speaking in the House of Commons, in 1839, I said that it would still require forty years to remove the evils of long standing which afflicted Ireland.

Thirty years have since passed, and great progress has been made.

The question is now, — shall we continue that progress on the principles of justice and equality, or shall we adopt the scheme of Irish independence recommended by the Fenian partisans?

It is as clear that Dublin and Cork must belong to the United Kingdom of England and Ireland, as that Lyons and Toulon must belong to France, and Richmond and New Orleans to the United States.

The plain question, then, is, — are the Irish agitators

prepared for civil war, with all its horrors and all its results?

Supposing the wishes of Ireland to be represented fairly by the monster meetings on tenant-right and on the grant of an amnesty for the convicted Fenians, the wishes and the wants of Ireland must be carefully separated.

It is the right of a people to represent its grievances. It is the business of a statesman to devise remedies.

The wants of Ireland are real, and must be supplied. Her wishes are transitory and intemperate; they must be filtered till all impure and noxious matter is cleared away, and nothing left but what is pure and wholesome. Then, indeed, we shall have, not only *Hibernia Pacata*, but *Hibernia Felix*.

Some of the most fruitful causes of the misery of small and poor tenants in Ireland have disappeared. When the elective franchise was conferred upon Roman Catholics, landlords gave forty-shilling freeholds to multitudes of miserable cottiers, and drove them by thousands to the poll, in exchange for the titles and offices they obtained for themselves at the Castle. The Act of 1829, abolishing the forty-shilling freehold franchise, took away the temptation to create these fictitious tenures. Forty years have elapsed since the abolition of the forty-shilling freeholds. But it is not time only which has been at work. The great potato famine, the immense emigration which ensued, and the Encumbered Estates Act, have cleared many estates of the pauper tenantry.

The Government can have no difficulty in obtaining valuable suggestions from official and independent sources. The large and liberal mind of the Lord Chancellor of Ireland, the legal knowledge of the law-officers

of the Crown, the long experience and enlightened suggestions of Dr. Hancock, who dispelled the fictions of
those who maintained that Ireland was declining, may all
be drawn upon by the Cabinet in framing a measure upon
Irish land, If rightly framed, it would be a still greater
blessing than the abolition of the Irish Church ; but the
course proposed by the 'Spectator' would produce,
instead of fertility, desolation ; instead of hatred, contempt. Here would be a fine result of statesmanship
applied to Ireland !

But worse might be apprehended, if the Ribbon
societies and their hired assassins are to dictate our
future policy.

In what Mr. Trench calls the Ribbon conspiracy
against his life, the chairman is reported to have
said : —

'Down with the Church, down with the landlords,
down with the agents, down with every thing, say I,
that stands in the way of our own green land coming
back to us again.'

' What wonderful grand fun we'll have fighting
among ourselves, when it does come ! ' said a thick-set,
herculean fellow at the lower end of the table.

' Well, now, I often thought of that,' replied his
neighbor in a whisper ; ' it'll be bloody work then in
airnest, as sure as you and I live to see it ; any thing
that has happen'd up to this will be only a joke to what
will happen then.'

' And what matter ? ' cried the advocate for fighting ;
' sure wouldn't it be better any day to be fighting
among friends than have no fighting at all, and be
slaves to our enemies ! ' [1]

---

[1] 'Realities of Irish Life,' p. 194.

The Scotch Highland Celts used to say among themselves, in their own cabins, and in their own language, 'Turn out the Saxon and take in the dog.' But the Highlands have been pacified without expelling the descendants of Gillespie Campbell, of Anglo-Norman origin, ancestor of the Duke of Argyll, or of John of Moravia, ancestor of the Duke of Atholl. So it will be with Ireland, if we use patience and moderation.

I cannot omit here some details upon the Encumbered Estates Act.

The proceeding was commenced in 1848; it was completed in the following year. Sir Robert Peel had proposed in the House of Commons a scheme for a new settlement of land in Ireland, framed apparently upon the settlement of Ulster by James I. The plan appeared to the Government and to members of Parliament generally to be too large and vague to be practicable, and it was consequently laid aside. A bill was introduced into the House of Lords by the Lord Chancellor, Lord Cottenham. Sir John Romilly, who had been recently appointed Solicitor-General, framed, in conjunction with Mr. Walter Coulson, a series of clauses which completely altered the character of the bill, and tended to make it far more effective. But when the bill went back to the House of Lords, Lord Cottenham so modified the clauses as to preserve to the first encumbrancer a power to nullify the whole bill. This Act passed in August, 1848; it is the 11th and 12th of Victoria, cap. 48, and is entitled 'An Act to facilitate the sale of Encumbered Estates in Ireland.' When the session was over, being very anxious on this subject, I went over to Ireland chiefly for the purpose of inquiring into the probable operation of this Act. Lord Clarendon, who was then Lord Lieutenant, requested

the Chancellor of Ireland to come to the Vice-regal
Lodge to confer with me. He told me that the Act
would probably be evaded, and I gathered from him
that, in his opinion, it would be a dead letter. When I
returned to England I sent for Sir John Romilly, and
instructed him to prepare a new Encumbered Estates
Bill for Ireland. I gave him full liberty to prepare it
as he thought desirable, both as to the scheme to be
adopted, and as to the provisions to be introduced for
working it, permitting, at his request, that the working
of the Act should be confided to a new court, to be
constituted for that purpose. When Sir John Romilly
introduced the bill in the House of Commons, he was
complimented very highly by Sir Robert Peel, who said
he was not one of those lawyers who took away the
key of knowledge, and prevented others from entering
in. Lord Cottenham waived his scruples; the Act
framed by Sir John Romilly and Mr. Coulson was confided to a court composed of very able men; and its
operation, extending over vast masses of property, and
changing the ownership of many estates, the owners of
which had been hopelessly encumbered, and the tenants
without means of improvement, proved, by the consent
of all parties, eminently beneficial.

The authorship of so large and useful a measure has
been attributed by many to Sir Robert Peel, and by
Lord St. Leonards to himself. But to the decision of
the Government overruling the technical views of their
own Lord Chancellor, and to the constructive skill of
Lord Romilly and Mr. Coulson, this enactment must
finally be attributed.[1] Pauperized owners of Castle
Rackrents have given place to prosperous tradesmen.

---

[1] See Letter of Lord Romilly in the 'Times' of March 13, 1869.

But there is some doubt whether the new owners, though generally more faithful sons of the Church of Rome, are kinder landlords than the heroes of Miss Edgeworth's tale.

I have only further to say on this head, that agrarian crimes must be put down by a vigorous hand. Sir George Grey, when Home Secretary, was fully alive to his duty in this respect. He acknowledged that Government was bound to protect the life of the subject, and he as explicitly discouraged all the wild notions regarding property which then, as now, were afloat. The measure which he introduced in 1847 was salutary, though severe.

Its effects may be estimated by taking, from official returns, the number of agrarian crimes committed respectively in the years 1844, 1845, 1861, 1865, 1866 : —

	Agrarian Outrages.
1844	889
1845	799
1861	198
1865	162
1866	83

I only hope that in 1870, the Home Secretary may take as high a tone as Sir George Grey, and introduce a measure as efficient in repressing agrarian crime and outrage as Sir George Grey introduced in 1847.

The present Government, soon after their entrance into office, seeing that the Fenian treason had been defeated by the promptitude and vigor of Lord Kimberley and the Duke of Abercorn, very naturally supposed that the least guilty of the offenders might be pardoned. But, however natural and however merciful this conduct on the part of the Government, it has clearly appeared that the measure was a mistaken one. The liberated

11

criminals have taken for granted that they were pardoned, not in the hope of their penitence, but as an
indemnity for past offences, and an encouragement to
fresh treasons.

The motives of the Executive Government were
laudable, but I am glad to hear that this mistake will
not be repeated.

In 1839, in order to comply with a wish of Lord Nor-
manby, whose experience in Ireland made him conversant
with internal government, I gave up the Home Department to him, and accepted the Colonial Office.

I soon became interested in Colonial affairs. It seemed
to me that the Imperial Government was bound, both in
honor and from the soundest views of national policy,
to protect, foster, and defend our Colonies. It may be
a matter of doubt whether or no to build up a Colonial
Empire. But it is evident that if Great Britain gives up
her supremacy from a niggardly spirit of parsimony, or
from a craven feeling of helplessness, other powers will
soon look upon the Empire, not with the regard due to
an equal, as she once was, but with jealousy of the height
she once held, without the fear she once inspired. To
build up an Empire extending over every sea, swaying
many diverse races, and combining many forms of religion, requires courage and capacity; to allow such an
Empire to fall to pieces is a task which may be performed by the poor in intellect, the pusillanimous in
conduct.

When I came into the Colonial Office, there was a
question regarding certain parties who were desirous of
founding in New Zealand a government having coercive
criminal jurisdiction. But I pointed out to them that
such conduct would be a violation of their duty as British subjects. The persons alluded to consulted Serjeant

Wilde, afterwards Lord Truro, and finding that I was right in point of law, desisted from their project. I told them, however, that they might be assured of the protection of the Crown, and, by the treaty of Waitangi, the Queen assumed the sovereignty of New Zealand. It was not, therefore, by chance, or without incurring obligations on the part of the Crown, that New Zealand was added to the British dominions.

I gave still stronger assurances to the British Provinces of North America, pledging to them the word of the Queen, that so long as they desired to remain her subjects they should receive the support of the Crown, and be defended as a part of the British dominions.

A faint-hearted Government in Great Britain may break these pledges, and depart from this policy. But from the day when they do so, the Decline and Fall of the British Empire may be dated.

At the same time, I do not think the relations of the Colonies to the mother country can be kept up precisely in their present form.

There is uneasiness growing up on both sides; the Colonies doubting as to the protection they may receive, and Great Britain complaining of the cost of the naval and military expenses incurred in defence of Colonial interests whenever they are in danger.

I am disposed to believe, that if a congress, or assembly representing Great Britain and her dependencies, could be convoked from time to time, to sit for some months in the autumn, arrangements reciprocally beneficial might be made.

I mean, that, on the one hand, the metropolitan State might promise protection to the Colonies, by her army and navy, against any foreign or barbarous enemy; and, on the other hand, a contribution of three or four mil-

lions towards our army and navy estimates might be
granted by the Colonial Parliaments, and an engagement
taken not to charge more than a certain percentage, say
ten per cent *ad valorem*, on British produce and manufactures; or they might propose, as New Zealand has
lately done, to ask for Imperial aid when absolutely
required, and propose to defray the expense of the aid
afforded, and not to interfere with the discretion of the
British commanders by sea and land. In such case, as
we have a Governor-General in India, and a Governor-
General of British North America, so we might have a
Governor-General of Australia and New Zealand, and a
Governor-General of Jamaica and of the West Indian
Islands.

This scheme may seem impracticable to many. But
so did the Reform Act of 1832; so did the total repeal
of the Corn-laws; so did the abolition of the Irish
Church. Great changes have been made; great changes
are impending; amid these changes, there is no greater
benefit to mankind, that a statesman can propose to
himself, than the consolidation of the British Empire.

In my eyes it would be a sad spectacle, it would be
a spectacle for gods and men to weep at, to see this
brilliant Empire, the guiding-star of Freedom, broken
up, — to behold Nova Scotia, the Cape of Good Hope,
Jamaica, and New Zealand, try each its little spasm of
independence, while France, the United States, and
Russia would be looking on, each and all willing to
annex one or more of the fragments to the nearest portion of their own dominions.

The difficulties, in detail, of such an arrangement
might be great.

Some further references to past occurrences may
serve to explain my meaning.

Mr. Baldwin, who had taken a prominent part in Canadian politics, came to England while Lord Glenelg was Secretary of State for the Colonies, and by his desire discussed with me the question of responsible government. I raised the objection that a responsible ministry in Canada might object to take part with England in a foreign war, in which she might be engaged.

Mr. Baldwin, who was a man of sense and ability, assured me that the Canadians had no such pretensions. They wished to manage their own local affairs, but had no desire to diminish the authority, or dim the lustre of the Crown of England in her external affairs.

With this assurance I was satisfied; and when I held the seals I practically acted upon it, though I did not concur in the theory. In 1854, I proposed to the House of Commons, on the part of the Government of Lord Aberdeen, to give free scope to the legislature of Canada in ecclesiastical affairs, and I have seen no reason to regret this policy.

It is the fashion to say that those Colonies which have adopted British institutions, whose ministers resign on a vote of want of confidence, and whose laws are framed on a British type, are virtually independent, and have no right to look for British protection. In my opinion nothing can be meaner in spirit, nothing less wise in policy, than such assertions.

There was a time when we might have stood alone as the United Kingdom of England, Scotland, and Ireland. That time has passed. We conquered and peopled Canada, we took possession of the whole of Australia, Van Diemen's Land, and New Zealand. We have annexed India to the Crown. There is no going back.

Tu regere imperio populos, Romane, memento.

For my part, I delight in observing the adoption of
our free institutions, and even of our habits and manners, in Colonies at a distance of 8,000 or 4,000 miles
from the Palace of Westminster.

During my tenure of the Colonial Office, a gentleman attached to the French Government called upon
me. He asked me how much of Australia was claimed
as the dominion of Great Britain. I answered, 'the
whole,' and with that answer he went away. A French
traveller of great quickness and power of observation
has lately given to the world his impression of the
friendly feeling of our Australian fellow-subjects towards the mother country.[1]

It is hardly necessary to say, that when the majority
in any of our dependencies declare by their representatives that they wish to separate from us, no attempt
should be made to detain them. The faults committed
by George Grenville, Charles Townshend, and Lord
North can never be repeated.

Of course, this remark does not apply to fortified
places, like Gibraltar and Malta. It has, however,
been too much the fashion for writers in the press, and
some members of the House of Commons, to overlook
the force of tradition, and the obligations of treaties,
and to assume that because France is bigger than
Belgium, Russia bigger than Sweden, therefore Belgium
must be annexed to France, Sweden to Russia. The
story of Brasidas might teach them better.

The Minister who tries to weaken the attachment of
our North American Provinces to Great Britain will

---

[1] See 'Australie, Voyage autour du Monde,' par le comte de Beau-
voir: Paris, 1869—a very interesting and amusing work. 'Greater
Britain,' by Sir Charles W. Dilke, is a very able work on a similar
subject.

be sure to rouse the generous indignation of the people of England, and will be punished, if not by impeachment, at all events by eternal infamy.

I pass on to other events.

In 1840, the Turkish Empire was threatened with dissolution. The treaty of Unkiar Skelessi erected a protectorate of Turkey on the part of Russia; a long course of intrigue, and the boldness of Mehemet Ali, a man of great genius and daring, had nearly separated Egypt and Syria from the Sultan's sovereignty. It became a question whether England should permit Russia and France to divide the Turkish Empire between them. The wise inaction of Lord Palmerston gave time to prepare the solution of a great crisis, his vigor shone forth at the decisive moment, and after the thunderbolt had fallen at Djune and at Acre, the air was cleared, and the sky was again serene.

The questions relating to political and municipal franchises were of so much difficulty, and excited so much political heat, that the Ministry of Lord Melbourne abstained for some years from attempting to promote those principles of free trade which had given rise to the honorable exertions of Huskisson and Canning. The attempt of Lord Althorp to lower the differential duties on timber, one of the grossest cases of Colonial protection, was received so coldly, and was so effectually thwarted by Sir Robert Peel, that the Government could not hope for any support from those Liberal Tories who had followed Mr. Huskisson during the Administration of Lord Liverpool. This was rather extraordinary, for Sir Robert Peel, although it was not generally known, had been, in Lord Liverpool's Cabinet, a warm advocate for free trade. Indeed, his liberal opinions upon this subject probably gave rise to Mr.

Canning's remark, that the Cabinet were divided, not by a straight, but by a serpentine line.

However, in 1840, the questions of franchise having been nearly all decided, a committee on the duties of imports, presided over by Joseph Hume, and informed by the accurate knowledge and sound judgment of Mr. Deacon Hume, revived the interest upon this subject. The question for the Cabinet to decide was, in reality, whether they would lower duties of a protective character on a great number of small articles, or whether they would attack the giant monopolies of sugar, of timber, and of corn. The latter course, the most gallant, though perhaps not the most prudent, was preferred; but, at the same time, the measures proposed were of the character of those brought forward by Mr. Huskisson, viz., that of a gradual approach to free trade rather than a complete repeal of protective duties. In this spirit, therefore, the Government proposed a reduction of the differential duties on sugar to 12s.; of the protective duties on timber to 10s.; and with respect to corn, a fixed duty of 8s.; to be relaxed from time to time by Order in Council, instead of the sliding-scale, which had been the favorite scheme of Lord Liverpool.

These proposals, however, excited quite as much animosity among the protected interests as if the Government had proposed the abolition of all differential duties on sugar and timber, and a total repeal of the Corn-laws. The landed gentry and the farmers were especially indignant, and they fondly looked to Sir Robert Peel and Sir James Graham to protect them from changes which the former had in public always strongly opposed, and which the latter had denounced as destructive to the position, and even to the existence of the land-owners of England. In spite of the symptoms of approaching defeat, I brought forward the question of the reduction of the duties on sugar. After a long debate, my motion was defeated by a majority of thirty-six.

This decision made it necessary for the Cabinet to consider their whole position, not only with reference to the measures they had announced, but also to their continuance as an Administration. It was obvious that there would be no public advantage in bringing forward the motion for a fixed duty on corn, of which notice had been given. There was no chance of obtaining a majority for such a motion; but if the whole budget of the year was to be thus defeated, it was plain that the only alternative which remained to the Cabinet was to dissolve or to resign. This question was anxiously considered, and it was deemed necessary to obtain some insight into the probable effect of a dissolution before resorting to such a measure. Among the letters which were received in the course of the next few days by members of the Government, was one from a very intelligent gentleman at the head of a great banking establishment in Lancashire, to the effect that in order to impress the country with a due sense of the importance of a change from protection to free trade, it was the duty of the Government to submit the question to the test of a general election. It was urged that, whatever might be the verdict as to majority or minority in the future House of Commons, the great question of freedom of trade could not fail to be thoroughly discussed, and especially the evils of inconvenient and vexatious restrictions on the supply of food to the people might be strongly denounced. Lord Grenville had said of the Corn-laws, in a memorable protest, that monopoly is the parent of uncertainty, of dearness, and of scarcity.   This great truth, and the injustice of such a monopoly in its bearing on a nation increasing in the extent of its manufactures, the expansion of its commerce, and the general diffusion of its wealth, could not escape a searching criticism and an ultimate condemnation.

These reasons prevailed, and the Cabinet, after several discussions, decided on dissolution in preference to immediate resignation.   It was thought best, however, for the sake of the convenient dispatch of business, and of a constitutional regard on the part of the Crown towards the House of Commons, to defer the announcement of this resolution.   Sir Robert Peel took advantage of the delay, as he had a perfect right to do, to bring forward a direct motion declaring a want of confidence, and this motion, after a long debate, was carried in a full House by a majority of one.   When, however, the Ministry announced, as they on their side were entitled to do, that in so divided a state of opinion the Crown would appeal to the people for a decision, Sir Robert Peel intimated that he would not interpose any obstacle to a dissolution ; but he made it a condition that, the elections over, the new House of Commons should be at once assembled.   With this condition I readily complied.

The dissolution took place.   The Ministry laid before the country for decision the question of Protection or Free Trade.   In the month of August the House of Commons met, and decided by a majority of ninety-one that the existing Ministers had not their confidence. Protection had been the bone of contention during the elections, and after the division of the Tory party looked forward, with sanguine hope, to the perpetuity of the

Corn-laws, and the eternal institution of a sliding-scale on the admission of foreign corn. Sir Robert Peel, however, skilfully avoided this issue; and while he pledged his supporters to an entire want of confidence in the Liberal Ministry, he left himself full latitude as to the measures which a future Ministry might think fit to adopt.

After the vote and the address, the Ministers at once resigned, and on September 3 a new Ministry, under Sir Robert Peel, was inaugurated.

Little was said, and less was done, in the remainder of the session of 1841.

In 1842, a new policy, both financial and commercial, was inaugurated. Much was done in the direction of free trade, but the dangerous topics of corn, sugar, and timber were tenderly touched or skilfully evaded.

Before the Parliament expired the Corn-laws were totally repealed, and the differential duties on sugar entirely abolished. But the Income-tax remained, and still remains, as the positive result of the Tory triumph in 1841.

In reviewing these proceedings, it may be thought that Lord Melbourne's Government showed great rashness when they proposed to touch the great monopolies of sugar, of timber, and of corn. Each of these monopolies was intrenched behind fortifications which were at that time impregnable. The West India interest was wealthy and commercial, possessing great influence at Liverpool and Glasgow, and ramified, through many branches, among members of the aristocracy and great mercantile firms, strongly represented in both Houses of Parliament. The timber monopoly, though eminently absurd, and defended by reasons obviously futile and unsound, was identified with a powerful Colonial interest, and had been covered by the shield of the Opposition leader when Lord Althorp had ventured to assail it. But, above all, the great monopoly of bread was identified, in the opinion of a great portion of the Lords and Commons, with the station, the dignity, and even the very existence of what is called ' the landed interest' of England. It had been said by Lord Bolingbroke, more than a century before, that while the Whigs might have occasional tenure of power, the Tories, resting upon the solid foundations of Church and land, were destined to hold the permanent government of the country. Burke, with the same opinion, though not with the same inclinations, had affirmed, in a letter to Fox, that the Whigs had never attained power but by a skilful use of opportunities. This doctrine, as to the solidity and the permanence of Tory power, was held by a numerous body of peers and country gentlemen, who cared nothing for the writings of Bolingbroke or Burke. Sir Robert Peel, therefore, showed much caution when, making a slight change in the Corn-laws, he left the great monopolies of sugar, timber, and corn practically untouched. He probably thought that to others, and not to him, would be left the enterprise of destroying the dragon whose ravages had spread famine among the people.

I have no need, and no inclination, to follow in detail the Administration of Sir Robert Peel. It was powerful, popular, and successful. Yet he did not hesitate, when he thought it essential for the public good, to risk the fate of his Ministry on behalf of an unpopular measure. He felt deeply that Ireland was his difficulty; he had abandoned, in 1829, those doctrines of Protestant ascendency and those exclusive laws which maintain a Protestant garrison in Ireland — doctrines and laws to which he had clung with so much tenacity in the earlier part of his political career. But he had not gained the confidence of the Roman Catholics of Ireland, and they obstinately refused favors at his hands which they would have been willing to accept from a Liberal Administration. To a man of the large mind of Sir Robert Peel, the alienation of Irish opinion and affection must have appeared a serious evil in the presence of domestic embarrassments and foreign complications. In this perplexity, he brought forward, as Prime Minister, a measure for a generous and sufficient endowment of the College of Maynooth. Much public discontent was excited among the fanatical parts of the Protestant population of England. I received several letters, assuring me that the confidence of my constituents of the city of London would be withdrawn from me if I continued to give my support to the measure of the Ministry. Yet I was persuaded then, as I am still persuaded, that the measure was one of broad and wise policy, tending to conciliate the Catholics of Ireland, and to prove to that portion of the Queen's subjects that their interests and their welfare were not indifferent to the statesmen and the people of England. It was thus considered by the Catholic body in general; and at the last reading of the bill in the House of Commons it was thus hailed by Lord Arundel, as the organ of his communion, and of the large numbers associated with him by faith, though not by race.

It was supposed at the time, openly stated by me, and as openly accepted by Sir Robert Inglis, that this measure was preparatory to one for the general endowment of the Roman Catholic Church in Ireland. Sir Robert Peel, in a private conversation at Nuneham a few years afterwards, suggested such a measure as fit to be adopted; but when Mr. Sheil, who was present, urged that Sir Robert himself ought to be the Minister to propose it, he declined any such responsibility. Nor is it likely that, had he returned to office, he would have ventured upon a course so repugnant to the predilections of his party, so distasteful to the Low Church and Nonconformists in England, and to the Presbyterians of Scotland. Be that as it may, the Maynooth Act was a work of wisdom and liberality, and must always be remembered to the honor of the Minister who proposed and carried it.

I now pause awhile in this sketch of my recollections, hoping to continue it at a later day.

In the mean time, I add some observations on topics which appear to me of public interest.

Belonging to the Whig party, the aim of that party has always been my aim — 'The cause of civil and religious liberty all over the world.' I have endeavored, in the words of Lord Grey, to promote that cause without endangering the prerogatives of the Crown, the privileges of the two Houses of Parliament, or the rights and liberties of the people.

According to my view, the Tory party cared little for the cause of civil and religious liberty, and the Radical party were not solicitous to preserve those parts of the Constitution which did not suit their speculative and theoretical opinions.

To hold a middle way, to observe the precept of Dædalus and to avoid the fate of Icarus, is at all times difficult, and, in certain conjunctures, perilous.

Happily, from 1830 to 1866, the Whigs and the Liberal Tories, who, like Lord Palmerston and Mr. Charles Grant, followed Mr. Canning, or who, like the Duke of Newcastle, Mr. Sidney Herbert, and Mr. Gladstone, followed Sir Robert Peel, have been able to accomplish great changes; to enlarge the limits of religious liberty; to promote the cause of freedom in Italy and Spain, in Belgium and Greece; to break the fetters of monopoly and restriction which bound our commerce; and to emancipate our Colonies from the ignorance and errors of the Home Government, without endangering any part of our Constitution.

The effects of this enlarged and liberal policy upon our finances and our trade have been very remarkable.

Thus to take only a few of the later changes.

In 1857, the receipts into the Exchequer amounted to 72,334,000*l.*

Since that time the amount of taxes repealed, compared with taxes imposed, gives a balance in favor of diminished taxation of 21,880,000*l.* The amount of revenue in March last was 72,592,000*l.*, thus showing an actual increase after the reduction.

The amount of the exports and imports, about 1853, was 268,000,000*l.*

In the year 1868, the two sums reached 568,000,000*l.*

In the year 1848, the Navigation Law was repealed, and Lord Derby and others predicted the total ruin of our commercial marine as the consequence. Mr. Lindsay, who believed in these prophecies, and has avowed his conversion, shall tell the result: —

	Vessels registered.	Tonnage.	Men employed.
1841	23,461	2,935,399	172,341
1867	40,942	7,277,098	346,606

Of British and Foreign tonnage in 1867: —

	British.	Foreign.
Entered inwards	11,197,685	5,140,952
Cleared outwards	11,172,205	5,245,090 [1]

---

[1] 'Log of my Leisure Hours,' by an Old Sailor, vol. iii. p. 204.

These figures have been taken from the Customs Returns.

Not only have these changes taken place without convulsion, but when, in 1848, all Europe was shaken by revolutions, the people of London rose on the 10th of April, not to overthrow, but to maintain our laws and institutions.

Among the most interesting speculations upon which an Englishman can enter, is the question whether the political Constitution under which we live is likely to endure. Montesquieu said that our Constitution would perish whenever the legislative power should become more corrupt than the executive. He was thinking, probably, of the danger arising from bribes, in the shape of offices, or lottery-tickets, or even in the grosser form of money, given by an incorruptible Minister to a corrupt majority of the House of Commons. But this kind of corruption had already diminished in the days of Walpole, had farther abated in the days of Pitt, and in our time has almost totally disappeared. Public opinion has stamped it out.

Let us see, then, what are the positive advantages of the British form of government, and what are the apparent dangers to which it is exposed.

1. There is complete personal liberty. A man may think what he pleases, write what he thinks, publish what he writes. Unless he commit some flagrant offence against the laws, and be convicted of that offence, he cannot be punished.

2. In case of reasonable suspicion of crime, he is entitled to have his case examined by a judge of integrity and learning, whose opinion of his guilt must be confirmed by a jury taken from among the householders of his county.

8. If a majority of the nation are dissatisfied with the administration of public affairs, their representatives can at once obtain a change of men and measures by a simple declaration of want of confidence.

This last advantage is one not enjoyed by the United States of America. . When a President has lost the confidence of his 'countrymen, and of Congress, he can only be removed by an impeachment, for which there may be no sufficient grounds, or by the expiry of his term of office, which may be in three months, or may not occur for more than three years.

The defects of the English Constitution affect chiefly the electoral constituents as a body which chooses the House of Commons, and the Parliament as a body empowered to make laws. The electors require to be restrained from bribery and excessive expenses, which affect our reputation, and poison representation at its source. The House of Commons must be compelled by public opinion to secure purity of election.

The United States, having Federal Legislatures intrusted with the business of making laws, are not subject to our defects.

In the House of Commons bills are postponed, year after year, for want of time. The financial periods are so· arranged that measures of general legislation are, except in rare cases, begun in that House early in February, and finished late in July. This is owing partly to the necessity of arranging expenditure and taxes before the end of March, and partly to the habit, which has increased, is increasing, and ought to be diminished, of making very long speeches. An old woman might now make to the House of Commons the prediction which an old woman once made to Horace : —

Hunc neque dira venena, nec hosticus auferet ensis,
Nec laterum dolor, aut tussis, nec tarda podagra ;
Garrulus hunc quando consumet cunque.[1]

But, supposing the House of Commons obstinately persists in calling for the budget in March, instead of postponing it till June, and members obstinately persist in talking through April, May, and June, then, not indeed the measures on which the fate of the country or of the Ministry depend, but measures of ordinary improvement relating to courts of justice, to the universities, to the public health, to education, to the Church, &c., &c., will continue to be sent to the House of Lords in the last half of July.

A body eager for plans of reform might, at that season, consider rapidly the wishes of the House of Commons. But the demand is hardly reasonable, and by an ancient and conservative Senate the task will probably be postponed till the next year.

There is, however, a defect in the personal composition of the House of Lords, which does not belong to its original constitution.

Since 1784, as we have seen, Pitt and his successors have so filled the House of Lords with Tory country gentlemen, that it has become a party body. Happily the good sense of the sons has supplied the deficiency of the fathers, and there can be little doubt that, while a Liberal Minister has the power of redressing the balance which Pitt so greatly disturbed, the House of Lords will be afraid of bringing down upon their heads a weight which might crush them altogether. If, therefore, a measure like the University Tests Bill is carried through the House of Commons by the Gov-

----

[1] Hor. 'Sat.' L ix. 81.

ernment, the Lords will not repeat their foolish vote of last session.[1] On the other hand, the House of Commons must not repeat the course which induced the House of Lords, in their just resentment, to throw out the Scotch Education Bill.

Some persons have endeavored to bring on at once such a collision as would either destroy the House of Lords, or induce the nation to rally round them as an integral part of the Constitution.

I beg to submit to such persons the two following remarks : —

The first is that, if the hereditary privileges of the peers are overthrown, the hereditary prerogative of the Sovereign will also be sacrificed. 'Do not,' said an accomplished orator in the House of Commons, many years ago, 'hang the Crown on the peg of an exception.' The particular application was mistaken, but the observation has truth to recommend it. The Sovereign does not inherit wisdom any more than the Duke of Norfolk.

The best Government consists in the union of liberty and order: we are at present in full possession of liberty, but order is sometimes in danger. Now, for the purpose of order, it is material that there should exist in the great bodies of the State the power which is called authority. Nothing more excites reverence than ancient prescriptive privilege ; nothing more moves the imagination than ancient lineage combined with recent achievement. Thus, to see in one assembly the descendants of the Talbots who fought for their country in the fourteenth century, with the Napier who so lately triumphed in Abyssinia, the heir of Marlborough,

---

[1] They did not do so.

who won the battle of Blenheim, and of Wellington, the victor at Waterloo, and of Nelson, who fell at Trafalgar, of Cecil, the wise counsellor of Elizabeth, and of Grey, the upright Minister of William IV., with the representatives of Mansfield, and of Camden, of Hardwicke, and of Somers, gives dignity and weight to the House of Peers.

It is true that every editor of a magazine can furnish at a few days' notice a better Senate than the British House of Lords.

Happily the people of England give little attention to those fanciful schemes. The nobility of England are not, like the French nobility before the Revolution, slavish sycophants of a court. They are known in their country houses as the free landlords of a free tenantry, promoting social good-will by a becoming hospitality. They are known in courts of justice as foremen of grand juries and magistrates at quarter-sessions. They share in national sports, and their wives and daughters visit the widows and the fatherless in their affliction.

Lastly, when a great question arises, which requires a display of more than ordinary knowledge of history, more accurate learning, more constitutional lore, and more practical wisdom than is to be found in the usual debates of Parliament, I know not where

> The general debate,
> The popular harangue, the tart reply,
> The logic, and the wisdom, and the wit

are to be found in greater perfection than among the prelates on the Episcopal bench, the peers of three centuries of nobility, and the recent occupants of the Woolsack.

Let me add what is, perhaps, the most important security of all — the prospect of any great democratic changes would shake public credit, and bring the nation to its senses — so that I cannot say I feel any alarm lest events should lead to the abolition of the House of Lords — involving, as no doubt it would, the fall of the Monarchy.

Lastly, to speak of my own work, I can only rejoice that I have been allowed to have my share in the task accomplished in the half-century which has elapsed from 1819 to 1869. My capacity, I always felt, was very inferior to that of the men who have attained in past times the foremost place in our Parliament, and in the councils of our Sovereign. I have committed many errors, some of them very gross blunders. But the generous people of England are always forbearing and forgiving to those statesmen who have the good of their country at heart ; like my betters, I have been misrepresented and slandered by those who know nothing of me ; but I have been more than compensated by the confidence and the friendship of the best men of my own political connection, and by the regard and favorable interpretation of my motives, which I have heard expressed by my generous opponents, from the days of Lord Castlereagh to these of Mr. Disraeli.

In political, as in other pursuits, men engage from various motives ; and as in the Church and at the Bar, in the Army and in the Navy, some are to be found who do no credit to the gown or to the uniform, so in the State. But, so far as I have been able to observe, I can sincerely say that I believe the public men of Great Britain, whatever diversity there may be in their views, have sincerely and honestly at heart the welfare of that great and free nation to which they belong.   R.

September 23, 1869.

POSTSCRIPT. — While these sheets have been going through the press, the news of the death of Lord Derby has afflicted his country, which saw in him a man, noble by character as well as by rank, always ready to sacrifice office for the sake of maintaining his opinions, and forming those opinions, if with the fallibility of human judgment, yet with an integrity which must in all future times command respect.   R.

November 23, 1869.

CHAPTER II.

POLICY OF LORD PALMERSTON IN THE EAST.

I WILL now refer to some occurrences which took place previously to 1841, when the Whig Government were defeated by the results of the general election.

The year 1840 saw the climax of Lord Palmerston's diplomatic ability and success as a statesman. For a long time he had observed a total silence with respect to his views on the complications of the East. At length he brought before the Cabinet a proposal, conceived with great foresight, and fully justified by the position of England. He asked from the Cabinet that he should be intrusted with power to conclude a treaty with Austria, Prussia, and Russia for the protection of the Turkish Empire, and resistance to the aggressive attempts of the Pacha of Egypt, supported by France, to destroy the integrity of the Turkish territory, by depriving the Sultan of his sovereignty over Egypt.

I concurred entirely in his plan, which seemed to me to afford the only alternative to abandonment of the Turkish Empire as a spoil to be scrambled for between Russia and France. On the one side was the treaty of Unkier-Skelessi, throwing its shield over Constantinople and the Dardanelles; on the other side were the intrigues of France and her Minister, M. Thiers, skilfully directed to the old French object, pursued by the first Napoleon before the Peace of Amiens, and carried on during the existence of that peace, of giving to France the dominion of Egypt.

But, although I fully concurred in the policy of Lord Palmerston, I saw that there was danger in forcing the Cabinet to an immediate decision. The Eastern question had been a topic of conversation for months among political parties. M. Guizot was the able and intelligent Ambassador of France in England. By his dispatches it was known to the French Government that Lord Holland and Lord Clarendon were strong advocates for the French Alliance, which they wished to be continued and strengthened. It was doubtful how many members of the Cabinet might espouse these views. I therefore urged delay, and obtained the consent of Lord Palmerston to a postponement of the decision of this mighty question to the Tuesday following. After the Cabinet, I went down to Buckhurst, a country house which I had hired, on the borders of Windsor Park. There, on the following morning, I received a messenger from Lord Palmerston, with a box containing a long letter in support of his views. I at once answered his letter, . telling him that I was fully convinced of the soundness of the policy he had explained to the Cabinet, but adding that I thought a short time was required to rally and to reconcile the opinions of our colleagues.

On the Monday morning I went to London, and had no sooner reached my office than Lord Melbourne came to me and consulted me on the impending decision. I told him that I completely embraced the opinions of Lord Palmerston, but that I thought it required an effort on his part to secure unanimity in the Cabinet. I told him that I thought he ought to tell Lord Holland that he was looked upon by Whig politicians as the representative of Mr. Fox, and that his resignation might

break up the Ministry or even dissolve the party. Lord
Melbourne consented. He had ·some doubts about the
policy, but said he thought Lord Palmerston would
resign if it were not adopted. The result of the meeting
on Tuesday was an entire agreement in the Cabinet, and
the signature of the Quadruple Treaty a few days afterwards.   ·

There were, however, still some difficulties to be overcome, both Parliamentary and naval. Lord Minto, as
head of the Admiralty, informed me that he should
require an additional number of seamen, and asked me
whether a vote of credit would not be necessary. I
said I thought not ; that an additional force of seamen
might be levied ; and if the policy of the Government
was successful the defect of form would be condoned.
A little later, during the recess, Lord Palmerston represented to Lord Melbourne that instructions ought at
once to be sent to the Mediterranean, directing Admiral
Stopford to attack Acre. Lord Melbourne wrote to me
asking my opinion. I answered that I thought Admiral
Stopford would attack Acre without special instructions,
but that to make things sure instructions such as Lord
Palmerston advised ought to be sent. This opinion was
sent to Lord Minto, who warmly concurred. Acre was
taken. A powder-magazine, which an Austrian Archduke had pointed out as likely to explode, exploded.
Concurrently with this event the famous army of Ibra-
him Pacha, supposed to be about to make an easy conquest of Constantinople, was defeated by the Turks.
The Turkish army passed over into Egypt ; Mehemet
Ali renounced his ambitious plans ; Louis Philippe,
at that time King of the French, renounced those of
Napoleon the First, and the peace of Europe was
assured.

When Parliament met I had no difficulty in obtaining their pardon for our victorious career.

In the course of these transactions I had occasion to do what I was in the habit of frequently doing, — I consulted the Duke of Wellington upon the state of our affairs. I asked him whether he thought there was any danger of an attack by the French fleet upon Malta or Gibraltar. He told me he thought our position was a very good one ; that he only regretted that we had not asked the French to be parties with us to the Quadruple Treaty. He did not apprehend any attack by a hostile fleet upon Malta or Gibraltar ; he thought the French would not like to touch a British garrison.

Thus the policy of Lord Palmerston, adopted by the Whig Cabinet, maintained the honor of the British name, kept Egypt out of the hands of France, and secured the peace of Europe.

Before I close this chapter I must allude, as briefly as I can, to the great event which occurred in the year 1837 ; namely, the death of King William the Fourth, and the accession of Queen Victoria. William the Fourth had made a memorable concession to the advice of his Ministers and the wishes of his people, when, upon hearing the views and explanations of Earl Grey, he gave his consent and approbation to the Reform Bill. He took an unusual and ill-considered step, when, upon the demise of Lord Spencer, he declared bluntly to Lord Melbourne that he had no further occasion for his services. It has since been explained that the King's mind was alarmed by some letters of Lord Duncannon on the subject of the Irish Church, and that he dreaded the proposals which his Ministers might submit to him on the subject of that Church. But, allowing that the alarm was natural, the King would have acted more in conformity with prudence, precedent, and constitutional usage, and with greater chance of success, if he had allowed his Ministers to bring forward their proposals, and had founded his opposition on the objections which he and the country might entertain to their boldness and subversive tendency.

The Queen who succeeded to the throne was a young Princess only eighteen years of age, and therefore only just entitled to wear the crown without a regency. Yet Queen Victoria, conscious of her own love of truth and justice, told her mother, the Duchess of Kent, that she ascended the throne without alarm. She relied, in the first place, on the loyal disposition and excellent character of the nation she was about to govern. She had in her uncle, King Leopold of Belgium, and his organ, Baron Stockmar, whose memoirs have lately been published, access to the wisest and most prudent advice. Her Minister, Lord Melbourne, whom she maintained in office, submitted to her decision counsels the most constitutional, free from any taint of self-interest or party prejudice. As I held the position of Secretary of State for the Home Department and leader of the Ministerial party in the House of Commons, it was incumbent on me to consider what was my duty to the Crown and to the country. We all know the prayer for the High Court of Parliament, to be read during their session, that ' Thou wouldst be pleased to direct and prosper all their consultations to the advancement of thy glory, the good of thy Church, the safety, honor, and welfare of our Sovereign and her dominions ; that all things may be so ordered and settled by their endeavors, upon the best and surest foundations, that peace and happiness, truth and justice, religion and piety, may be established among us for all generations.' This is not a prayer

'that all things may be so ordered and settled by their
endeavors, that peace and happiness, truth and justice,
religion and piety,' may endure for a quarter of a century, or half a century, or even for a century, but 'that
they may be established among us for all generations.'

I had felt the value and efficacy of this prayer, and
had endeavored to observe its purport in the measures
I proposed and the language I held, as conductor of
the business of the Government for the Crown in the
House of Commons. But I could not disguise from
myself or from Parliament the knowledge that there
were in the House of Commons men who departed very
widely from those principles which, under the lead of
the Whig party, had maintained the House of Hanover
upon the throne, had promoted civil and religious
liberty, had allowed every man to worship according
to the dictates of his own conscience, and which had
preserved among all changes loyalty to the Crown and
to the Constitution.

I could neither hear in silence nor abet the progress
of measures intended to destroy the aristocracy and up-
root the Church of England : my resistance was crowned
with success, and before the Ministry was changed, Mr.
Grote, Sir W. Molesworth, and Mr. Charles Buller were
entirely discomfited. But Mr. Grote and Mr. Henry
Warburton did not desert the principles of government
which they had embraced after reflection and inquiry.
The Poor Law Amendment Act, brought forward in
spite of popular dislike and the powerful opposition of
the 'Times' newspaper, which was neither scrupulous
nor temperate, was warmly supported by Mr. Grote.
It is thus noticed in the work entitled 'Personal Life
of George Grote ' : —

' The most important measure, however, brought for-

ward during the session of 1834 was the Poor Law
Amendment Act; perhaps the most creditable achievement of the Whig party. It was carried, after active
discussions and considerable opposition, by a large majority. I doubt whether, at any period *since* 1834, so
thorough and sound a change in our domestic machinery
could have been brought about. That it should at the
present time have become partially ineffective, is owing
to the altered tone of public opinion, on the character
of which, however, it is beside my province here to
enter.' [1]

The policy of the Philosophical Radicals at this time
is well defined in a letter of Mr. Henry Warburton's:—

' Expression is to be given to public opinion, and the
Whigs are to be made to feel the force of it, in constit-
uencies, by keeping them constantly in a state of alarm
of being ousted by Radical competitors — in Parliament,
by occasional threats of being voted against by their
Radical allies. In a certain state of disquietude it is
our business always to keep them; the pressure is to be
heightened or moderated according to circumstances,
and the magnitude and proximity of the objects we
hope to carry. But so long as there exists any material
difference in the weight of liberal measures which the
Whigs and Tories severally are willing to offer to us,
the highest bidder, if in possession, is not to be ousted
from the Government.' [2]

Mr. Warburton, usually called ' Philosopher Warburton,' acted loyally in support of the opinions here set
forth. I often saw him, and he did not grudge his
advice to the Government. In 1839, I think it was, he

---

[1] 'Personal Life of George Grote,' by Mrs. Grote, pp. 90–91.
[2] Ibid. p. 110.

urged upon me the adoption by the Government of the plan of penny-postage which had been made known to the public by Mr. Rowland Hill. I said I thought the plan very ingenious, and likely to confer great benefits upon the public, but that it would make a temporary deficit in the revenue, which would probably require to be filled up by new taxation. Mr. Warburton said that a new tax was a great evil, and he hoped it would be avoided. No further conversation passed at that time.

Unfortunately, the Government adopted both parts of Mr. Warburton's advice. The Cabinet was unanimous in favor of the ingenious and popular plan of a penny-postage ; but they ought to have enacted at the same time such measures as would have secured a revenue sufficient to defray the national expenditure. Failing to do this, there was for three years together a deficit, which exposed the Government to the powerful reproaches and unanswerable objections of Sir Robert Peel. Public opinion echoed those reproaches and those objections, and produced such a degree of discontent as was in itself a sufficient ground for a change of Administration.

There was, however, another ground of party hostility, which the Government were willing to provoke and eager to encounter. The Chancellor of the Exchequer had pointed out to the Cabinet that a large revenue might be derived from the admission of foreign sugar, giving, at the same time, the advantage of a protecting duty to the British Colonies. He likewise proposed the admission of foreign timber on terms more favorable than had hitherto been accorded. By one of the clumsy contrivances of the system of protection, the timber of Norway was sent to Canada and brought back to England, with a view to evade the high duty on foreign timber.

But there was another article which, since the year 1815, had been a favorite object of protection — this was corn. By the ingenious machinery of a sliding-scale, corn was only admitted at a low duty when British corn was at a high price, and was charged with an enormous duty when British corn was cheap, or at a moderate price in the market.

I pointed out to the Cabinet that, of all the grievances inflicted upon the British consumer by the system of monopoly and protection, that which arose from the corn duties was the most grievous and oppressive. Lord Grenville, in a memorable protest, had declared that monopoly was the parent of dearness and of scarcity. The best writers on political economy, several of the highest statesmen and members of the House of Commons, had argued powerfully for the repeal, or at least modification, of the corn duties.

I proposed, not a total repeal, but, in accordance with some of the best authorities, a moderate fixed duty on the admission of foreign corn.

The whole project, however, raised a clamorous uproar from West Indian planters, Colonial growers of timber, and, above all, from the land-owners, farmers, and agricultural laborers of England.

The Ministry were defeated by a majority of thirty-six on their proposal with regard to sugar duties. The Government resolved to dissolve Parliament. Sir Robert Peel, who was not aware of the intention of the Cabinet, then brought forward a vote of want of confidence, which he carried, after a long debate, by a majority of one. The general election, decided by the constituent bodies of freeholders in the counties, and 10l. householders in boroughs, gave to Sir Robert Peel a majority of ninety-one over the existing Ministry.

The Whig Ministers, however, thought it due to themselves and fair to the country to place on record their intention, had they been successful in the general election, to pursue the path of free trade, with regard to corn, sugar, and timber, by making some immediate reductions, thus opening the way to further changes which would save the people at a future period from monopoly prices on behalf of the West Indian planters, the Canadian producers of timber, and the land-owners and farmers of England, who insisted upon prices of sugar, timber, and corn sufficient to protect their own interests.

It was thus that, as the patrons and favorers of protection, in reference to sugar, timber, and corn, the Tory Ministry accepted office in September, 1841.

CHAPTER III.

1846.

FAULTS OF SIR ROBERT PEEL'S POLICY. — HIS RESIG-
NATION IN 1846. — TRIUMPH OF FREE TRADE.

THE faults which led to the fall of the Whig Ministry
in 1841, and the causes which led to the election of a
great majority ready to support Sir Robert Peel as a
Minister — a majority of not less than ninety-one — are
sufficiently known. Lord Melbourne's Government
had committed the error of conferring a benefit on the
people by lowering the duty on letters to one penny,
without at the same time making adequate provision
to supply the temporary deficiency in the public income.
Sir Robert Peel was not slow to perceive and to take
advantage of this error, but in laying down the principles by which his Government was to be guided he
neglected the demands which were sure to be made
upon him for a repeal or reduction of the duties on
corn, sugar, and timber. When, in the course of the
following session, a great number of manufacturers and
tradesmen came to me to complain of the abolition of
protection, I remember that, among others, a bootmaker
said, 'I work very hard all the week, but only on one
day of the week can I afford for my wife and myself a
dish of meat for dinner. It is very hard that I should
be deprived of protection for my trade, while the great
owners of land have the fullest protection for the corn

which their tenants produce.' I could only say that I could not give him hope of immediate relief, but that the protection given to corn was a grievance so palpable and so enormous that the House of Commons could not long leave him without a remedy.

This defect made, in fact, the weakness of Sir Robert Peel's position — a defect of which one of his colleagues, Lord Aberdeen, was fully sensible.

On the part of the Whigs, I had declared my intention of proposing a fixed duty on corn. This was likewise an error. Cobden and Bright proposed the only natural course, that of a total repeal of the duties on corn. But the Whig country gentlemen were not prepared for so bold a measure.

I have already remarked that the Tory party made a great mistake, when, in 1815, the war being over, and the power of Napoleon, for a time at least, extinguished, they did not entirely change their policy, and, instead of keeping up the defence and promotion of measures which war alone could justify, and which the influence of Pitt caused to prevail in the House of Commons, they did not consider wisely, liberally, and maturely what was the policy which in days of peace might be expected to prevail in Parliament and in the nation.

Pitt himself, from 1784 to 1792, had espoused large and popular principles; he had, in 1782, and even so late as 1786, proposed parliamentary reform. In 1786 he gave his sanction, by a treaty of commerce with France, to those principles of free trade which he had imbibed from Adam Smith. Even during the war, by combining the admission of Roman Catholics to office and to Parliament with the measures rendered necessary for the Union, he gave his solemn and deliberate sanction to the principle of religious liberty.

A statesman who could approve of parliamentary reform, however mitigated, of free trade, however modified, and of religious liberty, however guarded, cannot be esteemed other than a Liberal politician. But, as Canning truly said, the great bulk of the Tory party, professing to worship Pitt, adored him as the Pagans of the East adore the sun — only in his eclipse.

In 1817, Lord Castlereagh advised Parliament to suspend the Habeas Corpus Act. But, as Sir Samuel Romilly well remarked, the measure that was well fitted to defeat a few secret conspirators was entirely out of place as a weapon with which to contend against the discontented mass of a nation.

The Tory policy from 1819 to 1829 was in conformity with inspirations of Tory prejudice. In 1829, the Roman Catholic claims were conceded, but they were conceded rather to avert the danger of civil war than as a homage to the great principle of religious liberty. The Tory party still clung to the maintenance of the exclusive and intolerant Protestant Church of Ireland; to the exclusion, by heavy duties, of foreign corn; to the refusal of parliamentary reform; to the refusal of admission of even the highest of the working-classes to the privilege of giving votes for the choice of representatives in Parliament.

It is true that by fits and starts, when public opinion has been too strong for them, the Tory party, in the disguise of Conservatives, have made large concessions. In 1829, Sir Robert Peel, after a long and fruitless battle, in the course of which he contended that those who held the doctrine of transubstantiation were unfit to sit in Parliament, admitted the Roman Catholics to legislative and ministerial power. In 1846, the same Sir Robert Peel ceased to defend the Corn-laws, which he had upheld from the time of his entrance into Parliament. In 1865, Mr. Disraeli, who had succeeded to the lead of the Tory party, and had applauded the House of Commons for having refused to degrade the suffrage, seemed prepared still to defend the entrenchments of 1831. But in the following year he gave up the whole question, and lowered the franchise, not, as his predecessors had proposed, by a gradual widening of the gate of admission, but by a jump — which was called by his chief and master a leap in the dark — to all the householders in the towns. It remained to be considered whether a great party which shared, with the Whigs and Radicals, the representation of England, which has for many years asked for and enjoyed the confidence of hundreds of thousands of its people, is entitled to retain that confidence, on the ground that it has violated all its pledges, renounced its most cherished principles, and exposed the country to dangers at which it affected to be seriously alarmed, and whether, on the plea of its ability and dexterity, it shall govern the country on principles for the profession of which it held up its adversaries to odium at each recurring session, and shall obtain followers on the ground that there are still some principles to which it is sincerely attached, and which neither the clamor of a mob nor the prospect of power and office will induce it to abandon.

Experience, so far as it has gone, shows that public opinion is unfavorable to these sudden turns of policy, and to the relinquishment of doctrines which had been professed for years, enforced by all the cogency of argument, and illustrated by all the splendor of eloquence. It is to be noted that these great concessions of principle, hitherto a mark of Tory policy, have not been approved by the nation.

In 1829, Sir Robert Peel yielded the Roman Catholic claims. In 1830, the House of Commons changed the Ministry. In 1846, Sir Robert Peel gave up the Corn-laws. In the same year the House of Commons refused him their confidence, and the Ministry was changed. In 1867, Mr. Disraeli gave up his opposition to further reform, and, to use his own phrase, 'degraded the suffrage' to household voters. But, in 1868, upon a dissolution of Parliament, his Ministry was so thoroughly discomfited that he retired from office without waiting for a Parliamentary defeat.

Thus, it appears that either the House of Commons or the nation at large have used their power of rejection to condemn Ministers who, after long resistance, have conceded measures which for many years they had represented in their speeches as treason to their country, as outrage to all principle, and as destruction to the party of which they were the leaders. On what ground has this Parliamentary and popular withdrawal of confidence been pronounced? Lord Cottenham, a direct man and a straightforward statesman, expressed to me his opinion on Sir Robert Peel's assent to the repeal of the Corn-laws. 'Either,' he said, 'Sir Robert Peel foresaw the necessity of giving up his opposition to the repeal of the Corn-laws, or he did not. If he foresaw it, he was wanting in honesty when he persevered in his opposition. If he did not foresee it, he was wanting in wisdom, and is not fit to be intrusted with the supreme direction of this great Empire.'

The House of Commons in two instances, and the electors of the House of Commons in a third instance, have confirmed the logical conclusion of Lord Cottenham, and have withdrawn their confidence from Ministers who had made themselves remarkable by reprobation of all the doctrines on the maintenance of which they paraded their claims to confidence. It must be admitted, however, that a time of condonation comes, and I could not refuse assistance to Sir Robert Peel in 1846 on the sole ground of his change of opinion.

I did not, therefore, act on this ground alone, in voting against the Protection of Life Bill, introduced by Sir Robert Peel's Government in 1846; but I objected to the bill on Irish grounds. I then thought, and I still think, that it is' wrong to arrest men and to put them in prison on the ground that they *may* be murderers and house-breakers. They may be, on the other hand, honest laborers going home from their work. I think every means should be adopted for discovering the perpetrators of crime and bringing them to justice. I think that for this purpose it is right to give the majority of a jury power to convict, upon sufficient evidence, a man accused of murder. But I do not think that it is right to send a man to prison upon evidence that he has been out at night without any further offence. The Ministry of Sir Robert Peel were defeated in 1846 by a majority of more than seventy on the second reading of the Bill for the Protection of Life in Ireland. Her Majesty was pleased to intrust to me the task of forming a new Ministry. I endeavored to obtain the assistance of Lord Dalhousie, Lord Lincoln, and Mr. Sidney Herbert. Failing in that attempt, I had to consider whether I could propose a junction with the party which had deserted Sir Robert Peel on account of his repeal of the Cornlaws, but neither principle nor prudence would allow me to do so. It was on account of our adherence to the policy of free trade that we had been driven out of office in 1841, and the only course which I could honestly pursue was to go forward with measures extending the principles of commercial policy to which Sir Robert Peel had now given his assent. But I could have no hope of the assistance of the protectionists in such a policy. I therefore, after a long and friendly conference with the Duke of Beaufort, declined to ask for the assistance of his friends in the formation of a new Ministry. In the Administration which I then formed, I assumed the office of First Lord of the Treasury, Lord Cottenham became Lord Chancellor, Lord Lansdowne, President of the Council, and Sir George Grey, Home Secretary; Lord Palmerston, Foreign Secretary; Earl Grey, Colonial Secretary; Mr. Charles Wood, Chancellor of the Exchequer; Lord Clarendon, President of the Board of Trade; and Mr. Macaulay, who did not like to accept any office which would divert him from his literary work, Paymaster of the Forces. Mr. Sheil was Master of the Mint; Sir John Jervis, Attorney-General; Mr. Dundas, Solicitor-General; the Earl of Bessborough, Lord Lieutenant of Ireland; and Mr. Labouchere, Chief Secretary to the Lord Lieutenant.

One of the first questions I undertook to settle was that of the admission of foreign sugar, on which I had been so signally defeated in 1841. But on July 28, 1846, when Lord George Bentinck proposed not to go into Committee of Ways and Means on the sugar duty, the ayes, who, with Sir Robert Peel, Mr. Goulburn, Lord Lincoln, and Mr. Sidney Herbert, voted in our support, were 265; while the noes, led by Lord George Bentinck and Mr. Disraeli, were only 130. The bill I then introduced was far more favorable to the admission of foreign sugar than that which had been rejected in 1841.

The monopoly which had been enjoyed in favor of Colonial sugar having thus failed, it was obvious that the progress of free trade would have the active support of Sir Robert Peel and his friends. Sir Robert, after the fall of his Ministry, behaved to me and to my Administration in the most fair and honorable manner. Sir James Graham likewise gave his important and valuable support to the cause of free trade whenever its principles were in question. In 1848, on the proposal to repeal the Navigation Laws, which Adam Smith held ought to be an exception to his theory, the speech of Sir James Graham was the best that was made for the repeal. In fact, Sir Robert Peel and his friends devoted all their energies to the promotion of free trade, and gave their handsome support to the Ministers who had now become the leaders and chiefs in that great cause.

I may take this opportunity of adverting to the progress of free trade, to the caution with which it was first proposed as a principle to guide our policy, the bitterness with which it was assailed, the triumphs it has won, the benefits it has conferred upon the country, the refutation experience has given to all the arguments by which it was opposed, the prosperity it has introduced into our finance, and the prospect it gives that trade will spread over the world its powerful and beneficent influence.

It is bare justice to acknowledge that Mr. Huskisson and Mr. Canning were the first to make a breach in the wall of prohibition and protection, which was defended with so much obstinacy by the old Tory party, and by many prejudiced Whigs. The proposal of Mr. Huskisson in regard to silk goods was apparently modest and timid : he proposed that after three years' interval the prohibition of foreign silk goods should be exchanged for a duty of thirty per cent *ad valorem.* Mr. Huskisson was attacked, not only with argument, but with invective, as a man whose proposal of admission of foreign silks, on any terms, proved him to have a bad heart. It was in vain that Mr. Canning declared that those who opposed improvement because it was innovation would have to submit to innovation which was no improvement. I had the satisfaction, with Mr. Brougham and many others, of assisting in the triumph of Mr. Huskisson over prejudice and ignorance. Mr. Huskisson came to the Commons one day, with a small octavo volume in his hand, which he was proud to declare contained the whole tariff of customs' duty left existing on the statute-book. The Reform Act of 1832 was favorable to enlightened views of commercial policy, and opened the way to further reforms. Mr. Cobden and Mr. Bright obtained seats in the House of Commons, the former for Yorkshire, the latter for the city of Durham. My Whig friends, who represented counties, alarmed at the proposal of subjecting corn to a fixed duty of no more than eight shillings, contributed to the defeat of the Ministry, by a vote of want of confidence, in 1841. The leaders of the Whigs advised me, in 1845, not to vote for a total repeal of the Corn-laws; but domestic affairs having taken me to Edinburgh, I there wrote a letter to my constituents, declaring myself in favor of total repeal, which produced a great effect. Mr. Cobden and Mr. Bright, sacrificing their health for the public good, obtained in that year, for the first time, the adherence of the working-classes. The 'Times' newspaper proclaimed that the Anti-Corn-Law League was a great fact.

Sir Robert Peel proposed that the duty on corn should be reduced to one shilling per quarter, which amounted to about two per cent on the current price of wheat. I considered myself bound to carry on the march of the free trade army against monopolies in favor of Colonial sugar, of Canadian timber, and of English ships. Lord Derby predicted that this last concession to free trade would utterly ruin the merchant-shipping of England. An English ship-builder, who had defended with perseverance the monopoly of England, showed his spirit by immediately ordering the building of twelve new ships for the mercantile marine.

The progress of free trade has been constant, victorious, and irresistible.

It was supposed, and boldly asserted, that the exchange of high duties on foreign manufactures would destroy the revenue of customs and excise. The returns of the revenue for the year ending on December 31, 1873, sufficiently prove the fallacy of this expectation. It was expected that on the 31st of March, 1874, a surplus of upwards of five millions would exhibit the flourishing state of our finances. Men who consult the Parliamentary history of England from 1823 to 1873 will rejoice to acknowledge that the most enlightened members of our Parliament, the Liberal Tories of 1846, Sir Robert Peel, Mr. Sidney Herbert, Sir James Graham, and Lord Aberdeen, together with the Whigs, who for half a century have held the position of her Majesty's Ministers and her Majesty's Opposition, together with Mr. Cobden and Mr. Bright, and many Radical members of the House of Commons, have labored to destroy the restrictions which fettered British industry and British trade, and have thereby conferred immense benefits on their country. An old French merchant said to Colbert, when he was imposing restrictions on the entry of Dutch manufactures, and thereby cramping the silk manufactures of France, ' *Laissez faire et laissez passer*,' meaning thereby that he should not prescribe the length and breadth of the loom, or impose penalties on workmen who did not adhere to the ministerial measurement; that he should not forbid the entry of Dutch toys into France, or indirectly discourage the exportation of French wines to Holland.

These facts, which have been much misunderstood, contain the very simple secret of free trade. In speaking to my constituents of the city of London of the repeal of the Corn-laws, I said that it was barbarous to prevent the manufacturer of Lancashire from sending his yard of cotton cloth to Ohio, or to prevent the farmer in Ohio from sending his bushel of corn to Lancashire.

Nor can I foresee a time when the British manufacturer will no longer find a market for his goods in other parts of the world. The population of Great Britain is so cabined, cribbed, confined to the land of the British Isles, that our manufacturing towns will always be very populous, and there will exist for a long time vast territories in North and South America, in the plains of Buenos Ayres, in the hills and dales of Australia and New Zealand, where herds of cattle may find plentiful pasture, and the grower of corn receive an ample remuneration for his labor. The evil genius of protection may prevail in the Senate and the Congress of the United States, may animate selfish parties in the Legislatures of the British Colonies, but these obstacles must be overcome. Poets have sung the advantages of trade. Vir-

gil has said, that on one soil the growth of corn may
flourish, and that on another the grape will find its
proper nutriment: 'Hic segetes, illic veniunt felicius
uvæ.' Waller has said, speaking of English commerce: —

> The taste of hot Arabia's spice we know,
> Free from the scorching sun that makes it grow;
> Without the worm, in Persian silks we shine;
> And, without planting, drink of every wine.[1]

Pope, in a later age, has said: —

> The time shall come when, free as seas or wind,
> Unbounded Thames shall flow for all mankind;
> Whole nations enter with each swelling tide,
> And seas but join the nations they divide.

Man has contrived, not only by sanguinary wars, but
by the poison of commercial duties and vexatious pro-
hibitions in time of peace, to bar the intercourse between
nations. It belongs to benevolent humanity and friendly
policy to find a remedy for these evils, to make the com-
mandment, 'to fill the world,' the source of new blessings, and forge a chain of love which shall unite all the
races of mankind.

---

[1] 'Panegyric to my Lord Protector.'

CHAPTER IV.

DEFEAT OF THE PHILOSOPHICAL RADICALS. — SUP-
PRESSION OF THE CHARTIST RIOTS, 1848.

QUESTIONS still more urgent, if not more important,
than those debated in 1846 were agitated in 1848.
A strong attack was made by the Economists, headed
by Mr. Hume, and by the Philosophers, led by Sir
William Molesworth, upon the expenditure of the
State. The motion made by Mr. Hume on the 25th
of February was exceedingly vague; it was to this
effect: —

'That it is expedient that the expenditure of the
country should be reduced, not only to render an increase
of taxation in this session unnecessary, but that the
expenditure should be further reduced as speedily as
possible, to admit of a reduction of the present large
amount of taxation.'

The circumstances in which this motion was brought
forward were somewhat critical for me. During the
winter I had been afflicted with an illness which,
although not alarming, was a warning to me to be cautious in regard to my health. My medical adviser insisted on my having rest and change of air. I went to
St. Leonards, and after a few days' repose there returned,
much restored, to London with Charles Buller.

I spoke in the debate on Hume's motion, and said
'that among the opponents of the Government were

some who wished to see the prevalence of low establishments, low estimates, and low views.' On a division
the majority who supported the Government were one
hundred and fifty-seven, the noes in the minority, fifty-
nine ; giving a majority of ninety-eight in favor of the
Government. In the majority were Mr. Gladstone, Sir
James Graham, and Sir Robert Peel ; in the minority
were Sir William Molesworth, Mr. Bright, and Mr.
Cobden. Most people felt that the majority of ninety-
eight showed the adherence of the House of Commons
to the cause of constitutional freedom, hereditary monarchy, and national independence. The Opposition
received the support of members who were not really
their allies, but the undisguised abettors of violence,
anarchy, and disorder. This question requires further
elucidation.

The events on the Continent, in the early part of this
year, were striking and calamitous. In Paris, King
Louis Philippe, who had reigned for eighteen years, was
compelled to abdicate, and a Republic was, by popular
violence, installed at the Hotel de Ville. At Vienna,
the Imperial Government was overthrown, and the
leaders of the mob, whom Prince Windischgrätz styled
' la canaille,' were substituted for the regular authorities. In Prussia, the garrison of Berlin was ordered by
the King to withdraw from the capital ; and the King's
brother, the present Emperor of Germany, sought in
Buckingham Palace a place of refuge.

In London, threats of disorder and announcements
of an impending revolution were not wanting. It was
reported that Count Metternich, whose mind was intent
upon all the movements of the machine he had so long
directed, said, at his whist-table, that of all the revolutions threatening Europe, the most violent and destruc-

tive would be that of England, giving as his reason that Jacobinism had already done its worst to a great extent in France, Austria, Prussia, and Italy, but that in England the Church and the aristocracy had immense revenues still untouched, and ready to be the spoil of the ravenous democracy which was working its will over the European monarchies. It was proclaimed that a petition containing three millions of signatures would be presented to the House of Commons, and that a numerous assemblage, followed by multitudes of the people of London, would accompany the bearers of this petition to the House of Commons.

My first notion was, that the bearers of the petition, with their sympathizers, might be allowed to cross Westminster Bridge, and after delivering their petition at the doors of Parliament, might be turned off by the police to Charing Cross and the Strand. But a friend of mine, of great experience and acknowledged sagacity, deemed that there was some danger in this course, and that a better measure of precaution would be to prevent the expected crowd from crossing the bridges. Perceiving the wisdom of this advice, I requested the Commissioners of Police, Sir Charles Rowan and Sir Richard Mayne, to prepare a programme of proceedings for the appointed day, the 10th of April, and to attend a Cabinet fixed for a previous day. I requested the Duke of Wellington also to do me the favor to attend the Cabinet.

When the Cabinet met, Sir George Grey, the Home Secretary, being fully prepared for the duties incumbent upon him, I asked Sir Charles Rowan to read the programme proposed by the Commissioners of Police. When he had done reading, I asked the Duke of Wellington if the arrangement appeared to him to be judicious, and I had the good fortune to obtain the approbation of that great man. It was understood that the troops to be brought to London were to be kept out of sight, and that no military force was to appear unless action on their part should be absolutely necessary. On the evening of April 9 I received two anonymous letters, which convinced me that the leaders of the movement, either hopeless of success or awed by our preparations, had renounced any intention of using physical force.

Accordingly, on the 10th of April, great numbers having gone from every part of the town to Kennington Common, Sir Richard Mayne went on horseback to the scene of action. He told a policeman to go to Fergus O'Connor, who had taken up his position on a magnificent car, and request him to descend from his height and come to his stirrup on foot. The part of the mob which surrounded the car remonstrated with Fergus O'Connor, and desired him not to attend to the message. O'Connor called out to his followers, ' Be silent, you fools ; don't say a word to prevent my going to my best friend, Sir Richard Mayne.' He then descended from his seat and went to Sir Richard Mayne, who told him that he could go no further, but that if he would deliver the petition to the police, a cab should be furnished to three of the petitioners, who, if unaccompanied by any force, might cross Westminster Bridge in safety and deliver the petition at the door of the House of Commons. After this every thing was quiet. No great numbers followed the cab which contained the petition ; there was no mob at the door of the House of Commons, and London escaped the fate of Paris, Berlin, and Vienna. For my own part, I saw in these proceedings a fresh proof that the people of England were satisfied with the government under which they had the happiness to live, did not wish to be instructed by their neighbors in the principles of freedom, and did not envy them either the liberty they had enjoyed under Robespierre or the order which had been established among them by Napoleon the Great.

On May 8, 1849, the bill for the repeal of the Navigation Laws was read a second time in the House of Lords by a majority of ten. In the majority were the Duke of Wellington, the Earl of Aberdeen, and the Earl of Ripon. There were likewise three archbishops and eleven bishops, while in the minority there were only six bishops, making a majority of eight of the archbishops and bishops out of the total majority of ten.

I had on this occasion, as on many others, the advantage of the support of the House of Lords, which I should not have received if I had introduced into the House of Commons measures of a more radical complexion. If, for instance, I had coupled with the proposals of the Government a bill affecting the Irish Protestant Church, I should have encountered the hostility of the whole Tory majority in the House of Lords upon those measures, and should probably have been defeated by the Earl of Derby, who made a vigorous and powerful speech against the repeal of the Navigation Laws.

My enemies, of course, pointed with the satisfaction of spite at the absence of measures of a more decided stamp, such as the admission of a larger number of the working-classes to the mass of electors, and the reduction of the revenues of the Church of Ireland. But there are times when it is prudent for Whigs, moderate Tories, and Radicals to join in measures of reform and progress, upon which they can agree, and to leave for a

more favorable season measures of progress for which
there is only a slender majority in the House of Commons, and upon which they are sure to be defeated in
the House of Lords.   The Tory party is sometimes represented as obstructing every step in political progress.
But this is not so.   In a speech in the city of London,
I described the Liberal party, alluding chiefly to the
Whigs, as anxious to reform and to preserve, while I
described the Tories as desirous to preserve and to
reform.   The cause of truth and justice gains nothing
by unfair exaggerations.   The names of Pitt, Huskisson, Canning, Sir Robert Peel, Sir James Graham, and
Mr. Gladstone, must always be inscribed with honor in
the annals of free trade.

I do not think it necessary to enter into any minute
explanation of my reasons for introducing a bill for the
Prevention of the Assumption of Ecclesiastical Titles by
Prelates appointed by the Pope.   The object of that
bill was merely to assert the supremacy of the Crown.
It was never intended to prosecute any Roman Catholic
bishops who did not act in glaring and ostentatious defiance of the Queen's title to the Crown.   Accordingly,
a very clever artist represented me in a caricature as a
boy who had chalked up ' No Popery ' upon a wall and
then run away.   This was a very fair joke.   In fact, I
wanted to place the assertion of the Queen's title to
appoint bishops on the statute-book, and there leave it.
I kept in the hands of the Crown the discretion to prosecute or not any offensive denial of the Queen's rights.
My purpose was fully answered.   Those who wished to
give the Pope the right of appointing bishops in England
opposed the bill.   When my object had been gained, I
had no objection to the repeal of the Act.

During my temporary resignation of office, which took

place in the month of February, 1851, on the question of Mr. Locke King's motion for an alteration of the county franchise, Lord Aberdeen and Sir James Graham endeavored to persuade me not to persevere with the bill, but to be satisfied with Parliamentary resolutions asserting the rights of the Crown. I did not like to retire from the position I had assumed. But in substance the course suggested by Lord Aberdeen would have been as effectual and less offensive than that which I adopted.

A more serious question arose with respect to Lord Palmerston's conduct as Secretary for Foreign Affairs. Baron Stockmar, whose memoirs have been published, seems to have acquiesced in the opinion that my conduct on that occasion was dilatory and undecided. My own judgment upon it is that it was hasty and precipitate. I ought to have seen Lord Palmerston, and I think I could, without difficulty, have induced him to make a proper submission to her Majesty's wishes, and agree to act in conformity with conditions to which he had already given his assent. I felt it to be my duty to declare the political connection between Lord Palmerston and myself to be dissolved. But I felt at the same time that my Government was so much weakened that it was not likely to retain power for any long time.

Accordingly, I took the first opportunity to resign office. On February 23, 1852, I announced the resignation of the Ministry in the House of Commons. Just before the resignation, Lord Naas made a violent attack on Lord Clarendon, which I thought it my duty to rebut in the strongest language. On a division, the ayes were 137, and the noes 229; majority, 92.

Mr. Tierney used to say, as the fruit of his experience, that it was very difficult for a member of the House of

Commons to attain high office, but that it was still more difficult to leave high office with credit on sufficient grounds. The latter is, in fact, the more difficult operation of the two. I cannot say that in breaking up my own Administration, or in leaving Lord Aberdeen's Administration, or in leaving office in 1865, I have been satisfied with the reasons which determined me to give up the high position in which I had been placed by my Sovereign.

It may not be any loss to the reader if I give, in the next chapter, some observations on the course of the Executive Government of England since the Great Revolution of 1688.

CHAPTER V.

CONSTITUTION OF THE HOUSE OF COMMONS. — CHOICE OF LEADERS.

LORD MACAULAY has, in his review of the conduct of William Pitt, made a remark of so much importance, coming from such a man, that, if it be erroneous or overcharged, it ought not to be left without comment. I will give his remarks in full : —

'Parliamentary government, like every other contrivance of man, has its advantages and its disadvantages. On the advantages there is no need to dilate. The history of England during the one hundred and seventy years which have elapsed since the House of Commons became the most powerful body in the State; her immense and still growing prosperity; her freedom, her tranquillity, her greatness in arts, in sciences, and in arms; her maritime ascendency, the marvels of her public credit, her American, her African, her Australian, her Asiatic Empires, sufficiently prove the excellence of her institutions. But those institutions, though excellent, are assuredly not perfect. Parliamentary government is government by speaking. In such a government, the power of speaking is the most highly prized of all the qualities which a politician can possess; and that power may exist in the highest degree, without judgment, without fortitude, without skill in reading the characters of men or the signs of the times, without any knowledge of the principles of legislation or of political economy, and without any skill in diplomacy or in the administration of war. Nay, it may well happen that those very intellectual qualities which give a peculiar charm to the speeches of a public man may be incompatible with the qualities which would fit him to meet a pressing emergency with promptitude and firmness. It was thus with Charles Townshend. It was thus with Windham. It was a privilege to listen to those accomplished and ingenious orators. But in a perilous crisis they would have been found far inferior in all the qualities of rulers to such a man as Oliver Cromwell, who talked nonsense, or as William the Silent, who did not talk at all. When Parliamentary government is established, a Charles Townshend or a Windham will almost always exercise much greater influence than such men as the great Protector of England, or as the Founder of the Batavian Commonwealth.'[1]

From long experience in the House of Commons, I think I am entitled to say that in these remarks Macaulay is greatly mistaken. Charles Townshend and William Windham were listened to in the House of Commons with delight and applause. But there are other qualities which the House of Commons more imperatively requires. They require that the speaker who assumes to lead them should be himself persuaded that the course he recommends will prove beneficial to the country. Mr. Windham was unstable and irresolute. He said one day to Lord Henry Petty, who was sitting beside him, towards the end of his speech, ' Which way did I say I would vote ? ' Such a man can never lead the House of Commons. Lord Castlereagh was a very

---

[1] Macaulay's 'Review of William Pitt.'

tiresome, involved, and obscure speaker; Lord Althorp
was without any powers of oratory; yet I never knew
two men who had more influence in the House of Commons than Lord Castlereagh and Lord Althorp.   There
are qualities which govern men, such as sincerity, and
a conviction on the part of the hearers that the Minister
is a man to be trusted, which have more to do with influence over the House of Commons than the most
brilliant flights of fancy and the keenest wit.

Macaulay goes on to say that 'from the Book of
Dignities a curious list might be made out of Chancel-
lors ignorant of the principles of equity, and First Lords
of the Admiralty ignorant of the principles of navigation.'   Yet there are other qualities which Lord Spencer
and Lord Melville possessed, such as decision and calmness in days of peril, and power to enforce their own
persuasion upon others, which, proceeding from men
ignorant of the principles of navigation, have done
much to augment the British Empire, to promote British
prosperity, to avert danger from our shores, to make
our wars successful and our treaties honorable.

My grandfather, Lord Torrington, told me that the
first William Pitt sent a message to the Admiralty that
the Channel fleet must sail on the Tuesday following.
The Board of Admiralty answered, that it was impossible that the fleet could be ready by Tuesday.   Mr. Pitt
rejoined, that in that case he should recommend to the
King to name a new Board of Admiralty.   The Channel
fleet sailed on the Tuesday, and perhaps this was the
occasion when a great victory was gained on the coast
of France.

It would not be difficult, by going over our Parliamentary history from the Revolution of 1688 to the
present time, to show that the policy pursued has not

been a policy recommended merely by flashy or lively orators, but one adopted, from time to time, wisely or unwisely, in accordance with national views, and aimed at some intelligible object. Never did an expedition leave the English shores with more pomp of preparation, with higher expectation of great achievement, than the Walcheren expedition. Never was an expedition worse commanded, or attended with more disastrous failure. Yet, after a long inquiry, the House of Commons rejected a vote of censure upon the Ministers who directed the expedition. Mr. Elliot, of Wells, told me that, according to his belief, the House of Commons, in rejecting the censure, rightly interpreted the wishes of the country. The fact I believe to have been, that the country looked upon the contest with France as a contest of life and death, and was ready to forgive any error, except that of shrinking from the sacrifices required to prevent Napoleon from being as much the conqueror of England as he was the master of Europe.

Such, then, is the British House of Commons. In its worst days, when Addington was its Prime Minister, and the country gentlemen were supposed by a satirist to exclaim, —

They think we're honest, for they know we're dull,

the heart of Britain was sound, and Lord Hawkesbury refused, with becoming pride, to listen to the dictation of the great tyrant.

The House of Commons likes a man who can be trusted; that is to say, whose honesty is not questioned, and whose common sense can be expected to guide him at a moment of difficulty.

A review of political affairs from 1701 to 1800, or to the present day, will confirm what I have said.

Lord Macaulay has truly stated that during the reign of William III. that wise and sagacious prince took the management of foreign affairs into his own hands. I cannot think, however, that he did well to ally himself with Louis XIV., for the purpose of regulating the succession to the Crown of Spain on the death of the Spanish King. Two consequences were pretty sure to follow any such interference. The Spaniards would be indignant at the interference of any foreign power, and especially of an heretical power, in the disposal of the dominions united under the Spanish Crown. Louis XIV., the most faithless prince of his time, was sure to set at nought his own solemn promises, to renounce the renunciation made upon his marriage, and to look to his own aggrandizement and that of his family as full compensation for any load upon his conscience which he might incur by perjury. Accordingly these two consequences flowed as necessary results from the treaties made by William. With respect to domestic affairs, William endeavored to unite in one Council the best and cleverest statesmen of his day. His own preference was given to the Tories; but when he told one of his confidential servants that he thought the Tories were more friendly to the royal prerogative than the Whigs, that statesman quickly answered, ' Yes, but your Majesty is not King of the Tories.' At the end of his reign, the anger of the British nation against the French King, who, on the death of James II., had presumed to dispose of the Crown of England, united all parties in the King's favor.

The mind of Queen Anne was for a long time absolutely directed by Marlborough and Godolphin; but when the Duchess of Marlborough, from partiality to the Whigs and regard for her son-in-law, Sunderland,

had given a preponderance to the Whigs in the Cabinet,
the Tory prejudices of the Queen made her revolt
against this predominance, and by skilful intrigues Lord
Bolingbroke, Harley, and Mrs. Masham obtained complete power over the domestic and foreign policy of
Great Britain. Yet this superiority did not rest upon
any secure foundation. Harley was a skilful manager
of Parliamentary interests, and St. John an eloquent
orator, always able to command the cheers of his supporters; but they were bitterly hostile to each other.
Harley wished to support the Protestant succession, St.
John to pave the way for a Popish Pretender. Harley
aspired to an earldom, Bolingbroke could not be content
with a less dignity. Queen Anne thought to finish the
strife by making Bolingbroke Lord High Treasurer in
the place of Harley ; but in the very agony of the contest, Queen Anne died, and in place of a war of succession England fell into the hands of the Whigs, and
welcomed, amid the joy of the Dissenters, a German
Elector, as King of Great Britain. The Church recon-
ciled itself to a Protestant prince, and the Dissenters
readily promised to support the Church, as a barrier
against a Jacobite revolution.

Lord Oxford and Lord Bolingbroke had quarrelled
whether one or both should be Earls; but Robert Walpole, a country gentleman of Norfolk, had the sagacity
to perceive that the rule of Great Britain was about to
pass from the House of Lords to the House of Commons. He refused the title of Earl and the white staff
of Lord High Treasurer. As First Lord of the Treasury in the House of Commons, he ruled England for
more than twenty years ; and when at last he retired
to the House of Lords he said to Pulteney, who had
accepted the title of Earl of Bath, ' You and I, my

Lord, are now two of the most insignificant fellows in England.'

The next great leader of the House of Commons was William Pitt, like Walpole and like Churchill, a member of a country gentleman's family. William Pitt, unlike Henry Fox, who regarded money more than power, was bold, disinterested, and lofty in his aims. He said of his chief, the Duke of Newcastle, ' The Duke of Newcastle lent me his majority to carry on the Government.' He commanded his expeditions against France by placing a sheet of paper over the orders he gave, and leaving at the bottom of the page on which they were written only room for the signatures of the Lords of the Admiralty. In contradiction to his former declamations against Hanover, he gave large subsidies to Frederick of Prussia; and when he got possession of Canada said, ' I have conquered America in Germany.'

When Lord Chatham disappeared, the Tories obtained a majority in the Cabinet. They lost America; and, under the guidance of William Pitt the younger, fought against frenzy embodied in the democracy of France. By playing on the fears of England they were enabled to make gigantic efforts, and to raise her debt from one hundred and thirty millions to eight hundred millions. The two athletes who contended on the floor of the House of Commons were Pitt and Fox. Pitt, like his father, had the power of commanding men; his ruinous policy did not prevent his obtaining in the House of Commons attached friends, unbounded admiration, and a majority of two-thirds of the representatives of the people.'

Fox was a great speaker, and, in the words of Burke, the greatest debater the world ever saw. Not place or

power, but reputation as an orator, was the object of
his ambition, as he declares in one of his earliest letters to an intimate friend and relation. He inspired
affection rather than admiration. In his worst days an
observer said of his party, 'There are only forty of
them, but every one of them is ready to be hanged for
Fox.' In his earlier days, Lord Mansfield being asked
who that young man was whom he saw in Westminster
Hall, answered, 'That is the son of old Harry Fox,
with twice his parts and half his sagacity.'

These two men, Charles Fox and William Pitt, set
a proper value upon each other's great abilities. Pitt
said of Fox, ' Whenever I have made a better speech
than usual, I observe that Fox in his reply surpasses
himself.' Of Pitt's great speech on the renewal of the
war with France, Fox remarked that he had spoken
with an eloquence which Demosthenes would have admired, perhaps have envied.

The errors of Fox — his coalition with Lord North,
and his India Bill — were grave ; but the warmth of
his feelings and his passionate love of liberty should
obtain for his memory indemnity for these or even
greater faults. His affectionate temper, combined with
his love of liberty, won him the attachment of devoted
friends. His memory ought to be consecrated in the
heart of every lover of freedom throughout the globe.

I think I have shown that the faculty of leading the
House of Commons does not consist merely in making
flashy speeches, but is founded upon qualities which
entitle men to obtain as followers a majority in the
noblest assembly of freemen in the world.

CHAPTER VI.

MINISTRY OF LORD ABERDEEN. — ORIGIN OF THE CRIMEAN WAR.

I THINK I have said in a former chapter that I committed an error in resigning my office under Lord Aberdeen at the time and in the manner in which I did it.

But I had, in fact, committed a much greater error in consenting to serve under Lord Aberdeen as Prime Minister. I had served under Lord Grey and Lord Melbourne before I became Prime Minister, and I served under Lord Palmerston after I had been Prime Minister. In no one of these cases did I find any difficulty in allying subordination with due counsel and co-operation. But, as it is proverbially said, ' Where there is a will, there is a way,' so in political affairs the converse is true, ' Where there is no will, there is no way.'

As an instance of failure, I may mention that Lord Aberdeen earnestly wished to preserve peace between Russia and Turkey. I had pointed out a way in which this might be done. The Austrian Government had framed a note of conciliation, which the Emperor of Russia had accepted as a settlement of all difficulties. I proposed to Lord Clarendon that the Turkish Government should be told that if they would accept this note, *totidem verbis*, we could arrange a peace between

Turkey and Russia; but that if Turkey altered the note, we could not befriend her any further. Lord Aberdeen, although he saw very clearly that by this means peace would be insured, declined to use his authority to enforce the condition. Lord Clarendon recommended the Austrian note, but not in such a manner as to oblige Turkey to accept it, *totidem verbis*. Lord Stratford de Redcliffe failed in persuading the Turkish Ministers to accept the Austrian note. Alterations were made with a view to make it more palatable to the Oriental taste. But the Emperor of Russia, in his turn, was peremptory. In his turn he was unreasonable. He declared the alterations were made by the Padishah, a name he was wont to apply to Lord Stratford de Redcliffe. He refused the amended note, and war was the consequence.

Had I been Prime Minister at that time, I should have insisted on the acceptance of the Austrian note. I may add that had war then been averted, the Reform Bill of 1854, to which Sir James Graham had most willingly, and Lord Palmerston most reluctantly, assented, would in all probability have passed through Parliament recommended by Lord Aberdeen and his Cabinet. The franchise would have been given to 5*l.* householders; several boroughs which now return members would have been disfranchised. The gang who many years later skulked in the Cave of Adullam would never have existed, and the Reform Act would have been completed by its original promoters.

Thus has the course of history been changed by my weakness —

, Ambition should be made of sterner stuff.

Lord Aberdeen always told me that, after being Prime

Minister for a short time, he meant to make way for me, and give up the post. But somehow the moment never came for executing his intentions.

When I had accepted the mission to Vienna, with the hope of making peace, I found that neither my proposal for reducing the Russian fleet to three sail of the line, nor the French and British proposal for neutralizing the Black Sea, would be accepted by Russia. The Emperor of Austria wished to limit the Russian fleet to its former number. When I was about to depart from Vienna, the Austrian Minister of Foreign Affairs asked me to recommend the proposals of his Court to the British Ministers. I said I would advise Lord Palmerston and Lord Clarendon to continue the negotiations with Austria, but that neither Lord Palmerston nor Lord Clarendon would accept the proposals which he had mentioned to me.

I found, accordingly, that those proposals were rejected at home; and, as soon as they were rejected, I declared myself ready to continue the war, in conformity with the views of Lord Palmerston and Lord Clarendon. My notion was, that if the British Ministers had listened to the Austrian overtures, they might have replied that they could not agree to such terms; but that if Russia would make further concessions, Great Britain, with the agreement of France, would make peace on fair terms.

Had my plans prospered, the treaty of 1856, stipulating a reduction to three sail of the line, instead of a neutralization of the Black Sea, would probably have been accepted by Russia.

It is always a mistake to impose upon a great power conditions inconsistent with its sense of honor. The title of King of France, assumed by the English kings, was given up at the Peace of Amiens; and the articles relative to the demolition of Dunkirk added nothing to the security of England, however much they may have offended the pride of France.

The conduct of Lord Granville, in consenting to renounce the article of the treaty of 1856 relating to the Black Sea, has been much blamed; but it was notorious that none of the Great Powers were inclined to insist upon the retention of that part of the treaty. Had England insisted upon going to war to maintain the neutralization of the Black Sea, she would have gone to war without allies, and even Turkey would have insisted upon a large loan from the United Kingdom to enable her to sustain the expenses of war. Lord Palmerston himself did not expect that the treaty of 1856 would last fourteen years, which was the actual time of its duration. He was anxious to press upon Turkey the reform of her finances, and an honest administration of justice, which I had constantly urged in my dispatches; and he did not disguise his opinion that Great Britain could not go to war to defend a dead carcase.

The present state of affairs portends further changes. Servia and Roumania have nearly emancipated themselves from the Turkish yoke. In European Turkey, the population of the Christians increases far more rapidly than that of the Turkish subjects of the Sultan; so that, before the end of the century, Constantinople, Adrianople, and Bosnia will probably constitute the whole of the Turkish Empire in Europe; while the King of Greece, the Prince of Servia, with Belgrade for his capital, and the Prince of Roumania, with his relation the Emperor of Germany for his ally, will be the Christian Sovereigns of European Turkey.

Our only interest in this matter is to see that the Emperor of Russia observes the remaining articles of the treaty of 1856, and that the interests of trade are not injured by new treaties of commerce imposing heavy duties on the import of British goods at Constantinople and other parts of the Turkish provinces.

15

CHAPTER VII.

FOREIGN POLICY FROM 1859 TO THE DEATH OF LORD PALMERSTON.

I HAVE, in the Introduction to my Speeches and Despatches, marked 'Introduction II.,' in the second volume, given an account of the general course of foreign policy conducted by me, under the auspices of Lord Palmerston, from 1859 till the death of Lord Palmerston, which occurred in October, 1865. I have only a few remarks to add to the summary of foreign affairs there given.

When we first heard of the seizure of the two Confederate Commissioners on board the 'Trent,' Lord Palmerston asked me privately what we should do. I answered shortly, quoting what Grattan said, with reference to another power, and on another occasion, 'The United States Government are very dangerous people to run away from.' Lord Palmerston immediately proposed to the Cabinet to refer to the Law Officers of the Crown the question of the seizure of the two Commissioners which had taken place on board the 'Trent.' The Law Officers gave their opinion that the seizure was not justified by the law of nations. Lord Palmerston ordered such naval and military preparations as he thought urgent. The result I have stated in Introduction II. in the following terms : 'The British Government were far from pressing hard on the United

States, and, in spite of remonstrances from Lord Grey, Lord Clanricarde, Mr. Gregory, and others, put no impediment in the way of the capture of British merchant-ships, and placed full reliance on the courts of America for redress in cases of wrongful capture by American ships of war. But when British honor was clearly assailed, as in the case of the Commissioners who were passengers in the " Trent," reparation was promptly demanded, and honorably granted. If some delay occurred in giving that reparation, it must be attributed to the anxiety which President Lincoln and Secretary Seward naturally felt to allay American indignation before they fulfilled what they felt to be an imperative international obligation.'[1] It may be said further, that after this reparation had been granted — honorably demanded, and honorably granted —the relations of the two nations, the United Kingdom and the United States, were more cordial and more friendly than they had previously been. I state this fact on the authority of Lord Lyons, at that time Minister for Great Britain at Washington.

I have further to state, that when Mr. Mason, one of the two Confederate Commissioners, came to England, I received him in my own house. He at once declared that the object of his mission was to ask for the recognition of the Southern Confederate States as an independent power. I told him for answer, that if the military operations of the Southern States had been attended with great success ; if their victories had been brilliant and decisive ; and if the powers of Europe were generally disposed to acknowledge that they had fairly acquired the position of an independent power, the

---

[1] ' Speeches and Despatches,' vol. ii. p. 249.

British Government might fairly be asked for recognition. But none of these facts were proved, and there was no case to justify the British Government in acceding to the proposal he had made.

Mr. Mason answered me that the Government of England was a wise Government, and that he would not press his proposition any further. I shall later have some comments to make on the subsequent negotiations between the Cabinet of Mr. Gladstone and the Cabinet of President Grant.

I have stated in the former Introduction that there were two grounds on which I declined to submit the question of the ' Alabama ' to arbitration by a foreign power: ' It appeared to me that we could not, consistently with our position as an independent state, allow a foreign power or state to decide either that Great Britain had been wanting in good faith, or that our own Law Officers did not understand so well as a foreign power or state the meaning of a British statute.' [1] If Mr. Adams, in his answer to me, had stated that the American Government neither wished to call in question the good faith of Great Britain, nor to deny that our own Law Officers were the best authorities to decide the meaning of a British statute ; if, I say, Mr. Adams, who is a man of high honor and unblemished character, had given me these assurances, I should at once have agreed to arbitration ; but Mr. Adams knew perfectly well that he could give me no such assurances. In fact, Mr. Fish, who succeeded Mr. Seward as Secretary of State, did not scruple to allege that Lord Palmerston and I, the Prime Minister and Secretary of State, Sir Roundell Palmer and the Law Officers of the Crown, Sir

---

[1] 'Speeches and Despatches,' vol. ii. p. 259.

Thomas Fremantle, and the Commissioners of Customs, were all guilty of falsehood and hypocrisy. But I must reserve this matter for a future chapter.

In a former volume I related the course which Lord Palmerston's Cabinet had pursued in reference to the contest which was carried on for some years with a view to establish the union, the independence, and the freedom of Italy. In a dispatch of October 27, 1860, I evinced the sympathy which the British Government felt towards the people of Italy, and confirmed, by the authority of Vattel, the maxim, ' That when a people from good reasons take up arms against an oppressor, it is but an act of justice and generosity to assist brave men in the defence of their liberties.' But I will here give the entire dispatch : —

Lord J. Russell to Sir J. Hudson.

'Foreign Office, October 27, 1860.

' SIR, — It appears that the late proceedings of the King of Sardinia have been strongly disapproved of by several of the principal Courts of Europe. The Emperor of the French, on hearing of the invasion of the Papal States by the army of General Cialdini, withdrew his Minister from Turin, expressing at the same time the opinion of the Imperial Government in condemnation of the invasion of the Roman territory.

' The Emperor of Russia has, we are told, declared in strong terms his indignation at the entrance of the army of the King of Sardinia into the Neapolitan territory, and has withdrawn his entire mission from Turin.

' The Prince Regent of Prussia has also thought it necessary to convey to Sardinia a sense of his displeasure; but he has not thought it necessary to remove the Prussian Minister from Turin.

'After these diplomatic acts, it would scarcely be just to Italy, or respectful to the other Great Powers of Europe, were the Government of Her Majesty any longer to withhold the expression of their opinions.

'In so doing, however, Her Majesty's Government have no intention to raise a dispute upon the reasons which have been given, in the name of the King of Sardinia, for the invasion of the Roman and Neapolitan States. Whether or no the Pope was justified in defending his authority by means of foreign levies; whether the King of the Two Sicilies, while still maintaining his flag at Capua and Gaeta, can be said to have abdicated — are not the arguments upon which Her Majesty's Government propose to dilate.

'The large questions which appear to them to be at issue are these: Were the people of Italy justified in asking the assistance of the King of Sardinia to relieve them from governments with which they are discontented, and was the King of Sardinia justified in furnishing the assistance of his arms to the people of the Roman and Neapolitan States?

'There appear to have been two motives which have induced the people of the Roman and Neapolitan States to have joined willingly in the subversion of their governments. The first of these was, that the governments of the Pope and the King of the Two Sicilies provided so ill for the administration of justice, the protection of personal liberty, and the general welfare of their people, that their subjects looked forward to the overthrow of their rulers as a necessary preliminary to all improvements in their condition.

'The second motive was, that a conviction had spread since the year 1849, that the only manner in which Italians could secure their independence of foreign control was by forming one strong government for the whole of Italy.

'The struggle of Charles Albert in 1848, and the sympathy which the present King of Sardinia has shown for the Italian cause, have naturally caused the association of the name of Victor Emmanuel with the single authority under which the Italians aspire to live.

'Looking at the question in this view, Her Majesty's Government must admit that the Italians themselves are the best judges of their own interests.

'That eminent jurist, Vattel, when discussing the lawfulness of the assistance given by the United Provinces to the Prince of Orange when he invaded England, and overturned the throne of James II., says: "The authority of the Prince of Orange had doubtless an influence on the deliberation of the States-General, but *it* did not lead them to the commission of an act of injustice; for when a people from good reasons take up arms against an oppressor, it is but an act of justice and generosity to assist brave men in the defence of their liberties."

'Therefore, according to Vattel, the question resolves itself into this: Did the people of Naples and of the Roman States take up arms against their governments for good reasons?

'Upon this grave matter Her Majesty's Government hold that the people in question are themselves the best judges of their own affairs. Her Majesty's Government do not feel justified in declaring that the people of Southern Italy had not good reasons for throwing off their allegiance to their former governments; Her Majesty's Government cannot, therefore, pretend to blame the King of Sardinia for assisting them. There remains, however, a question of fact. It is asserted by

the partisans of the fallen governments that the people
of the Roman States were attached to the Pope, and
the people of the kingdom of Naples to the dynasty
of Francis II., but that Sardinian agents and foreign
adventurers have by force and intrigue subverted the
thrones of those sovereigns. It is difficult, however,
to believe, after the astonishing events that have been
seen, that the Pope and the King of the Two Sicilies
possessed the love of their people. How was it, one
must ask, that the Pope found it impossible to levy a
Roman army, and that he was forced to rely almost
entirely upon foreign mercenaries? How did it happen,
again, that Garibaldi conquered nearly all Sicily with
two thousand men, and marched from Reggio to Naples
with five thousand? How but from the universal disaffection of the people of the Two Sicilies?

'Neither can it be said that this testimony of the
popular will was capricious or causeless. Forty years
ago the Neapolitan people made an attempt regularly
and temperately to reform their government under the
reigning dynasty. The Powers of Europe, assembled
at Laybach, resolved, with the exception of England, to
put down this attempt by force. It was put down, and
a large foreign army of occupation was left in the Two
Sicilies to maintain social order. In 1848, the Neapolitan people again attempted to secure liberty under the
Bourbon dynasty, but their best patriots atoned, by an
imprisonment of ten years, for the offence of endeavoring to free their country. What wonder, then, that in
1860 the Neapolitan mistrust and resentment should
throw off the Bourbons, as in 1688 England had thrown
off the Stuarts?

' It must be admitted, undoubtedly, that the severance
of the ties which bind together a sovereign and his sub-

jects is in itself a misfortune. Notions of allegiance become confused; the succession to the throne is disputed; adverse parties threaten the peace of society; rights and pretensions are opposed to each other, and mar the harmony of the state. Yet it must be acknowledged, on the other hand, that the Italian revolution has been conducted with singular temper and forbearance. The subversion of existing power has not been followed, as is too often the case, by an outburst of popular vengeance. The extreme views of democrats have nowhere prevailed. Public opinion has checked the excesses of the public triumph. The venerated forms of constitutional monarchy have been associated with the name of a prince who represents an ancient and glorious dynasty. Such have been the causes and concomitant circumstances of the revolution of Italy. Her Majesty's Government can see no sufficient ground for the severe censure with which Austria, France, Prussia, and Russia have visited the acts of the King of Sardinia. Her Majesty's Government will turn their eyes rather to the gratifying prospect of a people building up the edifice of their liberties, and consolidating the work of ·their independence, amid the sympathies and good wishes of Europe.

 'I am, &c.,

   ' (Signed) J. RUSSELL.

' P. S. — You are at liberty to give a copy of this dispatch to Count Cavour.'

It was in acknowledgment of this dispatch that I was presented, by the generous kindness of some Milanese gentlemen, with a gift for which I am proud here to record my gratitude, — a beautiful marble statue by

Carlo Romano, representing young Italy; she holds in her hands a diadem embossed with the arms of the various Italian States, thenceforward to be one. This statue has ever since adorned my study.

In the same spirit I rejected, with the assent of Lord Palmerston and the Cabinet, and with the sanction of the Queen, a proposal of the French Government that the British navy should concur with that of France in preventing the passage of Garibaldi from Sicily to the mainland of Italy. On March 30, 1861, I wrote the following dispatch to the Marquis d'Azeglio:—

'Foreign Office, March 30, 1861.

'M. Le Marquis,—I have had the honor to receive your letter of the 19th inst., informing me that the National Parliament has voted, and the King, your august Sovereign, has sanctioned, a law by virtue of which His Majesty Victor Emmanuel II. assumes, for himself and for his successors, the title of "King of Italy."

' Having laid your communication before Her Majesty the Queen, I am commanded to state to you that Her Majesty, acting on the principle of respecting the independence of the nations of Europe, will receive you as the Envoy of Victor Emmanuel II., King of Italy.

' Corresponding instructions will be given to Sir James Hudson, Her Majesty's Envoy Extraordinary at the Court of Turin.

' I request you, M. le Marquis, to accept the assurances of my highest consideration.

' I have, &c.,
' (Signed)   J. Russell.'

I am happy to say that my dispatch of October 27,

1860, was warmly approved by Count Cavour and General Garibaldi, who, with the magnanimity of great men, instead of attributing to themselves the whole merit of rescuing Italy from her centuries of servitude and depression, and securing to her the blessings of independence and freedom, were ever willing to acknowledge with gratitude the efforts made by British statesmen to help on the good work.

The American Civil War was a calamitous event. Lord Campbell, then Lord Chancellor, was of opinion that the Government could not do otherwise than recognize the belligerent rights of the Southern States, important as they were, both in regard to the number of States, the extent of their commerce, and the population arrayed against the central Government.

We, therefore, proclaimed neutrality as the policy we ought to pursue. In a single instance, that of the escape of the 'Alabama,' we fell into error. I thought it my duty to wait for the report of the Law Officers of the Crown; but I ought to have been satisfied with the opinion of Sir Robert Collier, and to have given orders to detain the 'Alabama' at Birkenhead.

When another ship was constructed with a view to break the blockade of the American navy, I gave orders to detain it. I should have ordered the prosecution of the owners of the vessel, had not the principal Law Officer of the Crown given me reason to think that it would fail in an English court of justice. I, therefore, obtained the sanction of the Cabinet to purchase the two 'rams,' as they were called, which were intended for hostile purposes against the United States.

With regard to the good faith with which our neutrality was observed, I refer to the opinion of Mr. Grote, who was not unduly partial to the English Government, and whose testimony I believe to be founded in truth and justice. Writing to Sir George Lewis, December 29, 1862, he says : —

'The perfect neutrality of England in this destructive civil war now raging in America appears to me almost a phenomenon in political history.

'No such forbearance has been shown during the political history of the last two centuries. It is the single case in which the English Government and public, generally so over-meddlesome, have displayed some prudent and commendable forbearance, in spite of great temptations to the contrary. And the way in which the Northern Americans have requited such forbearance is alike silly and disgusting. I never expected to have lived to think of them so unfavorably as I do at present. Amidst their very difficult present circumstances, they have manifested little or nothing of those qualities which inspire sympathy and esteem, and very much of all the contrary qualities; and among the worst of all their manifestations is their appetite for throwing the blame of their misfortunes on guiltless England.' [1]

Upon Lord Palmerston's death, in 1865, the Queen was pleased to confer upon me the office of First Lord of the Treasury. When I had been received by the Cabinet in that capacity, I proposed to them to consider whether it was possible with public advantage to confer the right of voting upon the best of the working-classes. This was agreed to; and it was likewise decided that it would be best ·to separate the question of the franchise from that of the disfranchisement of

---

[1] 'Personal Life of George Grote,' p. 262.

boroughs. After much inquiry, we agreed to fix the suffrages of boroughs at an occupation of 7*l.* value.

The House of Commons did not agree with us as to the separation of the question of suffrage from that of disfranchisement. We had not quite made up our minds as to the shape in which this disfranchisement should be adopted.

Our whole course, however, was disturbed by the formation of a party which aimed, not so much at the improvement of a Reform Bill, as the defeat of the Ministry. They owe the name by which they are known to the wit of Mr. Bright, who likened them to the occupiers of the Cave of Adullam. The band may be said to have been divided into three columns or gangs, the first consisting of the selfish, the second of the timid, and the third of those who were both selfish and timid. They had a leader, who, like the Achitophel of Dryden, was

> Sagacious, bold, and turbulent of wit.

Of him, as of Achitophel — supposing his object was to destroy the Ministry — it might also be said —

> To further this, Achitophel unites
> The malcontents of all the Israelites ;
> Whose differing parties he could wisely join,
> For several ends to serve the same design.

There were no doubt some honest men in the Cave of Adullam ; but, upon the whole, I have never, in my long political life, known a party so utterly destitute of consistent principle or of patriotic end ; they were indifferent to the state of the suffrage, or the disfranchisement of boroughs, provided their own selfish objects were attained.

When these bandits, uniting themselves to the Tories,

had put the Government in a minority, the Cabinet thought it right to offer their resignation. It was not that they could not bear a defeat on a detail of the Reform Bill, but that it was obvious that the band of Adullam would never be satisfied till, by wiles and stratagems, they had driven the Ministry from office.

Of the three gangs which issued from the Cave of Adullam, the timid inspire pity, the selfish indignation, the timid and selfish contempt.

CHAPTER VIII.

REFORM BILL OF 1867. — MR. GLADSTONE'S SPEECH ON
THE IRISH CHURCH. — GENERAL ELECTION. — CHANGE
OF MINISTRY. — RETIREMENT FROM THE LEAD THAT
I HAD HELD SINCE 1834.

WHEN Lord Derby and Mr. Disraeli succeeded me and
Mr. Gladstone as First Lord of the Treasury and
Chancellor of the Exchequer, in 1865, they had before
them a task of no small difficulty. They had met our
proposal to admit the working-men who lived in houses
of 7*l.* value with every kind of obstruction, cavil, and
quibble. They had maintained strongly that there
ought to be no reduction, or, as Mr. Disraeli styled it,
no degradation of the franchise. They had raised the
objection that there was no disfranchisement of boroughs,
and therefore the measure could not be styled a complete Reform Bill. They had, lastly, suggested the
objection that rated value, not actual value, ought to
be taken as the test.

This question had been fully considered when the
original Reform Bill was introduced in 1831. It was
then found that rated value furnished a very uncertain
criterion, and that while in one borough 6*l.* rated value
meant an actual value of 8*l.* or 9*l.*, in half a dozen
other boroughs it meant 10*l.* or 12*l.* Lord Derby was
a man who might have been deterred by these difficulties from proceeding with his task; Mr. Disraeli

had no such fears. . After a time he resolved to disregard what was called a 'hard and fast line,' and to admit every rated householder, though he might be rated at only 1*l.* or 10*s.*, to an equal suffrage with the 10*l.* householder.

Some of the Tory leaders have not only protested as loudly as Mr. Disraeli against any reduction of the suffrage, but have conscientiously felt the truth of the objections which Mr. Disraeli only assumed as a convenient cloak. Three members of the Cabinet — Lord Cranborne, Lord Carnarvon, and General Peel — left the Cabinet. Relieved from these inconvenient colleagues, who were troubled with a conscience, Mr. Disraeli threw his net over Lord Derby and Lord Stanley, and held out the finality of household suffrage as a reason for its adoption.

Disregarding, as Mr. Disraeli and Lord Derby disregarded, all the principles which they had pretended to uphold, it is clear to me that the right of voting for a representative body can only be founded upon one of two principles. One is, the Radical principle that every adult male who is subject to the laws of a country ought to have a share in electing its representatives. The other is, the Whig principle that the persons endowed with the right of voting for the members of the House of Commons, by whom the whole state of the country is guided and directed, ought to be persons qualified by property and education for the discharge of so important a trust.

Lord Derby's Reform Bill answered neither of these descriptions. It did not comply with the Radical requirement, as hundreds of thousands of adult males were not admitted to the franchise. It did not comply with the Whig test, as many thousands of rated householders were in a state of ignorance and dependence.

In short, the measure was, as Lord Derby truly called it, a leap in the dark. Still, it was brought forward by a Government which had always professed Conservative principles, and it could not safely be resisted. I therefore advised my friend Mr. Forster, who was then a leading man of the House of Commons, to support the measure, and to persuade all those politically connected with him to do so likewise. My Whig friends, in a small committee, advised me to withhold this opinion from the public. I myself wished to practise no concealment on the subject. Mr. Gladstone had, in the same session which saw the introduction of the Reform Bill of 1867, made an admirable, eloquent, and convincing speech on the Irish Church. This speech produced a profound impression on the minds of the new electors. I had myself, for reasons which shall be mentioned hereafter, retired from the leadership of the Whig-Radical party. Mr. Disraeli's recent conversion had won as little favor on his behalf as had been won on behalf of Sir Robert Peel by his conversion on the Roman Catholic question and on the repeal of the Corn-laws. So that, at the general election in the autumn of 1868, the Ministry were defeated by a majority of over one hundred. Mr. Disraeli resigned without meeting Parliament, and Mr. Gladstone was desired by the Queen to form a Ministry.

This task was performed with little tact or discrimination. As Mr. Gladstone did not himself assume the office of Chancellor of the Exchequer, he ought to have placed in that post a confidential friend on whose judgment he could rely. Mr. Cardwell was admirably fitted for the post; he was sent to the War Office. Mr. Lowe was made Chancellor of the Exchequer. Mr. Bruce was well qualified to organize and direct the education of the poorer classes throughout the country; he was sent to the Home Office, where he soon became unpopular — unjustly, no doubt, for his conduct was prudent and judicious; but still he was not the man for that office.

I will go no farther. Lord Clarendon was admirably qualified to be Secretary of State for Foreign Affairs; and some other posts were well filled.

I cannot think that I was mistaken in giving way. to Mr. Gladstone as head of the Whig-Radical party of England. During Lord Palmerston's Ministry I had every reason to admire the boldness and the judgment with which he directed our finances. I had no reason to suppose that he was less attached than I was to national honor; that he was less proud than I was of the achievements of our nation by sea and land; that he disliked the extension of our Colonies; or that his measures would tend to reduce the great and glorious Empire of which he was put in charge to a manufactory of cotton cloth and a market for cheap goods, with an army and navy reduced by paltry savings to a standard of weakness and inefficiency.

CHAPTER IX.

JUSTICE TO IRELAND.

THE question of the government of Ireland is a very large one. I think I cannot do better than lay down the propositions which I wish to establish with a view to the better government of that country.

I. That murders in Ireland are not the insulated crimes of persons excited by covetousness or revenge, but the deliberate acts of a powerful confederacy which, in defiance of the Queen and Parliament, orders the infliction of a criminal law more formidable than the law of the State. This proposition can be demonstrated both by authority and by numerous instances.

II. That the Roman Catholic clergy, in the capacity of parish priests, have great sway over the minds of the people of Ireland ; but being entirely dependent upon the voluntary offerings of their flocks, are, from sympathy or from fear, unwilling to appear as the prosecutors of the confederacy that directs and executes murders.

III. That the remedy for these evils is to be sought in such a reform of the criminal law as would place convictions for murder in the hands of a majority of the jury ; and, secondly, in making a provision for the Roman Catholic parish priests of Ireland out of the revenues of the Protestant Church, after the expiry of life-interests, with a provisional grant in the interval from the Consolidated Fund.

IV. That the Secretary of State for the Home Department of Great Britain ought to have in Ireland the same powers of administration which he exercises in England and in Scotland.

V. That Scotland, before the Union of England and Scotland, suffered from evils not very different from those to which Ireland is now exposed, but by the wisdom of Lord Somers and Lord Chatham, the Lowlands of Scotland have been led to prosperity, and the Highlands of Scotland have been pacified. A similar policy applied to Ireland will probably be attended with similar effects.

VI. Home Rule must be met with as peremptory a refusal as that which Lord Grey and Lord Althorp gave to repeal of the Union in 1830.

I. In Mr. Nassau Senior's 'Journals upon Ireland,' there occurs, in the narrative of the year 1852, a very interesting conversation between Lord Rosse and Mr. Senior, in which Lord Rosse is asked what he would do if he were Minister, and had a fair working majority. After stating that he ' would make the Disarming Act general and permanent, and allow very few exceptions,' Lord Rosse goes on to say: 'I would then reform the stipendiary magistracy. On this institution the security of the country mainly depends. As soon as an outrage has been committed it is the duty of the stipendiary magistrate to collect into a focus the slight and transitory indications, which, if acutely perceived and sedulously followed up, will lead to detection. No function requires more zeal, vigor, and intelligence. The men selected for it are generally elderly *roués*, with broken fortunes and damaged reputations, who are made stipendiaries because their patrons do not venture to make them any thing else. I have implored Lord Lieutenant

after Lord Lieutenant not to allow so important an office
to be thus jobbed away. All that I could get from any
one of them were promises that the appointments should
be as little bad as they could make them. . . . The
appointments should be made in England, or, if in Ireland, two persons should concur, and I would require
them to be chosen from the police — that is to say,
from the officers of the constabulary. This would secure their having some experience in the investigation
of crime, and would, besides, raise the character of the
police force. . . . I would endeavor to extend the
field of summary convictions. Juries are fit only for
countries in which the people are the friends of the law.
In Ireland it is difficult to find a jury that dares, or even
wishes, to do its duty. Where juries must be retained,
I would adopt the Scotch plan, and make them decide
by a majority, and make it penal to reveal how each
juryman voted. Among the mischiefs of requiring a
unanimous verdict is its publicity. . . . The prevention
and punishment of crime are all that we want. Emigration will restore the proportion between population
and subsistence. Under the National School system
education is rapidly spreading. The physical resources
of Ireland are vast and almost untouched. But we are
under two different and repugnant systems of law. One
is enacted by Parliament and enforced by the courts,
the other is concocted in the whiskey-shop and executed
by the assassin. And the law of the people is far better
enforced than that of the Government. Those who
break it are generally sure to be detected, for their
offences are generally public; the punishment is as
severe as any that man can inflict or suffer, and the
chances of escaping it are few. The popular law, therefore, is obeyed, the Government law is disregarded.

Give us merely security. Let the proprietor be master of his land, the manufacturer of his capital, and the laborer of his strength and skill, and the virtues which we now seem to want — industry, frugality, and providence — will spring up as soon as they can depend on their reward.'[1]

Three examples may be here given of murders in Ireland. The first is extracted from Mr. Trench's 'Realities of Irish Life.'[2]

Mr. Trench, in his 'Realities of Irish Life,' relates the occurrence of a robbery at the house of a Mr. Hall, in the year 1838. He goes on to say : —

'Thenceforth, without any reasonable cause that I could ascertain, Mr. Hall became exceedingly unpopular and obnoxious to the peasantry.'

He then proceeds, with reference to the same year : —

'A few months after this occurrence, on the 18th of May, a beautiful bright sunny day, at noon, I was riding with a friend to the sessions at Borrisokane. I heard a faint report at a little distance in the fields as of a gun or pistol, but took no notice of it, when, almost immediately afterwards, a man came running up a lane to meet us, saying, " Oh! sir, Mr. Hall has just been shot."

' " Shot!" cried I, pulling up my horse ; " do you mean murdered ?"

' " Oh! yes, sir," replied the man, " he is lying there in the field."

' " Is he dead ?" I asked.

' " Stone dead!" was the man's reply ; and as he said so I never shall forget the strange mixture of horror and of triumph which pervaded his countenance.

---

[1] Nassau Senior's 'Ireland,' vol. ii. pp. 32-34.

[2] 'Realities of Irish Life.' By W. S. Trench. Boston : Roberts Bros.

'I turned to a gentleman of well-known courage, and a daring rider, and said, "Can we do nothing, Mr. Smith? The murderer cannot have gone far. Surely we might make a circuit round the place across the country; and though no one will tell us which way he ran, we may by this means come up with him or see him. We are both well-mounted and armed — let us try."

'"Hush! my dear sir," replied he, "the murderer never ran; that would at once betray him. He is surely in the field with us at this moment, and is probably one of those now looking at the body and expressing his wonder at who did it."'

Mr. Trench proceeds to describe the murder: —

'Mr. Hall was still walking in the fields, enjoying the freshness of this sunny day in May. The young man came up unperceived within twenty yards of him. Mr. Hall heard him, and turned round and faced him. The murderer walked on, still without speaking or showing his pistol, straight up to Mr. Hall. Mr. Hall was amazed; but seeing him still coming steadily and silently on, he half drew his sword-cane, at last suspecting that mischief must be intended. The man still continuing to approach, Mr. Hall sprang back a step or two in order to get his sword-cane free, and in doing so stumbled over a tussock and fell. The young man then went up, and before Mr. Hall could get up or recover himself, he put the pistol down close to his head and shot him dead upon the spot. The moment he had done so he threw the pistol into the adjoining hedge, walked quietly to meet his companion, put his hands into his pockets, never left the ground, and was one of those whom we afterwards saw standing near the body.

'Such was the story as told by the man who had been originally hired to murder Mr. Hall, but who had now turned informer; and his testimony was corroborated by a chain of evidence so clear and conclusive, that not a doubt of its truth was left upon the mind of a single grand juror who heard him.

'The trial was rather a peculiar one; and, contrary to general expectation, the judge's charge was decidedly in favor of the prisoner. The jury were evidently puzzled, but they threw the benefit of the doubts entertained by the majority in favor of the prisoner at the bar, as they were justly bound to do; and it was afterwards openly announced that eleven were for the acquittal, and only one for a conviction. Nothing could turn this man from his unwavering belief that the prisoner had done the deed; and after the usual time the jury was discharged, and the prisoner remanded to gaol.

'Such scenes as these could not fail to produce a strong effect upon the gentry resident around, and urgent letters were written by myself and other gentlemen to the Government; and at last a "Special Commission" was ordered at Clonmel for the trial of several Ribbon cases, and of Mr. Hall's murderer in particular, of the guilt of whom the authorities had not a doubt.

'The Special Commission was looked upon, and justly so, as a very formidable affair. The judges chosen by the Government to preside were Judges Doherty and Pennefather. They sat together, as is usual in a Special Commission. Almost all the gentlemen in the county attended, and were prepared to serve as jurors; and Clonmel, where the Commission was held, was crowded to excess. The opening of the Commission had a very solemn effect. The first trial was that of Mr. Hall's murderer. The prisoner was again brought to the bar and arraigned; he was paler than when tried before at Nenagh, but he still preserved the same impassive resolution. The grand jury was duly sworn, the bills were found, and then came the swearing-in of the petty jury who were to try the case, and on whom the cause of justice and the life of the prisoner depended. The prisoner was allowed twenty challenges peremptorily, and as many more as he could show cause for. It was an exciting scene, and great quickness and knowledge of character were required on the part of the prisoner's counsel and attorney. Of course their object, so far as their right of challenge would allow them, was to challenge and reject all the firm, fair, and upright men in the county, and to place upon the jury the timid, or those whose sympathies, from political, religious, or other reasons, might be supposed to lean towards the prisoner.

' But they had not much time to decide. As the name of each juror resounded through the court, and the person called answered to his name, the crier handed the small Testament to the man now about to be sworn, and said aloud, slowly and solemnly, " Prisoner, look upon the juror, — juror, look upon the prisoner ; " and then he commenced the oath. At this moment, and with no more time to consult or determine than I have stated, the prisoner's attorney cried out in a loud voice, " Challenge ! " if he thought the juror likely to be unfavorable to his cause. The effect was very striking. And as gentleman after gentleman were " challenged," it became a decided compliment to be rejected. At length my name was called. I answered, came forward to the front, and took the Testament in my hand. I felt that all eyes were upon me. It was well known that the murder had been committed near my residence, and that I had been almost present at the scene. " Prisoner, look upon the juror, — juror, look upon the prisoner." We both looked steadily at each other, and just as I thought the oath was about to be administered, " Challenge ! " resounded through the court. I cannot describe my emotion as I felt relieved from the onus of such a trial.

' At length a jury — and by no means a bad one — was sworn. So many good jurors had attended, that the prisoner had no great choice ; his challenges were soon exhausted, and a jury — admitted in general to be a fair one — proceeded now to listen to the intensely interesting statement of the Attorney-General, who began to open his case. The trial proceeded with all the grave solemnity which was suited to such an occasion. The witnesses gave their evidence clearly, consistently, and well ; nor did the cross-examination of the prisoner's counsel, though conducted in the ablest manner, shake their testimony in the least. All who heard the evidence plainly saw that a conviction must ensue.

' The disclosures which the informer had necessarily made, when examined on the previous trial, gave the prisoner's counsel a great advantage over him. He now knew the whole of the informer's story, and made the most of his knowledge in his cross-examination ; but still he failed to shake the frightful truthfulness of his evidence. One scene struck me much. After the witness had detailed how he had himself undertaken to be the murderer, and had twice stolen behind Mr. Hall for the purpose of shooting him in the back, and had only given up his design because he fancied it was " unlucky," the prisoner's counsel said, " Then it was not your conscience which smote you ? "

' " *Not a bit !* " replied the man.

' " And you stole up behind the poor old gentleman to shoot him for money ? " said the lawyer.

' " *I did.*"

' " I suppose you would do any thing for money ? "

' " *I would*," replied the man, quite unappalled, and growing desperate.

' The lawyer still continued to excite him.

' " You would shoot your *father* for money, I suppose ? "

' " *I would*," exclaimed the man furiously.

' " *Or your mother ?* "

' " *I would.*"

' " *Or your sister ?* "

' " *I would.*"

' " *Or your brother ?* "

' " *Ay, or yourself either !* " cried the infuriated ruffian.

' The prisoner was condemned, and executed a fortnight after his conviction.

' Tipperary for a long time after was quiet.' [1]

I will now give two instances of murder where no conviction took place.

But before doing this, I will take an instance of a person who just missed falling a victim to a plan for his assassination.

Mr. Nicholson, being a man of large means, spent 40,000*l.* in endeavors to improve his estate by fencing, draining, restoring the fertility of districts left almost barren by the exhaustion of overcropping, and the removal of cabins left vacant by emigration.

Casserly the elder occupied a miserable cabin, which was the residence of Casserly himself and his wife,

---

1 ' Realities of Irish Life,' p. 51.

a married daughter, with her husband and several children, and of an unmarried son. When this son wished to marry, Casserly proposed to remove him to a wretched hole, which was only fit for an ass, and had been occupied for that purpose. Mr. Nicholson offered young Casserly twelve guineas to enable him to emigrate, and on his refusal to accept the offer determined to remove him as a tenant. Hence the attempt to hold him up to odium, and then the attempt to murder him.

But the case which was the immediate cause of a conspiracy to assassinate Mr. Nicholson arose on a notice to quit being given to a man named Lanham, who occupied fourteen acres, at a rent of 18*l*. 10*s*., as tenant from year to year.

After being frequently defeated in courts of law, and finally in the House of Lords, Lanham resolved to obtain, if not victory, at least revenge, and hired men to murder Mr. Nicholson on his return from Dublin. On the necessary particulars being obtained, two men were told off with loaded fire-arms to await the passing of the carriage from the railway station to Mr. Nicholson's house.

The following particulars are taken from a pamphlet entitled ' A Chapter of Irish Landlordism ' : —

' On the afternoon fixed for the tragedy, Mr. Nicholson drove in an open carriage from Kells, accompanied by his niece, Miss Staples. In the rear of the carriage a seat was placed, the occupant of which — a well-armed guard, who was an ex-constable of the constabulary — sat with his back to the carriage. On previous occasions the guard was in the habit of sitting on the box-seat with the coachman ; the change of position having been made for supposed greater security. As the carriage was driven forward to the place where the intended assassins were in ambush, the change of position of the guard appears to have induced them to fire as the carriage was approaching, instead of waiting till it came up, when they might be unpleasantly confronted with the guard. This alteration of arrangement proved fatal to the success of the scheme, the guns having been discharged so that their contents completely riddled the unfortunate coachman; only two stray slugs reached Mr. Nicholson and Miss Staples; the former being struck on the forearm and the latter on the shoulder, the wound in either case not being of a dangerous character. The guard immediately fired after the assassins, whom he saw moving off, but, as it appeared, without effect. The horses, finding themselves liberated from control, commenced to plunge, but Mr. Nicholson soon obtained possession of the reins; and Miss Staples, with great presence of mind, at once went to the assistance of the guard in supporting the dying coachman. In this way the beleaguered party proceeded to their destination. These events occurred in the month of October, 1869.'

The complicity of the people with the Ribbon conspiracy seems not to admit of question. ' A thatcher, who had been at work during the day on the roof of one of the cottages, retired inside and shut himself up before the carriage came forward. An old pensioner of the family, whose father was also a dependant on Balrath House, made an observation in the early part of the day in Kells that " if the ould gentleman lived through that day he would live for ever." Another circumstance proving complicity is, that at two o'clock on the day of the attempt, a countryman in the town of Balbriggan, more than thirty miles from Balrath, announced that Mr. Nicholson had been shot. Another circumstance worth recalling was, that although the village had the appearance of being deserted up to the time of the outrage, people were seen passing in crowds immediately after the shots had been fired. With respect to the punishment of so foul and notorious a crime, several arrests were made of supposed guilty parties; but as no satisfactory evidence was procured, the prisoners were all eventually discharged.'

I wish to compare the circumstances already related with any thing that can be supposed to happen in England upon the perpetration of a similar crime. Could any attempt at assassination occur in the case of a gentleman returning in his carriage to his country house from the railway station? Would not all the neighborhood be alarmed? and would not the assassins be captured and made subject to the law? Is it possible that when a land-owner has been murdered, his murderer should gaze quietly on the dead body and mix familiarly with all the laborers in the field?

What is now the state of affairs at Balrath?

In December, 1872, Mr. Nicholson died at a good old age, the establishment was broken up, and Mr. Christopher Nicholson, the present owner, has gone to reside in England.

I will further remark, that a pair of white gloves have been given to the judge at Kells, but that those gloves would have more properly been given to the chiefs of the Ribbon confederacy in Ireland; for to them it is owing that Mr. Christopher Nicholson is safe in England, and has not been murdered in the county of Meath. I must, however, ask how it is that, more than seventy years after the Union with England, the supreme force in Ireland is vested, not in the judges

and ministers of the law, but in the Ribbon confederacy? Remedies are not far to seek. If giving to the
majority of a jury, as in Scotland, the power of conviction should prove inadequate, let tribunals be created
of men sufficiently intelligent to weigh the value of
evidence, and sufficiently independent not to be swayed
by relationship with the criminal, or fear of the Ribbon
confederacy.

Another instance of a crime perpetrated with impunity by the members of the Ribbon confederacy oc-.
curred the year before last. Mrs. Neill, who lived in
her own house, at 5 Sydenham Terrace, Rathmines, a
suburb of Dublin, had interfered in a dispute between
two of her tenants. The dispute arose about a right
of way. The cattle of one tenant having trespassed on
the land of another, Mrs. Neill sanctioned a proposal
to put a gate to prevent the trespass; and as the other
tenant refused to submit she served on him herself a
process of ejectment. It was ascertained at the office
of Mrs. Neill's solicitor that an affidavit of the service
of ejectment would be made on a certain day. On the
day previous to that arranged for making the affidavit,
which was on May 27, 1872, two men knocked at her
door at Rathmines. Mrs. Neill hearing the knock
went herself to open the door; upon her doing so one
of the men fired a pistol at her breast, causing her immediate death. No legal evidence could be procured
of this murder. The coroner's verdict of ' Wilful murder against some person or persons unknown ' was
returned, and no one was made amenable for the
crime.

It might be supposed that so horrible a crime, committed in open day, in a suburb of the great city of
Dublin, would have spread terror and alarm, and that

the Government, by large offers of reward and by extraordinary means, would have sought to punish so horrible an outrage. But the crime seems to have been passed over as an ordinary occurrence, and the criminal law of the Ribbon society seems to have had its sentence of death executed without difficulty, and the crime was allowed to pass without special inquiry. If the late Government of Ireland earned approbation by the abolition of a Church Establishment which had no root in the affections of the people, and by giving a remedy to tenants who are evicted from their homes without any justifiable cause, so much the more is it necessary to carry into effect, with strictness and impartiality, that protection of life and property which is the first duty of a Government. No hospitality, however princely, no magnificence of banquets and of balls, no urbanity of manners, no observance of state ceremonials, can excuse a Government for allowing murder to be committed with impunity at the will of a lawless confederacy, whose agents are unpunished, and whose orders seem to be implicitly obeyed. At the end of the seventeenth century, Scotland was infested by troops and bands of men to whom murder, incest, and robbery were familiar. The Government of Great Britain knew its duties and performed them with resolution. Before many years had expired the farmers and manufacturers of Scotland could pursue their occupations in peace, and assert the rights of property with advantage to the owner of land and his tenants. In 1780, law and order were observed in Scotland. In 1872, law and order could not run their course in Ireland.

We shall be told, no doubt, by a powerful portion of the press of London, that the people of Ireland are incurable barbarians, and that the spirit of anarchy cannot be exorcised by any magic which human wit can devise. But there is no truth in this allegation. An admirable body of constabulary, devised by Sir Robert Peel, performs its duties with fidelity and discipline; the administration of the Poor-law, opposed by the great demagogue of Ireland, works its way with regularity and directs its machinery more efficiently than a similar administration in England. The judges perform their functions without disturbance; and although they may be hooted or burned in effigy, if they perform their duties as the judges of Queen Victoria, and not in compliance with the dictates of a seditious press, their judgments are carried into effect without resistance.

I now proceed to my second proposition: that the Roman Catholic clergy, in the capacity of parish priests, have great sway over the minds of the people of Ireland, but, being entirely dependent upon the voluntary offerings of their flocks, are, from sympathy or from fear, unwilling to appear as the prosecutors of the confederacy that directs and executes murders.

It should be the study of wise rulers to govern the states over which they are supreme according to the disposition of the nations they have to govern, but always in such a manner as to foster their virtues and to repress their vices.

Mr. Froude, in the able work upon Ireland which he has published, has observed that after the conquest of Ireland by the Normans, the difficulty of Ireland from first to last has been 'because the effort of the conquerors was to govern the Irish, not as a vassal province, but as a free nation; to extend the forms of English liberty — her trials by jury, her local courts, her Parliaments — to a people essentially unfit for them; and,

17

while governing Ireland, to teach her at the same time the harder lesson — how to govern herself.'[1]

In considering the Irish character, I have to observe that the Irish have two remarkable virtues and two prominent defects. The two virtues are, a sincere love of religion and a strong sense of justice; the two defects are, vanity and pugnacity. It has been the mistake of the English rulers of Ireland to check, to curb, and to misguide the sense of religion and the love of justice, and to indulge the vanity and pugnacity of the nation. In the reign of Henry II. titles were granted by Pope Adrian to the King of England. The Roman Catholic religion continued without interruption to be the faith of the nation till the period of the Reformation; but at the period of the Reformation, Elizabeth, without any preparatory steps, decreed that the nation should be Protestant. The Reformation deepened the animosity which the Irish felt towards England. To the animosities of race and the dispossession of the Irish, guilty of rebellion, from their lands, were added the animosity of an oppressed religion. Down to the year 1778, a priest who celebrated the mass according to his own faith and that of the people to whom he administered was liable to imprisonment for his offence. Lord Shelburne, the great-grandfather of the present Marquis of Lansdowne, when Secretary of State, was obliged to implore the mercy of the Crown to save a priest from the legal penalty which he had incurred by saying mass. The Protestant Church had always been a sickly exotic, and had never taken root in the soil.

It was obvious that when, in 1830, the Whigs came

---

[1] 'The English in Ireland,' by J. A. Froude, vol. i. p. 18.

into power, the difficulty of the Irish Church was to be encountered; and Lord Ripon was not wrong in stating that the appointment of a Commission to inquire was equivalent to an Act of Parliament to abolish. But there were evidently four courses to pursue.

The first course was that of Lord Lansdowne—to diminish the church revenues gradually and partially, to find some kindred object to which the surplus revenues could be applied, and to content ourselves with that imperfect remedy. The second course was to secularize the church revenues, and to give the whole of those revenues to secular purposes, such as hospitals and lunatic asylums. The third course was to transfer the revenues, after the expiry of life-interests, to the Roman Catholic clergy. The fourth would be not very different in principle from the third; it would consist of an endowment for the Roman Catholics in the provinces of Leinster, Munster, and Connaught, and for the Presbyterians in Ulster.

I do not include the absurd proposal of making a grant to every sect, however small its numbers.

The first of these proposals was that which I submitted to Parliament for some years, and which I only abandoned from seeing that a small majority in the House of Commons would never prevail over a strong majority in the House of Lords. In fact, the people of England never took up warmly the appropriation clause, and, indeed, were not persuaded that the Protestant Church in Ireland could be that miserable, monopolizing minority which Fox had described it to be.

The second course is stated by a committee of Mr. O'Connell in very clear terms as follows:—

'Your committee claim that the ecclesiastical state revenues should (as the existing vested interests dropped off) be applied for the general benefit of the community; that is, for the support of the poor, for the promotion of education, and in works of charity, equally and without distinction, to all sects and persuasions.'[1]

On this proposal it may be remarked, that the support of the poor has been provided for by separate Acts of Parliament, and that education is supplied by large annual grants of Parliament.

As to hospitals, it is to be supposed that the nurses would be after the model of Mrs. Quickly, who is much shocked that Falstaff, when not in immediate danger, should mention the name of God.

'"How now, Sir John?" quoth I; "what, man! be of good cheer." So 'a cried out, "God, God, God!" three or four times. Now I, to comfort him, bid him 'a should not think of God; I hoped there was no need to trouble himself with any such thoughts yet.'[2]

The setting up of hospitals and lunatic asylums in all the great towns of Ireland would doubtless furnish an opening for many jobs, and the Patronage Secretary of the Treasury might gain several converts from Home Rule by promising large endowments for charitable foundations for their constituents.

The third proposal has many advantages to recommend it. First, it would be in accordance with the statutes of the time of Henry II., when Pope Adrian issued a bull by which the King of England was made Lord of Ireland, and tithes were granted to him.

'There can be no reasonable doubt of the authenticity of this document. Baronius published it from the 'Codex Vaticanus;' John XXII. has annexed it to his

---

[1] 'Past and Present Policy of England towards Ireland,' by C. Greville, p. 283.

[2] 'King Henry V.,' act ii. scene 3.

brief addressed to Edward II.; and John of Salisbury states distinctly, in his *Metalogicus*, that he obtained this bull from Adrian. (*Metal.*, I. 4.)[1] From this time (1154) till the reign of Elizabeth, that is to say, for four centuries, we must suppose that, however irregularly levied, the tithes of Ireland were appropriated to the Roman Catholic clergy of Ireland. If the words *plunder* and *blunder* have any significance, they should be applied, not to Mr. Gladstone and his Cabinet, but to Queen Elizabeth and the Protestant Church of Ireland.

The endowment of the Roman Catholic clergy of Ireland has, therefore, the plea of antiquity to recommend it.

It has likewise its accordance with the character of the Irish people; they are described by Mr. Froude as 'passionate in every thing; passionate in their patriotism, passionate in their religion.'[2] He likewise, while with the spirit of a severe historian he pities the imperfections of their character, says of the nation, that 'they appeal to sympathy in their very weakness, and they possess, and have always possessed, some qualities, the moral worth of which it is impossible to over-estimate, and which are rare in the choicest races of mankind.'[3]

If such is the moral worth of the Irish people, and if they are passionate in their attachment to religion, it can hardly be denied that a large provision ought to be made to enable the parish priests to attend to their spiritual wants, and give spiritual comfort on those frequent occasions of feasts and fasts, of illness and of worship, when the Roman Catholic gentleman and the

---

[1] See 'Illustrated History of Ireland,' p. 273. 'Religious History of Ireland,' by James Godkin.

[2] 'The English in Ireland.' Froude. Vol. I. p. 23.

[3] Ibid., vol. i. p. 21.

Roman Catholic peasant alike require that his priest should be able to attend him easily and conveniently. The priest should neither have a long distance to travel, nor want means to obtain the food and the clothing necessary for his maintenance. I will quote one authority to make good the proposition I have laid down. It is the deliberate judgment of Dr. Arnold. His large and liberal views are thus explained in the volume of his 'Life and Letters':—

'I think that a Catholic is a member of Christ's church just as much as I am, and I could well endure one form of that Church in Ireland and in England. We are suffering here from that accursed division among Christians of which I think the archfiend must be the author. The good Protestants and bad Christians have talked nonsense and more than nonsense so long about popery and the beast and antichrist, that the simple, just, and Christian measure of establishing the Roman Catholic Church in three-fifths of Ireland seems removed by common consent. The Protestant clergy ought not to have their present revenues in Ireland; so far I agree with Lord Grey, but not in a narrow, low, economical view of their pay being over-proportioned to their work, but because church property is one of the most sacred trusts of which the sovereign power in the church, *i.e.*, the King and Parliament, not the bishops and clergy, is appointed by God trustee. It is a property set apart for the advancement of direct Christian principles; first, by furnishing religious comfort and instruction to the grown-up part of the population; next, by furnishing the same to the young in the shape of religious education. Now the Christian people of Ireland have a right to have the full benefit of their church property, which now they cannot have, because Protestant clergy-

men they will not listen to. I think, then, that it ought
to furnish them with Catholic clergymen. . . . I have
one great principle which I never lose sight of, to insist
strongly on the difference between Christian and anti-
Christian, and to sink into nothing the difference between Christian and Christian.'[1]

I should, for my own part, object very strongly to the
setting up of a Roman Catholic Church establishment
in Ireland, with its archbishops, bishops, and deans, its
preposterous pretensions, and its ultramontane doctrines;
but the Roman Catholic parish priests ought, I think, to
have provided for each of them a manse or rectory, with
a few acres of land; in short, sufficient pasture for a
cow or a horse. That we should confine our grants to
the parochial clergy was the opinion of the late Mr.
Tierney.

Dr. Arnold was not the first person who perceived
that reasons, even stronger than those I have mentioned, exist for endeavoring to range the Roman Catholic priesthood on the side of peace and order. Bishop
Law, a man of great comprehension of mind, and not
less liberality, has spoken to the following effect of the
conduct of the Roman Catholic priests of Ireland:
'The almost total dependence of the Roman Catholic
clergy of Ireland upon their people for the means of
subsistence is the cause, according to my best judgment,
why, upon every popular commotion, many priests of
that communion have been, and, until measures of better policy are adopted, always will be, found in the ranks
of sedition and opposition to the established Government. The peasant will love a revolution, because he
feels the weight of poverty, and has not often the sense

---

[1] Dr. Arnold's 'Life and Letters,' vol. i. p. 382.

to perceive that the change of masters may render it
heavier ; the priest must follow the impulse of the popular wave, or be left behind on the beach to perish.'[1]

I am aware that there are many obstacles in the way
of an endowment for the parish priests of the Roman
Catholic Church in Ireland, yet the reasons in its
favor are exceedingly strong.   They may be thus
summed up : —

1. It is a restoration of property conferred by
Henry II. and the Pope on the Roman Catholic Church
of Ireland.   2. It is in accordance with the religion of
the great majority of the people of Ireland.   3. It
would relieve the farmers and peasants of Ireland from
very heavy demands.   4. It would separate the Roman
Catholic clergy from all sympathy and connivance with
the Ribbon confederacy, and give the best hope of
checking murder, carried on, as it is at present, in the
spirit of established regular criminal law, ' ut pœna ad
paucos, metus ad omnes, perveniat.'

Thus recommended, it is to be hoped that some
great Minister, or some wise Parliament, may at length
provide for the prospect of ' Hibernia pacata.'

I now come to my fourth proposition : —

That the Secretary of State for the Home Department
of Great Britain ought to have in Ireland the same
authority as in Scotland.

In order to place in contrast the two systems, it will
be necessary to compare the government of Scotland
from 1707 to 1829 with the government of Ireland for
a similar period.

The proposal I make is justified by the course which
was adopted with regard to Scotland by the Union of

---

[1] Plowden, vol. iii. p. 716.

1707, and the prodigious success of the policy enforced by that Union.

The Union of Scotland confirmed in the most solemn manner the establishment of a National Church on principles to which the Scotch nation were deeply attached. Courts of justice administered laws to which the Scotch Parliament had given its assent. The distribution of property, which had been made with the assent of the nobility, gentry, and commonalty of Scotland, provided a decent though frugal maintenance for the parochial ministers of the National Church, for the repair of their dwellings, and the means of education for the poor, which John Knox had taken care should include religious instruction, in which he and the majority of the people of Scotland could willingly concur.

The administration of law and the establishment of a religious worship agreeable to the conscience of the people being thus provided for, and guaranteed by special enactments binding on the Sovereign, Lord Somers applied the resources of his wisdom to the maintenance of order and liberty by the Executive Government.

A strong desire was entertained to preserve the Privy Council of Scotland, and to place in the hands of its members powers of state and justice, but Lord Somers, by a speech in the House of Lords, averted the mischiefs which would have resulted from the establishment of two political administrations, one in England and another in Scotland. The following notes contain briefly the heads of the speech in the House of Lords made by this great statesman : ' True concern for preserving the public peace. Heartily desirous of the Union. No less desirous to make it entire and complete. Not at all perfect while two political administrations subsist. The true argument for the Union was the danger to both kingdoms from a divided state. *Principally by the help of one to enslave the other, and to effect another sort of union.* The advantage of Scotland is to have the same easy access to the Prince, to be under the immediate personal care of the Prince, and not to owe their protection and countenance to any subordinate institution. This was my argument at the Union. Will not prevaricate. Worse state after the Union if a distinct Administration continue.'[1]

The policy of Lord Somers was successful; the seat of government was placed in England, and the government of the Church was confided to a general assembly composed partly of the ministers of the 'Kirk' and partly of lay elders popularly elected.

The administration of justice was intrusted to the most eminent members of the bar of Scotland chosen by the Crown.

Thus constituted, the government of Scotland has withstood most dangerous storms. When the young Pretender landed in Scotland, in 1745, the destinies of England were confided to two ministers, of whom it was said with truth and wit, that the one, Lord Carteret, made a trifle of every difficulty, and the other, the Duke of Newcastle, a difficulty of every trifle. Yet the Lowlanders of Scotland were true to their principles, and they had in President Forbes an able and sagacious leader. The history of Scotland from the time of the battle of Culloden shows that, whether in her manufacturing towns, as Glasgow, Paisley, and Dundee, or in her agricultural counties, as the Lothians, industry has its due reward, and that order and liberty flourish

---

[1] Lord Hardwicke's 'State Papers,' vol. ii. p. 473.

together. If there occurs anywhere in Scotland a riot or a conspiracy, the Home Secretary is prompt to direct the forces of Great Britain to the diseased part, and every one relies on the pacific termination of the disorder.

I have omitted to mention one blot which did much to diminish the merit of the Union between England and Scotland. The Parliamentary representation of Scotland was left in the hands, or placed in the hands, of a miserable, monopolizing minority, as odious and as exclusive as the church minority which deformed the Union between Great Britain and Ireland.

A few owners of land held, under the title of superiorities, the whole Parliamentary representation of Scotland in their hands. The supremacy of Dundas and his followers was not even mitigated by the influence of a majority of numbers, which in Ireland belonged so manifestly to the Roman Catholics, as to break in some degree the tyranny of law. Lord Archibald Hamilton was almost the only man who dared in Parliament to raise his voice in the cause of right and justice. During the early days of the French War, a lawyer or man of letters who spoke against the excesses of arbitrary power could, if a lawyer, hardly obtain a brief; or if a philosopher, scarcely use his literary talent without the fear of being oppressed and excluded from the legitimate use of his freedom by the oppressive mandate of an intolerant majority. Such men as Mr. Jeffrey, Mr. Cockburn, and Mr. Fletcher were the targets at which all the arrows of exclusion, of abuse, and of calumny were directed. One lady, the wife of Mr. Fletcher, was said to keep on her toilet table a miniature guillotine, with which she slew the ducks and chickens for her husband's table. These absurd inventions were suited to the prevailing palate, and made it difficult for Mr. Fletcher to maintain his independence. This tyranny was not finally overcome till Lord Grey's accession to power in 1830.

I have seen private letters which have been preserved describing the enthusiasm, the popular joy, and the sense of deliverance from the yoke of Toryism which animated the crowds of Edinburgh when they welcomed Mr. Abercrombie and Mr. Jeffrey, or, more properly, James Abercrombie and Francis Jeffrey, when they were elected under the Reform Act as members for Edinburgh. The Dundases had been as intolerant, as corrupt, and as powerful in the Scotch, as the Beresfords in the Irish community.

I am allowed to copy from the diary of Mrs. Fletcher her commemoration of the triumph of political liberty in Scotland : —

'It was during that winter, 1832–3, that the hustings were erected for the first time at the cross of Edinburgh for the popular election of the members for the city, under the new Reform Bill. I often took my three grandsons, and explained to them how their grandfather and father would have rejoiced to see that day, for the sake of the improvement of their country, and the security of its future freedom.

'At length, in March, 1833, came the day of election, and we were kindly invited by the Lord Advocate and Mrs. Jeffrey to their house in Moray Place, to see the members brought home in triumph. The citizens of Edinburgh did themselves honor in choosing two such representatives as James Abercrombie, the Speaker of the House of Commons, and Francis Jeffrey, then Lord Advocate ; men not less eminent for their talents than for their public spirit and courage in supporting

the cause of civil and religious liberty, both in and out
of Parliament. I scarcely felt equal to go, leaving
Mary alone on that day in our lodgings. Our kind
Mrs. Thompson secretly consulted her husband, and
came with a cheery face early in the day, to say Dr.
Thompson allowed his patient to go with me to the
chair or sofa offered her near the window by Mrs.
Jeffrey. It was a glorious sight for us to see these
truly honest men borne home amidst the acclamations
of tens of thousands of their grateful and emancipated
countrymen. We stood by them on the balcony of
Mr. Jeffrey's house while they shortly returned thanks
to the people. Few events ever excited me more than
those which took place in Edinburgh at that time.'[1]

While it must be said of Mr. Fletcher that he sacrificed the honest earnings of his profession, in order to
maintain the independence of his position, and preserve
the utterance of his free opinions in favor of civil liberty in the worst of times, it must be also recorded
that his widow Mrs. Fletcher never bated a jot of heart
or hope when deprived of her husband, and suffering
many afflictions of a domestic nature ; she was still one
of the most agreeable members of society, and assembled Mr. Jeffrey, Mr. Cockburn, and others at her
evening parties, which were distinguished amongst the
most agreeable resorts of the literary society of Edinburgh. I shall always remember with pleasure the
many evenings on which, with Professor Playfair and
others, who maintained opinions favorable to freedom,
I was associated with those parties.

Let us now turn to Ireland, taking the period from
1708 to 1829.

---

[1] 'Autobiography of Mrs. Fletcher,' p. 181, privately printed.

The Union of England with Scotland, and the Union
of Great Britain and Ireland have been consolidated
by two Acts of Union, — the Act of Union between
England and Scotland, passed in 1708, and the Act of
Union between Great Britain and Ireland, concluded
in 1801.

These two Acts were framed upon totally different
principles, and therefore we must not be surprised,
omitting all invidious contrast between the national
characters of the Scotch and the Irish, if we find that
the result has been totally different. While the Scotch
Union has established a confirmation of the Scotch
National Church, and the maintenance of the laws and
courts of justice prevailing in Scotland before the
Union, and while Scotland has made wonderful progress in manufactures, in agriculture, and every species
of industry, the picture presented by Ireland is of a far
less agreeable nature.

After the Revolution of 1688 in England, after the
battle of the Boyne and the battle of Aughrim, the
Irish people wished to devote themselves to the growth
and manufacture of wool. The soil of Ireland is especially adapted to the feeding of sheep ; the price
of fleece-wool in Ireland, in 1733, was fivepence, of
combed wool, twelvepence a pound. In France, Irish
fleece-wool was sold for two shillings and sixpence a
pound ; combed wool from four shillings and sixpence
to six shillings. It is obvious that if the Irish had
been allowed to export their fleece and combed wool
to France, they would have made an enormous profit
by their pastoral industry, and the anarchical spirit
would have been vanquished. What stood in the way
of these benefits ? — benefits for Ireland, benefits for
England, benefits for the Empire ? Why could not

the Irish build manufacturing towns, and erect manufactories of cloth in competition with the linen manufactories of Belfast, in rivalry of the towns of Leeds and Halifax in England? Was it the anarchical spirit of the Irish? No. When the Irish rebels with their French allies had been vanquished at the Boyne, when James had gone back to say his prayers and get absolution at St. Germains, the English Parliament, instead of making a flourishing United Kingdom, prohibited, by Act of Parliament (the 9th of William III.), the direction of the industry of the Irish to the manufacture of cloth, and, in a spirit of detraction and of selfishness, resolved to build on the poverty of Ireland the supremacy of English law and English administration. When this monopoly had gone on for nearly a century, and the Irish, deprived of a fair course for their industry, had resorted to illegal trade as the only defence against the injustice and impolicy of England, Mr. Hely Hutchinson, an Irish gentleman of noble family, the ancestor of the peer who commanded with distinction, after the death of Sir Ralph Abercrombie, the English army in Egypt, made, in 1779, the following statement before Lord Harcourt, the Lord Lieutenant: —

'As the law stands,' he said, 'we can sell our wool and woollen goods only to Great Britain. We can buy woollen cloths there only. If such a law related to two private men instead of two kingdoms, and enjoined that in buying and selling the same goods one individual should deal with one man only in exclusion of others, it would in effect ordain that both as buyer and seller that man should fix his own price and profit, and would refer to his discretion the loss and profit of the other dealer. You have defeated your own object. The exclusion of Ireland from the woollen trade has been more injurious to you than to us. One pack of Irish wool works up two packs of French wool. The French undersell the English, and, as far as they are supplied with Irish wool, the loss to England is double what it would be if the Irish exported their wool manufactured. . . . As to the practice of running wool, Ireland has paid to Great Britain for eleven years past double the sum she collects from the whole world in all the trade which Great Britain allows her — a fact not to be paralleled in the history of mankind. Whence did all this money come ? Our very existence is dependent on our illicit commerce.' [1]

Persons of all ranks in Ireland were principals or accomplices in smuggling. ' Distinctions of creed were obliterated, and resistance to law became a bond of union between Catholic and Protestant, Irish Celt and English colonist — from the great landlord whose sheep roamed in thousands over the Cork mountains, to the gauger who, with conveniently blinded eyes, passed the wool-packs through the custom-house as butter barrels ; from the magistrate whose cellars were filled with claret on the return voyage of the smuggling craft, to the judge on the bench who dismissed as frivolous and vexatious the various cases which came before the courts to be tried.' [2]

' If encountered at sea, the contraband vessels were sometimes armed so heavily that the government cutters and schooners hesitated to meddle with them. If unarmed and overhauled, they were found apparently

---

[1] 'Mr. Hely Hutchinson to Lord Harcourt, July 1, 1779,' MSS. Record, Office. Froude's ' The English in Ireland,' vol. i. pp. 447–48.

[2] Froude's ' The English in Ireland,' vol. i. pp. 448–49.

laden with some innocent cargo of salt provisions. The wool was pressed with screws into barrels, which were washed with brine, that they might pass for butter, herring, or salt pork casks. The more determined the authorities showed themselves, the more resolute were the Irish, the lawlessness and wildness of the trade giving it fresh zest. Driven from the Cork warehouses, the packs were stored in caves about the islands and cliffs and crags, where small vessels took them off at leisure ; or French traders, on signal from shore, sent in their boats for them. Chests of bullion were kept by the merchants at Rochelle and Brest to pay for them as they were landed. When the French Government forbade the export of so much specie, claret, brandy, and silks were shipped for Ireland in exchange on board the vessels which had brought the wool.'[1] Mr. Froude truly declares that this system worked the extremity of mischief commercially, socially, and politically ; but, happily for the political and commercial evils thus brought upon Ireland, a remedy was found.

Two men of extraordinary genius, both Irishmen, were about this time, that is, in 1778, taking a leading part in the commercial policy of England. The first of these, Edmund Burke, was descended from a family long settled in the south of Ireland. He was born in the year 1730 ;[2] in 1774 he was elected one of the representatives for the commercial city of Bristol. In 1778 he wrote a letter to 'Samuel Span, Esquire, Master of the Society of Merchant Adventurers of Bristol;' his letter related to resolutions of the House of Commons somewhat mitigating the exclusive spirit of the measures

---

[1] Froude's 'The English in Ireland,' vol. i. p. 450.
[2] 'Life of Edmund Burke,' by Peter Burke, Esq.

18

framed to secure the monopoly of trade and manufactures to England. Burke declared in his letter that he considered the resolutions merely as preparatory of better things, as a means of showing experimentally that justice to others is not always folly to ourselves. He went on to say, 'Too little dependence cannot be had at this time of day on names and prejudices. The eyes of mankind are opened, and communities must be held together by an evident and solid interest. God forbid that our conduct should demonstrate to the world that Great Britain can, in no instance whatsoever, be brought to a sense of rational and equitable policy but by coercion and force of arms.'[1] Further, 'Do we in these resolutions *bestow* any thing upon Ireland? Not a shilling. We only consent to *leave* to them, in two or three instances, the use of the natural faculties which God has given to them, and to all mankind.'

In a later passage, Burke asks: 'How much have you lost by the participation of Scotland in all your commerce? The external trade of England has doubled since that period.' He adds, 'Such liberality there is in virtue of sentiment that you have grown richer by the partnership of poverty.'

Finding that this letter had no success, he wrote to two gentlemen of Bristol, who had lamented that he had taken so decided a part against his constituents. In this second letter he declares, 'No Government ought to own that it exists for the purpose of checking the prosperity of its people, or that there is such a principle involved in its policy.'[2]

He concludes his letter with the following paragraph:

---

[1] Burke's Works, vol. iii. pp. 212–13.
[2] Ibid., p. 225.

' It is very unfortunate that we should consider those as rivals whom we ought to regard as fellow-laborers in a common cause. Ireland has never made a single step in its progress towards prosperity by which you have not had a share, and perhaps the greatest share, in the benefit. That progress has been chiefly owing to her own natural advantages and her own efforts, which, after a long time, and by slow degrees, have prevailed in some measure over the mischievous systems which have been adopted. Far enough she is still from having arrived even at an ordinary state of perfection; and if our jealousies were to be converted into politics, as systematically as some would have them, the trade of Ireland would vanish out of the system of commerce. But believe me, if Ireland is beneficial to you, it is so not from the parts in which it is restrained, but from those in which it is left free, though not left unrivalled. The greater its freedom, the greater must be your advantage. If you should lose in one way, you will gain in twenty.' [1]

There is an historical reason why I should make comments on this letter. The historical reason is, that in 1771 Oliver Goldsmith wrote of Burke : —

> Who, born for the universe, narrowed his mind,
> And to party gave up what was meant for mankind.

This couplet conveys a most unjust charge against Burke. In 1777, he wrote a public letter to the sheriffs of Bristol in favor of conciliation to America. In 1778, he wrote, as we have seen, in favor of granting free trade to Ireland. It was impossible to take a course more opposed to national and commercial prejudices, or more conducive to the interests of mankind. Gold-

---

[1] Burke's Works, vol. iii. pp. 227–28.

smith, on the other hand, was a Jacobite, and narrowed his mind in the Jacobite vice.

The second Irishman to whom I alluded was Henry Grattan. Henry Grattan was intended for the bar, but, by the influence of Lord Charlemont, was elected member for Charlemont in the place of Francis Caulfield, Lord Charlemont's brother. Grattan was born in 1746, in the city of Dublin, which his father represented in Parliament; he was educated at the University of Dublin, and in 1767 was entered a student of the Middle Temple. He admired, to the point of enthusiasm, the eloquence of Lord Chatham, and more than once reported his speeches. He was called to the Irish Bar in 1772. The first speech, of which we have any record in the collection of his speeches, was delivered in 1778; in 1779, in the Irish Parliament, he moved an amendment to the address to the King, asking for free trade for Ireland. The Prime Serjeant (Mr. Hussey Burgh) and Mr. Flood, in order to secure unanimity, moved, ' That we beg leave, however, humbly to represent to His Majesty that it is not by temporary expedients, but by a free trade alone, that this nation is now to be saved from impending ruin.' This was unanimously adopted, and the address, with this amendment, was agreed to. On the succeeding day it was moved by Mr. Conolly, seconded by Mr. Ponsonby, and resolved *nem. con.*, ' That the thanks of this House be given to the different volunteer corps in this kingdom for their spirited and (at this time) necessary exertions in its defence.'[1]

The formation of the volunteers, to the amount of forty thousand armed men, showed that Ireland was in

---

[1] 'Grattan's Speeches,' vol. i. p. 25.

earnest in asserting her rights. In April, 1782, the volunteers had augmented in numbers to nearly eighty thousand men, and in the month of February they assembled at a convention at Dungannon, to take into consideration the question of their country's freedom. The three most important resolutions agreed upon were these: —

'*Resolved:* That a claim of any body of men, other than the King, Lords, and Commons of Ireland, to make laws to bind this kingdom, is unconstitutional, illegal, and a *grievance.*

'*Resolved:* That the powers exercised by the Privy Council of both kingdoms, under, or under color or pretence of, the law of Poynings, are unconstitutional and a *grievance.*

'*Resolved:* That a Mutiny Bill, not limited in point of duration from session to session, is unconstitutional and a *grievance.*' [1]

Ireland had at length been driven into a course of armed resistance to the violent and tyrannical conduct of the English House of Commons and the English Ministry, which nothing but resistance could overcome. At the same time, a change of Ministry took place in England, and Charles Fox, who became Secretary of State, introduced into the British House of Commons a bill to repeal the 6th of George I. Thus was effected without bloodshed a great revolution. Ireland obtained a change by which her legislative independence was secured.

Unhappily, this victory was not fruitful of prosperity to Ireland. From 1772 to 1801 the Parliament of

---

[1] 'Grattan's Speeches,' vol. i. p. 121.

Ireland was remarkable chiefly for intolerance and corruption. Grattan in vain endeavored to obtain for the Roman Catholics, who formed the great majority of the people of Ireland, admission to the privileges of the British Constitution. In these efforts he was not supported by Lord Charlemont. In the name of Protestant ascendency, which was the official creed of all men who took part in the government of Ireland, a grasping, bigoted, and corrupt junto upheld a monopoly more narrow, more unjust, and more injurious to the Commonwealth than any of those which, in her last days, Queen Elizabeth had surrendered.

We have now to consider what was the new system established by George III. and Mr. Pitt at the beginning of the nineteenth century. In order to introduce that system, the Protestants of Ireland were bought with honors and with money, the Roman Catholics of Ireland' were deceived and betrayed. Lord Cornwallis, who, as a loyal man, was bound to carry into effect the will of his Sovereign, said he was obliged to pay compliments to men whom he should like to kick. A more disgusting process than the transactions connected with the Irish Union could not well be. Mr. Pitt, indeed, not only held out hopes to the Roman Catholics of Ireland, but sincerely wished to give effect to those hopes ; he no doubt reckoned that having been more than sixteen years at the head of the councils of the King, having a decided majority in the two Houses of Parliament, the advice he should be prepared to give his Sovereign, in order to unite the hearts of his people in the throes and struggles of a great war, would be accepted. Mr. Pitt was entirely mistaken. The King's answer was in these words : —

'Queen's House, February 1, 1801.

'I should not do justice to the warm impulse of my heart if I entered on the subject most unpleasant to my mind without first expressing that the cordial affection I have for Mr. Pitt, as well as high opinion of his talents and integrity, greatly add to my uneasiness on this occasion; but a sense of religious as well as political duty has made me, from the moment I mounted the throne, consider the oath that the wisdom of our forefathers has enjoined the Kings of this realm to take at their Coronation, and enforced by the obligation of instantly following it in the course of the ceremony with taking the Sacrament, as so binding a religious obligation on me to maintain the fundamental maxims on which our Constitution is placed, namely, the Church of England being the established one, and that those who hold employments in the State must be members of it, and consequently obliged, not only to take oaths against Popery, but to receive the Holy Communion agreeably to the rites of the Church of England. This principle of duty must, therefore, prevent me from discussing any proposition tending to destroy this groundwork of our happy Constitution, and much more so that now mentioned by Mr. Pitt, which is no less than the complete overthrow of the whole fabric. When the Irish propositions were transmitted to me by a joint message from both Houses of the British Parliament, I told the lords and gentlemen sent on that occasion that I would with pleasure and without delay forward them to Ireland; but that, as individuals, I could not help acquainting them that my inclination to a Union with Ireland was principally founded on a trust that the uniting the Established Churches of the two kingdoms would for ever shut the door to any further measures with respect to the Roman Catholics.'[1]

The consequences of this declaration on the part of George III. was the resignation of Mr. Pitt, Lord Grenville, Mr. Dundas, Lord Spencer, Mr. Windham, and Mr. Canning; the defeat of the hopes which the Roman Catholics of Ireland had entertained; and the postponement of · Roman Catholic Emancipation till 1829.

Fox, Pitt, and Burke were three of the ablest men who have applied their minds to the administration of England and Ireland. Fox and Burke made two immense mistakes when they coalesced with Lord North, and proposed a government of India with party views. Mr. Pitt made a blunder of no less importance and more fatal when, in 1804, he surrendered to the King his own project of a coalition. I will give here a note of a combined Administration, recorded by Lord Stanhope, as planned by Mr. Pitt in May, 1804 : —

Treasury	Mr. Pitt.
Secretaries of State	{ Lord Melville. Mr. Fox. Lord Fitzwilliam.
Admiralty	Lord Spencer.
Lord President	Lord Grenville.
Privy Seal	Duke of Portland.
Lord Chancellor	Lord Eldon.
M. General of Ordnance	Lord Chatham.
Chancellor of Duchy	Mr. Windham.
Board of Control	Lord Castlereagh.
Lord Steward	Lord Camden.
Committee of Trade	Lord Harrowby.
Secretary at War	Mr. Grey.
Secretary to Ireland	Mr. Canning.

---

[1] Stanhope's 'Life of Pitt,' vol. iii. App. 28, 29.

It may safely be said, that never in difficult circumstances was there so bright a prospect of a strong Ministry, for all the foreign and domestic interests of England, as at the hour when the project of Mr. Pitt was laid before the King of England. Fox, although he afterwards observed that he would not have served under Pitt, had, in reality, only two conditions on which, in his letters to his friends, he would have insisted — one, that a coalition was clearly right; the other, that no mediocrities should be admitted into the Cabinet. Pitt, after his interview with the King, humbly declared that he had never been so vanquished. Yet, in fact, there never was an argument so weak as that which George III. opposed to him. He reminded Pitt that he had himself proposed to exclude Fox from the Privy Council; but the only ground for that exclusion was, that Fox had put forward as an abstract theory the sovereignty of the people. The real ground of difference between Pitt and Fox had arisen from the democracy of France. From the moment when Napoleon Bonaparte became First Consul, all danger of democracy in France had disappeared, and a despotism, resting upon a military dictator, whether under the name of First Consul or Emperor, was a form of government against which Pitt and Fox would with equal spirit and equal abhorrence have contended. Burke had said of Lord Chatham, that a peep into the King's closet intoxicated him; and Lord Chatham's son, with all his abilities and all his eloquence, seems to have been subject to a similar intoxication. Had Fox been at the Foreign Office in 1804, Austria would not have been hurried into war, the battle of Austerlitz would not have been fought, and Pitt would not have died in 1806. Pitt and Fox would have agreed not to force on the Catholic question, and, in 1810, the policy of those two great men would have prevailed in Ireland. What actually happened was very different.

In January, 1806, Pitt died. In September of the same year Fox died. George III. said to his daughter, the Princess Mary, afterwards Duchess of Gloucester, who told it to me, that he never thought he should have regretted the death of Fox so much as he found he did. In the following year a very moderate proposal with respect to the army was made by Lord Grenville's Ministry. Not only did the King reject this proposal, but he made a demand inconsistent with the Constitution.

'He required an assurance, in writing, from the Ministers, that they would never press upon him in future any measure connected with the Catholic question;' in other words, that his advisers would never give him advice upon one great and important branch of public affairs, involving in their opinion the character and 'even the safety of the Empire.'[1]

This condition implied that not even in the immediate prospect of civil war — a prospect that made the Duke of Wellington advise his Sovereign to yield — would the Minister give any advice respecting the Roman Catholic question.

Of course neither Lord Grenville nor Lord Spencer, neither Lord Holland nor Lord Fitzwilliam, neither Mr. Grey nor Lord Henry Petty could assent to such degrading terms. The Ministers resigned; and not till twenty-three years afterwards did any of the Ministers of that day, with the exception of Lord Sidmouth, enter the Cabinet.

---

[1] 'Memoirs of the Whig Party.' Lord Holland. Vol. ii. p. 203.

'The No Popery' cry of 1807, and the general election of that year, was the proceeding most discreditable to the English people of any that has occurred in my time. Several of the ablest men in Parliament, the chief ornaments of the House of Commons, were obliged to take refuge in small boroughs. Mr. Grey, then Lord Howick, went from Northumberland to Appleby ; Mr. Windham went from Norwich to Romney.

Mr. Perceval was the author of the 'No Popery' cry, and did his utmost to arouse the people to religious hatred.

The flame did not subside till 1829, when O'Connell agitated the people of Ireland to assemble in their thousands, and impressed upon the Duke of Wellington the fear of civil war.

In 1829, the Catholic claims were granted, and from that time till 1868 it was the object of the advisers of the Crown of England to increase the privileges and promote the happiness of the people of Ireland. This has been well stated by Lord Mayo, in his speech of 1868 ; but any one who knows the history of national feelings must be aware that long and fatal injuries are not forgiven till after many years of conciliation and repentance. The wound still rankles, the injuries are still remembered, and the stronger the feelings of the nation, the deeper the wound and the longer the cure. It is acknowledged by Lord Mayo himself, that in 1868 the hostile feelings of the Irish people against English government were not changed ; yet, he says, ' Professor Ingram has truly remarked, that changes so great, and made within so short a period, constitute the largest peaceful revolution in the history of the world.' [1]

---

[1] Lord Mayo's Speech on the state of Ireland, March 10, 1868.

Yet the Union with Ireland preserved and crystallized some of the worst wrongs which had aggravated the miseries of conquest.

One of these wrongs was the Protestant Church establishment. I have seen a letter written by one of the descendants of the conquerors, himself the owner of a large landed estate, which contained the advice of the writer to his Sovereign Queen Elizabeth. He says that there were two ways in which the Irish people could be governed; the one was by extirpating all the Roman Catholics in the country; the other, the conversion of all the Roman Catholics to the Protestant religion. The writer says that the Queen is too humane and too tender to adopt the first method, he therefore recommends the second.

The second was, in fact, the mode adopted, but it entirely failed. After three hundred years of trial, not above one-seventh or one-eighth of the people of Ireland were Protestants of the Established Church. In 1867, when Mr. Gladstone and I were both in Italy, I ascertained the opinions and sentiments of Mr. Gladstone upon this important subject. I found that he was as little disposed as I was to maintain Protestant ascendency in Ireland; and from that time I judged that this great question would be safer in his hands than in mine. This last observation requires some development.

In 1833, when Lord Melbourne told me that all the members of the Cabinet wished me to take the lead of the Liberal party in the House of Commons, I willingly consented to do so.

The question of the maintenance, diminution, or abolition of the Protestant Established Church in Ireland had long attracted my attention. Upon this ques-

tion, in 1835, I had overthrown the Administration of
Sir Robert Peel. I was of opinion that unless some
great change was made in the Established Church,
justice to Ireland could not be done. I was not, indeed,
in 1869, physically equal to a much longer continuance
of the labor imposed upon a leader of the House of
Commons. But there was a further consideration.

My political character is very much the reverse of
that which Sydney Smith, in an angry temper and a
witty mood, attributed to me. I never was ready either
to take the command of the Channel fleet or to behold
the loss of that fleet with equanimity. My disposition
has always been favorable to compromise and moderation. I had acted in that temper on this very subject
of the Irish Church. I had listened to Lord Lansdowne,
who had maintained that if any property was taken
from the Church of Ireland it should not amount to the
whole of that property, and should be given to some
kindred purpose, such as that of education.

I felt, however, that boldness, which, according to
Lord Bacon, is the first quality of a statesman, was required as the primary quality for dealing with the Irish
Church, and that no man could dispute the pre-eminence
in that quality of Mr. Gladstone.

I knew that Mr. Gladstone had an eloquence equal
to that of Mr. Canning, and I believed that he was endowed with integrity fit to be compared with that of
Lord Althorp. I knew that Mr. Gladstone was prepared to take a large and liberal view of the question
of the Irish Church; to him, therefore, I was ready to
transfer the mantle which I had worn for thirty years.
I have only one remark to add to my estimate of the
qualities of the late Prime Minister. I was not wrong
in attributing to him eloquence equal to that of Mr.

Canning, and integrity on a par with that of Lord
Althorp. But I had omitted in my observation one
important quality. Lord Macaulay says of William
Lord Russell, and his influence in the House of Commons: 'He had long exercised there an influence
resembling the influence which, within the memory
of this generation, belonged to the upright and benevolent Althorp; an influence derived, not from superior
skill in debate or in declamation, but from spotless integrity, from plain good sense, and from that frankness, that simplicity, that good nature, which are
singularly graceful and winning in a man raised by
birth and fortune high above his fellows.'[1] So it was
of Lord Althorp; it was his fearless frankness which,
above all, gave him the confidence of the House of
Commons. He was not afraid to call a spade a spade,
and make his hearers understand, in a few plain words,
the policy he meant to pursue. In that quality Mr.
Gladstone is greatly his inferior.

In defining the policy to be adopted by the nation
with regard to the Irish Established Church, there
were two objects to be considered. One was, the disposition to be made of the property and privileges of
the Church; the other, the use to be made of the property, whether the amount were large or small, after
the expiry of the life-interests of the existing Protestant clergy.

With respect to the first of these objects, nothing
could be more wise or more complete than the demon-
stration of Mr. Gladstone. The Irish Protestant Church
had been from its beginning in the reign of Elizabeth
foreign to the soil, ill-planted and ill-nurtured, a scarc-

---

[1] Macaulay's 'History of England,' vol. iii.

crow rather than a tree, a fountain of bitterness and
animosity rather than a fertilizing stream. Mr. Gladstone illustrated most happily the fall of such a Church
by the fall of Lear, when he thinks himself falling
down a precipice, and is, in fact, only throwing himself
down on the flat ground on which he stands.

The second object was the wise and judicious disposal of the revenues which the total destruction of
the Church of Ireland would place within his reach.
But this matter has been already elucidated.

What I have here to ask is, whether the time has
not arrived for placing in the Home Department in
Whitehall the administration of the internal government of Ireland? Whether the evils which Lord
Somers foresaw would have happened to England and
Scotland if separate administrations had been granted
to them, have not actually happened to Ireland?
Whether there is any reason for refusing to the Irish
people the benefits of English rule?

I remember that, in 1819, after the Manchester
meeting, known by the name of Peterloo, I was stay-
ing in the house of Sir James Mackintosh, in the country. We read every day in the newspapers accounts
of meetings; it was generally stated that the meeting
at Manchester, although legal, had been attacked and
dispersed by military force. Sir James said to me, ' It
will be worth while to look at my law-books and see
whether this assumption that the meeting at Manchester was legal is founded in law.' We soon found reason to conclude that the Manchester meeting was an
illegal meeting. Sir James Mackintosh and I agreed
that in the approaching session of Parliament we would
not affirm the legality of the Manchester meeting.
Accordingly, when the prisoners arrested at Manches-.

ter were brought to trial, Mr. Justice Bailey and Chief Justice Tindal pointed out, in the clearest terms and on the highest authorities, the circumstances which made the meeting an illegal one.

Yet only two years ago, a meeting was held in the neighborhood of Belfast, marked by similar illegalities in a far more offensive form; and it seems never to have occurred to the Irish Government that they had permitted, with the most insulting publicity and with the most disastrous consequences, that which had called down the censure of Mr. Justice Bailey and Lord Chief Justice Tindal. A year after, Mr. Justice Lawson pointed out, amid the ruins of houses, and after many wounds had been given and suffered on both sides, the illegality of the Belfast meeting.

Now, I ask, why is not the power and the duty of maintaining internal peace in Ireland transferred to our present Home Secretary, who, by his answer respecting the condemned Fenians, has given promise that he will not go to sleep over his charge? I may add here that this was the change recommended in 1850 by Sir Robert Peel.

I should say, at the same time, that while it is the duty of England to preserve internal peace in Ireland, she is bound to look with regret to her four hundred years, from 1430 to 1829, during which period she did every thing in her power to check the industry, to repress the manufactures, to persecute the religion, and to confiscate the rights of the Irish people.

It has been said and repeated that the spirit of anarchy in Ireland is so inherent in the people that it is impossible to subdue it.

But we have seen that the government of Scotland from 1707 to 1829 was guided by political wisdom and by civil and religious liberty, while the review of the government of Ireland from 1707 to 1829 shows it to have been directed by commercial jealousy, by political corruption, and by religious intolerance. Is it, then, so certain that the nature of the two races makes the one incapable of submitting to government, and the other tranquil and obedient? May it not be that such different prescriptions — political wisdom with civil and religious liberty to the one, and political corruption with commercial jealousy and religious intolerance to the other — may have caused the difference?

I now arrive at my sixth proposition, viz., ' " Home Rule " must be refused in as peremptory a manner as repeal of the Union was rejected by Lord Grey and Lord Althorp in 1830.' I should have been very glad if the leaders of popular opinion in Ireland had so modified and mollified their demand for ' Home Rule ' as to make it consistent with the unity of the Empire. There can be no doubt that the existing legislation by Private Bills is exceedingly cumbrous and expensive ; that great funds are wasted in purchasing private interests, and in giving fees to lawyers for services which are neither conducive to the public good nor advantageous to property. It would have been a great advantage in lightening the labors of Parliament, and in promoting useful public legislation, if the rural parts of England, Scotland, and Ireland had been divided and distributed into municipalities springing from a popular origin, and invested with local powers. The principle of our Constitution, that no taxes or rates should be levied except by popular consent, is grossly violated by the raising of large sums by virtue of the orders of magistrates, named by the Crown upon the advice of the Lord Chancellor. The Private Bills of Lords and Commons do not violate this

19

principle, but are in many instances very costly. The late Mr. Brassey was enabled to construct a railway from Turin to the Alps at no greater expense than was incurred in carrying a bill through Parliament to sanction the Great Northern Railway of England.

It is, however, useless at present to discuss the project of provincial corporations. The favorers of 'Home Rule' in Ireland have declared very distinctly that what they propose is to convert the legislative Union of England, Scotland, and Ireland into a federal Government, on the model of the old Republic of Holland, or the modern federal union of the United States of America.

This would be to open a source of civil war over England and Ireland, not against law, but by virtue of law, owing its authority to the Imperial Parliament itself.

No matter how well devised the restrictions which might be framed to prevent the province of Ireland encroaching on the central power, the earliest efforts of a popular demagogue at Dublin would be directed to the enlargement of local privileges, to the absorption of one part after another of the central authority by the local assemblies. The taxes, the poor-rates, the funds for education, the private property consecrated by the Act of Settlement, the right of Protestants to their churches and chapels, nay, the privileges of Protestants to enjoy their own places of worship and their own religious ceremonies, would all be matters of dispute, and the 'Home Rulers,' to whom Great Britain would have given power, would then throw in the teeth of their partners in London the concessions which had been made by themselves.

I own I can see no hope that Ireland would be well and quietly governed under the dispensation of 'Home Rule.' In my opinion, the prisoners convicted of

treason-felony under the rule of Lord Kimberley and
the Duke of Abercorn were too easily let off by the
Cabinet of Mr. Gladstone. But peace was not thereby
obtained. There can be no doubt that the policeman
murdered at Manchester was slaughtered, not from
private malice, but for the sake of obtaining impunity
for high treason. Thereupon it was alleged that the
murder was a political offence, and as such entitled to
indemnity. How could we expect that there would be
peace and harmony between two assemblies, one of
which, in Ireland, would assert the right to impunity,
and the other, in London, which would look to punishment as the retribution for murder? It will be as well,
therefore, that we should look to the declarations of
Lord Grey and Lord Althorp, when Mr. O'Connell demanded the repeal of the Union as a compliance with
his petition for justice to Ireland. Lord Althorp said
on that occasion that he could not agree to the repeal
of the Union, as he considered it a dismemberment of
the Empire.

Lord Grey as openly and firmly declared that he
might support the Union on the ground, 'quod fieri
non debuit factum valet;' but, without availing himself
of that plea, that he gave his unhesitating and uncom-
promising adherence to the Act of Union.

Let me here assert that there can be no greater
mistake in the government of Ireland than to yield upon
points where justice is against the popular demand. I
have said that the Irish have a character rather resembling that of the French than that of the English nation.
At all events, we may safely lay down in regard to
Ireland, that every just petition ought to be granted,
and that every unjust demand ought to be refused.
The abolition of the Protestant Established Church, the

education of Protestant and Catholic together on secular subjects, ought to be maintained. The parish priests of Ireland of the Roman Catholic Church ought to be supported from the property now at the disposal of Parliament. A Roman Catholic University should be founded. The power to grant degrees should be confined to the Queen's University, and the colleges founded upon the advice of Sir Robert Peel and Sir James Graham should be maintained. Those who insist upon having a University where, by an *Index Expurgatorius*, modern history and moral philosophy are not taught, should be considered as the partisans of bigotry and ignorance.

But, while every attempt to revive the University Bill, rejected in 1873 by the House of Commons, should be resisted, the utmost care should be taken not to keep up the disdainful and contemptuous tone which has been too long the prevailing language of the government press. Government can exercise, and does exercise, a great influence over part of the press, by communicating from authority intelligence which has been received, and the decisions which have been arrived at by persons holding high office. It is an abuse of that influence when decisions, which have not been arrived at, are suggested by leading persons as likely to be the course of policy of the existing Ministers. I remember a time when the late Duke of Richmond said he could always tell what the Cabinet were about to do by reading the 'Times' of the day when the Cabinet was summoned. But without thus abusing the right of a Government, and putting a gag on the mouths of those Ministers who have not been consulted on the views communicated to the 'Times' or 'Daily Telegraph,' it would be easy to make it a condition of communicating intelligence that the tone of the newspapers thus favored should not be one of scorn and insult towards the people of Ireland. There is no harm in using towards angry people the soft language which turns away wrath. Kindness towards the Irish people will do more to extinguish bad passions than bitter invectives and boastful claims to superiority on the part of the English press and the English nation.

In answer to all I have urged, it may be said that the inhabitants of Scotland are Scotchmen and Protestants, and that the inhabitants of Ireland are Irishmen and Roman Catholics; and that a policy which was successful in Scotland might have totally failed in Ireland.

It may, therefore, be useful to examine what has been the policy pursued by the Governments of France and Italy, and in what respects it differs from the policy pursued by the English in Ireland.

France and Italy, it is well known, have a great majority of Roman Catholic inhabitants.

I will not touch upon Germany, as there are questions still pending in that country. But France and Italy have for some time adopted a policy which appears to be now, and promises to be hereafter, successful.

This policy forms a striking contrast to the course long pursued by the English in Ireland.

For instance, both in France and Italy the clergy have the means of living afforded them. In France, these means are afforded by a grant of the Representative Assembly. In Italy, where tithes are as much abolished as they are in France, the clergy are sustained on moderate salaries by endowments and voluntary contributions from the principal towns.

But there are two subjects sedulously kept apart from priestly interference. These are marriage and education.

The English in Ireland have pursued a totally different course. They have left the parish priests to voluntary contributions, to fees on baptism, on marriage, and on funerals. Marriage and education they have left almost entirely in the hands of the Roman clergy. In the year 1831, an effort was made to introduce large portions of the Bible to be read in the National Schools. Archbishop Whately has recorded, by the pen of Mr. Senior, what were his expectations from his agreement with Archbishop Murray on this subject. Dr. Whately said, ' Archbishop Murray and I agreed in desiring large portions of the Bible to be read in our National Schools, but we agreed in this because we disagreed as to its probable results. He believed that they would be favorable to Romanism; I believed that they would be favorable to Protestantism; and I feel confident that I was right. . . . Though the priest may still, perhaps, denounce the Bible collectively as a book dangerous to the laity, he cannot safely object to the Scripture extracts which are read to children, with the sanction of the prelates of his own church. But these extracts contain so much that is inconsistent with the whole spirit of Romanism, that it is difficult to suppose that a person well acquainted with them can be a thorough-going Roman Catholic. The principle upon which that Church is constructed, the duty of unenquiring, unreasoning submission to its authority, renders any doubt fatal. A man who is commanded not to think for himself, if he finds he cannot avoid doing so, is unavoidably led to question the reasonableness of the command; and when he finds that the Church which claims a right to think for him has preached doctrines, some of which are inconsistent with, and others are opposed to, what he has read in the Gospel, his trust in its infallibility, the foundation on which its whole system of faith is built, is at an end. The education supplied by the National Board is gradually undermining the vast fabric of the Irish Roman Catholic Church.'[1]

But Archbishop Whately was not immortal, nor had the Irish Board of Education the perpetuity of the Roman Church; consequently it has become entirely a tool in the hands of the Roman Catholic clergy. The case of Father O'Keefe has shown that when a man is degraded from the position of parish priest he is sure to lose his rank as manager of parish schools. The Education Board in this case have found out new offences to lay upon the head of Father O'Keefe; but this is one of the usual tricks and devices of the Jesuit school. The Institution of Irish Education, once so bright a wreath on the brow of the late Lord Derby, has become of late years a weapon in the hands of Cardinal Cullen and the Ultramontane clergy of Ireland. The number of pupils on the rolls were : —

Year.	Number on the Rolls.	Average daily attendance.
1869	991,335	358,560
1870	998,999	359,199
1871	1,021,700	363.850

That is to say, the average daily attendance but slightly exceeded one-third of the number of children nominally attending the schools. The Parliamentary grant to these schools last year amounted to 542,222*l.*, and the voluntary contributions from the whole of Ireland were only 14,955*l.* That is to say, the property of Ireland contributed less than one shilling, while the State expended more than a pound.

---

[1] Senior's Journals relating to Ireland, 1868.

I am told that it is not uncommon, in the National Schools of Ireland, when the Protestant children are withdrawn for their own religious instruction, to take, from cases in the wall, the graven images which the Roman Catholics use to enliven or, as some would say, supply the object of their worship.

The question of marriage need not here be dwelt upon. Had Mrs. Fitzherbert had a male child, the question of a disputed succession might have been serious; but as that misfortune did not happen, we may for the present omit the reflections which would have arisen.

The question of the state of the Roman Catholic Church in Ireland ought to attract the serious consideration of our statesmen. Not many years ago an Irish priest, taught at Maynooth, wished to devote to learning the chief employment of a studious life. I saw such a priest in France last year, who, with his small library, and his bachelor *ménage*, enjoyed the delights of a picturesque country, and the regard of his friendly parishioners. No such good fortune was reserved for the priestly scholar of Ireland. His sleep was broken by the seditious or indecent songs of the farmers who occupied a room close by his bedroom in the small farmhouse where he had obtained a lodging. Driven to distraction by these interruptions, he gave up his plan of study, and was content to live with his neighbors as a thoughtless and unlearned priest. Another parish priest received a message requiring his attendance from a dying penitent, whose house was separated from his own dwelling by a river and a mountain. He arrived at the bedside, but the penitent was no more.

Is it to be supposed that these privations and disturbances, which the parish priests of Ireland suffer, have had no effect on their equanimity and their tempers? Can we imagine that the priest who trudged along the road weary and exhausted would see, with wholly charitable feelings, the Protestant rector pass by in his chariot and pair, enjoying the luxury of his comfortable position and his light labors? Is it enough to say that the Protestant clergy have their incomes only for life? Have three hundred years of proscription and persecution passed by without leaving bitter dregs in the cup from which he was condemned to drink? Why must we suppose that the men who recollect these things with anger, and perhaps with hatred, are incurably barbarous and irreclaimable? Why should we not try the experiment which in France and Italy has been found successful? Why not provide a frugal maintenance for the parochial clergy of the people, and assert for the State the control of marriage and education?

It is no question of the supremacy of the Pope, or of permission to the Church of Rome to draw the line as it pleases between spiritual and temporal, leaving ' to God that which is God's, and to Cæsar that which is Cæsar's.' It is a question of the happiness of a people long vexed by religious injustice and political oppression.

Fortunate the Ministry whose fate it shall be —

To scatter plenty o'er a smiling land
And read their history in a nation's eyes.

CHAPTER X.

TENANTS IN IRELAND.

LET us now consider the treatment of tenants in Ireland. We have seen that Mr. Grattan described the Government and the people of Ireland as a people ill-governed and a Government ill-obeyed.

Towards the end of the last century a fit of liberality, or a fit of panic, induced the Parliament of Ireland to grant new franchises to the Roman Catholics. Not that a Roman Catholic, the son of a gentleman of property, or a leading barrister in the courts of law, was permitted to sit in Parliament to represent any portion of his countrymen, but the Roman Catholic was allowed to choose a Protestant knight of the shire or borough member. The consequences of this boon were most calamitous. Thousands of freeholds were created, thousands of freeholders were marched to the poll, to purchase for a great proprietor a deanery for his brother, a place at the Board of Customs for his son. In 1829, Sir Robert Peel denounced the mischief of this large extension of the franchise, and proposed its abolition.

It happened to me to be present at a small meeting of Members of Parliament, mostly Whigs, at the house of Sir Francis Burdett. Alarmed at the prospect of the destruction of a popular franchise, we asked Lord Althorp to wait upon Sir Robert Peel to propose for the retention of the forty-shilling freeholders, coupled with

the great measures which we intended warmly to support. Lord Althorp returned, bringing a negative to
our proposal. But I remember that Sir Francis Burdett
said, 'It seems that the abolition of the forty-shilling
freeholders, instead of being a punishment, will be a
benefit to Ireland.' We most of us took a similar view.

But we little knew the character of the miserable,
monopolizing minority who, by aid of the prejudices
of George III. and the cry of 'No Popery,' had so long
governed Ireland. Thousands of human beings, who
from their wretched huts had swarmed to the elections,
men with wives and helpless children, were rooted out
as noxious weeds when they had served their purpose
as ladders, whereby their landlords might climb to
wealth and to power. They were now useless instruments, and hundreds of them were driven out in the
cold days or bleak nights of winter, their miserable
cabins levelled with the ground, and they themselves,
scantily clothed, left to struggle with the inclemency
of the elements, to die by the roadside, or to perish of
famine after weeks of suffering and exhaustion. Is it
the 'fickleness, the perversity, and the levity of Irishmen' that has caused the great mass of the people to
recollect with pain and with resentment the heedless
laxity with which their freeholds were bestowed upon
them, and the cruelty with which they were driven out,
when their votes were no longer available, to pine and
to perish? Or is it not rather a proof that the people
have been ill-governed? Is it wonderful that such
injuries, apparent benefits so fallacious, real sufferings
so undeserved, should have sunk deeply into their
minds, and created a feeling of revenge, against which
the lounger in St. James's may protest, while he re-
peats, after the London newspaper, a declamation

against 'the fickleness, the perversity, the levity of
Irishmen'?

It is true that these evils have been in a great degree
remedied. After many years a poor-law was enacted,
and the wretched families driven out of their homes
found temporary shelter and food, if they could get
nothing better. But at length, with the boldness which
belongs to him, and the genius which inspires him, Mr.
Gladstone devised a remedy.

In order to understand the nature of this remedy,
the reader should be aware that in England the landlord usually undertakes, in some districts by established
custom, in the country generally by a prevailing sense
of obligation, to keep in repair, or to provide for the
repair of, the houses and farm-buildings of his tenants.
Often the tenant does not wish for a lease, but relies
on the continuance of a practice by virtue of which
his father and his grandfather have flourished, and he
hopes to continue, neither burdened by a great rise of
rent nor fettered by written obligations.

In Ireland the tenant was often left to provide for his
own comfort. If he had built a good house, with a
roof of slate and beams of timber, and was suddenly
turned out for giving a vote to the popular candidate,
he had no claim in law for any compensation. In Mr.
Trench's volume on the 'Realities of Irish Life,' a
sturdy, rebellious farmer is introduced, who boasts that
he has put at his own expense every stick in his house,
and planted every cabbage in his garden, without any
means of legal redress.

Mr. Gladstone saw that it was of no use to spend his
time on legal refinements, or to show that in the course
of law and equity the victim of political or religious
enmity could obtain no redress. He saw that rough

justice was better than no justice at all; and he gave a remedy for disturbance, even where no positive injury had been inflicted.

If Mr. Gladstone has met with scanty forbeârance from his opponents, it cannot be said, as some Liberal agitators are fond of repeating, that the House of Lords have unfairly obstructed this great measure. For instance, the bill of the Government proposed that a tenant should receive seven years' rent for a wilful act of ejection. The House of Lords proposed to reduce the seven years to six; so that a man who paid 5*l.* a year rent would have received 30*l.* instead of 35*l.* But this cannot be said to be a fatal obstruction, nor would the disturbance have been compensated very inadequately. The seven years may be a fairer limit than the six; but it is a strong instance of party injustice to complain of the Duke of Richmond, of Lord Derby, of Lord Salisbury, and Lord Cairns, as the obstinate and pertinacious opponents of every Liberal improvement. This amendment was afterwards withdrawn, and the seven years' compensation restored.

Of course the alterations in the tenure of land do not cause the disappearance of an old hereditary feud, or prevent altogether those acts of violence which are sanctioned by the code of the Ribbon confederacy. In 1839 I ventured to say, in Parliament, that I trusted that in forty years the grievances of Ireland would be redressed. That time has not yet come, and I am not sanguine that those who are witnesses of the state of Ireland in 1879 will see an end of Ireland's evils, while no sufficient remedy is proposed by authority, and while a portion of the press makes it a pastime to calumniate the Irish people, and to provoke enmity between the two portions of the British Empire.

A work of great ability and likewise of great research, entitled 'The English in Ireland,'[1] has lately appeared. The work is in three thick octavo volumes. Unfortunately, the ability is misapplied, and the research is adapted to reconcile the English people to the worst instances of intolerance and corruption on the part of the English Governments which succeeded each other from 1700 to 1829.

The general view of the writer, worked out with elaborate detail, is, that the Irish people, in asking that Roman Catholics should not be disqualified and degraded on account of their religion, that abuses should be reformed, and that honesty should be introduced into the administration, asked that which it was preposterous to ask, and which it was justice to refuse. The author exalts Lord Clare as a hero, and lowers Mr. Grattan as the utterer of 'glittering declamations.' Mr. Grattan, as I have already mentioned, spoke of Ireland as 'a people ill-governed, and a Government ill-obeyed.' I must be excused for my want of perception, but I own I cannot see any glitter or any declamation in this picture. Mr. Grattan, in his speeches in the Irish Parliament, described in minute detail the hardships suffered by Irish cottagers, who were forced to pay tithes for their wretched vegetables till they were left in a state of impoverishment, ruin, and despair. It may be called glittering declamation to describe these sufferings of the Irish peasant, but I own that neither the adjective nor the substantive appears to me to be justly applied.

On April 14, 1788, Mr. Grattan said: 'In three-fourths of this kingdom potatoes pay no tithe; in the

---

[1] 'The English in Ireland in the Eighteenth Century.' James Froude.

south they not only pay, but pay most heavily. They pay frequently in proportion to the poverty and helplessness of the countrymen ; for in the south it is the practice to crouch to the rich and to encroach upon the poor ; hence, perhaps, in the south the mutability of the common people. What so galling, what so inflammatory as the comparative view of the condition of His Majesty's subjects in one part of the kingdom and the other ! In one part their sustenance is free, and in the other tithed in the greatest degree ; so that a grazier coming from the west to the south shall inform the latter that with him neither potatoes nor hay are tithed ; and a weaver coming from the north shall inform the south that in his country neither potatoes nor flax are tithed ; and thus are men, in the present unequal and unjust state of things, taught to repine, not only by their intercourse with the pastor, but with one another.

' To redress this requires no speculation, no extraordinary exercise of the human faculties, no long fatiguing process of reason and calculation, but merely to extend to the poor of the south the benefits which are enjoyed by His Majesty's subjects in the other parts of Ireland ; it is to put the people of the south on a level with their fellow-creatures. If it shall be said that such an exemption would cause a great loss to the parson, what a terrible discovery does that objection disclose ! that the clergy of the south are principally supported by the poor ; by those whom they ought, as moral men, to relieve, and, as Christian men, support, according to the strictest discipline of the Church.' This, I suppose, is what Mr. Froude calls ' glittering declamation ! ' I confess I do not perceive the glitter or the declamation.

It is true, that equal rights given to the Catholics and reform of Parliament, obtained previously to the Act of Union with Ireland, might have raised to power such men as Lord Fitzwilliam, Mr. Grattan, and Sir Ralph Abercrombie, and might have prevented such a man as Lord Clare from taking his seat in the English House of Lords. Lord Clare was a man of splendid talents, and was successful in resisting the Irish Rebellion; but I confess I cannot see that in giving bribes to a majority of the Irish Parliament, Mr. Pitt and Lord Westmoreland used the necessary means of government. If such men as I have mentioned, Lord Fitzwilliam, Sir Ralph Abercrombie, Lord Cornwallis, and Mr. Grattan had been employed to govern the Irish people by honest means, who can convince me that such means must have failed? Who can prove that large salaries and prodigal pensions, unfit appointments to offices of trust and honor, the sale of peerages for money, and the support of the Roman Catholics extorted by promises, not afterwards kept, were the only means by which Ireland could be governed?

I must reject this apology for a system of intolerance and corruption; I hold it to have been cruel to Ireland to inflict it, and shameful to England to permit it.

Lord Edward Fitzgerald and other victims incurred, no doubt, the penalties of high treason; but, however successful the attempt to blacken and to blast the memory of the men who at that time were driven by despair to appear in arms against the Government of their country, it will be impossible for history, if fairly written, to justify the broken promises of Pitt, and to sink in oblivion the iniquity of his colleagues, Castlereagh and Dundas.

CHAPTER XI.

NATIONAL EDUCATION.

DURING the reign of the House of Hanover till a period within my memory the faith of the Church of England was professed by all the graduates of the English Universities. About 1820 an agitation sprang up for the purpose of abolishing religious tests as a condition for admission to degrees. But this agitation was condemned by the authorities of the Universities, and the Whigs had recourse, in despair of a successful change in Oxford and Cambridge, to an address to the Crown to allow a separate University to be erected, where religious tests should not be required. This question came on for discussion during Sir Robert Peel's short administration of 1835, and the Minister was defeated by a majority of eighty votes. At a more recent time, Mr. Heywood, brother of Sir Benjamin Heywood, brought forward a proposal for a Commission to inquire into the state of the English Universities. As the organ of the Government, I supported Mr. Heywood, and, notwithstanding the powerful and able opposition of Mr. Gladstone, I succeeded in procuring the inquiry. Into the history of more recent events it is not necessary to enter.

The ancient Universities of Oxford and Cambridge required only amendments and reforms in conformity with the spirit of their institutions, and with a view to those liberal studies which must from time to time be made suitable to the spirit of the age.

But the education of the great mass of the people was so deficient as to require new measures, which became the subject of fierce party debate.

In 1808, the Duke of Sussex, the Duke of Bedford, Lord Somerville, and others, established a society for the purpose of teaching the poorer classes, and especially with the view of giving to the whole population of England Scriptural education. This society received from the first the cordial patronage of George III.

A bystander might have supposed that an object so simple and so benevolent as that of teaching the people to read and understand the Bible, if it had not met with warm support, would have encountered no opposition. But the party-spirit of the Church was roused, and the clergy thought that it was superfluous, if not dangerous, to teach the poorer classes to read. However, the desire for instruction among all classes grew wider and deeper, and a resolute opposition to the general education of the people became unpopular and unpalatable.

The friends of the Church, therefore, in 1811, three years after the foundation of the British and Foreign School Society, set up the National Society, in order to educate the population in the principles of the Established Church. Every scholar was to learn the Catechism, and to attend divine worship on Sundays in the Established Church, where he was to pray for God's blessing upon the bishops and clergy, and the congregations committed to their charge, with an entire omission of the Dissenting sects, however pious and however religious they might be. The clergy were, however, permitted to allow the children of Dissenting parents to come to the schools of the National Society, and even to go on Sundays to worship with their parents if the clergyman of the parish did not forbid so great a latitude of religious liberty. The exertions of the National Society, supported by the large funds of the great proprietors of England in addition to the wealth of the Church, were, of course, successful. But, in spite of the exertions of the two societies, the education of the general population of England was lamentably deficient. I, therefore, soon after Her Majesty's accession to the throne, drew her attention to the great want of education among her subjects, and engaged Lord Lansdowne, the President of the Council, to co-operate with me in the endeavor to extend, to improve, and to organize the education of the people of Great Britain. Lord Lansdowne, however, desired to confine our official duties and responsibilities to the supervision of the funds voted by Parliament.

I, therefore, submitted to the Queen a proposal that a Committee of Privy Council, consisting entirely of persons holding office in the Administration, should be formed to superintend the funds voted by Parliament. I humbly advised that Her Majesty should express her wish that the youth of her kingdom should be religiously brought up, and that the rights of conscience should be respected. Her Majesty was graciously pleased to approve of these suggestions. It was a part of the plan submitted that a Normal School should be founded, where the young of the Established Church, and of various religious sects, should be educated together.

Early in the session of 1839 the heads of this scheme were communicated to the House of Commons. It is difficult to understand at this time the storm that was raised. I explained in the simplest terms, without any exaggeration, the want of education in the country, the deficiencies of religious instruction, and the injustice of subjecting to the penalties of the criminal law persons who had never been taught their duty to God and man.

The proposal of a Normal School, especially, excited the most vehement opposition, and we were obliged to renounce that part of the plan. But the throwing out of one of our children to the wolf did little to appease his fury. The violence of bigotry and fanaticism excited the numbers brought together by party hostility. Lord Stanley, in a long and animated speech, proposed to overthrow our whole plan, and to rely upon the Church as the recognized and legitimate teacher of religious and secular knowledge. On a division, he was defeated by a majority of five. The grant of 30,000*l*., in a Committee of Supply, was carried by a majority of only two. In the House of Lords, the Archbishop of Canterbury carried, by a majority of one hundred and eleven, resolutions condemnatory of our whole scheme.

It is very well for Mr. Lowe to censure us for not proposing at that time a scheme comprehending the whole population, and expelling ignorance from the realm. But Mr. Lowe at that time had only to deal with Australia, we had to deal with England.

The Bishop of London, Dr. Blomfield, who was very sincerely friendly to education, suggested to me that if the State and the Church went on fighting, we should only injure one another, without promoting the great object we both had in view. Seeing the justice of this remark, I agreed to a meeting at Lansdowne House, where the Archbishop of Canterbury, and the Bishops of London and Salisbury, met Lord Lansdowne and me.

After a conference we agreed to a treaty, of which the principal terms were that the inspectors of the schools of the National Society should send their reports to the English bishops as well as to the Committee of Privy Council, and that we should co-operate on the most friendly terms in the great work of education. In this manner the Committee of Privy Council of Education was confirmed, and has lasted till the present year.

Lord Lansdowne attached, with justice, the greatest importance to the appointment of inspectors, and to the choice of a chief or head to direct and guide the whole machine of education. Lord Lansdowne found a person so well fitted for this office (Dr. Kaye, now Sir James K. Shuttleworth), that, whether in his office at White-hall or in his journeys in the country, he was capable of organizing and directing the whole plan according to which the public funds could be brought to aid the system of education.

Lord Brougham had, in 1833, proposed a grant to the National Society, and an equal grant to the British and Foreign School Society, of a sum of 10,000*l*. each, for the purpose of assisting those two societies. For six years the amount remained unchanged. It was in 1846 that the Liberal Ministry, having been restored to office, gave fresh vigor to the cause, and inspired new efforts for the promotion of general education. Sir Robert Peel, when he came into power, so far from continuing the spiteful war which the Tory party had commenced in 1839, expressed to Sir James Kaye Shuttleworth his great satisfaction that, through the channel of the British and Foreign School Society, the Government would obtain a means of communicating with the Dissenting bodies.

It was about the year 1846, I think, that I recommended to the Committee of Council a capitation grant in proportion to the attendance of the different scholars.

It was long intended to establish a general system of education for England, and I frequently spoke of the intention both in the House of Commons and at the meetings of the British and Foreign School Society.

In my opinion the Act of 1870 was not brought forward too late, but rather too soon. Many difficulties might have been obviated, many objections avoided, and some unpopular provisions omitted, if the Government had taken more time for consideration, and then made its plan more comprehensive. In 1870 there was accommodation for 1,878,584 children in schools receiving grants from Government; and in 1870–71, there was accommodation for 2,012,679. Now, when it is considered that this school accommodation had been provided, not by the State, but only by the assistance of the State; that the clergy of the Church of England had shown unremitting zeal and unflagging attention in the work of education, it is no wonder that Mr. Forster has said that his work, and that of his colleagues, was to supplement the existing education, and not build a new house from the beginning. Indeed, if such had been the attempt, the Government would have been guilty not only of a large superfluity of grants and much waste, but of great ingratitude.

That there are some faults in the Education Act of 1870 is not to be denied. No time will be lost if I submit for consideration some of the improvements that may be required, and how the edifice may be rendered complete.

I am encouraged to make some criticisms by the speech of Mr. Stansfeld, the late President of the Board of Local Government, at Liverpool. He declares that none of the Cabinet, nor Mr. Forster himself, ever supposed that the Education Act of 1870 was a perfect or permanent measure. Such is the view that I have always taken of it. I have considered the Act of 1870 as an excellent Act, but as one that would be improved, and possibly perfected, by the lessons of experience, and the patient observations of the Committee of Council.

I will remark, in the first place, that although the Government were quite right to avail themselves of the voluntary efforts that had been made between 1846 and 1870, a period of twenty-four years, it was neither in the spirit of Mr. Forster's declaration nor in the spirit of sound progress to commence a great scaffolding of new Voluntary Schools of a denominational or sectarian character. There was this fault in such an attempt, that the Board Schools intended by the Act of 1870 were to be schools in which the Bible would be read in its integrity, and no formularies were to be admitted. The Voluntary Schools newly to be set up were to receive instruction according to catechisms of the Church of England, the very first questions in which could not be answered with truth by the children of Baptists, who deny the propriety of infant baptism, and in which a paraphrase of the Lord's Prayer is given, which omits some of the most essential words of Christ, and inserts words which Christ never used, in the Prayer. This paraphrase is followed by an explanation of the sacraments, which no child of eight or ten years old is able to comprehend.

Instead of these sectarian formularies, encouragement

ought to be given, in schools aided by the State, to the daily reading of the Bible, with such simple explanations as an intelligent and discreet school-master is fully competent to give.

It is well known that in rural districts the clergy, the country gentlemen, and the farmers, intent upon avoiding rates, and hoping to escape with a very moderate subscription, do all they can to avoid a school board, and augment the number of what, by a misnomer, are called Voluntary Schools; but this is not the way to found a national system of education.

There is, however, a much greater defect introduced into our system by the 25th clause or section of the Education Act. By that clause, or section as it is properly called, the only voluntary act is performed by the parent of the child to be taught. Before the Act of 1870 Voluntary Schools were really voluntary, and were supported by voluntary subscriptions; but now the parent of the child is told, 'If you have got any money in your pocket, or if one of your neighbors is willing to subscribe for a National or Church School, the payment may be voluntary; but if no such sum can be procured, the power of the State will help you; and if your neighbor, who is a Baptist, does not choose to subscribe to a Church School, his chair and his table will be seized, and sold by auction, to procure a sum to promote the teaching of infant baptism.' The Presbyterian and the Congregationalist, in the same manner, will undergo compulsion to compel them to support a Voluntary School.

It is obvious that in this manner a great injustice is committed.

In the last century Dissenters were fined for not accepting municipal offices, which they could not hold without receiving the Sacrament according to the rites

of the Church of England. But Lord Mansfield, in his
memorable judgment of 1767, abolished these fines as
illegal in the name and in the spirit of religious liberty.

Unhappily, the present payments by Dissenters to
Church Schools are legal, being sanctioned by Act of
Parliament. There is, however, a precedent, which is
apt and appropriate.

In the year 1868, on July 31, an Act was passed,
called an ' Act for the Abolition of Compulsory Church
Rates.' The preamble and the first section of this Act
are as follows : —

' Whereas Church Rates have for some years ceased
to be made or collected in many parishes by reason of
the opposition thereto ; and in many other parishes,
where Church Rates have been made, the levying
thereof has given rise to litigation and ill-feeling :

' And whereas it is expedient that the power to compel payment of Church Rates by any legal process should
be abolished :

' Be it therefore enacted by the Queen's Most Excellent Majesty, by and with the advice and consent of the
Lords spiritual and temporal, and Commons, in this
present Parliament assembled, and by the authority of
the same as follows : —

' I. From and after the passing of this Act no suit
shall be instituted, or proceeding taken, in any ecclesiastical or other court, or before any justice or magistrate,
to enforce or compel the payment of any Church Rate
made in any parish or place in England or Wales.'

This precedent is the more applicable, as it was
originally entertained on the suggestion of Mr. Gladstone.

I will here give a rough sketch of the measures which
appear to me suitable for the completion of a plan for
National Education in England and Wales : —

I. England and Wales should be divided into five or six hundred districts, each having its own name and title.

II. Each district should have a board elected in the manner now prescribed by Act of Parliament.

III. Each district should have a central school; and, where necessary, two or more central schools.

IV. Each central school should be a free school, where no payment should be required.

V. A portion of the Bible should be read daily in each central school.

VI. The central school or schools should be maintained by payments from the Consolidated Fund, to be voted annually by grants of the House of Commons.

VII. Denominational or sectarian schools should be divided into two classes; the first class consisting of schools which were built and founded before the year 1870, and the latter of schools which have been built and founded since that year. To the schools of the first class grants should be made during each year for ten years; to schools of the second class for five years from the year of the proposed enactment. To schools of the first class half the yearly cost of the schools should be voted; to schools of the second class one-fourth of the yearly cost.

VIII. The Committee of Privy Council, which should direct the whole plan, should consist of the President and Vice-President of the Council and three other members. Ordinary business should be conducted by the President and Vice-President of the Council; extraordinary business by the whole five members of the Committee.

IX. The school-rates, enacted by the 25th section of the Education Act, should be treated as church-rates are treated by the Act of 1868.

I subjoin a few remarks on the principles upon which this scheme is founded.

The people of England and Wales are not pagans, or infidels, or atheists. The School Boards have already declared, in answer to official inquiries, their preference for a religious education. I have no doubt that, in answer to similar inquiries, they would declare their wish that the rights of conscience should be respected. It would, therefore, be necessary that the Roman Catholic schools should be allowed their own catechism and their own version of the Bible ; and that they should have the same grant from Government as other denominational schools.

It would be necessary that, as in Saxony, Switzerland, and Scotland, geography and history, and the elementary parts of political economy, should be taught in the upper schools ; or, in small districts, in the upper parts of the elementary schools. The revised code should not be permitted or revived.

I have endeavored to reconcile the homage and regard due to the Bible with the consideration which is due to the ministers of religion, who have exhibited so much zeal and liberality in the cause of education. With the exception of Roman Catholics, all Christian sects in England profess faith in the Bible. The working-men of England have neither the time nor the capacity to give religious instruction to their children.

There is no question of greater interest to be settled by Parliament than the question of National Education. In the present tranquil state of our foreign relations, there is no object of greater importance to which the attention of the country can be called than the establishment of a sound, universal system of education of the people.

But, unhappily, there is no question upon which there seems less prospect of general agreement. The clergy will not yield an inch of their pretension to tax the Baptist to pay for the teaching of infant baptism, and the Presbyterian to call for God's blessing upon the bishops and clergy, and the congregations committed to their charge, with the marked omission of the vast population who are not under the charge of the bishops and clergy of the Established Church. Who are these Protestant Dissenters? Before the glorious Revolution of 1689, James II. offered a bribe to Protestant Dissenters in the shape of indulgence and dispensations if they would separate their cause from that of the Established Church. They firmly refused to do so.

At another period, upon the accession of the House of Hanover, there was an opportunity for the eminent men who at that time were at the head of Protestant dissent to appeal to King George I. for liberty to themselves, accompanied with restrictions on the Protestant Church. They resolved that as the Protestant Church was a barrier against Popery, they were bound to support and uphold it.

It seems to have occurred to the High Church party that an opportunity had come for revenging themselves upon the Nonconformists, whose benefits are too heavy to bear, whose hostility they are happy to provoke, and whose downfall they hope to offer up as a sacrifice to the Ritualists, the affinity of whom to the Church of Rome they delight to recognize.

The position of Dissenters is more fully explained and recognized in the famous speech I have already referred to, of Lord Mansfield in the case of the Chamberlain of London against Allen Evans. It had been the practice, the intolerant practice, of the city of London to name

Dissenters to certain offices in their gift, knowing that they could not take the Sacrament according to the rites of the Church of England for a year before their election, and reckoning upon the fine which they would be able to levy to increase the funds of the corporation.

When the case came to be heard, seven judges gave their opinion that the defendant was at liberty to object to the validity of his election, and only one judge, Mr. Baron Perratt, gave his opinion that the defendant was not at liberty to object to the validity of his election.

Lord Mansfield stated that as the Corporation Act was originally framed, the disability ' was owing to what was then in the eye of the law a crime; every man being required by the canon law, received and confirmed by statute law, to take the Sacrament in the church at least once a year; the law would not permit a man to say that he had not taken the Sacrament in the Church of England, and he could not be allowed to plead it in bar of any action brought against him.'

But Lord Mansfield went on to state in noble terms, ' that Nonconformity being no longer a crime, the natural liberty of the subject was in favor of the Dissenter. There is no usage or custom, independent of positive law, which makes Nonconformity a crime. The eternal principles of natural religion are part of the common law; the essential principles of revealed religion are part of the common law, so that any person reviling, subverting, or ridiculing them may be prosecuted at common law. But it cannot be shown from the principles of natural or revealed religion that, independent of positive law, temporal punishments ought to be inflicted for mere opinions with respect to particular modes of worship. Persecution for a sincere, though erroneous, conscience is not to be deduced from reason or the fitness of things; it can only stand upon positive law. . . . The Toleration Act renders that which was illegal before, now legal; the Dissenters' way of worship is permitted and allowed by this Act; it is not only exempted from punishment, but rendered innocent and lawful; it is established, it is put under the protection, and is not merely under the connivance, of the law. In case those who are appointed by law to register Dissenting places of worship refuse on any pretence to do it, we must, upon application, send a mandamus to compel them.' [1]

Lord Mansfield was able to say that the requiring the payment of a fine by the Dissenters was both unjust and illegal. But the Dissenters who now say, ' We will not pay denominational fees, because it does violence to our religious scruples,' may say, indeed, that it is unjust to compel them to do so; but they cannot say that it is illegal. It is for this reason that Lord Cairns cannot follow in the steps of Lord Mansfield, while he may entertain sentiments as liberal as those of the great Tory judge.

It may be said that the precedent of Lord Mansfield's judgment does not apply, as in that case Dissenters were singled out for penalty and fined as Dissenters. But there is a more recent precedent which is clearly applicable. Church-rates, when voted by a majority of rate-payers, were payable by all householders. The present school-rates are payable by the Baptist householder on the demand of a Churchman parent who wishes his son to acknowledge, in the words of the Catechism, the efficacy of infant baptism, and the teaching given to the infant by his godfather and godmother.

---

[1] 'Parliamentary History,' 1767.

The difference between the two parties is clearly pointed
out by a writer in the 'Pall Mall Gazette' of Jan. 28,
1874; that writer says: ' " We will not pay denominational fees because it does violence to our religious
scruples," and "you must pay denominational fees,
because to refuse them does violence to other peoples'
religious scruples; " these represent the positions respectively occupied by the two parties.'

There is, indeed, in one of the States of New England,
if not more than one, a way out of the difficulty. In
the State of Massachusetts there is no compulsion on
the parent to send his boy or girl to school. It is left
to him to find out the advantage of having his children
educated in reading, writing, and arithmetic. The
schools are all free schools. At the end of the year
the expenses of all the schools are charged as an article
in the Budget upon the revenue of the State, and the
amount is generally the heaviest item in the State
Budget.

I am told, however, that such a scheme would not be
palatable in England, and that parents would not take
advantage of the opportunity of sending their sons and
daughters to school.

It seems to me, therefore, that what was done as
regards church-rates ought to be done in regard to
school-rates. Any deficiency in the payment of rates
could be made good, if public opinion approved of it,
by an additional grant in the House of Commons.
The amount required would not be large, and the poor
parents, who wanted to send their sons to Church
schools, would probably be better off than they are
now.

Let me here say, that I do not look upon Denominational Schools with any of the horror with which they

are regarded at Birmingham. For many years I proposed large grants in the House of Commons for schools
mainly supported by the clergy of the Church of England. There is much to be learned in the Catechism
which will do no one any harm. With liberal grants
from Parliament, the elementary facts of history and
geography might be easily and well taught. If the
children under fourteen years of age were taught on
three days of the week, and allowed to apply the other
three to industry, recompensed by wages, the cause of
education and the cause of labor and industry would
be both promoted.

June 15, 1874. — I perceive that in a recent debate in
the House of Commons, Lord Frederick Cavendish and
Mr. Salt each proposed a scheme by which the religious
difficulty in the schools would be solved. One scheme
is, that a large additional grant should be made for education by Parliament. The other scheme is, that Voluntary Schools should be required out of their existing
funds to educate the sons and daughters of pauper
Churchmen. Either of these schemes seems to me to
furnish an easy solution of a difficulty which has created much ill-will, and may produce further discord.
Unless the High Church party desires as a Christian
object, and the Prime minister desires as a political
object, to put down Dissenters, one of these schemes
will be accepted, and the cause of peace and good-will
towards men will make new progress.

To return once more to the question of the Dissenters:
I see it is repeated over and over again, that it would
be very hard to compel a man to send his boy to school,
and then not to allow him to choose the school to which
his boy shall be sent. Very hard, indeed, I answer, if
the parent can afford to pay for the school he chooses,

mate most nearly to the middle of the channel, and
allow of an open passage. But unfortunately it occurred to the British Commissioners that the line
through the middle of the channel was to be found
in a channel close to the American shore, departing
altogether from the words of the Treaty. It occurred,
on the other hand, to the American Commissioners,
that the proper line through the middle of the strait
was to be found close to the shore of Vancouver's
Island. It was quite evident that neither a line which
went close to the American shore, nor a line which
went close to Vancouver's Island, could be the line
intended by the Treaty.

It is perfectly obvious that a line that was to go to
the midst of the channel which separates the Continent from Vancouver's Island, and then southerly to
the middle of the channel of Fuca's Straits, and then
to the Pacific, could not approach the American shore ;
nor, on the other hand, could a line which, leaving the
middle of the channel, approached Vancouver's Island,
be the channel intended by the Treaty of 1846. So
that neither the channel called Rosario, nor the channel
called the Canal de Haro, was the channel intended by
the Treaty. Moreover, the British Government was
perfectly aware that the Canal de Haro would be unfavorable to the British Government. This is stated
in the case of the Government of Her Britannic Majesty : —

'An interpretation, therefore, of the Treaty which
would declare the Canal de Haro to be the channel
down which the boundary line is to be carried, would
be to declare that Her Britannic Majesty's Government,
when it concluded the Treaty of 1846, *intended to favor
the United States Government to its own prejudice*, for

it would be to declare that Her Britannic Majesty's Government intended to *abandon the use of the only channel leading to its own possessions* which it knew to be navigable and safe, and to confine itself to the use of a channel respecting which it had no assurance that it was even navigable in its upper waters for sea-going vessels ; nay, respecting which it is not too much to say, that Her Britannic Majesty's Government *had a firm belief that it was a dangerous strait.*' [1] Her Majesty's Ministers being thus fully persuaded that the choice of the Canal de Haro would favor the United States Government to the prejudice of Great Britain, deliberately resolved to leave the Emperor of Germany no alternative, but to bind him to choose between a boundary through the Rosario Straits or through the Canal de Haro. Had the British Government submitted the whole Treaty of 1846 to the arbitration of the Emperor of Germany, there might have been a decision favorable to the interest of Great Britain ; but, pinned to the choice between two lines, both inconsistent with the Treaty, the learned men to whom the Emperor of Germany referred the question decided it against Great Britain. They probably thought that Great Britain could well bear an additional humiliation. Therefore it was, that not only were the wives of Canada left widows, not only were the mothers of Canada left childless, without compensation, but it was determined to complete the surrender of British honor and of British character.

If we look back to the transactions of former times, it appears that in 1793–94 there was a complaint made, on the part of Great Britain, that British merchant

---

[1] Case of the British Government.

ships had been captured within the jurisdiction of the
United States. A correspondence between the Governments of London and Washington accordingly took
place. It so happened that at that time each Government was presided over by a man of high honor and
integrity. At the head of the Foreign Office of England was Lord Grenville, descended from an ancient
and honorable English family. At the head of the
Government of America was George Washington, descended from a family of the Cavaliers of the time of
Charles I. These two men were determined to pursue
the paths of truth and justice. Mr. George Hammond,
the father of the respected Under-Secretary of State
for Foreign Affairs, wrote, in May, 1793, that several
ships belonging to British merchants had been captured
by the French frigate the 'Embuscade,' and had been
condemned as lawful prize by the French Consul. On
May 15, Mr. Jefferson wrote in the following terms to
Mr. Hammond : 'Sir, — Your several memorials of the
8th instant have been laid before the President, as had
been that of the 2d, as soon as received. They have
been considered with all the attention and impartiality
which a firm determination could inspire, to do what
is equal and right between all the belligerent Powers.'

Mr. Jefferson goes on to state that the condemnation
as legal prize of a British vessel captured by a French
frigate was, as Mr. Hammond had justly stated, ' not
warranted by the usage of nations, nor by the stipula-
tions existing between the United States and France.'

In a subsequent part of his letter, Mr. Jefferson
states, ' The capture of the British ship " Grange," by
the French frigate " l'Embuscade," has, on inquiry,
been found to have taken place within the Bay of Dela-
ware, and jurisdiction of the United States, as stated in
your memorial of the 2d instant; the Government is.

therefore, taking measures for the liberation of the crew and restitution of the ship and cargo.'

The correspondence between the two Governments was carried on in the same friendly spirit in which it had been commenced. There was no question of arbitration ; a convention was signed, by which commissioners were appointed to estimate the value of the British vessels captured, and their cargoes, which had been brought as prizes into the ports of the United States, and it is stated to be much underrated at the amount of 195,548*l.* sterling, and the compensation was paid in due course.

The relations of amity between the two countries of England and the United States were not disturbed, and not even the oldest of the old women of Great Britain expressed any apprehension of war between the two nations. But then General Washington had no inclination to calumniate Lord Grenville, and the Secretary of the Treasury in England was not concerned in raising a panic in England for the sake of obtaining a majority in the House of Commons.

Had Lord Granville agreed to see me before he sent his mission to Washington, I should have pointed out to him the weak parts of our case ; I should have said, as Lord Chief Justice Cockburn has since done, that after I had received the opinion of Sir Robert Collier, there was a *primâ facie* case for detaining the ' Alabama,' and that I had failed in not doing so during the interval of four days which elapsed before I received the legal opinion of the Law Officers of the Crown. General Washington, in like manner, had, from mistake, allowed British ships to be captured within the jurisdiction of the United States.

Had Lord Granville and Mr. Gladstone conducted themselves as General Washington and Mr. Jefferson had done in 1793, compensation would have been paid, at a moderate and not a fancy value, for the ships captured and destroyed by the 'Alabama.' There would have been no war, no panic, and no arbitration.

I only trust that if any similar case should arise of mistakes in regard to the law of nations, or the exact sense of treaties, the official correspondence will be conducted in the tone of George Washington and Mr. Jefferson, of Lord Grenville and Mr. Hammond, and not in the language of Fish and Cushing, of Lord Granville and the Marquis of Ripon. In any such case, I shall say to Lord Granville, as Sir Peter Teazle said to Mrs. Candour, 'If my character is attacked, I only beg of you not to undertake my defence.'

There can be no better testimony to the honesty with which the neutrality of England was observed than that of Mr. Grote.

I must confess that the conduct of Lord Granville and Mr. Gladstone on this occasion deeply wounded my feelings. I was not quite satisfied with the behavior of Lord Clarendon, when he left, without notice, the original dispatch of Mr. Fish. But our characters were safe in the hands of the British Parliament and the British people. It was a different question when the accusation of falsehood and hypocrisy was laid in the name of the Government of the great Republic before five arbitrators of different nations.

The Prime Minister and the Foreign Secretary took for their model, apparently, the character of Donna Inez in the poem of 'Don Juan' : —

Calmly they heard each calumny that rose,
And saw *his* agonies with such sublimity,
That all the world exclaimed ' What magnanimity ! '

So let it be.

The more I respect the constitution and the character of the great American Republic, the more am I inclined to feel calumnies from such a source. Happily, neither the memory of Lord Palmerston nor my character are likely to suffer from the charges of Mr. Fish. It is to be hoped that, on any similar occurrence, the British nation will have better defenders than those who held the offices of First Lord of the Treasury and Secretary of State for Foreign Affairs in the years 1871 and 1872.

Had Lord Granville remembered his promise to see me before the President of the Council departed for Washington, I should have advised him not to insist on the weak parts of our case.

I assent entirely to the opinions of the Lord Chief Justice of England, that the ' Alabama ' ought to have been detained during the four days in which I was waiting for the opinion of the law officers. But I think that the fault was not that of the Commissioners of Customs; it was my fault, as Secretary of State for Foreign Affairs.

I should have been glad to have admitted that fault as plainly and as explicitly as General Washington admitted his mistake in 1793.

I have only further to say, that I do not wish to impute to Mr. Gladstone and Lord Granville any personal ill-will to me in all this matter. But they seem to have been quite unaware that the United Kingdom is a great country, and that its reputation ought to be dear to every British heart.

CHAPTER XIII.

POLICY FOR THE FUTURE.

WHEN I first came into public life, the great Empire of Napoleon was tottering to its downfall. Yet his insane confidence in his star was scarcely abated. Having been successful in a trifling action in the interior of France, he said to three of his marshals who were with him at supper, ' In six weeks we shall be on the Vistula.' The abdication of Fontainebleau put an end to these dreams. He himself had said, with his wonderful sagacity, ' If the Emperor of Austria were driven five times out of Vienna he would come back with undiminished strength; but if I am once driven out of Paris, I may never sit on the throne again.'

In expectation of the fall of Napoleon, there were two great problems to be solved: Who should be the Sovereign of France? What should be the boundaries of France?

The restoration of the Bourbons was agreed to without much difficulty.

The future extent and limits of France seem to have been decided by the advice of England.

The Emperor Alexander told Count Pozzo de Borgo that Lord Aberdeen had spoken to him of the Alps, the Pyrenees, and the Rhine as the future limits of France. Pozzo de Borgo replied that neither the Prince Regent nor his Ministers would consent to such frontiers.

Not long after this Lord Castlereagh wrote to Lord Aberdeen to instruct him that the English Ministers would grant the limits of the French Monarchy in 1792 as the boundaries of the kingdom of Louis XVIII.

Upon this question hung the decision then made, and perhaps the future history of France. Napoleon wrote to his brother Joseph, the mock-King of Spain, that if it fell to his fortune to sign peace with the allies, and they granted him the natural frontiers of France, meaning the Alps, the Pyrenees, and the Rhine, he would do all in his power to observe that peace; but if they gave him a restricted frontier, he should seize the first opportunity of making a quarrel, and endeavor to recover the whole of the left bank of the Rhine.

Such was the quarrel upon which, after fifty-six years of peace, Napoleon III., the nephew of the great Napoleon, fastened, in July, 1870, as a fit cause for renewed war in Europe. Napoleon III. — inferior to the first Napoleon in preparing for war, in collecting his armies for war, and in making war — fell in 1870 as his uncle had done in 1814. But the contest is not yet over. The French nation is hungry for the recovery of Alsace and the surrendered parts of Lorraine.

As soon as Napoleon III. took the command of his army at Metz, he informed them, in an order of the day, that they would have many sieges to undertake. Those sieges were, doubtless, the sieges of Cologne, of Coblentz, of Mentz, of Landau. His hopes were disappointed, his projects defeated. But the quarrel remains for the present or for a future generation. The objects to be sought are, a restored French Empire on the one side, a powerful and united Germany on the other.

It is easy to see on which side are the interests of England and of Europe.

and his boy's maintenance there, or if he can get a subscription from a friend for that payment. But that the man should have a right to put his hand into his neighbor's pocket, and take out of it such a sum as will enable him to send his boy to a school which teaches opinion to which that neighbor has a conscientious objection, is unjust. It would be better to abolish compulsion in the matter of education altogether than to inflict such injustice. The fact is, that the Church of Rome and the Protestant Dissenters of England have practices totally distinct on the subject of religion. The Church of Rome indulges in absolutions and dispensations ; she declares it is wrong for a man to marry his niece, or his first cousin, and then she grants a special dispensation for the purpose. At the beginning of Lent a proclamation is made that on certain days the strictest fast is to be observed. Not only meat and fowls, but butter, milk, and cream are prohibited. But then both men and women of weak constitution can easily obtain a license dispensing with these severe rules.

The Protestant Dissenters of England have a totally different view. I can give an instance of the scruples they entertain. I asked Mr. John Wood, the Chairman of the Board of Inland Revenue, whether his father had acted as a magistrate during the time the Corporation and Test Acts had been in force. His answer was, ' No,' his father had no objection to take the Sacrament according to the rites of the Church of England, but he did not like to do it for a purpose which by the law was prohibited.

The late Mr. Henry Drummond said, in the House of Commons, that two centuries ago every man was governed by the word *credo*, but that in the present

21

century the governing word was changed to *credit*. It is thus that at the present time the grievance which affects the consciences of Dissenters is declared by the most powerful organ of the press to be a ' blot which is very minute.' In fact, some of the organs of public opinion care little for a cause which does not affect the price of the Three per Cents, and makes only a very minute difference in the price of Erie shares.

CHAPTER XII.

TREATY OF WASHINGTON.

IT is a painful part of my task to discuss the foreign policy of the late British Ministry, and especially the Treaty of Washington, with its antecedents and accompaniments. But this task cannot be avoided.

I shall, in the first place, refer to the opinions recorded by Baron de Hübner. Baron de Hübner is an intelligent traveller, who has been more than once in the United States. But, besides this, he has had great diplomatic experience, having been for some time the Ambassador of Austria in France, and is universally esteemed for his good sense and sagacity. He thus puts on record the opinions he gathered from Englishmen and citizens of the United States on his last voyage to America: 'The English 'regret unanimously that there was any necessity to make concessions, but in their opinion the satisfaction outweighs the discontent. If I am not much mistaken, that is the feeling which predominates in England. American statesmen appear uncertain as to the value they ought to attach to the Treaty. . . . In the opinion of the public at large, the Treaty of Washington is, on the part of the English Government, an act of deference — the acknowledgment of the superiority of the power of the United States. England has submitted — she has capitulated; neither more nor less. If this erroneous interpretation is spread throughout the Union, and takes root in the conviction of the masses, the conciliatory dispositions which have animated the English negotiators are ill-understood, and this Treaty, while removing present difficulties, will have prepared the minds of men for future complications.' [1]

This last remark of Baron Hübner is of great importance. If it is believed, in the opinion of the public at large in America, that the Treaty of Washington is, on the part of the people of England, 'an acknowledgment of the superiority of the power of the United States: England has submitted and has capitulated;' such a conviction in the mind of a nation so proud and self-sufficient as the Republic of the United States is no doubt a bad preparation for peace. It is a great mistake to suppose that a concession, even the most abject to a foreign nation, is certain to conciliate their good-will. The power which conceives that a great Empire has confessed its inferiority, is apt to make demands which a nation having a lively sense of honor is certain to reject. For instance, the present Government of the United States might ask from the present Government of England the annexation of Canada with the States of the Union. Some members of the late Cabinet might think this a cheap mode of securing peace. But Lord Palmerston always considered the retention of Canada essential to the maintenance of British honor, and the nation at large would assuredly agree with Lord Palmerston in this opinion. Thus the danger of war would not be averted, but increased by the proposal of this concession.

It remains to be considered, however, whether there

---

[1] 'Promenade Autour du Monde,' vol. ii.

are any just grounds for the opinion, that the concessions made in and by the Treaty of Washington, or in
consequence of that Treaty, were ' an act of deference
and an acknowledgment of the superiority of the power
of the United States.' If not, the opinion is a mere
bravado on the part of the American people, but the
following points may be quoted in support of the
American opinion : —

I. That instead of subjecting the conduct of the
British Government, during the civil war in the United
States, to the known rules of International Law and
the provisions of the Foreign Enlistment Act, an *ex
post facto* law was invented, by which, and by the arbitrary interpretation of which, the conduct of the
British Government was tried many years after the
event.

II. That that part of the Treaty of 1846 which respects the channel between the American continent and
Vancouver's Island was subjected to a perversion of its
plain words, whereby British interests were exposed to
the risk of a wrong decision by the arbiter pointed out
by the Treaty of Washington.

III. That while the British Government professed
to give redress for any wrongs inflicted on either side
during the civil war, the injuries inflicted on the
Canadian subjects of the Queen, killed or wounded,
by the Fenian invasion from the United States were
not provided for, either by the demands of the British
Government or by the provisions of the Treaty of
Washington.

On June 12, 1871, Lord Granville, alluding to an
assertion of mine, said —

' The noble Earl said that the United States has
made no concessions; but, in the very beginning of the

protocols, Mr. Fish, renewing the proposition he had made before to much larger national claims, said : —

'" The history of the 'Alabama,' and other cruisers which had been fitted out or armed, or equipped, or which had received augmentation of force in Great Britain or in her Colonies, and of the operations of those vessels, showed extensive direct losses in the capture and destruction of a large number of vessels with their cargoes, and in the heavy national expenditures in the pursuit of the cruisers ; and indirect injury in the transfer of a large part of the American commercial marine to the British flag, in the enhanced payments of insurance, in the prolongation of the war, and in the addition of a large sum to the cost of the war and the suppression of the rebellion; and also showed that Great Britain, by reason of failure in the proper observance of her duties as a neutral, had become justly liable for the acts of those cruisers and of their tenders ; that the claims for the loss and destruction of private property which had thus far been presented amounted to about fourteen millions of dollars, without interest ; which amount was liable to be greatly increased by claims which had not been presented."

' These were pretensions which might have been carried out under the former arbitration ; but they entirely disappear under the limited reference which includes merely complaints arising out of the escape of the "Alabama."'

Who would have supposed that, after this solemn declaration of the Secretary of State for Foreign Affairs, made in the House of Lords, these 'Indirect Claims' for the prolongation of the war, and various other preposterous claims which had never been heard of before, would ever be heard of again ? Every one would have supposed that all these claims would have been withdrawn from the decision of the arbitrators, and that the British Government, if the American Government had not consented to their withdrawal, would have refused to appear in the Hall of Arbitration. But so far was this from being the case, that the British arbitrator, it is true, did not appear to arbitrate on the Indirect Claims; but a decision was come to by the arbitrators, and the claims, which Lord Granville declared had entirely disappeared, were dismissed, not as being consistent with the Treaty, or expunged from the American case, but as inconsistent with the law of nations.

That a Government should sign a Treaty, and should afterwards allow to go before arbitrators articles which that Government had declared not to be contained in the Treaty, appears to me entirely inconsistent with the national honor.

So, likewise, the omission to insist upon compensation for the wives who had lost their husbands, and the mothers who had lost their sons, by the Fenian invasion of Canada, was a desertion of that protection to life and property of the Queen's subjects upon which Her Majesty's Ministers were bound to obtain redress. It is to be remarked that, although many American merchants lost property by the aggressions of the ' Alabama,' the only injuries to life and limb were inflicted on British subjects. Sir John Macdonald, the late Prime Minister of Canada, expressed, in a public speech, his surprise and dissatisfaction at this neglect.

2. The surrender of the Island of Juan, and the retreat from the line which General Scott, an honorable American officer, had fixed of his own accord, was a serious and wanton loss; and, on the whole, it is no wonder that the American public should have con-

cluded that ' the Treaty of Washington is, on the part
of the English Government, an act of deference — the
acknowledgment of the superiority of the power of the
United States.   England has submitted — she has capitulated; neither more nor less.'

One is tempted to ask, Why should England have
performed this act of deference?   Have English troops
surrendered at Saratoga?   Has an English army capitulated at Yorktown?   Have hostile fleets paraded
the British Channel in defiance of England?

So far was it from true that such or similar events
have happened, that one of the last transactions that
took place between the two countries before Mr. Gladstone acceded to office was, that Great Britain, having
demanded the liberation of American citizens captured
in the ' Trent,' and having intimated that a refusal
of her demands might produce serious consequences,
those demands were complied with, promptly and un-
conditionally.

3. The position taken by Her Majesty's representatives with regard to the Treaty of 1846, signed by
Mr. Pakenham, was singularly, if not intentionally,
calculated to produce a decision adverse to the claims
of the British Commissioners.   The Treaty of 1846
said, in plain terms, that persons named by the two
Powers were to draw a line across the strait which
separates the American shore from Vancouver's Island,
that upon arriving at the point which intersects that
line, at the 49th parallel of latitude, a line was to be
drawn through the middle of the channel to the south
till the line should reach the open sea.

It might have been difficult to find a passage free
from obstacles in the middle of the channel, but the
obvious resource was to take a line that would approxi-

Perhaps it will be enough for the United Kingdom in 1874, as it would have been enough in 1792, to refuse the most tempting offers of France, and to keep aloof from the quarrel.

We may rely upon the prudence of Germany, of Austria, and of Russia, that these three Powers will remain banded together in spirit, if not in form. Some eight or ten months before the war of 1870 broke out, Lord Clarendon informed me of his own knowledge that Prussia had an understanding with Russia, according to which Russia would have an army of sufficient strength, on the frontier of Polish Galicia, to prevent Austria from assisting France in the coming war. That Russia was prepared so to act, that Austria was fully aware of it, and that, forewarned, she meant to be forearmed, are facts which have lately been given in an authentic shape to the English public.

We may, I trust, be confident that when the crisis comes, our Minister of Foreign Affairs will neither be taken by surprise nor omit the measures which the emergency will require.

There are some who suppose that the Sovereigns of Europe will look only to their own advantage, and will be only anxious to divide Belgium, Holland, and Luxemburg among them as a magnificent banquet.

But, in the first place, the Sovereigns of Europe are not in these days such plunderers and murderers as the newspapers imagine them to be. In the next place, it would be difficult to satisfy the various pretensions of the Sovereigns, and give to each the slice that would appease his appetite.

It is, indeed, not difficult, but impossible, to say what may be the circumstances in which a new war in Europe may arise. If Germany should attempt to annex Hol-

22

land, I trust that the arm of England will be lifted in defence of Holland. If France, or any other Power, should conspire to destroy the independence of Belgium, I trust that Lord Palmerston's Treaty of 1839 will bring England to the aid of Belgium. If the dreams of Napoleon I. should inspire some future Bonaparte, and induce him to attempt to recover what are called the natural frontiers of France, I trust that the revival of another hundred days will lead to a third overthrow of France. But at present all is dark; and we can only trust that when the day of danger arrives, England will prove true to her engagements, conscious of her great power, and mindful of her duties to mankind.

CHAPTER XIV.

GENERAL ELECTION. — FALL OF MR. GLADSTONE'S MINISTRY.

THE crisis has arrived. The General Election has given a majority of upwards of fifty to the Tory Opposition ; and it is reported that Mr. Gladstone's Cabinet have determined to resign.

With respect to the result of the General Election, there are numbers of precedents for such an event. In 1690, only one year after the glorious Revolution, complaints were made that the Whigs had gone too far in a spirit of exclusiveness, all the members of corporations who had accepted King James's rule being excluded for seven years from office. This was done by what was called the Sacheverell Clause. King William prorogued Parliament with a view to an immediate dissolution. When the General Election came, the turn of the tide against the Whigs was conspicuous. The four members for the city of London were replaced by four Tories. Sir Isaac Newton, who had been elected for the University of Cambridge, resigned his seat, and gave his vote in favor of Sir Robert Sawyer, a very prominent Tory. The elections went, generally, in the same channel ; and, although it was not then the custom to change the entire Ministry as the effect of a General Election, many Whigs retired from the Executive, and many Tories succeeded to their places.

In the reign of Queen Anne, the name of Sacheverell again occurs, as that of a man impeached by foolish zeal and Whig proscription. In 1710, when Dr. Sacheverell was rashly impeached, and Queen Anne had given to Tory Ministers the predominance which, in the days of Marlborough and Godolphin, had been enjoyed by the Whigs, four Tories of the High Church party came in for the city of London at the General Election.

But the most signal example of a change of popular feeling, and the downfall of Whig power, occurred in 1784 — Fox and Burke were dismissed from office. The most prominent men of that day thought the attempt to make a new Ministry of the Opposition so foolish as to be ridiculous ;[1] yet Pitt, by the exercise of extraordinary patience, and by keeping his footsteps in the narrow path of the Constitution, gained a great triumph. The coalition of Fox and North had disgusted the people; the India Bill, with its oligarchy of seven party men to be rulers of India, alarmed the King for the safety of his prerogative.

Where Fox and Burke were defeated, it can be no disgrace to Gladstone to have failed.

The General Election of 1841, which drove the Whigs from office, and gave a majority of ninety-one to Sir Robert Peel, is fresh in the recollection of all our elder statesmen.

We come now to the fall of Mr. Gladstone.

There can be no doubt that Mr. Gladstone, by his great eloquence, by his power of developing the most abstruse propositions, and embracing at once, in his large capacity, the most logical demonstrations with the most captivating and dazzling rhetoric, has made for himself

---

[1] See 'Letters of Sir Gilbert Elliot,' lately published.

a fame which, in the lapse of centuries, will suffer no
eclipse.   The only man whom I have heard in Parliament who combined to an equal degree the most severe
reasoning with the most wonderful flights of imagination
was Mr. Plunket in his speeches for Catholic emancipation.   But Mr. Gladstone will be renowned not only
for his parliamentary eloquence, but for his legislative
acts.

For three hundred years the Protestant Established
Church of Ireland has been the most odious and offensive emblem of the corruption and the intolerance of
England.   To have quietly removed this monopoly so
offensive to the Irish nation, the target against which
the arrows of Ireland's best archers were always aimed,
without any of the *rabbling* which marked the expulsion
of the English liturgy from Scotland, without disorder,
without riot, is a great feat in the history of any statesman.   No man can complain that he has been wronged,
a nation may rejoice that she has been righted.   The
attempts to remedy this portentous injury, without
extinguishing the Church to turn the curse into a
blessing, were sure to prove, as Lord Althorp, Lord
Durham, and I contended in Lord Grey's Cabinet they
would be in 1833, stupendous failures.   Driving with
the Duke of Leinster one day, some miles from Carton,
we came to a very handsome new church, fit for the
reception of several hundred people.   That, said the
Duke of Leinster to me, is one of the churches erected
by the Commissioners, under Lord Stanley's Church
Reform Act.   The only Protestants of the parish are
the Duchess and I, and we always attend at the church
at Maynooth.

Not a less conquest over difficulties, perhaps a greater,
was Mr. Gladstone's Land Act.   A farmer, who had

built a house, roofed it with slate, put glass in the
windows and vegetables in the garden, might have
been turned out for giving a wrong vote at an election
without any legal claim for compensation of the smallest
amount. It was said that these instances were rare,
but the power to commit such injustice was an evil to
be remedied. Mr. Gladstone, doing rough justice to
the poor tenantry of Ireland, added to the right of the
evicted tenant to obtain shelter and food at the work-
house, the right to pecuniary compensation for disturbance, to the amount of seven years' rent of his
holding.

These reforms require the sanction of time to make
them fit and easy, and that advantage be taken of the
wise provision of Lord Cairns, that the Irish Church
Act should be subject to revision. The landlords of
Ireland, upon whom, by the Act of 1836, the obligation
of paying tithe rent-charge was imposed, have no right
whatever to claim the extinction of that rent-charge
in their own favor. It was a bribe to the landlords of
Ireland which may still be withdrawn. I am one of
those who have had the advantage of the Act of 1869,
but I am quite willing to give up that advantage and to
leave my heirs still subject, as I am now, to the payment of the tithe rent-charge.

I do not wish in this place to recite by rote the faults
of Mr. Gladstone as a statesman, but I feel bound to
do him justice with respect to another great act of his
career.

The Education Act of 1870 was a great and wise
measure, framed with a view to complete the assistance
which had already been given by Parliament to popular
instruction. Mr. Forster was wise as well as just in
proposing rather to complete by supplementary pro-

visions what had been done, than to kick down the
scaffolding which had been already erected, and build
from the ground a new edifice. But in the manner of
doing this, Mr. Forster adopted a very clumsy expedient, and made his measure offensive and insulting to
the Protestant Dissenters of England. It would have
been easy to supply the need of sectarian or denominational schools by grants from the House of Commons.
The Tory party would equally have assisted Mr. Forster, and a great cause of irritation would have been
spared. To tell a Baptist he must support a voluntary
school, and that if he does not choose to do so, his table
and chair will be sold by auction, was a revival of
church-rates in a more offensive form. It is said that
the Dissenters would object as much to a vote of Parliament in favor of denominational schools as to a school-
rate. But it is one thing to agitate against the payment
of a rate which offends his conscience, and another
thing to agitate at a public meeting for the repeal of an
Act of Parliament or a change of its provisions. The
Society of Friends never petition against the votes for
the army and navy.

I may as well proceed now to name two other prominent causes of Mr. Gladstone's defeat at the General
Election.

At the same time with Mr. Gladstone's manifesto
appeared declarations generally in favor of progress,
but urging the abolition of the Church Establishment,
and the proposal of free land, free church, free schools.

These proposals put me in mind of a note of Dean
Swift, on a remark of Bishop Burnet, that the Duke
of Monmouth was a man free of all vice. 'Yes,' said
Dean Swift, ' as a man is free of a club.'

Mr. Chamberlain, who is a leading apostle of this

school, reminds me, with his notions of progress, of Tony
Lumpkin, in the play of 'She Stoops to Conquer.' I
will copy part of a dialogue from that play, in which
Tony Lumpkin and his mother represent tolerably well
Mr. Chamberlain and John Bull. When asked to de-
scribe his journey, Tony answers : —

'*Tony.* You shall hear. I first took them down Feath-
erbed Lane, where we stuck fast in the mud. I then
rattled them crack over the stones of Up-and-down Hill.
I then introduced them to the gibbet on Heavy-tree
Heath ; and from that, with a circumbendibus, I fairly
lodged them in the horse-pond at the bottom of the
garden.

'*Hast.* But no accident, I hope ?

'*Tony.* No, no, only mother is confoundedly frightened.'[1]

So in this case, no harm, no accident has happened, but
John Bull was 'confoundedly frightened.' In fact, he
has been more frightened than hurt by the threats of the
advanced Liberals. Mr. Chamberlain was left at Sheffield at the bottom of the poll. Mr. Roebuck and Mr.
Mundella have been triumphantly returned. But the
want of plain speaking on the part of Mr. Gladstone
has ruined his cause. One opponent, indeed, attacked
Mr. Gladstone, of whom Mr. Gladstone, with more truth
than Ajax, may say, —

Et cum victus erit, mecum certasse feretur.

A third fault of his Ministry, however, was greater
than either of the others.

By his foreign policy he has tarnished the national
honor, injured the national interests, and lowered the

---

[1] 'She Stoops to Conquer,' act v.

national character.   Happily the strength of the Empire, as it is described in the Imperial Census, abridged in the 'Times' of February 19, 1874, is such, that no power will be in a hurry to quarrel with us.

And surely peace and happiness, truth and justice, religion and piety, are such blessings that we ought not to put a limit to the time we may hope to possess them. That future generations should have the same blessings, that there may be no rashness, no impatience, no greediness to catch the fruit before the sun of summer has matured it, is my earnest prayer for the country whose freedom I have worshipped, and whose liberties and prosperity I am not ashamed to say we owe to the providence of Almighty God.

CONCLUDING CHAPTER.

I PROPOSE in the present chapter to end this long and various narrative. I wish, in doing so, to review the present state of England and pending questions both as regards the external and the internal relations of the United Kingdom. But before I do so, it may be well to give in a summary my own view of the course I have pursued, and of the results I have obtained.

When I first began public life, the Tories of England, who were styled by Madame de Staël, with truth and justice, the Whigs of Europe, had achieved a decided and a successful victory. I could only say with Lord Byron,

> I greatly venerate the nation's glories,
> And wish they were not owing to the Tories.

At this time Lord Liverpool and Lord Castlereagh ruled the destinies of England. After the suicide of Lord Castlereagh and Mr. Canning's death, Mr. Peel became the real chief of the Tory party and of the majority which followed his lead. The chief heads of the policy which he adopted may be thus stated : —

(1) The Roman Catholics were to be permanently excluded from Parliament and from office.

(2) The Protestant Church of Ireland was to be maintained without diminution or alteration.

(3) Foreign corn was not to be admitted, except at a very high duty, into the United Kingdom till the corn of England had reached nearly a famine price.

(4) Other articles of foreign produce and manufacture were to be admitted with high duties, on the principle of protection.

It would be an injustice to Sir Robert Peel if these governing principles of policy were to be stated as the results of his own intelligent mind. But he was governed by the narrow views and intolerant principles of the Tory party, which had embraced measures expedient, and perhaps necessary, during war, but which were quite unfitted for a policy of peace.

The point to which I directed my efforts was the refusal to grant even the most moderate measure of parliamentary reform. I proposed as a minimum to give members to Manchester, Leeds, and Birmingham. This proposal was considered in the Cabinet in the time of Sir Robert Peel. But it was rejected, and from that time it became hopeless to extract even the smallest concession upon this subject of parliamentary reform through the Tory Administration.

The Duke of Wellington pronounced the existing system perfect, and in a few days was obliged to give up his post to Lord Grey.

At Lord Grey's desire I prepared a plan of reform, by which one hundred and fifty seats for close boroughs were to be transferred to the great manufacturing towns and populous counties of England. Although nothing had been heard of such proposals before, they were no sooner promulgated than popular enthusiasm rose in its strength and converted them into law. It happened soon after this event that I was called upon to lead the House of Commons, and then obtained in Lord Melbourne not so much a master as a friend and a co-operator.

I had carefully studied the history of the civil wars

of England and of the Revolution of France.   The best
men of England and the best men of France had been
carried forward by a current in which they knew not
how to guide the ship intrusted to their care.   I had
my own difficulties.   The Philosophical Radicals were
intent upon the destruction of the Church ; the Chartists
wished to create confusion.   With such dangers I had
to contend, and might have been overwhelmed in the
flood.   With the help of Sir Robert Peel and a majority
of the House of Commons I defeated the Philosophical
Radicals.   With the valuable aid and assistance of the
Duke of Wellington I reduced the Chartists to insignificance.

I do not wish to carry this narrative further.   It
seems to me that in 1873 the contest had been fully
decided : that we had carried into effect a change
which has given prosperity for more than forty years,
without convulsion, without infringing the prerogatives
of the Crown, the privileges of the two Houses of Parliament, or the rights and liberties of the people, which
Lord Grey, in the name of his Sovereign, had called
upon the nation to maintain and defend.

I should mention, however, that soon after the Reform Bill was carried, 20,000,000*l.* were granted as
compensation to the owners of slaves.   Mr. Stephen,
one of the ablest men whom I have known in the
course of political life, and Mr. Taylor, whose high
worth as a poet all England knows, and whom it is a
happiness to me to call my friend, had calculated at
20,000,000*l.* the loss which the planters would incur by
the abolition of slavery.   But it was one thing to estimate the loss ; it was another to obtain from Parliament
means to defray the 20,000,000*l.* charged upon the
national revenue.   This could only be done by Lord

Althorp, the guardian of the public finances, and the responsible Minister for the national exchequer.

Lord Althorp did not shrink from this appalling task. The British nation had been aroused to enthusiasm by agitation, and the continual distribution of pamphlets and addresses. Mr. Stephen said with great justice, 'That we ought to be thankful to God for having permitted us, even at such a cost, to atone for the sin of so many years of slavery.'

I have already given my views respecting the state of Ireland, and with respect to the past and future of education.

I have reserved for the last part of this account the sensual or symbolical worship of the Church of Rome and its imitators, the melodramatic representation of the Crucifixion.

We all know that when Christ was brought to trial for his life before Pontius Pilate he prayed to God that he might be spared this painful sacrifice, but concluded his prayer by saying to God, 'Not my will, but thy will be done.' We all know that the Jewish mob called out, 'Crucify him! Crucify him!' and that he underwent an ignominious and degrading death. But we have now to relate that men who are not required to endure an hour's pain for the benefit of mankind, put on all kinds of harlequin dresses, and perform all sorts of antics, to resemble, as they pretend, the great and memorable sacrifice of Christ's propitiation; and, without suffering pain in a little finger, pretend to imitate and assume the attitudes of our Saviour, and to accomplish in their own persons the mystery of a divine being who actually gave his life for the benefit of mankind. If this were only like one of the sacred plays of the Spanish theatre, we might be content to say that it was a contemptible farce, but assuming, as it does, to be an act to inspire devotion, and give to the Christian world a lively representation by clerical performers of the real tragedy which was performed in Jerusalem under the Roman government more than eighteen hundred years ago, we can only pronounce it to be a shocking profanation.

It will be enough to show that I am not exaggerating the assumptions or the pretences used to disguise this offensive spectacle by alluding to, and quoting a writer in the ' *Directorium Anglicanum*,' an authorized publication of the Ritualist section of our religious community. The whole service, indeed, instead of being a compliance with the command of our Saviour to his friends and companions at his Last Supper, ' Do this in remembrance of me,' is a sacrifice offered up by a priest who performs this melodrama before retiring to dine, after the fatigues of the day. Thus we learn that the *amice* represents the *linen rag* wherewith the Jews blindfolded our Saviour; the *alb*, the white garment in which Herod clothed him ; the *girdle*, *stole*, *and maniple*, the cords and fetters with which he was bound ; the *chasuble*, the seamless vest of Christ ; *the cross embroidered on its back*, that which our Lord carried up the hill of Calvary.

But surely this is enough of the masquerade dresses which our Ritualist priests use for the purpose of parodying a solemn and sacred event in history.

For my part, I am ready to forgive the members of an ancient and venerable Church which, in the dark middle ages of Europe, thought to symbolize the creed of Christians, and to awaken the devotion of millions who could neither read nor write by statues to attract worship, and by pictures to represent the Virgin Mary and the disciples of Christ, who followed his preaching and inculcated his doctrine.

But at the present time the question is totally altered. The millions who, before the revival of letters, could only be taught by signs and emblems, have now been replaced by millions who have learned to read the Bible, who have been taught the words of Christ in their own native language, and are no longer bound by the theology of subtle logicians. I remember once calling upon a Spanish canon in his native town. I found him at dinner, and he kindly invited me to join him. But not being in very good health, I declined to drink a second glass of wine. ‘ What,’ he said, ‘ don’t you know the syllogism : “ Qui bene bibit bene dormit ; qui dormit non peccat ; qui non peccat salvatus erit ” ? ’ He told me that this syllogism, though popular at Salamanca, was a *silogismo cancioso*, or, in other words, a hoax.

But I believe the syllogism was quite as good and as sound theology as many of the dogmas which have pervaded scholastic theology.

Indeed, it is absurd to suppose that we are on the brink of a great contest between those who have learnt the principles of the Reformation and those who wish to lead us by crooked paths, and windows that shut out the light, to the temples where truth is lost amid a blaze of light, a great pomp of dresses, and the strains of melodious music.

It is very evident that the disciples of the Church of Rome wish to lead us from confession and absolution to the doctrine of transubstantiation ; from thence to the worship of images, and from thence to all the abuses which at the end of the fifteenth century and at the beginning of the sixteenth excited the anger and the scorn of Luther, Calvin, Zwinglius, and others.

We may now define the difference between the Reformers who hold to the fundamental doctrines of the Reformation, and the Ritualists, whether of the Church of England or of the Church of Rome. The difference is, then, that the Reformers hold to the faith in Christ, not as explained by Thomas Aquinas, or Duns Scotus, or even by Luther and Calvin, but as laid down by Christ himself in the Gospels. With this faith the Reformers combine great respect for the authority of Aristotle.

The Ritualists, on the other hand, combine faith in Aristotle with great respect and even veneration for the character of Jesus Christ. The primary faith of the Reformers is in the words of Christ. The primary faith of the Ritualists is in Aristotle.

It is not doubtful which way the Protestants of England will decide. They will follow in the footsteps of the Reformers.

It is to be noted that the sentiments of devotion awakened by fine dresses, fine music, and dark mysteries, figured in symbols and ceremonies, are not confined to any particular religious faith. Devotion to Mahomet, or to Buddha, may be excited by the same means which prevail with the Ritualists of England in favor of the name of Christ.

But another course has been taken by the leaders who laid the foundation of what we in England call the Reformation.

It has been the object of the English Reformers, whether attached to the Established Church or belonging to the various bodies of Christians known as the three denominations of Presbyterians, Baptists, and Independents, or belonging to the sect of Unitarians, or to various other religious bodies who are established

in England, to inform the minds and consciences of
their hearers by the doctrine, commandments, and
teaching of Christ.

Luther began the campaign against Rome by calling
upon men publicly to read the Holy Scriptures.

The theologians of the Roman Church were not prepared to meet him on this challenge. Learned doctors,
who bore sway as theologians at Rome, were quite
ignorant of the Gospel, and while they could contend
in favor of Thomas Aquinas against Duns Scotus, in
favor of Duns Scotus against Melancthon or Zwinglius,
they could not venture to quote the words of Jesus
Christ, or to support their doctrines by the words of
St. John or of St. Paul.[1]

Men, however, were informed by the New Testament, read 'audibly and distinctly,' that Christ taught
his disciples to love all men; that a man ought to love
his neighbor as himself; that if he had any personal
quarrel with any man he should seek reconciliation,
and offer to forgive them who had trespassed against
him, before he placed his gift upon the altar.

A follower of Christ would likewise be taught that
a Samaritan guilty of schism became the true neighbor
of a man lying wounded and naked, by attending to
his wounds, and giving money to provide for his care
and sustenance.

A hearer of Christ's word would also be taught that
of two men who went into the temple to pray, the rich
man who boasted that he gave tithes of all he possessed,
and that he was not as other men were, would not be
so surely justified as the man who said humbly, 'Lord,
be merciful to me a sinner.'

---

[1] Paolo Sarpi.

He would likewise hear that the man who forgave trespasses against him, and not he who refused to forgive, would be excused and pardoned. Above all, he would be taught that love between man and man was the true way to make peace prevail on the earth. He would not, indeed, conceal the prediction of Christ that mankind would persecute those who taught this doctrine, and thereby a sword and not good-will would be the first consequence of his appearance upon earth. But he would also learn that the song of the angels who proclaimed on earth peace and good-will would be the final result of Christ's teaching. He would hear from the Bible that the sabbath was made for man, and not man for the sabbath.

Beyond all these lessons, the Reformers were taught that Christ was cruelly put to death by a degrading and disgraceful mode of punishment; that he gave his life for mankind, and submitted humbly to all the insults which those who called out ' Crucify him ! Crucify him ! ' thought were the due punishment of a person who was a model of virtue, of kindness, of love of his kind.

Is there not something to excite devotion in the repetition of a narrative so sublime, so touching, so useful for the improvement of mankind? Yet more than one device has been put in force to conceal these lessons from the knowledge of mankind.

It may be said that the Protestant congregations of England may adopt the music and the pomp of Ritualistic service and still attend to the sublime lessons of charity and humility of our Lord. This is certainly possible, but not probable. Those who adopt the mummeries of the Ritualists are apt to forget that they ought not to boast that they are not as other men are, and to reject the exclamation of the publican, 'Lord, be merciful to me a sinner.'

The English nation must choose between the two. Either they must adopt the Ritualistic mode of worship, and set aside the Acts of Parliament by which the country is now governed, or they must, with the Archbishop of Canterbury, adhere to the principles of the glorious Reformation begun by Henry VIII., and established by his daughter Elizabeth, Queen of England and of Ireland.

There is one gift bestowed by Jesus Christ upon his people which we still enjoy, and which I hope we may continue to enjoy.

When Jesus Christ was asked whether he was the Saviour for whom they looked, or whether they should look for another, he gave instances of the miracles he had performed; that the blind had been made to see, that the paralytic had been told to take up his bed and walk, and that even the dead had been bidden to appear in his grave-clothes with life restored.

All this power of miracles has departed from us. We do not, like the Roman Church, pretend to restore the broken limb or make whole the wounded body. But there was one concluding sentence in Christ's declaration which we still preserve. He terminated his message by saying, 'and the poor have the Gospel preached to them.' This we preserve. The Bible Society could tell how many copies of the Gospel they distribute every year among all the nations of the world. Only a few years ago, by the exertions of a zealous minister of the Gospel, the price of the Bible was reduced in Scotland from 5s. to 10d.

Thus the people of Great Britain have inherited a privilege worthy of the divine author of the religion

which has its name and its teaching from Christ. If
the British nation is wise, it will not allow the Roman
Church with its infallible head, or the Ritualists with
their mimic ornaments, nor those who are deaf to the
teachings of Socrates and of Cicero, of Bacon and of
Newton, to deprive them of the inestimable blessing
of the Gospel.

From this great and sublime question we may proceed to matters which have obtained of late years more
or less of public attention.

In preparing a conclusion to ' Recollections and Suggestions,' which have been the object of memory or
meditation for sixty years, it is fit that I should make
a general avowal of the impression I have received
with regard to my own part in public life, and that
which others have taken with whom I have been associated, or to whom I have been opposed.

My persuasion is that I have been received with
quite as much favor as I deserved. I think what I
have done well has been honestly supported ; and that
where my measures have miscarried, the failure has
been owing not to undue animosity or malignant mis-
representation, but to errors which I have committed
from mistaken judgment or a mistaken appreciation of
facts.

I believe I may say, with many other of the leading
men who, since the Revolution of 1689, have had the
direction of public affairs, that my ends have been
honest, and that I have looked to the happiness of my
countrymen as the object to which my efforts ought to
be directed.

Speaking generally, and with some exceptions, I am
willing to give the same testimony to those with whom
I have been associated and to the chief leaders to

whom I have been opposed. I relied, and I believe justly relied, on the integrity and sound principles of Lord Althorp; and while I believe that Sir Robert Peel erred from over-caution, I see no reason to doubt that his great capacity was at all times employed for what he believed to be the welfare of his country. Indeed, I do not doubt that with the exception of the small band who were said to occupy the Cave of Adullam, the parties I have had to act with or to confront have been animated with the sincere desire to devote their talents to the public good.

Among the questions which may or may not occupy the attention of the House of Commons in the approaching sessions, the question of parliamentary reform deserves to be noted. It was inevitable that the growth of large towns, the seats of the manufactures of cotton, of wool, and of linen, could not be permanently excluded from that which called itself, the Commons House of Parliament; and that the representation of the people which excluded all those seats of manufacture could not be, as the Duke of Wellington supposed, a perfect system of representation. We to a great extent remedied the evil in 1832. But there is an observation which cannot escape either legislators or their constituents.

When Oliver Cromwell was Lord Protector of the United Kingdom, he framed a new instrument of government, and united with it a new system of representation. Disregarding the divisions which separated Scotland from England, and Ireland from both, he framed a scheme by which the counties of the three nations should have four, six, eight, or ten members each, as the circumstances of the time seemed to demand, by which great towns were represented by one member each, and small boroughs were totally omitted.

In the list of members I find for Middlesex four members, for the city of London six, for Westminster two. The number of members for Devonshire I find to be eleven, for Plymouth two, Exeter two, Totness one, Barnstable two, Honiton one, Dartmouth one. For Cambridgeshire I find four members, for Cambridge town one, and for Cambridge University one ; for the Isle of Ely two. For Lincolnshire I find ten members, one for Stamford, Boston one. In Lancashire the number of members is four, but there is one for Manchester, which, after the restoration of 1660 till 1832, had no member. For Liverpool there is one member, one for Preston, and one for Lancaster.

The representation was extended to Scotland and Ireland on the same principles which were applied to England, but Cromwell's dislike to Scotland, of which he said that he was told ' that it was a poor country inhabited by honest people,' but that he found that the country was not poor, and that the people were not honest, was visible in this scheme of representation.

Ireland had been too recently ground down by civil war to admit of a fair representation. But of this whole scheme Lord Clarendon says ' that it was generally thought a warrantable alteration, and fit to be made in better times.'

It is a marked feature in this scheme of representation, that the boroughs which in those days were small were totally omitted.

I confess it appears to me that if the question of parliamentary reform is again touched, Parliament ought not to content itself with giving to householders in counties the same right of voting which they have in boroughs, lopping off a few small towns, but that the scheme of Cromwell should be revived in these better times.

The difficulties which prevented a union with Scotland for so long a time after the Restoration, and the mismanagement which so long afflicted Ireland, ought to be kept out of sight in a large and capacious view of the union of Great Britain and Ireland. The populous counties of Ireland, with her cities of Belfast and Cork, ought to have a fair representation, and the miserable small towns of Ireland ought to be at once disfranchised.

As the scheme of Disestablishment and Disendowment of Churches, which was so popular with the Cabinet a few years ago, seems to have been now finally relinquished, Ireland ought to have for her Roman Catholic people an establishment of parish priests governed by a single Metropolitan, as the Church of England is governed by its Metropolitans of Canterbury and of York, and Scotland by her General Assembly of clerical ministers and lay members, which meets every year under the authority of a high commissioner appointed by the Crown, and which invokes the spirit and the guidance of our Lord Jesus Christ.

Whether a Tory Ministry will ever undertake such a task, or whether a Whig Ministry will ever again be called to the councils of the Sovereign, I am unable to say; I only wish to point out what in my opinion the public interest demands.

There are many topics to which the attention of the present Ministry must be directed. I think myself they would have done better if, instead of introducing a number of important measures in the late session of Parliament, they had made an excuse of the suddenness with which the burden of government had been thrown upon them, and had reserved for the coming session of 1875 the development of their whole foreign and domestic policy. Twelve gentlemen who, though bound by party ties, have been acting independently for five or six years are not at once inspired with oracular systems of policy; with a regular plan of finance; with a plan for the army and navy; or with a judgment upon the precedents left by their predecessors, distinguishing those acts which may be accepted as permanent alterations and those which may admit of alteration or reversal. The late Lord Brougham, for instance, had devoted much attention to endowments. Many of these, such as hospitals for the cure of leprosy, and sums to be devoted to the redemption of captives made by the Dey of Algiers, might properly be otherwise applied. But it is not enough to say that a man who devoted the savings of a long life to the education of the poor in the city of London or Westminster, was a pious founder, in order to disendow his schools, and make the caprice of a Minister the new rule for charitable foundations.

There are in the air of public opinion, besides errors to be corrected with temper and moderation, other schemes which have no solid foundation, and are sure to pass away with the bubbles of the day's froth; for instance, certain unions have declared that if farmers had more capital and more agricultural skill, the land would have a greater produce and the country be more flourishing. This is quite true. But who is to furnish the capital, and who the agricultural skill? The unions will not furnish the one, and are unable to furnish the other. The inexorable law of demand and supply extinguishes the whole scheme.

A farmer in Scotland, with his nineteen or twenty-one years' lease, accumulates profits sufficient to become the tenant and the improver of a new farm. Thus gradually and thus surely does agriculture improve, and thus insensibly will the landlords and tenants in England accumulate the wealth and the science which have distinguished Scotland.

When Sir Robert Peel imposed the income-tax in 1842, several farmers of Berwickshire and the neighboring counties intrusted to my hands a petition, praying to have the proportion of income-tax paid by tenants lowered. On looking over the list of the tenants who signed their names to the petition, I found some who paid 2,000*l.* a year of rent, and others who paid 1,500*l.* and 1,200*l.* yearly. The landlords and tenants of England have not generally acquired the spirit or the knowledge which would enable them to cultivate their farms well. I have heard that on the estate of Londesborough, sold by the late Duke of Devonshire, the *incuria* of low rents and lazy farming produced at the period of the sale bad cultivation and contented indolence. But these changes are not to be made on a sudden; 'Rome was not built in a day,' says the English proverb. 'No se tomó Zamora, En una hora,' says the Spaniard.

With regard to our security from foreign invasion, it must be said, in the first place, that the invasion of the British Isles would require immense preparation, and that immense preparation could not not be made without such expense, so many ships, and so many regiments, that the population of Great Britain would have full time to organize their forces, and to make the battle of Dorking a signal victory for the British against an invading army.

We may, therefore, put out of the question the dangers of an invasion of the British Islands by a foreign enemy. We must call to mind, however, that we have a land frontier of 1,200 miles in North America, open in many passages, and a land frontier of 12,000 miles in our Indian Empire, which good military judges have pronounced to be defensible at every point of its vast extent. It is worth while, however, to weigh and estimate the dangers to which our Empire may be exposed both in the West and in the East.

There occurs from time to time in the press of the United States an explosion of ambition and envy, prompted by the desire of adding the Dominion of Canada to the territory of the United States.

That is, however, far from being a deliberate intention of aggrandizement on the part of the Great Western Republic.

Mr. Cobden, who was friendly to our giant son, expressed his opinion that if the lust of dominion should ever possess the government and the people of the United States, they would look rather to the south than to the north for the gratification of their ambition. He pointed out that the territory to the north gave a return to the efforts of a laborious and frugal workman of only moderate crops of corn, while the great table-land of Mexico produced cotton and sugar, and her mines were rich with silver. He, therefore, reckoned the risk of a war with Great Britain, which might, as in 1812, prove destructive to the trade of the United States, while the land of Mexico, divided by civil war, would, as in the days of General Scott, be easily subdued and as easily held in subjection.

I know not whether he was acquainted with the saying of a French statesman, engaged in framing the treaty of Versailles of 1763, that those who were masters of North America would, in the end, be masters of the South.

Be this as it may, the honor of the British Crown

is pledged to defend the Queen's dominions in North
America with the utmost forces of the Empire; and it
is very improbable that, with such a prospect before,
them, the President and Secretary of State at Washington will coolly contemplate a hostile invasion of the
Queen's possessions in Canada.

It is true, that the late Government committed a
folly when they evacuated the new and expensive fortifications at Quebec, and abandoned the garrison at
Halifax. Very few years have elapsed since part of the
garrison at Halifax furnished the means of preserving
the Island of Jamaica to the British Crown, and it is
not likely that a Canadian garrison would be dispatched
to Jamaica with the same readiness, or act with equal
efficiency, against a negro insurrection.

But this error can easily be repaired by a Government
which is prepared to defend the Queen's possessions,
and which has a proper sense of the value of British
honor. I should, therefore, pay little regard to the
speeches which in the United States are called 'Bun-
come,' and which are as void of meaning as they are
hollow in sound.

I have said that the British Empire of India has a
frontier of 12,000 miles, and is, according to the judgment of military men, in every point of that frontier,
defensible. But still, the commander of 800,000 men,
the autocrat of a vast Empire, possessed with a spirit

Like Macedonia's madman or the Swede,

may be tempted by the riches of India, by the rumors
of disaffection to British rule, by intrigues constantly
springing up, and by the hope of glory to the Russian
name, to undertake the vast enterprise of depriving
Great Britain of her Indian possessions, and annexing

them to the crown of the Muscovite. Let us consider what are the reasons to be thrown into the opposite scale.

In the first place, there is the danger and the disgrace of initiating a great disturbance of the peace of the world. When Napoleon failed in his task of completing the conquest of Europe, England became the friend of Russia, and for more than half a century the bonds of friendship, broken only by the blunder of the Crimean war, have united the two nations.

It will be said by the surrounding spectators, 'Asia is surely large enough to contain two European powers.' Each power is strong and independent; they are not, like Cæsar and Pompey, contending for rule or the same empire. Russia has carried her conquests to the shore of the Black Sea, and her power is only bounded by an ocean limit and the river Danube. Her trade in Central Asia is not disturbed by England.

Why, it will be said, destroy peace, the greatest blessing of nations, by new aspirations, by new alliances, and by making an open wound on the fair body of Europe?

Other considerations must intervene. England can at any time borrow, on moderate terms, one hundred millions in the market of London. The capitalists of Europe would expect that if the Russian Emperor would be ready to borrow he would be equally ready to violate his engagements. A high rate of interest would be demanded, and the people of Russia would complain of unwonted and unexpected burdens. Nor is the state of a large military empire, a stratocracy, as it was formerly termed, without its separate dangers.

If Alexander the Great had lived longer he might have found his favorite generals rebel against his authority. When Napoleon the Great sent his legions into Portuguese territory, they were greatly inclined, and even conspired, to make one of his marshals King of Portugal.

Dangers such as these, obstacles such as these, might 'stop the path of a Hannibal, but Hannibal was a soldier of fortune sworn to hate the Roman name. A Czar of Russia, filled with anxieties every morning, and dreading every night the fate of Peter or of Paul, might well be induced to prefer the ease and security of a tranquil reign to the prospect of unceasing dangers and an uninterrupted anxiety.

But I am not so very confident of our security as to advise that any precautions should be neglected.

It was well said by Tippoo Saib, ' that what he dreaded was not so much the British army then in India, as the British army that might arrive from England.'

None of the advantages that modern science has furnished in the way of weapons, of railroads, of discipline, and intelligent officers, should be neglected.

Lord Salisbury has well advised that a railway along the course of the Indus should enable the Governor-General of India to pour an overwhelming force on the points most likely to be threatened by an enemy.

The genius of Clive and the unscrupulous policy of Warren Hastings, the far-seeing view of Lord Wellesley and the peaceable watchfulness of Lord Minto, have created, have strengthened, and have preserved our Indian Empire.

I cannot myself believe that we shall be overcome in the effort to maintain that which we have with so much difficulty acquired. The mutiny of the Indian army threatened our Empire with extinction. A wise Viceroy guided our councils with unshaken firmness. A skilful general traversed vast tracts of the country with victory in his hand; intrepid soldiers rescued beleaguered garrisons. Beautiful women implored their husbands to put them to death, rather than leave them victims to infamy and dishonor.

By such virtues the Indian Empire was saved; but it would be idle to suppose that such an Empire can be maintained by virtues less resolute, by qualities less exalted, by courage less invincible, than the virtues, the qualities, and the courage which have founded and preserved it.

I have stated in the House of Lords, that by the Treaty of Washington the honor of the British nation was tarnished, her character lowered, and her interests endangered. But as every prominent candidate at the late general election had blamed the foreign policy of Mr. Gladstone's Cabinet, and as that general election had for its result a majority of fifty for Mr. Disraeli in the place of a majority of sixty for Mr. Gladstone, I also stated that in my opinion the British people, by giving a majority to the Conservative candidates, had passed a sentence of condemnation against the authors of the concession which had tarnished the honor, lowered the character, endangered the interests of the British nation.

In 1856, England obtained at Paris a treaty by which Russia bound herself to make the Black Sea a neutral sea, and not to send her ships of war to navigate that sea. Considering that a large number of the subjects of Russia live on the borders of the Black Sea, this was a very harsh and unusual stipulation. No one would have been surprised to learn that Russia, when her naval and military losses were repaired, had asked the Powers of Europe to meet and to modify that harsh

condition of the Treaty of 1856, to which all the principal Powers had agreed. Nothing could have been
more reasonable than such a request. Is that what she
did? did she propose that the Powers should come
together under the leadership of Great Britain? Quite
the contrary: Prince Gortchakoff, on behalf of the
Emperor of Russia, declared this humiliating part of
the Treaty of Paris to be null and void. He declared
it would no longer be submitted to by his Imperial
master.

It is true that a conference took place, and that a
condition was inserted in the articles, according to
which, in case of the violation of the other parts of the
Treaty of 1856, England and France would be at
liberty to assist Turkey by their naval power. This
was to put a decent mask on the harsh features of the
Russian dictator. But it seems to be admitted, that if
Russia finds any treaty to which she has given her
public and solemn assent injurious to her interests, she
is at liberty to declare that treaty null and void, and to
proceed as if it did not exist.

For the injuries to property inflicted by the 'Alabama' on American merchant vessels, an ample compensation, not to say an extravagant and inordinate
compensation, of upwards of three millions sterling has
been paid, and I will not say any thing further upon
this subject.

Eighty-five years ago, the French nation determined
to reform its constitution, and to aim at the blessings
of a free government. For eighty-five years they have
struggled in vain; they have tried putting to death,
without form of trial, the highest of their nobility, the
fairest ladies of their aristocracy, the bravest of their
generals, the most accomplished of their men of science,

the most virtuous of their princesses, and the best of all classes. Robespierre declared that 200,000 heads must fall before France could be free and happy. They put him to death, and interrupted the reign of terror. They then accepted as their ruler a great military chief who governed tyrannically, and carried 600,000 men to Moscow to perish in an insane expedition. The nation then put him aside, and restored the brother of Louis XVI. He governed like Charles II., caring nothing for moral principles, but understanding his own enjoyments, and delighting in witty conversation. I have heard Prince Talleyrand describe the scene of his death-bed. Charles X., his successor, was, like James II., a bigot, and it was part of his religion to break faith with his subjects.

I was riding in Hyde Park at Easter, 1830, with the Duke of Laval, the French ambassador, when I said to him, ' We are going to have a revolution in France.' ' What,' he said, ' are we going to have a Republic?' I said, ' No, you will have the Duke of Orleans as your king.' I knew what was about to happen from living much with the French Whigs.

One of the cleverest of them had said at dinner when I was present, ' None but so stupid a king as Charles X. would have appointed as his Minister so stupid a man as the Prince of Polignac.' The event occurred as I had expected, and at the end of July the Duke of Orleans was made King of the French, but he neglected the maxim of one of the ablest of French statesmen, ' not to govern too much.' He attempted to govern by corruption, but not the corruption of Sir Robert Walpole, with a great end in view. The corruption of Louis Philippe was a sordid traffic of places and honors, of dinners and entertainments, in order to control the

members of an assembly chosen by 200,000 electors for
the whole of France.

Thiers has lately pointed out this fault, which led
to the abdication of the citizen King. Had the French
been English they would have kept their King, but
compelled him to adopt reform.

The subsequent events in France are well known.
The choice of the French nation now lies between
several alternatives. One recommended by M. Thiers,
and favored by a large popular support, would consist
of confirming and consolidating the present form of
government, with a President ·chosen for a term of
years, a senate or House of Lords calculated to give
steadiness to the action of the Representative Assembly,
and laws intended to perpetuate the public liberties of
the nation.

Its advocates affirm that this form of government
would institute and maintain a Conservative Republic.
Its adversaries deny that a Republic in France can ever
be conservative; they say it would always be violent
and revolutionary, and they point to the examples of
1793 and of 1873 with a shudder, to express their fears
and confirm their objections.

I do not venture to give a decided opinion upon a
judgment which must, after all, depend on the will of
a nation so numerous and so enlightened as that of
France; but I will not conceal my opinion upon another
alternative which is about to be submitted to the decision of the French nation; that alternative involves the
restoration of the French Empire, with its despotic government and its passion for foreign wars.

Napoleon I. was a man of the most extraordinary
talents for strategy and tactics in war, and for administration in peace. His preparations for war are related

in detail in the history of Thiers, and show an energy and activity by day and night which have never been equalled by kings the most celebrated for their warlike achievements, or by the most famous generals who have led the armies of ambitious sovereigns. In peace, his great maxim of administration was ' that every thing should be done for the people, but nothing by the people.' Whether a man should be raised to the highest honors and intrusted with the highest commands, or whether he should be put to death without trial and without inquiry, Napoleon thought ought to be left to his sole will and his sole decision. It was said of him by a woman of genius, ' he traversed crimes and virtues as he traversed mountains and rivers, because they were on his road.'

Napoleon III. had neither the talents nor the energy, neither the errors nor the ambition, of his uncle. For a long time he followed the path of peace, maintained friendly relations with the great enemy of his predecessor, and sought in the lessons of political economy the road to riches and to peace. But the curse of his family was upon him. We have found it recorded that Napoleon I. had declared to his brother that if France had her natural frontiers he would abide by a treaty of peace; but if she had not those frontiers, he would make war upon the first convenient opportunity. Thus, after twenty years of successful power, Napoleon III. made a war the most unjust, the most senseless, the most ill-prepared, and the worst conducted which this generation has seen. The omens which attend upon such a war are fearful. At the beginning of June, 1815, Napoleon I. reckoned with certainty upon entering Brussels before the month was over. On June 18 he was defeated at Waterloo. In the beginning of

July, 1870, Napoleon III. announced to his army the approaching capture of all the fortresses on the left bank of the Rhine. At the beginning of September he capitulated with all his troops, and was dethroned by force at Paris. These precedents are surely enough to induce the French nation not again to place a member of the family of Bonaparte on the throne of France. The one hundred days of 1815 are commemorated with the battle of Waterloo. The war of 1870 is associated in our lively recollection with the defeat and fall of the Second Empire. The French nation may well shrink from the fear of incurring a second Waterloo, or from being exposed to a renewal of the surrender of Sedan.

Whatever may be the mature decision of the French nation, the other Powers of Europe are sufficiently warned; England and Italy, Germany and Prussia, Austria and Russia will do well, when the Imperial Eagle flies from the towers of Notre Dame, to make treaties of alliance and prepare for action.

I leave to future consideration the measures that will be necessary.

Various events, to which it is needless to recur, have since prevented the introduction of a complete measure of reform. In 1867, Mr. Disraeli, then Prime Minister, proposed the law of the right of election in boroughs to a simple rated household suffrage, and this proposal, with the addition made by Lord Cairns of a minority clause, borrowed from the Bill of 1854, was adopted by both Houses of Parliament.

How, then, do we stand at present?

Let us first consider the immediate requirements of political expediency, and next what is fitted to the permanent welfare of the country.

With regard to the first of these questions, it is

obvious that there are two demands, one of which has already received much popular support, and which was thrown open by Mr. Gladstone to any member who chose to take it up — this was the admission of rated householders to vote in counties as they are now admitted to do in boroughs.

The other demand which is put forward by the Radical party is a further disfranchisement of small boroughs. My own opinion is, that if ever there should come a time when public opinion should be favorable to the destruction of the small boroughs and the admission of householders to vote in counties, it will be well not to make some paltry changes which would whet the appetite for fresh designs, but to make a warrantable alteration which may stand the test of time, and be fitted to serve the purposes of the coming generation.

For this purpose, it is well to look back to the project of Oliver Cromwell. His frame of government provided for a protector who, upon his death, was to be replaced by another chief of the State, to be elected likewise for life.

What part of Cromwell's plan of representation Lord Clarendon would have thought fit to adopt in better times is quite uncertain, but it is obvious that Cromwell was a man of large conceptions, and that if he had had any one fit to succeed him in the Protectorate he might have founded a commonwealth which John Milton and Algernon Sydney would have contributed to support, the one with his extensive learning, the other with his high spirit, and both by their lofty and unblemished characters.

Those things are past; we have happily contrived to join with the rights of hereditary Monarchy as large a scheme of popular freedom as any of the ancient Republics ever devised. That it may long endure, is my fervent and humble prayer.

I will not attempt to review the changes which have taken place in Europe from the days of Charles V. and Louis XI. to the present time. But there is some advantage in having attained to old age in a period of happy progress, and to be able to bear testimony to the advances which have been made in the cause of civil and religious liberty during the half century which has elapsed since 1824 to the present year. At the former of these periods, it was laid down as an axiom, which no one could venture to contradict, that changes introduced by Sovereigns from above would be productive of peace and improvement, but that if introduced from below, by the initiative of popular movements, they could produce nothing but anarchy and confusion.

In 1874, we see institutions introduced in Germany by universal suffrage, planted in Italy by popular revolution, resting in France, as in Germany, upon universal suffrage.

Generally speaking, the authority of governments in Europe is based upon those principles which in 1824 were pronounced to be the parents of anarchy and disorder. No one can say that, with the exception of England, the Powers of Europe have yet attained a settled condition ; but there are many signs which give hope of the prevalence of religious liberty. In the course of this retrospect, it is impossible not to recollect that the Madiai were severely punished for reading in a family circle some chapters of the Holy Gospel, and that in Spain some few scattered Protestants were punished for a similar profanation.

We hear now of Protestant places of worship at

Cordova and Seville, in Spain, and at Florence and Rome, in Italy.

When the great truths of the Gospel are thus admitted and allowed to reach the public ear, we may have good hopes for the cause of civil and religious liberty. With this sentiment I conclude my work. John Milton has said: —

> What more oft in nations grown corrupt,
> And by their vices brought to servitude,
> Than to love bondage more than liberty,
> Bondage with ease than strenuous liberty.

Such is happily not now our case. From 1815 to 1873 there has been a course of gradual progress towards civil and religious liberty. There is nothing so conservative as Progress. England is in the full enjoyment of civil and religious freedom. I hope she may never descend from this height, and that the wish of the great poet, under whose roof I conclude, may see his vision fulfilled, and become the creed and the confidence of a better and a stronger age of mankind: —

> Of old sat Freedom on the heights,
>   The thunders breaking at her feet;
> Above her shook the starry lights,
>   She heard the torrents meet.
>
> There in her place she did rejoice,
>   Self-gather'd in her prophet-mind,
> But fragments of her mighty voice
>   Came rolling on the wind.
>
> Then stept she down thro' town and field,
>   To mingle with the human race,
> And part by part to men revealed
>   The fulness of her face.

RUSSELL.

ALDWORTH, *October* 29, 1874.

APPENDICES.

IN the progress of liberal opinions, it is important to record the relaxation of the chains by which the Church of England has been bound. The Low Church endeavor to confine the Established Church within the strict letter of its Calvinistic Articles; the High Church, especially the Ritualistic portion of the body, wish to condemn all who do not follow with servile obedience the syllogisms of Aristotle and the abuses of the Roman Church; the Broad Church, alone, wish to give that full liberty to the Church of England which the late Bishop Wilberforce delighted to boast of and to celebrate.

One of the first cases which, after Lord Brougham's Act of Parliament, came before the Ecclesiastical Committee of Privy Council was the case of Mr. Gorham. Mr. Gorham had been appointed to a living in Cornwall. In looking over the new scene of his labors, he found in a corner of his church a square stone altar which had been used before the Reformation. He moved the altar back from its corner and replaced it by a communion table suitable to the reformed Church. But his offence was not overlooked by the High Church party. On his being appointed to another living in Devonshire, the Bishop of Exeter summoned him to appear before him to answer for a heresy, into which he was said to have fallen, in the subject of baptism. Mr. Gorham, who was poor and in weak health, was compelled to walk between four and five miles each day, and was kept fasting while he was exposed to the dialectics, divinity, and metaphysics of his inexorable enemies. They found, of course, that he was unable to hold the living to which he had been appointed. But happily for Mr. Gorham, the case came before the Judicial Committee, the members present of which were Lord Larydale, Lord Campbell, Sir James Parke, Dr. Lushington, Sir J. L. Knight Bruce, and Mr. Pemberton Leigh. The Archbishops of Canterbury (Sumner), and York (Musgrave), and the Bishop of London (Blomfield), assisted by special command of Her Majesty.

On the 8th of March, 1850, the judgment of the Judicial Committee was read in the Council Chamber by Lord Larydale. The Lords of the Council did not decide that the opinions of Mr. Gorham were the opinions of the Church of England, but they declared 'that it appears that opinions, which we cannot in any important particular distinguish from those entertained by Mr. Gorham, have been propounded and maintained without censure or reproach by many eminent and illustrious prelates and divines, who have adorned the Church from the time when the Articles were first established. We do not affirm that the doctrines and opinions of Jewell, Hooker, Usher, Jeremy Taylor, Whitgift, Pearson, Carlton, Prideaux, and many others, can be received as evidence of the doctrines of the Church of England; but their conduct, unblamed and unquestioned as it was, proves, at least, the liberty which has been allowed of maintaining such doctrine.'

On the 9th of March, 1850, the Privy Council was held, at which were present Her Majesty the Queen, Prince Albert, the Lord President, Lord John Russell, Viscount Palmerston, and Sir George Grey. The Queen, having taken the judgment of the Committee of the Privy Council into consideration, 'was pleased to approve thereof, and of what is therein recommended, and to order, as it is hereby ordered, that the same be duly and punctually observed, complied with, and carried into execution.'

The committee say in their judgment: 'The case not requiring it, we have abstained from expressing any opinion of our own upon the theological correctness or error of the doctrine held by Mr. Gorham, which was discussed before us at such great length and with so much learning.' This judgment was a great enlargement of the liberty of the Church of England, and influenced many other cases. I proceed to one of these upon a matter of very great importance.

II.

In 1864, the judgment of the Judicial Committee of Privy Council was delivered upon a case affecting the opinions of two of the authors of the work entitled 'Essays and Reviews.'

It is well known that the authors of these Essays declared publicly, that they were not collectively responsible for any one of the Essays contained in their work. But the point of the judgment pronounced by Lord Westbury, in 1864, is still of very great importance, and affected very seriously the position and reputation of two of the authors, namely, Dr. Williams, Vicar of Broad-Chalke, in Wiltshire, and Henry Bristow Wilson, B.D., Vicar of Great Staughton, Hunts.

The points on which they were arraigned are so clearly defined in an opinion signed by Sir Roundel Palmer, now Lord Selborne, and Sir Hugh Cairns, now Lord Cairns, that I think I can do nothing better than copy the opinions signed by them: —

'We understand the Lord Chancellor to have, in substance, founded his judgments upon a negative answer to the inquiry, whether every clergyman of the Church of England was strictly bound to affirm the two following propositions:

'"1. That every part of every book of Holy Scripture was written under the inspiration of the Holy Spirit, and is the Word of God."

' " 2. That it is impious or heretical to entertain or express a hope that even the ultimate pardon of the wicked, who are condemned in the day of judgment, may be consistent with the will of Almighty God."

' These are the exact propositions referred to in our opinion.

(Signed) {
ROUNDEL PALMER
(now Lord Selborne).
H. M. CAIRNS
(now Lord Cairns).'
}

The members of the Judicial Committee present at these appeals were — the Archbishop of Canterbury (Longley), the Lord Chancellor (Westbury), the Archbishop of York (Thompson), the Bishop of London (Tait), now Archbishop of Canterbury, Lord Cranworth, Lord Chelmsford, Lord Kingsdown. Two of these, the Archbishop of Canterbury and the Archbishop of York, stated ' that they do not concur in those parts of this judgment which relate to the 7th article of charge against Dr. Williams, and to the 8th article of charge against Mr. Wilson.' All the others, namely, the Lord Chancellor (Westbury), the Bishop of London (Tait), Lord Cranworth, Lord Chelmsford, and Lord Kingsdown, must be reckoned as having concurred in the judgment.

I have quoted these opinions of Mr. Gorham in regard to baptism, and of Dr. Williams and of Mr. Bristow Wilson, without any thought of espousing the opinions either of Mr. Gorham in respect of baptism, Dr. Williams or Mr. Wilson in regard to the doctrine of eternal punishment. I have quoted them in order to show the liberty of opinion which is allowed by the judgments of the Committee of Privy Council to members of the Church who have endeavored to seek the truth, and have honestly exercised the right of private judgment which is exercised by all true Protestants.

An attempt was made in the House of Commons by some ritualistic members of Parliament to deprive the judgments of the Privy Council of ecclesiastical authority. By a very cunning artifice, it was proposed that a committee of Privy Council in ecclesiastical cases should consist entirely of laymen; this motion was carried unopposed, and almost unperceived, in a committee on the 'Bill of Judicature.' It is obvious what would have been the next step. It would have been contended that a judgment of laymen could have no weight with the bishops and archbishops, deans, rectors, and vicars, who had been admitted to ordination as priests. There is no saying how far this argument might have prevailed in producing schism in the Church, and confusion in the Law. Happily the trick was detected. Lord Cairns perceived that it was a stratagem with the Ritualists, and must be opposed in the House of Lords. Lord Selborne, then Lord Chancellor, proposed an amendment by which the poison of the amendment of the Commons was neutralized and rendered harmless. When I went to the House of Lords, I found that the Archbishops of Canterbury and of York had consented to the amendment of the Lord Chancellor, and that the subtle device of the Ritualists was sure to fail.

I rely upon the legal knowledge and the freedom from prejudice of Lord Selborne and Lord Cairns to defeat any similar artifice. It is clear that the Ritualists are not disposed to give up the contest. Dr. Pusey has publicly declared that the judgment in the case of Mr. Gorham was an error and ought to be reversed. Until the religion of the Church of England has been assimilated to the religion of Rome, of St. Thomas Aquinas and of Aristotle, the Ritualists will not be satisfied.

It remains to be seen what part Mr. Gladstone will take in this great contest. The principles of the Reformation are on one side, the adherents of the Church of Rome on the other.

INDEX.

A.

ABERCROMBIE, James, election of, 268.

Aberdeen, Lord, course suggested with regard to Ecclesiastical Titles Act, 211 ; his Ministry, 221.

Adams, Mr., his conduct with regard to the 'Alabama' claims, 228.

'Alabama' claims, Earl Russell on the, 228 ; Mr. Fish's proposition, 326.

Althorp, Lord, as Chancellor of the Exchequer, 56 ; speech on the resignation of ministers, 84 ; restoration of his Ministry, 89 ; introduces the Coercion Bill, 92 ; and Bill for the Reform of the Church of Ireland, 93 ; Bill for Reform of Poorlaws, 95 ; speech on the Irish Church question, 100 ; opposes the Coercion Act, 104 ; resignation, 104 ; restored to power under Lord Melbourne, 106 ; resignation and retirement from public life, 106 ; attempts to promote free trade, 167 ; influence in the House of Commons, 215 ; on the Union Act, 201 ; waits upon Sir R. Peel, 208 ; grants incurred by the abolition of slavery, 348.

America, opinions on the Treaty of Washington, 323 ; points in support of these opinions, 325 ; our land frontier in, 361.

American Civil War, a calamitous event, 235 ; neutrality of England, 235.

Anne. Queen, Parliament during the reign of, 217.

Australia, 166.

Austria, intentions of Russia towards, 337 ; aggression of, 364.

Azeglio, Marquis de, letter to, 234.

B.

BALDWIN, Mr., discussion on responsible government in the colonies, 165.

Baptism, Mr. Gorham's opinions on, 376.

Baring, Mr. Alexander, his objections to reform, 33 ; deputed by the Duke of Wellington to form a government, 84 ; opposition to the Reform Bill, 85 ; fails to form a government, 87.

Bedford, Duke of, 306.

Belfast, illegal meeting at, 288.

Bible, the, in national schools, 294 ; evidence against Ritualism, 353 ; use of, 355.

Bills, private, in Parliament, 289.

Births, registration of, 117.

Bissett, Mr., on Lord Wellington before the battle of Salamanca, 11.

Black Sea Treaty, 366.

Blomfield, Dr., treaty regarding education, 308.

Bonaparte, Emperor Napoleon, his downfall, 335 ; his character, 369.

Bonaparte, Louis Napoleon, his quarrel with Germany, 336 ; and results, 336 ; his character, 369.

Boroughs, origin of nomination, 29.

Boundary Bill, adoption of the, 74.

Bright, Right Hon. John, his interest in the Irish Church, 126.

Britain, Great, its constitution, 176, 177 ; advantages of government forms of, 176 ; her honor tarnished by the Treaty of Washington, 306.

British and Foreign School Society, foundation of, 306 ; grants to, 309.

British Isles, their security from invasion, 361 ; exposed to dangers, 362, 363.

Cambridge: Press of John Wilson and Son.

www.ingramcontent.com/pod-product-compliance
Lightning Source LLC
Chambersburg PA
CBHW051525100726
47898CB00005B/1573